Dear Reader,

It's one thing to know what you want. It's another entirely to realize what you need. In these two classic stories, bestselling author Nora Roberts shows us how wonderful life can be when what we want and what we need become one and the same.

In *Second Nature,* reporter Lee Radcliffe is a woman on a mission to land an exclusive interview with enigmatic writer Hunter Brown. When he agrees to the article on the condition that Lee accompany him on a camping trip, she reluctantly obliges. But after a few cozy nights under the stars, Lee discovers there's something she wants just as badly as the interview—Hunter himself!

In *Summer Desserts,* we meet Summer Lyndon, a gifted dessert chef at the top of her game. Despite her own ambitions, she can't turn down sexy hotel tycoon Blake Cocharan's demand that she work for him in the kitchen of his Philadelphia hotel. Summer's never been able to walk away from a challenge, especially when the man issuing it is so frustratingly attractive!

We hope these stories inspire you to always go after what you want...you never know when it might lead you to the love you've always desired.

The Editors

Silhouette Books

NORA ROBERTS

A Change of Plans

Silhouette Books

Published by Silhouette Books

America's Publisher of Contemporary Romance

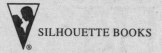

SILHOUETTE BOOKS

A CHANGE OF PLANS

ISBN-13: 978-0-373-28180-0

Recycling programs
for this product may
not exist in your area.

Copyright © 2014 by Harlequin Books S.A.

The publisher acknowledges the copyright holder
of the individual works as follows:

SECOND NATURE
Copyright © 1985 by Nora Roberts

SUMMER DESSERTS
Copyright © 1985 by Nora Roberts

This edition published by arrangement with Harlequin Books S.A.

For questions and comments about the quality of this book, please contact us
at CustomerService@Harlequin.com.

® and TM are trademarks of Harlequin Books S.A., used under license.
Trademarks indicated with ® are registered in the United States Patent
and Trademark Office, the Canadian Intellectual Property Office and in
other countries.

Visit Silhouette Books at www.Harlequin.com

Printed in U.S.A.

CONTENTS

SECOND NATURE   7

SUMMER DESSERTS   237

SECOND NATURE

To Deb Horm, for the mutual memories

Prologue

…with the moon full and white and cold. He saw the shadows shift and shiver like living things over the ice-crusted snow. Black on white. Black sky, white moon, black shadows, white snow. As far as he could see there was nothing else. There was such emptiness, an absence of color, the only sound the whistling moan of wind through naked trees. But he knew he wasn't alone, that there was no safety in the black or the white. Through his frozen heart moved a trickle of hot fear. His breath, labored, almost spent, puffed out in small white clouds. Over the frosted ground fell a black shadow. There was no place left to run.

Hunter drew on his cigarette, then stared at the words on the terminal through a haze of smoke. Michael Trent was dead. Hunter had created him, molded him exclusively for that cold, pitiful death under a full moon. He felt a sense of accomplishment rather than remorse for destroying the man he knew more intimately than he knew himself.

He'd end the chapter there, however, leaving the details of Michael's murder to the reader's imagination. The mood was set, secrets hinted at, doom tangible but unexplained. He knew his habit of doing just that both frustrated and fascinated his following. Since that was precisely his purpose, he was pleased. He often wasn't.

He created the terrifying, the breathtaking, the unspeakable. Hunter explored the darkest nightmares of the human mind and, with cool precision, made them tangible. He made the impossible plausible and the uncanny commonplace. The commonplace he would often turn into something chilling. He used words the way an artist used a palette and he fabricated stories of such color and simplicity a reader was drawn in from the first page.

His business was horror, and he was phenomenally successful.

For five years he'd been considered the master of his particular game. He'd had six runaway bestsellers, four of which he'd transposed into screenplays for feature films. The critics raved, sales soared, letters poured in from fans all over the world. Hunter couldn't have cared less. He wrote for himself first, because the telling of a story was what he did best. If he entertained with his writing, he was satisfied. But whatever reaction the critics and the readers had, he'd still have written. He had his work; he had his privacy. These were the two vital things in his life.

He didn't consider himself a recluse; he didn't consider himself unsociable. He simply lived his life exactly as he chose. He'd done the same thing six years before…before the fame, success and large advances.

If someone had asked him if having a string of best-sellers had changed his life, he'd have answered, why should it? He'd been a writer before *The Devil's Due* had shot to number one on the *New York Times* list. He was a writer now. If he'd wanted his life to change, he'd have become a plumber.

Some said his lifestyle was calculated—that he created the image of an eccentric for effect. Good promotion. Some said he raised wolves. Some said he didn't exist at all but was a clever product of a publisher's imagination. But Hunter Brown had a fine disregard for what anyone said. Invariably, he listened only to what he wanted to hear, saw only what he chose to see and remembered everything.

After pressing a series of buttons on his word processor, he set up for the next chapter. The next chapter, the next word, the next book, was of much more importance to him than any speculative article he might read.

He'd worked for six hours that day, and he thought he was good for at least two more. The story was flowing out of him like ice water: cold and clear.

The hands that played the keys of the machine were beautiful—tanned, lean, long-fingered and wide-palmed. One might have looked at them and thought they would compose concertos or epic poems. What they composed were dark dreams and monsters—not the dripping-fanged, scaly-skinned variety, but monsters real enough to make the flesh crawl. He always included enough realism, enough of the everyday, in his stories to make the horror commonplace and all too plausible. There was a creature lurking in the dark closet of his work, and that creature was the private fear of every man. He found it, always. Then, inch by inch, he opened the closet door.

Half-forgotten, the cigarette smoldered in the overflowing ashtray at his elbow. He smoked too much. It was perhaps the only outward sign of the pressure he put on himself, a pressure he'd have tolerated from no one else. He wanted this book finished by the end of the month, his self-imposed deadline. In one of his rare impulses, he'd agreed to speak at a writers' conference in Flagstaff the first week of June.

It wasn't often he agreed to public appearances, and when he did it was never at a large, publicized event. This particular conference would boast no more than two hundred published and aspiring writers. He'd give his workshop, answer questions, then go home. There would be no speaker's fee.

That year alone, Hunter had summarily turned down offers from some of the most prestigious organizations in the publishing business. Prestige didn't interest him, but he considered, in his odd way, the contribution to the Central Arizona Writers' Guild a matter of paying his dues. Hunter had always understood that nothing was free.

It was late afternoon when the dog lying at his feet lifted his head. The dog was lean, with a shining gray coat and the narrow, intelligent look of a wolf.

"Is it time, Santanas?" With a gentleness the hand appeared made for, Hunter reached down to stroke the dog's head. Satisfied, but already deciding that he'd work late that evening, he turned off his word processor.

Hunter stepped out of the chaos of his office into the tidy living room with its tall, many-paned windows and lofted ceiling. It smelled of vanilla and daisies. Large and sleek, the dog padded alongside him.

After pushing open the doors that led to a terra-cotta patio, he looked into the thick surrounding woods. They shut him in, shut others out. Hunter had never considered which, only knew that he needed them. He needed the peace, the mystery and the beauty, just as he needed the rich red walls of the canyon that rose up around him. Through the quiet he could hear the trickle of water from the creek and smell the heady freshness of the air. These he never took for granted; he hadn't had them forever.

Then he saw her, walking leisurely down the winding path toward the house. The dog's tail began to swish back and forth.

Sometimes, when he watched her like this, Hunter would think it impossible that anything so lovely belonged to him. She was dark and delicately formed, moving with a careless confidence that made him grin even as it made him ache. She was Sarah. His work and his privacy were the two vital things in his life. Sarah was his life. She'd been worth the struggles, the frustration, the fears and the pain. She was worth everything.

Looking over, she broke into a smile that flashed with braces. *"Hi, Dad!"*

Chapter 1

The week a magazine like *Celebrity* went to bed was utter chaos. Every department head was in a frenzy. Desks were littered, phones were tied up and lunches were skipped. The air was tinged with a sense of panic that built with every hour. Tempers grew short, demands outrageous. In most offices the lights burned late into the night. The rich scent of coffee and the sting of tobacco smoke were never absent. Rolls of antacids were consumed and bottles of eye drops constantly changed hands. After five years on staff, Lee took the monthly panic as a matter of course.

Celebrity was a slick, respected publication whose sales generated millions of dollars a year. In addition to stories on the rich and famous, it ran articles by eminent psychologists and journalists, interviews with both statesmen and rock stars. Its photography was first-class, just as its text was thoroughly researched and concisely written. Some of its detractors might have termed it quality gossip, but the word *quality* wasn't forgotten.

An ad in *Celebrity* was a sure bet for generating sales and interest and was priced accordingly. *Celebrity* was, in a tough, competitive business, one of the leading monthly publications in the country. Lee Radcliffe wouldn't have settled for less.

"How'd the piece on the sculptures turn out?"

Lee glanced up at Bryan Mitchell, one of the top photographers on the West Coast. Grateful, she accepted the cup of coffee Bryan passed her. In the past four days, she'd had a total of twenty hours' sleep. "Good," she said simply.

"I've seen better art scrawled in alleys."

Though she privately agreed, Lee only shrugged. "Some people like the clunky and obscure."

With a laugh, Bryan shook her head. "When they told me to photograph that red-and-black tangle of wire to its best advantage, I nearly asked them to shut off the lights."

"You made it look almost mystical."

"I can make a junkyard look mystical with the right lighting." She shot Lee a grin. "The same way you can make it sound fascinating."

A smile touched Lee's mouth but her mind was veering off in a dozen other directions. "All in a day's work, right?"

"Speaking of which—" Bryan rested one slim jean-clad hip on Lee's organized desk, drinking her own coffee black. "Still trying to dig something up on Hunter Brown?"

A frown drew Lee's elegant brows together. Hunter

Brown was becoming her personal quest and almost an obsession. Perhaps because he was so completely inaccessible, she'd become determined to be the first to break through the cloud of mystery. It had taken her nearly five years to earn her title as staff reporter, and she had a reputation for being tenacious, thorough and cool. Lee knew she'd earned those adjectives. Three months of hitting blank walls in researching Hunter Brown didn't deter her. One way or the other, she was going to get the story.

"So far I haven't gotten beyond his agent's name and his editor's phone number." There might've been a hint of frustration in her tone, but her expression was determined. "I've never known people so closemouthed."

"His latest book hit the stands last week." Absently, Bryan picked up the top sheet from one of the tidy piles of papers Lee was systematically dealing with. "Have you read it?"

"I picked it up, but I haven't had a chance to start it yet."

Bryan tossed back the long honey-colored braid that fell over her shoulder. "Don't start it on a dark night." She sipped at her coffee, then gave a laugh. "God, I ended up sleeping with every light in the apartment burning. I don't know how he does it."

Lee glanced up again, her eyes calm and confident. "That's one of the things I'm going to find out."

Bryan nodded. She'd known Lee for three years, and she didn't doubt Lee would. "Why?" Her frank, almond-shaped eyes rested on Lee's.

"Because—" Lee finished off her coffee and tossed the empty cup into her overflowing wastebasket "—no one else has."

"The Mount Everest syndrome," Bryan commented, and earned a rare, spontaneous grin.

A quick glance would have shown two attractive women in casual conversation in a modern, attractively decorated office. A closer look would have uncovered the contrasts. Bryan, in jeans and a snug T-shirt, was completely relaxed. Everything about her was casual and not quite tidy, from her smudged sneakers to the loose braid. Her sharp-featured, arresting face was touched only with a hasty dab of mascara. She'd probably meant to add lipstick or blusher and then forgotten.

Lee, on the other hand, wore a very elegant ice-blue suit, and the nerves that gave her her drive were evident in the hands that were never quite still. Her hair was expertly cut in a short swinging style that took very little care—which was every bit as important to her as having it look good. Its shade fell somewhere between copper and gold. Her skin was the delicate, milky white some redheads bless and others curse. Her makeup had been meticulously applied that morning, down to the dusky blue shadow that matched her eyes. She had delicate, elegant features offset by a full and obviously stubborn mouth.

The two women had entirely different styles and entirely different tastes but oddly enough, their friendship had begun the moment they'd met. Though Bryan didn't always like Lee's aggressive tactics and Lee didn't always approve of Bryan's laid-back approach, their closeness hadn't wavered in three years.

"So." Bryan found the candy bar she'd stuck in her jeans pocket and proceeded to unwrap it. "What's your master plan?"

"To keep digging," Lee returned almost grimly. "I do

have a couple of connections at Horizon, his publishing house. Maybe one of them'll come through with something." Without being fully aware of it, she drummed her fingers on the desk. "Damn it, Bryan, he's like the man who wasn't there. I can't even find out what state he lives in."

"I'm half-inclined to believe some of the rumors," Bryan said thoughtfully. Outside Lee's office someone was having hysterics over the final editing of an article. "I'd say the guy lives in a cave somewhere, full of bats with a couple of stray wolves thrown in. He probably writes the original manuscript in sheep's blood."

"And sacrifices virgins every new moon."

"I wouldn't be surprised." Bryan swung her feet lazily while she munched on her chocolate bar. "I tell you the man's weird."

"*Silent Scream*'s already on the bestseller list."

"I didn't say he wasn't brilliant," Bryan countered, "I said he was weird. What kind of a mind does he have?" She shook her head with a half-sheepish smile. "I can tell you I wished I'd never heard of Hunter Brown last night while I was trying to sleep with my eyes open."

"That's just it." Impatient, Lee rose and paced to the tiny window on the east wall. She wasn't looking out; the view of Los Angeles didn't interest her. She just had to move around. "What kind of mind *does* he have? What kind of life does he live? Is he married? Is he sixty-five or twenty-five? Why does he write novels about the supernatural?" She turned, her impatience and her annoyance showing beneath the surface of the sophisticated grooming. "Why did you read his book?"

"Because it was fascinating," Bryan answered immediately. "Because by the time I was on page three, I was so into it you couldn't have gotten the book away from me with a crowbar."

"And you're an intelligent woman."

"Damn right," Bryan agreed and grinned. "So?"

"Why do intelligent people buy and read something that's going to terrify them?" Lee demanded. "When you pick up a Hunter Brown, you know what it's going to do to you, yet his books consistently spring to the top of the bestseller list and stay there. Why does an obviously intelligent man write books like that?" She began, in a habit Bryan recognized, to fiddle with whatever was at hand—the leaves of a philodendron, the stub of a pencil, the left earring she'd removed during a phone conversation.

"Do I hear a hint of disapproval?"

"Yeah, maybe." Frowning, Lee looked up again. "The man is probably the best colorist in the country. If he's describing a room in an old house, you can smell the dust. His characterizations are so real you'd swear you'd met the people in his books. And he uses that talent to write about things that go bump in the night. I want to find out why."

Bryan crumpled her candy wrapper into a ball. "I know a woman who has one of the sharpest, most analytical minds I've ever come across. She has a talent for digging up obscure facts, some of them impossibly dry, and turning them into intriguing stories. She's ambitious, has a remarkable talent for words, but works on a magazine and lets a half-finished novel sit abandoned in a drawer. She's lovely, but she rarely dates for any purpose other than business. And she has a habit of twisting paper clips into ungodly shapes while she's talking."

Lee glanced down at the small mangled piece of

metal in her hands, then met Bryan's eyes coolly. "Do you know why?"

There was a hint of humor in Bryan's eyes, but her tone was serious enough. "I've tried to figure it out for three years, but I can't precisely put my finger on it."

With a smile, Lee tossed the bent paper clip into the trash. "But then, you're not a reporter."

Because she wasn't very good at taking advice, Lee switched on her bedside lamp, stretched out and opened Hunter Brown's latest novel. She would read a chapter or two, she decided, then make it an early night. An early night was an almost sinful luxury after the week she'd put in at *Celebrity*.

Her bedroom was done in creamy ivories and shades of blue from the palest aqua to indigo. She'd indulged herself here, with dozens of plump throw pillows, a huge Turkish rug and a Queen Anne stand that held an urn filled with peacock feathers and eucalyptus. Her latest acquisition, a large ficus tree, sat by the window and thrived.

She considered this room the only truly private spot in her life. As a reporter, Lee accepted that she was public property as much as the people she sought out. Privacy wasn't something she could cling to when she constantly dug into other people's lives. But in this little corner of the world, she could relax completely, forget there was work to do, ladders to climb. She could pretend L.A. wasn't bustling outside, as long as she had this oasis of peace. Without it, without the hours she spent sleeping and unwinding there, she knew she'd overload.

Knowing herself well, Lee understood that she had a tendency to push too hard, run too fast. In the quiet of her bedroom she could recharge herself each night so that she'd be ready for the race again the following day.

Relaxed, she opened Hunter Brown's latest effort.

Within a half hour, Lee was disturbed, uncomfortable and completely engrossed. She'd have been angry with the author for drawing her in if she hadn't been so busy turning pages. He'd put an ordinary man in an extraordinary situation and done it with such skill that Lee was already relating to the teacher who'd found himself caught up in a small town with a dark secret.

The prose flowed and the dialogue was so natural she could hear the voices. He filled the town with so many recognizable things, she could have sworn she'd been there herself. She knew the story was going to give her more than one bad moment in the dark, but she had to go on. That was the magic of a major storyteller. Cursing him, she read on, so tense that when the phone rang beside her, the book flew out of her hands. Lee swore again, at herself, and lifted the receiver.

Her annoyance at being disturbed didn't last. Grabbing a pencil, she began to scrawl on the pad beside the phone. With her tongue caught between her teeth, she set down the pencil and smiled. She owed the contact in New York an enormous favor, but she'd pay off when the time came, as she always did. For now, Lee thought, running her hand over Hunter's book, she had to make arrangements to attend a small writers' conference in Flagstaff, Arizona.

She had to admit the country was impressive. As was her habit, Lee had spent the time during the flight from L.A. to Phoenix working, but once she'd changed to the small commuter plane for the trip to Flagstaff, her work had been forgotten. She'd flown through thin clouds over a vastness almost impossible to conceive after the skyscrapers and traffic of Los Angeles. She'd looked down on the peaks and dips and castlelike rocks of Oak Creek Canyon, feeling a drumming excitement that was rare in a woman who wasn't easily impressed. If she'd had more time...

Lee sighed as she stepped off the plane. There was never time enough.

The tiny airport boasted a one-room lobby with a choice of concession stand or soda and candy machines. No loudspeaker announced incoming and outgoing flights. No skycap bustled up to her to relieve her of her bags. There wasn't a line of cabs waiting outside to compete for the handful of people who'd disembarked. With her garment bag slung over her shoulder, she frowned at the inconvenience. Patience wasn't one of her virtues.

Tired, hungry and inwardly a little frazzled by the shaky commuter flight, she stepped up to one of the counters. "I need to arrange for a car to take me to town."

The man in shirtsleeves and loosened tie stopped pushing buttons on his computer. His first polite glance sharpened when he saw her face. She reminded him of a cameo his grandmother had worn at her neck on special occasions. Automatically he straightened his shoulders. "Did you want to rent a car?"

Lee considered that a moment, then rejected it. She hadn't come to do any sightseeing, so a car would hardly be worthwhile. "No, just transportation into Flagstaff." Shifting her bag, she gave him the name of her hotel. "Do they have a courtesy car?"

"Sure do. You go on over to that phone by the wall there. Number's listed. Just give 'em a call and they'll send someone out."

"Thank you."

He watched her walk to the phone and thought he was the one who should have said thank-you.

Lee caught the scent of grilling hot dogs as she crossed the room. Since she'd turned down the dubious tray offered on the flight, the scent had her stomach juices swimming. Quickly and efficiently, she dialed the hotel, gave her name and was assured a car would be there within twenty minutes. Satisfied, she bought a hot dog and settled in one of the black plastic chairs to wait.

She was going to get what she'd come for, Lee told herself almost fiercely as she looked out at the distant mountains. The time wasn't going to be wasted. After three months of frustration, she was finally going to get a firsthand look at Hunter Brown.

It had taken skill and determination to persuade her editor-in-chief to spring for the trip, but it would pay off. It had to. Leaning back, she reviewed the questions she'd ask Hunter Brown once she'd cornered him.

All she needed, Lee decided, was an hour with him. Sixty minutes. In that time, she could pull out enough information for a concise, and very exclusive, article. She'd done precisely that with this year's Oscar winner, though he'd been reluctant, and a presidential candidate, though he'd been hostile. Hunter Brown would probably be both, she decided with a half smile. It would only add spice. If she'd wanted a bland, simple life, she'd have bent under the pressure and married Jonathan. Right now she'd be planning her next garden party rather than calculating how to ambush an award-winning writer.

Lee nearly laughed aloud. Garden parties, bridge parties and the yacht club. That might have been perfect for her family, but she'd wanted more. More what? her mother had demanded, and Lee could only reply, Just more.

Checking her watch, she left her luggage neatly stacked by the chair and went into the ladies' room. The door had hardly closed behind her when the object of all her planning strolled into the lobby.

He didn't often do good deeds, and then only for people he had a genuine affection for. Because he'd gotten into town with time to spare, Hunter had driven to the airport with the intention of picking up his editor. With barely a glance around, he walked over to the same counter Lee had approached ten minutes before.

"Flight 471 on time?"

"Yes, sir, got in ten minutes ago."

"Did a woman get off?" Hunter glanced at the nearly empty lobby again. "Attractive, midtwenties—"

"Yes, sir," the clerk interrupted. "She just stepped into the restroom. That's her luggage over there."

"Thanks." Satisfied, Hunter walked over to Lee's neat stack of luggage. Doesn't believe in traveling light, he noticed, scanning the garment bag, small Pullman and briefcase. Then, what woman did? Hadn't his Sarah taken two suitcases for the brief three-day stay with his sister in Phoenix? Strange that his little girl should be two parts woman already. Perhaps not so strange, Hunter reflected. Females were born two parts woman, while males took years to grow out of boyhood—if they ever did. Perhaps that's why he trusted men a great deal more.

Lee saw him when she came back into the lobby. His

back was to her, so that she had only the impression of a tall, leanly built man with black hair curling carelessly down to the neck of his T-shirt. Right on time, she thought with satisfaction, and approached him.

"I'm Lee Radcliffe."

When he turned, she went stone-still, the impersonal smile freezing on her face. In the first instant, she couldn't have said why. He was attractive—perhaps too attractive. His face was narrow but not scholarly, raw-boned but not rugged. It was too much a combination of both to be either. His nose was straight and aristocratic, while his mouth was sculpted like a poet's. His hair was dark and full and unruly, as though he'd been driving fast for hours with the wind blowing free. But it wasn't these things that caused her to lose her voice. It was his eyes.

She'd never seen eyes darker than his, more direct, more…disturbing. It was as though they looked through her. No, not through, Lee corrected numbly. Into. In ten seconds, they had looked into her and seen everything.

He saw a stunning, milk-pale face with dusky eyes gone wide in astonishment. He saw a soft, feminine mouth, lightly tinted. He saw nerves. He saw a stubborn chin and molten copper hair that would feel like silk between the fingers. What he saw was an outwardly poised, inwardly tense woman who smelled like spring evenings and looked like a *Vogue* cover. If it hadn't been for that inner tension, he might have dismissed her, but what lay beneath people's surfaces always intrigued him.

He skimmed her neat traveling suit so quickly his eyes might never have left hers. "Yes?"

"Well, I…" Forced to swallow, she trailed off. That

alone infuriated her. She wasn't about to be set off into stammers by a driver for the hotel. "If you've come to pick me up," Lee said curtly, "you'll need to get my bags."

Lifting a brow, he said nothing. Her mistake was simple and obvious. It would have taken only a sentence from him to correct it. Then again, it was her mistake, not his. Hunter had always believed more in impulses than explanations. Bending down, he picked up the Pullman, then slung the strap of the garment bag over his shoulder. "The car's out here."

She felt a great deal more secure with the briefcase in her hand and his back to her. The oddness, Lee told herself, had come from excitement and a long flight. Men never surprised her; they certainly never made her stare and stammer. What she needed was a bath and something a bit more substantial to eat than that hot dog.

The car he'd referred to wasn't a car, she noted, but a Jeep. Supposing this made sense, with the steep roads and hard winters, Lee climbed in.

Moves well, he thought, and dresses flawlessly. He noted, too, that she bit her nails. "Are you from the area?" Hunter asked conversationally when he'd stowed her bags in the back.

"No. I'm here for the writers' conference."

Hunter climbed in beside her and shut the door. Now he knew where to take her. "You're a writer?"

She thought of the two chapters of her manuscript she'd brought along in case she needed a cover. "Yes."

Hunter swung through the parking lot, taking the back road that led to the highway. "What do you write?"

Settling back, Lee decided she might as well try her routine out on him before she was in the middle of two hundred published and aspiring writers. "I've done articles and some short stories," she told him truthfully enough. Then she added what she'd rarely told anyone. "I've started a novel."

With a speed that surprised but didn't unsettle her, he burst onto the highway. "Are you going to finish it?" he asked, showing an insight that disturbed her.

"I suppose that depends on a lot of things."

He took another careful look at her profile. "Such as?"

She wanted to shift in her seat but forced herself to be still. This was just the sort of question she might have to answer over the weekend. "Such as if what I've done so far is any good."

He found both her answer and her discomfort reasonable. "Do you go to many of these conferences?"

"No, this is my first."

Which might account for the nerves, Hunter mused, but he didn't think he'd found the entire answer.

"I'm hoping to learn something," Lee said with a small smile. "I registered at the last minute, but when I learned Hunter Brown would be here, I couldn't resist."

The frown in his eyes came and went too quickly to be noticed. He'd agreed to do the workshop only because it wouldn't be publicized. Even the registrants wouldn't know he'd be there, until the following morning. Just how, he wondered, had the little redhead with the Italian shoes and midnight eyes found out? He passed a truck. "Who?"

"Hunter Brown," Lee repeated. "The novelist."

Impulse took over again. "Is he any good?"

Surprised, Lee turned to study his profile. It was infinitely easier to look at him, she discovered, when those eyes weren't focused on her. "You've never read any of his work?"

"Should I have?"

"I suppose that depends on whether you like to read with all the lights on and the doors locked. He writes horror fiction."

If she'd looked more closely, she wouldn't have missed the quick humor in his eyes. "Ghouls and fangs?"

"Not exactly," she said after a moment. "Not that simple. If there's something you're afraid of, he'll put it into words and make you wish him to the devil."

Hunter laughed, greatly pleased. "So, you like to be scared?"

"No," Lee said definitely.

"Then why do you read him?"

"I've asked myself that when I'm up at 3:00 a.m. finishing one of his books." Lee shrugged as the Jeep slowed for the turn-off. "It's irresistible. I think he must be a very odd man," she murmured, half to herself. "Not quite, well, not quite like the rest of us."

"Do you?" After a quick, sharp turn, he pulled up in front of the hotel, more interested in her than he'd planned to be. "But isn't writing just words and imagination?"

"And sweat and blood," she added, moving her shoulders again. "I just don't see how it could be very comfortable to live with an imagination like Brown's. I'd like to know how he feels about it."

Amused, Hunter jumped out of the Jeep to retrieve her bags. "You're going to ask him."

"Yes." Lee stepped down. "I am."

For a moment, they stood on the sidewalk, silently.

He looked at her with what might have been mild interest, but she sensed something more—something she shouldn't have felt from a hotel driver after a ten-minute acquaintance. For the second time she wanted to shift and made herself stand still. Wasting no more words, Hunter turned toward the hotel, her bags in hand.

It didn't occur to Lee until she was following him inside that she'd had a nonstop conversation with a hotel driver, a conversation that hadn't dwelt on the usual pleasantries or tourist plugs. As she watched him walk to the desk, she felt an aura of cool confidence from him and traces, very subtle traces, of arrogance. Why was a man like this driving back and forth and getting nowhere? she wondered. Stepping up to the desk, she told herself it wasn't her concern. She had bigger fish to fry.

"Lenore Radcliffe," she told the clerk.

"Yes, Ms. Radcliffe." He handed her a form and imprinted her credit card before he passed her a key. Before she could take it, Hunter slipped it into his own hand. It was then she noticed the odd ring on his pinky, four thin bands of gold and silver twisted into one.

"I'll take you around," he said simply, then crossed through the lobby with her again in his wake. He wound through a corridor, turned left, then stopped. Lee waited while he unlocked the door and gestured her inside.

The room was on the garden level with its own patio, she was pleased to note. As she scanned the room, Hunter carelessly switched on the TV and flipped through the channels before he checked the air conditioner. "Just call the desk if you need anything else," he advised, stowing her garment bag in the closet.

"Yes, I will." Lee hunted through her purse and came up with a five. "Thank you," she said, holding it out.

His eyes met hers again, giving her that same frozen jolt they had in the airport. She felt something stir deep within but wasn't sure if it was trying to reach out to him or struggling to hide. The fingers holding the bill nearly trembled. Then he smiled, so quickly, so charmingly, she was speechless.

"Thank you, Ms. Radcliffe." Without a blink, Hunter pocketed the five dollars and strolled out.

Chapter 2

If writers were often considered odd, writers' conferences, Lee was to discover, were oddities in themselves. They certainly couldn't be considered quiet or organized or stuffy.

Like nearly every other of the two hundred or so participants, she stood in one of the dozen lines at 8:00 a.m. for registration. From the laughing and calling and embracing, it was obvious that many of the writers and would-be writers knew one another. There was an air of congeniality, shared knowledge and camaraderie. Overlaying it all was excitement.

Still, more than one member stood in the noisy lobby like a child lost in a shipwreck, clinging to a folder or briefcase as though it were a life preserver and staring about with awe or simple confusion. Lee could appreciate the feeling, though she looked calm and poised as she accepted her packet and pinned her badge to the mint-green lapel of her blazer.

Concentrating on the business at hand, she found a chair in a corner and skimmed the schedule for Hunter Brown's workshop. With a dawning smile, she took out a pen and underlined.

CREATING HORROR THROUGH ATMOSPHERE AND EMOTION
Speaker to be announced.

Bingo, Lee thought, capping her pen. She'd make certain she had a front-row seat. A glance at her watch showed her that she had three hours before Brown began to speak. Never one to take chances, she took out her notebook to skim over the questions she'd listed, while people filed by her or merely loitered, chatting.

"If I get rejected again, I'm going to put my head in the oven."

"Your oven's electric, Judy."

"It's the thought that counts."

Amused, Lee began to listen to the passing comments with half an ear while she added a few more questions.

"And when they brought in my breakfast this morning, there was a five-hundred-page manuscript under my plate. I completely lost my appetite."

"That's nothing. I got one in my office last week written in calligraphy. One hundred and fifty thousand words of flowing script."

Editors, she mused. She could tell them a few stories about some of the submissions that found their way to *Celebrity*.

"He said his editor hacked his first chapter to pieces so he's going into mourning before the rewrites."

"I always go into mourning before rewrites. It's after a rejection that I seriously consider taking up basket weaving as a profession."

"Did you hear Jeffries is here again trying to peddle that manuscript about the virgin with acrophobia and telekinesis? I can't believe he won't let it die a quiet death. When's your next murder coming out?"

"In August. It's poison."

"Darling, that's no way to talk about your work."

As they passed by her, Lee caught the variety of tones, some muted, some sophisticated, some flamboyant. Gestures and conversations followed the same wide range. Amazed, she watched one man swoop by in a long, dramatic black cape.

Definitely an odd group, Lee thought, but she warmed to them. It was true she confined her skill to articles and profiles, but at heart she was a storyteller. Her position on the magazine had been hard-earned, and she'd built her world around it. For all her ambition, she had a firm fear of rejection that kept her own manuscript unfinished, buried in a drawer for weeks and sometimes months at a time. At the magazine, she had prestige, security and room for advancement. The weekly paycheck put the roof over her head, the clothes on her back and the food on her table.

If it hadn't been so important that she prove she could do all this for herself, she might have taken the chance of sending those first hundred pages to a publishing house. But then… Shaking her head, Lee watched the people mill through the registration area, all types, all sizes, all ages. Clothes varied from trim professional suits to jeans to flamboyant caftans and smocks. Apparently style was a matter of taste and taste a matter of individuality. She wondered if she'd see quite the same variety anywhere else. Absently, she glanced at the partial manuscript she'd tucked into her briefcase. Just for cover, she reminded herself. That was all.

No, she didn't believe she had it in her to be a great writer, but she knew she had the skill for great reporting. She'd never, never settle for being second-rate at anything.

Still, while she was here, it wouldn't hurt to sit in on one or two of the seminars. She might pick up some pointers. More important, she told herself as she rose, she might be able to stretch this trip into another story on the ins and outs of a writers' conference. Who attended, why, what they did, what they hoped for. Yes, it could make quite an interesting little piece. The job, after all, came first.

An hour later, a bit more enthusiastic than she wanted to be after her first workshop, she wandered into the coffee shop. She'd take a short break, assimilate the notes she'd written, then go back and make certain she had the best seat in the house for Hunter Brown's lecture.

Hunter glanced up from his paper and watched her enter the coffee shop. Lee Radcliffe, he mused, finding her of more interest than the local news he'd been scanning. He'd enjoyed his conversation with her the day before, and as often as not, he found conversations tedious. She had a quality about her—an innate frankness glossed with sophistication—that he found intriguing enough to hold his interest. An obsessive writer who believed that the characters themselves were the plot of any book, Hunter always looked for the unique and the individual. Instinct told him Lee Radcliffe was quite an individual.

Unobserved, he watched her. From the way she looked absently around the room it was obvious she was preoccupied. The suit she wore was very simple but showed both style and taste in the color and cut. She was a woman who could wear the simple, he decided, because she was a woman who'd been born with style. If he wasn't very much mistaken, she'd been born into wealth as well. There was always a subtle difference between those who were accustomed to money and those who'd spent years earning it.

So where did the nerves come from? he wondered. Curious, he decided it would be worth an hour of his time to try to find out.

Setting his paper aside, Hunter lit a cigarette and continued to stare at her, knowing there was no quicker way to catch someone's eye.

Lee, thinking more about the story she was going to write than the coffee she'd come for, felt an odd tingle run up her spine. It was real enough to give her an urge to turn around and walk out again when she glanced over and found herself staring back at the man she'd met at the airport.

It was his eyes, she decided, at first not thinking of him as a man or the hotel driver from the previous day. It was his eyes. Dark, almost the color of jet, they'd draw you in and draw you in until you were caught, and every secret you'd ever had would be secret no longer. It was frightening. It was…irresistible.

Amazed that such a fanciful thought had crept into her own practical, organized mind, Lee approached him. He was just a man, she told herself, a man who worked for his living like any other man. There was certainly nothing to be frightened of.

"Ms. Radcliffe." With the same unsmiling stare, he gestured to the chair across from him. "Buy you a cup of coffee?"

Normally she would've refused, politely enough. But now, for some intangible reason, Lee felt as though she had a point to prove. For the same intangible reason, she felt she had to prove it to him as much as to herself. "Thank you." The moment she sat down, a waitress was there, pouring coffee.

"Enjoying the conference?"

"Yes." Lee poured cream into the cup, stirring it around and around until a tiny whirlpool formed in the center. "As disorganized as everything seems to be, there was an amazing amount of information generated at the workshop I went to this morning."

A smile touched his lips, so lightly that it was barely there at all. "You prefer organization?"

"It's more productive." Though he was dressed more formally than he'd been the day before, the pleated slacks and open-necked shirt were still casual. She wondered why he wasn't required to wear a uniform. But then, she thought, you could put him in one of those nifty white jackets and neat ties and his eyes would simply defy them.

"A lot of fascinating things can come out of chaos, don't you think?"

"Perhaps." She frowned down at the whirlpool in her cup. Why did she feel as though she was being sucked in, in just that way? And why, she thought with a sudden flash of impatience, was she sitting here having a philosophical discussion with a stranger when she should be outlining the two stories she planned to write?

"Did you find Hunter Brown?" he asked her as he studied her over the rim of his cup. Annoyed with herself, he guessed accurately, and anxious to be off doing.

"What?" Distracted, Lee looked back up to find those strange eyes still on her.

"I asked if you'd run into Hunter Brown." The whisper of a smile was on his lips again, and this time it touched his eyes as well. It didn't make them any less intense.

"No." Defensive without knowing why, Lee sipped at her cooling coffee. "Why?"

"After the things you said yesterday, I was curious what you'd think of him once you met him." He took a drag from his cigarette and blew smoke out in a haze. "People usually have a preconceived image of someone but it rarely holds up in the flesh."

"It's difficult to have any kind of an image of someone who hides away from the world."

His brow went up, but his voice remained mild. "Hides?"

"It's the word that comes to my mind," Lee returned, again finding that she was speaking her thoughts aloud to him. "There's no picture of him on the back of any of his books, no bio. He never grants interviews, never denies or substantiates anything written about him. Any awards he's received have been accepted by his agent or his editor." She ran her fingers up and down the handle of her spoon. "I've heard he occasionally attends affairs like this, but only if it's a very small conference and there's no publicity about his appearance."

All during her speech, Hunter kept his eyes on her,

watching every nuance of expression. There were traces of frustration, he was certain, and of eagerness. The lovely cameo face was calm while her fingers moved restlessly. She'd be in his next book, he decided on the spot. He'd never met anyone with more potential for being a central character.

Because his direct, unblinking stare made her want to stammer, Lee gave him back the hard, uncompromising look. "Why do you stare at me like that?"

He continued to do so without any show of discomfort. "Because you're an interesting woman."

Another man might have said beautiful, still another might have said fascinating. Lee could have tossed off either one with light scorn. She picked up her spoon again, then set it down. "Why?"

"You have a tidy mind, innate style, and you're a bundle of nerves." He liked the way the faint line appeared between her brows when she frowned. It meant stubbornness to him, and tenacity. He respected both. "I've always been intrigued by pockets," Hunter went on. "The deeper the better. I find myself wondering just what's in your pockets, Ms. Radcliffe."

She felt the tremor again, up her spine, then down. It wasn't comfortable to sit near a man who could do that. She had a moment's sympathy for every person she'd ever interviewed. "You have an odd way of putting things," she muttered.

"So I've been told."

She instructed herself to get up and leave. It didn't make sense to sit there being disturbed by a man she could dismiss with a five-dollar tip. "What are you doing in Flagstaff?" she demanded. "You don't strike me as someone who'd be content to drive back and forth to an airport day after day, shuttling passengers and hauling luggage."

"Impressions make fascinating little paintings, don't they?" He smiled at her fully, as he had the day before when she'd tipped him. Lee wasn't sure why she'd felt he'd been laughing at her then, any more than why she felt he was laughing at her now. Despite herself, her lips curved in response. He found the smile a pleasant and very alluring surprise.

"You're a very odd man."

"I've been told that, too." His smile faded and his eyes became intense again. "Have dinner with me tonight."

The question didn't surprise her as much as the fact that she wanted to accept, and nearly had. "No," she said, cautiously retreating. "I don't think so."

"Let me know if you change your mind."

She was surprised again. Most men would've pressed a bit. It was, well, expected, Lee reflected, wishing she could figure him out. "I have to get back." She reached for her briefcase. "Do you know where the Canyon Room is?"

With an inward chuckle, he dropped bills on the table. "Yes, I'll show you."

"That's not necessary," Lee began, rising.

"I've got time." He walked with her out of the coffee shop and into the wide, carpeted lobby. "Do you plan to do any sightseeing while you're here?"

"There won't be time." She glanced out one of the wide windows at the towering peak of Humphrey Peak. "As soon as the conference is over I have to get back."

"To where?"

"Los Angeles."

"Too many people," Hunter said automatically. "Don't you ever feel as though they're using up your air?"

She wouldn't have put it that way, would never have thought of it, but there were times she felt a twinge of what might be called claustrophobia. Still, her home was there, and more important, her work. "No. There's enough air, such as it is, for everyone."

"You've never stood at the south rim of the canyon and looked out, and breathed in."

Again, Lee shot him a look. He had a way of saying things that gave you an immediate picture. For the second time, she regretted that she wouldn't be able to take a day or two to explore some of the vastness of Arizona. "Maybe some other time." Shrugging, she turned with him as he headed down a corridor to the right.

"Time's fickle," he commented. "When you need it, there's too little of it. Then you wake up at three o'clock in the morning, and there's too much of it. It's usually better to take it than to anticipate it. You might try that," he said, looking down at her again. "It might help your nerves."

Her brows drew together. "There's nothing wrong with my nerves."

"Some people can thrive on nervous energy for weeks at a time, then they have to find that little valve that lets the steam escape." For the first time, he touched her, just fingertips to the ends of her hair. But she felt it, experienced it, as hard and strong as if his hand had closed firmly over hers. "What do you do to let the steam escape, Lenore?"

She didn't stiffen, or casually nudge his hand away as she would have done at any other time. Instead, she stood still, toying with a sensation she couldn't remember ever experiencing before. Thunder and lightning, she thought. There was thunder and lightning in this man, deep under the strangely aloof, oddly open exterior. She wasn't about to be caught in the storm.

"I work," she said easily, but her fingers had tightened on the handle of her briefcase. "I don't need any other escape valve." She didn't step back, but let the haughtiness that had always protected her enter her tone. "No one calls me Lenore."

"No?" He nearly smiled. It was this look, she realized, the secret amusement the onlooker could only guess at rather than see, that most intrigued. She thought he probably knew that. "But it suits you. Feminine, elegant, a little distant. *And the only word there spoken was the whispered word, 'Lenore!'* Yes." He let his fingertips linger a moment longer on her hair. "I think Poe would've found you very apt."

Before she could prevent it, before she could anticipate it, her knees were weak. She'd felt the sound of her own name feather over her skin. "Who are you?" Lee found herself demanding. Was it possible to be so deeply affected by someone without even knowing his name? She stepped forward in what seemed to be a challenge. "Just who are you?"

He smiled again, with the oddly gentle charm that shouldn't have suited his eyes yet somehow did. "Strange, you never asked before. You'd better go in," he told her as people began to gravitate toward the open doors of the Canyon Room. "You'll want a good seat."

"Yes." She drew back, a bit shaken by the ferocity of the desire she felt to learn more about him. With a last look over her shoulder, Lee walked in and settled in the front row. It was time to get her mind back on the business she'd come for, and the business was Hunter Brown. Distractions like incomprehensible men who drove Jeeps for a living would have to be put aside.

From her briefcase, Lee took a fresh notebook and two pencils, slipping one behind her ear. Within a few moments, she'd be able to see and study the mysterious Hunter Brown. She'd be able to listen and take notes with perfect freedom. After his lecture, she'd be able to question him, and if she had her way, she'd arrange some kind of one-on-one for later.

Lee had given the ethics of the situation careful thought. She didn't feel it would be necessary to tell Brown she was a reporter. She was there as an aspiring writer and had the fledgling manuscript to prove it. Anyone there was free to try to write and sell an article on the conference and its participants. Only if Brown used the words *off the record* would she be bound to silence. Without that, anything he said was public property.

This story could be her next step up the ladder. Would be, Lee corrected. The first documented, authentically researched story on Hunter Brown could push her beyond *Celebrity*'s scope. It would be controversial, colorful and, most important, exclusive. With this under her belt, even her quietly critical family would be impressed. With this under her belt, Lee thought, she'd be that much closer to the top rung, where her sights were always set.

Once she was there, all the hard work, the long hours, the obsessive dedication would be worth it. Because once she was there, she was there to stay. At the top, Lee thought almost fiercely. As high as she could reach.

On the other side of the doors, on the other side of the corridor, Hunter stood with his editor, half listening to her comments on an interview she'd had with an aspiring writer. He caught the gist, that she was excited about the writer's potential. It was a talent of his to be able to conduct a perfectly lucid conversation when his mind was on something entirely different. It was something he roused himself to do only when the mood was on him. So he spoke to his editor and thought of Lee Radcliffe.

Yes, he was definitely going to use her in his next book. True, the plot was only a vague notion in his head, but he already knew she'd be the core of it. He needed to dig a bit deeper before he'd be satisfied, but he didn't foresee any problem there. If he'd gauged her correctly, she'd be confused when he walked to the podium, then stunned, then furious. If she wanted to talk to him as badly as she'd indicated, she'd swallow her temper.

A strong woman, Hunter decided. A will of iron and skin like cream. Vulnerable eyes and a damn-the-devil chin. A character was nothing without contrasts, strengths and weaknesses. And secrets, he thought, already certain he'd discover hers. He had another day and a half to explore Lenore Radcliffe. Hunter figured that was enough.

The corridor was full of laughter and complaints and enthusiasm as people loitered or filed through into the adjoining room. He knew what it was to feel enthusiastic about being a writer. If the pleasure went out of it, he'd still write. He was compelled to. But it would show in his work. Emotions always showed. He never *allowed* his feelings and thoughts to pour into his work—they would have done so regardless of his permission.

Hunter considered it a fair trade-off. His emotions, his thoughts, were there for anyone who cared to read them. His life was completely and without exception his own.

The woman beside him had his affection and his respect. He'd argued with her over motivation and sentence structure, losing as often as winning. He'd shouted at her, laughed with her and given her emotional support through her recent divorce. He knew her age, her favorite drink and her weakness for cashews. She'd been his editor for three years, which was as close to a marriage as many people come. Yet she had no idea he had a ten-year-old daughter named Sarah who liked to bake cookies and play soccer.

Hunter took a last drag on his cigarette as the president of the small writers' group approached. The man was a slick, imaginative science fiction writer whom Hunter had read and enjoyed. Otherwise, he wouldn't be there, about to make one of his rare appearances in the writing community.

"Mr. Brown, I don't need to tell you again how honored we are to have you here."

"No—" Hunter gave him the easy half smile "—you don't."

"There's liable to be quite a commotion when I announce you. After your lecture, I'll do everything I can to keep the thundering horde back."

"Don't worry about it. I'll manage."

The man nodded, never doubting it. "I'm having a small reception in my suite this evening, if you'd like to join us."

"I appreciate it, but I have a dinner engagement."

Though he didn't know quite what to make of the

smile, the organization's president was too intelligent to press his luck when he was about to pull off a coup. "If you're ready, then, I'll announce you."

"Any time."

Hunter followed him into the Canyon Room, then loitered just inside the doors. The room was already buzzing with anticipation and curiosity. The podium was set on a small stage in front of two hundred chairs that were nearly all filled. Talk died down when the president approached the stage, but continued in pockets of murmurs even after he'd begun to speak. Hunter heard one of the men nearest him whisper to a companion that he had three publishing houses competing for his manuscript. Hunter skimmed over the crowd, barely listening to the beginning of his introduction. Then his gaze rested again on Lee.

She was watching the speaker with a small, polite smile on her lips, but her eyes gave her away. They were dark and eager. Hunter let his gaze roam down until it rested on her lap. There, her hand opened and closed on the pencil. A bundle of nerves and energy wrapped in a very thin layer of confidence, he thought.

For the second time Lee felt his eyes on her, and for the second time she turned so that their gazes locked. The faint line marred her brow again as she wondered what he was doing inside the conference room. Unperturbed, leaning easily against the wall, Hunter stared back at her.

"His career's risen steadily since the publication of his first book, only five years ago. Since the first, *The Devil's Due,* he's given us the pleasure of being scared out of our socks every time we pick up his work." At the mention of the title, the murmurs increased and heads began to swivel. Hunter continued to stare at Lee, and she back at him, frowning. "His latest, *Silent Scream,* is already solid in the number-one spot on the bestseller list. We're honored and privileged to welcome to Flagstaff—Hunter Brown."

The effusive applause competed with the growing murmurs of two hundred people in a closed room. Casually, Hunter straightened from the wall and walked to the stage. He saw the pencil fall out of Lee's hand and roll to the floor. Without breaking rhythm, he stooped and picked it up.

"Better hold on to this," he advised, looking into her astonished eyes. As he handed it back, he watched astonishment flare into fury.

"You're a—"

"Yes, but you'd better tell me later." Walking the rest of the way to the stage, Hunter stepped behind the podium and waited for the applause to fade. Again he skimmed the crowd, but this time with such a quiet intensity that all sound died. For ten seconds there wasn't even the sound of breathing. "Terror," Hunter said into the microphone.

From the first word he had them spellbound, and held them captive for forty minutes. No one moved, no one yawned, no one slipped out for a cigarette. With her teeth clenched tight, Lee knew she despised him.

Simmering, struggling against the urge to spring up and stalk out, Lee sat stiffly and took meticulous notes. In the margin of the book she drew a perfectly recognizable caricature of Hunter with a dagger through his heart. It gave her enormous satisfaction.

When he agreed to field questions for ten minutes,

Lee's was the first hand up. Hunter looked directly at her, smiled and called on someone three rows back.

He answered professional questions professionally and evaded any personal references. She had to admire his skill, particularly since she was well aware he so seldom spoke in public. He showed no nerves, no hesitation and absolutely no inclination to call on her, though her hand was up and her eyes shot fiery little darts at him. But she was a reporter, Lee reminded herself. Reporters got nowhere if they stood on ceremony.

"Mr. Brown," Lee began, and rose.

"Sorry." With his slow smile, he held up a hand. "I'm afraid we're already overtime. Best of luck to all of you." He left the podium and the room, under a hail of applause. By the time Lee could work her way to the doors, she'd heard enough praise of Hunter Brown to turn her simmering temper to boil.

The nerve, she thought as she finally made it into the corridor. The unspeakable nerve. She didn't mind being bested in a game of chess; she could handle having her work criticized and her opinion questioned. All in all, Lee considered herself a reasonable, low-key person with no more than her fair share of conceit. The one thing she couldn't, wouldn't, tolerate was being made a fool of.

Revenge sprang into her mind, nasty, petty revenge. Oh, yes, she thought as she tried to work her way through the thick crowd of Hunter Brown fans, she'd have her revenge, somehow, some way. And when she did, it would be perfect.

She turned off at the elevators, knowing she was too full of fury to deal successfully with Hunter at that moment. She needed an hour to cool off and to plan.

The pencil she still held snapped between her fingers. If it was the last thing she did, she was going to make Hunter Brown squirm.

Just as she started to push the button for her floor, Hunter slipped inside the elevator. "Going up?" he asked easily, and pushed the number himself.

Lee felt the fury rise to her throat and burn. With an effort, she clamped her lips tight on the venom and stared straight ahead.

"Broke your pencil," Hunter observed, finding himself more amused than he'd been in days. He glanced at her open notebook, spotting the meticulously drawn caricature. An appreciative grin appeared. "Well done," he told her. "How'd you enjoy the workshop?"

Lee gave him one scathing look as the elevator doors opened. "You're a font of trivial information, Mr. Brown."

"You've got murder in your eyes, Lenore." He stepped into the hall with her. "It suits your hair. Your drawing makes it clear enough what you'd like to do. Why don't you stab me while you have the chance?"

As she continued to walk, Lee told herself she wouldn't give him the satisfaction of speaking to him. She wouldn't speak to him at all. Her head jerked up. "You've had a good laugh at my expense," she grated, and dug in her briefcase for her room key.

"A quiet chuckle or two," he corrected while she continued to simmer and search. "Lose your key?"

"No, I haven't lost my key." Frustrated, Lee looked up until fury met amusement. "Why don't you go away and sit on your laurels?"

"I've always found that uncomfortable. Why don't you vent your spleen, Lenore. You'd feel better."

"Don't call me Lenore!" she exploded as her control slipped. "You had no right to use me as the brunt of a joke. You had no right to pretend you worked for the hotel."

"You assumed," he corrected. "As I recall, I never pretended anything. You asked for a ride yesterday. I simply gave you one."

"You knew I thought you were the hotel driver. You were standing there beside my luggage—"

"A classic case of mistaken identity." He noted that her skin tinted with pale rose when she was angry. An attractive side effect, Hunter decided. "I'd come to pick up my editor, who'd missed her Phoenix connection, as it turned out. I thought the luggage was hers."

"All you had to do was say that at the time."

"You never asked," he pointed out. "And you did tell me to get the luggage."

"Oh, you're infuriating." Clamping her teeth shut, she began to fumble in her briefcase again.

"But brilliant. You mentioned that yourself."

"Being able to string words together is an admirable talent, Mr. Brown." Hauteur was one of her most practiced skills. Lee used it to the fullest. "It doesn't make you an admirable person."

"No, I wouldn't say I was, particularly." While he waited for her to find her key, Hunter leaned comfortably against the wall.

"You carried my luggage to my room," she continued, infuriated. "I gave you a five-dollar tip."

"Very generous."

She let out a huff of breath, grateful that her hands were busy. She didn't know how else she could have prevented herself from slapping his calm, self-satisfied face. "You've had your joke," she said, finding her key at last. "Now I'd like you to do me the courtesy of never speaking to me again."

"I don't know where you got the impression I was courteous." Before she could unlock the door, he'd put his hand over hers on the key. She felt the little tingle of power and cursed him for it even as she met his calmly amused look. "You did mention, however, that you'd like to speak to me. We can talk over dinner tonight."

She stared at him. Why should she have thought he wouldn't be able to surprise her again? "You have the most incredible nerve."

"You mentioned that already. Seven o'clock?"

She wanted to tell him she wouldn't have dinner with him even if he groveled. She wanted to tell him that and all manner of other unpleasant things. Temper fought with practicality. There was a job she'd come to do, one she'd been working on unsuccessfully for three months. Success was more important than pride. He was offering her the perfect way to do what she'd come to do, and to do it more extensively than she could've hoped for. And perhaps, just perhaps, he was opening the door himself for her revenge. It would make it all the sweeter.

Though it was a large lump, Lee swallowed her pride.

"That's fine," she agreed, but he noticed she didn't look too pleased. "Where should I meet you?"

He never trusted easy agreement. But then Hunter trusted very little. She was going to be a challenge, he felt. "I'll pick you up here." His fingers ran casually up to her wrist before he released her. "You might bring your manuscript along. I'm curious to see your work."

She smiled and thought of the article she was going to write. "I very much want you to see my work." Lee stepped into her room and gave herself the small satisfaction of slamming the door in his face.

Chapter 3

Midnight-blue silk. Lee took a great deal of time and gave a great deal of thought to choosing the right dress for her evening with Hunter. It was business.

The deep blue silk shot through with thin silver threads appealed to her because of its clean, elegant lines and lack of ornamentation. Lee would, on the occasions when she shopped, spend as much time choosing the right scarf as she would researching a subject. It was all business.

Now, after a thorough debate, she slipped into the silk. It coolly skimmed her skin; it draped subtly over curves. Her own reflection satisfied her. The unsmiling woman who looked back at her presented precisely the sort of image she wanted to project—elegant, sophisticated and a bit remote. If nothing else, this soothed her bruised ego.

As Lee looked back over her life, concentrating on her career, she could remember no incident where she'd found herself bested. Her mouth became grim as she ran a brush through her hair. It wasn't going to happen now.

Hunter Brown was going to get back some of his own, if for no other reason than that half-amused smile of his. No one laughed at her and got away with it, Lee told herself as she slapped the brush back on the dresser smartly enough to make the bottles jump. Whatever game she had to play to get what she wanted, she'd play. When the article on Hunter Brown hit the stands, she'd have won. She'd have the satisfaction of knowing he'd helped her. In the final analysis, Lee mused, there was no substitute for winning.

When the knock sounded at her door, she glanced at her watch. Prompt. She'd have to make a note of it. Her mood was smug as, after picking up her slim evening bag, she went to answer.

Inherently casual in dress, but not sloppy, she noted, filing the information away as she glanced at the open-collared shirt under his dark jacket. Some men could wear black tie and not look as elegant as Hunter Brown looked in jeans. That was something that might interest her readers. By the end of the evening, Lee reminded herself, she'd know all she possibly could about him.

"Good evening." She started to step across the threshold, but he took her hand, holding her motionless as he studied her.

"Very lovely," Hunter declared. Her hand was very soft and very cool, though her eyes were still hot with annoyance. He liked the contrast. "You wear silk and a very alluring scent but manage to maintain that aura of untouchability. It's quite a talent."

"I'm not interested in being analyzed."

"The curse or blessing of the writer," he countered. "Depending on your viewpoint. Being one yourself, you should understand. Where's your manuscript?"

She'd thought he'd forget—she'd hoped he would. Now, she was back to the disadvantage of stammering. "It, ah, it isn't…"

"Bring it along," Hunter ordered. "I want to take a look at it."

"I don't see why."

"Every writer wants his words read."

She didn't. It wasn't polished. It wasn't perfect. Without a doubt, the last person she wanted to allow a glimpse of her inner thoughts was Hunter. But he was standing, watching, with those dark eyes already seeing beyond the outer layers. Trapped, Lee turned back into the room and slipped the folder from her briefcase. If she could keep him busy enough, she thought, there wouldn't be time for him to look at it anyway.

"It'll be difficult for you to read anything in a restaurant," she pointed out as she closed the door behind her.

"That's why we're having dinner in my suite."

When she stopped, he simply took her hand and continued on to the elevators as if he hadn't noticed. "Perhaps I've given you the wrong impression," she began coldly.

"I don't think so." He turned, still holding her hand. His palm wasn't as smooth as she'd expected a writer's to be. The palm was as wide as a concert pianist's, but it was ridged with calluses. It made, Lee discovered, a very intriguing and uncomfortable combination. "My imagination hasn't gone very deeply into the prospect of seducing you, Lenore." Though he felt her stiffen in outrage, he drew her into the elevator. "The point is, I don't care for restaurants and I care less for crowds and interruptions." The elevator hummed quietly on the short ascent. "Have you found the conference worthwhile?"

"I'm going to get what I came for." She stepped through the doors as they slid open.

"And what's that?"

"What did you come for?" she countered. "You don't exactly make it a habit to attend conferences, and this one is certainly small and off the beaten path."

"Occasionally I enjoy the contact with other writers." Unlocking the door, he gestured her inside.

"This conference certainly isn't bulging with authors who've attained your degree of success."

"Success has nothing to do with writing."

She set her purse and folder aside and faced him straight on. "Easy to say when you have it."

"Is it?" As if amused, he shrugged, then gestured toward the window. "You should drink in as much of the view as you can. You won't see anything like this through any window in Los Angeles."

"You don't care for L.A." If she was careful and clever, she should be able to pin him down on where he lived and why he lived there.

"L.A. has its points. Would you like some wine?"

"Yes." She wandered over to the window. The vastness still had the power to stun her and almost…almost frighten. Once you were beyond the city limits, you might wander for miles without seeing another face, hearing another voice. The isolation, she thought, or perhaps just the space itself, would overwhelm. "Have you been there often?" she asked, deliberately turning her back to the window.

"Hmm?"

"To Los Angeles?"

"No." He crossed to her and offered a glass of pale gold wine.

"You prefer the East to the West?"

He smiled and lifted his glass. "I make it a point to prefer where I am."

He was very adept at evasions, she thought, and turned away to wander the room. It seemed he was also very adept at making her uneasy. Unless she missed her guess, he did both on purpose. "Do you travel often?"

"Only when it's necessary."

Tipping back her glass, Lee decided to try a more direct approach. "Why are you so secretive about yourself? Most people in your position would make the most of the promotion and publicity that's available."

"I don't consider myself secretive, nor do I consider myself most people."

"You don't even have a bio or a photo on your book covers."

"My face and my background have nothing to do with the stories I tell. Does the wine suit you?"

"It's very good." Though she'd barely tasted it. "Don't you feel it's part of your profession to satisfy the readers' curiosity when it comes to the person who creates a story that interests them?"

"No. My profession is words—putting words together so that someone who reads them is entertained, intrigued and satisfied with a tale. And tales spring from imagination rather than hard fact." He sipped wine himself and approved it. "The teller of the tale is nothing compared to the tale itself."

"Modesty?" Lee asked with a trace of scorn she couldn't prevent.

The scorn seemed to amuse him. "Not at all. It's a matter of priorities, not humility. If you knew me better, you'd understand I have very few virtues." He smiled, but Lee told herself she'd imagined that brief predatory flash in his eyes. Imagined, she told herself again and shuddered. Annoyed at her own reaction, she held out her wineglass for a refill.

"Have you any virtues?"

He liked the fact that she struck back even when her nerves were racing. "Some say vices are more interesting and certainly more entertaining than virtues." He filled her glass to just under the rim. "Would you agree?"

"More interesting, perhaps more entertaining." She refused to let her eyes falter from his as she drank. "Certainly more demanding."

He mulled this over, enjoying her quick response and her clean, direct thought patterns. "You have an interesting mind, Lenore. You keep it exercised."

"A woman who doesn't finds herself watching other people climb to the top while she fills water glasses and makes the coffee." She could have cursed in frustration the moment she'd spoken. It wasn't her habit to speak that freely. The point was, she was here to interview him, Lee reminded herself, not the other way around.

"An interesting analogy," Hunter murmured. Ambition. Yes, he'd sensed that about her from the beginning. But what was it she wanted to achieve? Whatever it was, he mused, she wouldn't be above stepping over a few people to get it. He found he could respect that, could almost admire it. "Tell me, do you ever relax?"

"I beg your pardon?"

"Your hands are rarely still, though you appear to have a great deal of control otherwise." He noted that at his words her fingers stopped toying with the stem of her glass. "Since you've come into this room, you haven't stayed in one spot more than a few seconds. Do I make you nervous?"

Sending him a cool look, she sat on the plush sofa and crossed her legs. "No." But her pulse thudded a bit when he sat down beside her.

"What does?"

"Small, loud dogs."

He laughed, pleased with the moment and with her. "You're a very entertaining woman." He took her hand lightly in his. "I should tell you that's my highest compliment."

"You set a great store by entertainment."

"The world's a grim place—worse, often tedious." Her hand was delicate, and delicacy drew him. Her eyes held secrets, and there was little that intrigued him more. "If we can't be entertained, there're only two places to go. Back to the cave, or on to oblivion."

"So you entertain with terror." She wanted to shift farther away from him, but his fingers had tightened almost imperceptibly on her hand. And his eyes were searching for her thoughts.

"If you're worried about the unspeakable terror lurking outside your bedroom window, would you worry about your next dentist appointment or the fact that your washer overflowed?"

"Escape?"

He reached up to touch her hair. It seemed a very casual, very natural gesture to him. Lee's eyes flew open as if she'd been pinched. "I don't care for the word *escape*."

She was a difficult combination to resist, Hunter thought, as he let his fingertips skim down the side of her throat. The fiery hair, the vulnerable eyes, the cool gloss of breeding, the bubbling nerves. She'd make a fascinating character and, he realized, a fascinating lover. He'd already decided to have her for the first; now, as he toyed with the ends of her hair, he decided to have her for the second.

She sensed something when his gaze locked on hers again. Decision, determination, desire. Her mouth went dry. It wasn't often that she felt she could be outmatched by another. It was rarer still when anyone or anything truly frightened her. Though he said nothing, though he moved no closer, she found herself fighting back fear— and the knowledge that whatever game she challenged him to, she would lose because he would look into her eyes and know each move before she made it.

A knock sounded at the door, but he continued to look at her for long silent seconds before he rose. "I took the liberty of ordering dinner," he said, so calmly that Lee wondered if she'd imagined the flare of passion she'd seen in his eyes. While he went to the door, she sat where she was, struggling to sort her own thoughts. She was imagining things, Lee told herself. He couldn't see into her and read her thoughts. He was just a man. Since the game was hers, and only she knew the rules, she wouldn't lose. Settled again, she rose to walk to the table.

The salmon was tender and pink. Pleased with the choice, Lee sat down at the table as the waiter closed the door behind him. So far, Lee reflected, she'd answered more questions than Hunter. It was time to change that.

"The advice you gave earlier to struggling writers about blocking out time to write every day no matter how discouraged they get—did that come from personal experience?"

Hunter sampled the salmon. "All writers face discouragement from time to time. Just as they face criticism and rejection."

"Did you face many rejections before the sale of *The Devil's Due?*"

"I suspect anything that comes too easily." He lifted the wine bottle to fill her glass again. She had a face made for candlelight, he mused as he watched the shadow and light flicker over the cream-soft skin and delicate features. He was determined to find out what lay beneath, before the evening ended.

He never considered he was using her, though he fully intended to pick her brain for everything he could learn about her. It was a writer's privilege.

"What made you become a writer?"

He lifted a brow as he continued to eat. "I was born a writer."

Lee ate slowly, planning her next line of questions. She had to move carefully, avoid putting him on the defensive, maneuver around any suspicions. She never considered she was using him, though she fully intended to pick his brain for everything she could learn about him. It was a reporter's privilege.

"Born a writer," she repeated, flaking off another bite of salmon. "Do you think it's that simple? Weren't there elements in your background, circumstances, early experiences, that led you toward your career?"

"I didn't say it was simple," Hunter corrected. "We're all born with a certain set of choices to make. The matter of making the right ones is anything but simple. Every novel written has to do with choices. Writing novels is what I was meant to do."

He interested her enough that she forgot the unofficial interview and asked for herself, "So you always wanted to be a writer?"

"You're very literal-minded," Hunter observed. Comfortable, he leaned back and swirled the wine in his glass. "No, I didn't. I wanted to play professional soccer."

"Soccer?"

Her astonished disbelief made him smile. "Soccer," he repeated. "I wanted to make a career of it and might have been successful at it, but I had to write."

Lee was silent a moment, then decided he was telling her precisely the truth. "So you became a writer without really wanting to."

"I made a choice," Hunter corrected, intrigued by the orderly logic of her mind. "I believe a great many people are born writer or artist, and die without ever realizing it. Books go unwritten, paintings unpainted. The fortunate ones are those who discover what they were meant to do. I might have been an excellent soccer player. I might have been an excellent writer. If I'd tried to do both, I'd have been no more than mediocre. I chose not to be mediocre."

"There're several million readers who'd agree you made the right choice." Forgetting the cool facade, she propped her elbows on the table and leaned forward. "Why horror fiction, Hunter? Someone with your skill and your imagination could write anything. Why did you turn your talents toward that particular genre?"

He lit a cigarette so that the scent of tobacco stung the air. "Why do you read it?"

She frowned; he hadn't turned one of her questions back on her for some time. "I don't as a rule, except yours."

"I'm flattered. Why mine?"

"Your first was recommended to me, and then..." She hesitated, not wanting to say she'd been hooked from the first page. Instead, she ran her fingertip around the rim of her glass and sorted through her answer. "You have a way of creating atmosphere and drawing characters that make the impossibility of your stories perfectly believable."

He blew out a stream of smoke. "Do you think they're impossible?"

She gave a quick laugh, a laugh he recognized as genuine from the humor that lit her eyes. It did something very special to her beauty. It made it accessible. "I hardly believe in people being possessed by demons or a house being inherently evil."

"No?" He smiled. "No superstitions, Lenore?"

She met his gaze levelly. "None."

"Strange, most of us have a few."

"Do you?"

"Of course, and even the ones I don't have fascinate me." He took her hand, linking fingers firmly. "It's said some people are able to sense another's aura, or personality if the word suits you better, by a simple clasp of hands." His palm was warm and hard as he kept his eyes fixed on hers. She could feel, cool against her hand, the twisted metal of his ring.

"I don't believe that." But she wasn't so sure, not with him.

"You believe only in what you see or feel. Only in what can be touched with one of the five senses that you understand." He rose, drawing her to her feet. "Everything that is can't be understood. Everything that's understood can't be explained."

"Everything has an explanation." But she found the words, like her pulse, a bit unsteady.

She might have drawn her hand away, and he might have let her, but her statement seemed to be a direct challenge. "Can you explain why your heart beats faster when I step closer?" His face looked mysterious, his eyes like jet in the candlelight. "You said you weren't afraid of me."

"I'm not."

"But your pulse throbs." His fingertip lightly touched the hollow of her throat. "Can you explain why when we've yet to spend even one full day together, I want to touch you, like this?" Gently, incredibly gently, he ran the back of his hand up the side of her face.

"Don't." It was only a whisper.

"Can you explain this kind of attraction between two strangers?" He traced a finger over her lips, felt them tremble, wondered about their taste.

Something soft, something flowing, moved through her. "Physical attraction's no more than chemistry."

"Science?" He brought her hand up, pressing his lips to the center of her palm. She felt the muscles in her thighs turn to liquid. "Is there an equation for this?" Still watching her, he brushed his lips over her wrist. Her skin chilled, then heated. Her pulse jolted and scrambled. He smiled. "Does this—" he whispered a kiss at the corner of her mouth "—have to do with logic?"

"I don't want you to touch me like this."

"You want me to touch you," Hunter corrected. "But you can't explain it." In an expected move, he thrust his hands into her hair. "Try the unexplainable," he challenged before his lips closed over hers.

Power. It sped through her. Desire was a rush of heat. She could feel need sing through her as she stood motionless in his arms. She should have refused him. Lee was experienced in the art of refusals. There was suddenly no wit to evade, no strength to refuse.

For all his intensity, for all the force of his personality, the kiss was meltingly soft. Though his fingers were strong and firm in her hair, so firm if she'd tried to move away she'd have found herself trapped, his lips were as gentle and warm as the light that flickered on the table beside them. She didn't know when she reached for him, but her arms were around him, bodies merging, silk rustling. The quiet, intoxicating taste of wine was on his tongue. Lee drank it in. She could smell the candle wax and her own perfume. Her ordered, disciplined mind swam first with confusion, then with sensation after alluring sensation.

Her lips were cool but warmed quickly. Her body was tense but slowly relaxed. He enjoyed both changes. She wasn't a woman who gave herself freely or easily. He knew that just as he knew she wasn't a woman often taken by surprise.

She seemed very small against him, very fragile. He'd always treated fragility with great care. Even as the kiss grew deeper, even as his own need grew surprisingly greater, his mouth remained gentle on hers, teasing, requesting. He believed that lovemaking, from first touch to fulfillment, was an art. He believed that art could never be rushed. So, slowly, patiently, he showed her what might be, while his hands stayed only in her hair and his mouth stayed softly on her.

He was draining her. Lee could feel her will, her strength, her thoughts, seeping out of her. And as they drained away, a flood of sensation replenished what she lost. There was no dealing with it, no...explaining. It could only be experienced.

Pleasure this fluid couldn't be contained. Desire this strong couldn't be guided. It was the lack of control more than the flood of feeling that frightened her most. If she lost her control, she'd lose her purpose. Then she would flounder. With a murmured protest, she pulled away but found that while he freed her lips, he still held her.

Later, he thought, at some lonely, dark hour, he'd explore his own reaction. Now he was much more interested in hers. She looked at him as though she'd been struck—face pale, eyes dark. Though her lips parted, she said nothing. Under his fingers he could feel the light tremor that coursed through her—once, then twice.

"Some things can't be explained, even when they're understood." He said it softly, so softly she might have thought it a threat.

"I don't understand you at all." She put her hands on his forearms as if to draw him away. "I don't think I want to anymore."

He didn't smile as he let his hands slide down to her shoulders. "Perhaps not. You'll have a choice to make."

"No." Shaken, she stepped away and snatched up her

purse. "The conference ends tomorrow and I go back to L.A." Suddenly angry, she turned to face him. "You'll go back to whatever hole it is you hide in."

He inclined his head. "Perhaps." It was best she'd put some distance between them. Very abruptly, he realized that if he'd held her a moment longer, he wouldn't have let her go. "We'll talk tomorrow."

She didn't question her own illogic, but shook her head. "No, we won't talk anymore."

He didn't correct her when she walked to the door, and he stood where he was when the door closed behind her. There was no need to contradict her; he knew they'd talk again. Lifting his glass of wine, Hunter gathered up the manuscript she'd forgotten and settled himself in a chair.

Chapter 4

Anger. Perhaps what Lee felt was simple anger, without other eddies and currents of emotion, but she wasn't certain whom she felt angry with.

What had happened the evening before could have been avoided—should have been, she corrected as she stepped out of the shower. Because she'd allowed Hunter to set the pace and the tone, she'd put herself in a vulnerable position *and* she'd wasted a valuable opportunity. If Lee had learned anything in her years as a reporter, it was that a wasted opportunity was the most destructive mistake in the business.

How much did she know of Hunter Brown that could be used in a concise, informative article? Enough for a paragraph, Lee thought in disgust. A very short paragraph.

She might have only one chance to make up for

lost time. Time lost because she'd let herself feel like a woman instead of thinking like a reporter. He'd led her along on a leash, she admitted bitterly, rubbing a towel over her dripping hair while the heat lamp in the ceiling warmed her skin. Instead of balking, she'd gone obediently where he'd taken her. And had missed the most important interview of her career. Lee tossed down the towel and stalked out of the steamy bathroom.

Telling herself she felt nothing but annoyance for him and for herself, Lee pulled on a robe before she sat down at the small writing desk. She still had some time before room service would deliver her first cup of coffee, but there wasn't any more time to waste. Business first…and last. She pulled out a pad and pencil.

HUNTER BROWN. Lee headed the top of the pad in bold letters and underlined the name. The problem had been, she admitted, that she hadn't approached Hunter—the assignment—logically, systematically. She could correct that now with a basic outline. She had, after all, seen him, spoken to him, asked him a few elementary questions. As far as she knew, no other reporter could make such a claim. It was time to stop berating herself for not tying everything up neatly in a matter of hours and make the slim advantage she still had work for her. She began to write in a decisive hand.

APPEARANCE. Not typical. Now there was a positive statement, she thought with a frown. In three bold strokes, she crossed out the words. Dark; lean, rangy build, she wrote. Like a long-distance runner, a cross-country skier. Her eyes narrowed as she brought his face to the foreground of her memory. Rugged face, offset by an air of intelligence. Most outstanding feature—eyes. Very dark, very direct, very…unnerving.

Was that editorializing? she asked herself. Would those long, quiet stares disturb everyone? Shrugging the question away, Lee continued to write. Tall, perhaps six-one, approximately a hundred sixty pounds. Very confident. Musician's hands, poet's mouth.

A bit surprised by her own description, Lee went on to her next category.

PERSONALITY. Enigmatic. Not enough, she decided, huffing slightly. Arrogant, self-absorbed, rude. Definitely editorializing. She set down her pen and took a deep breath, then picked it up again. A skilled, mesmerizing speaker, she admitted in print. Perceptive, cool, taciturn and open by turns, physical.

The last word had been a mistake, Lee discovered, as it brought back the memory of that long, soft, draining kiss, the gentleness of the mouth, the firmness of his hands. No, that wasn't for publication, nor would she need notes to bring back all the details, all the sensations. She would, however, be wise to remember that he was a man who moved quickly when he chose, a man who apparently took precisely what he wanted.

Humor? Yes, under the intensity there was humor in him. She didn't like recalling how he'd laughed at her, but when she had such a dearth of material, she needed every detail, uncomfortable or not.

She remembered every word he'd said on his philosophy of writing. But how could she translate something so intangible into a few clean, pragmatic sentences? She could say he thought of his work as an obligation. A vocation. It just wasn't enough, she thought in frustration. She needed his own words here, not a translation of his meaning. The simple truth was, she had to speak to him again.

Dragging a hand through her hair, she read over her orderly notes. She should have held the reins of the conversation from the very beginning. If she was an expert on anything, it was on channeling and steering talk along the lines she wanted. She'd interviewed subjects more closemouthed than Hunter, more hostile, but she couldn't remember any more frustrating.

Absently, she began to tap the end of her pencil against the table. It wasn't her job to be frustrated, but to be productive. It wasn't her job, she added, to allow herself to be so utterly seduced by an assignment.

She could have prevented the kiss. It still wasn't clear to Lee why she hadn't. She could have controlled her response to it. She didn't want to dwell on why she hadn't. It was much too easy to remember that long, strangely intense moment and in remembering, to feel it all again. If she was going to prevent herself from doing that, and remember instead all the reasons she'd come to Flagstaff, she had to put Hunter Brown firmly in the category of assignment and keep him there. For now, her biggest problem was how she was going to manage to see him again.

Professionally, she warned herself. But she couldn't sit still thinking of it, or him. Pacing, she tried to block out the incredibly gentle feel of his mouth on hers. And failed.

A flood of feeling; she'd never experienced anything like it. The weakness, the power—it was beyond her to understand it. The longing, the need—how could she know the way to control it?

If she understood him better perhaps... No. Lee lifted her hairbrush, then set it down again. No, understanding Hunter would have nothing to do with fighting her desire for him. She'd wanted to be touched by him, and though she had no logical reason for it, she'd wanted to be touched more than she'd wanted to do her job. It was unprecedented, Lee admitted as she absently pushed bottles and jars around on her dresser. When something was unprecedented, you had to make up your own guidelines.

Uneasy, she glanced up and saw a pale woman with sleepy eyes and unruly hair reflected in the glass. She looked too young, too…fragile. No one ever saw her without the defensive shield of grooming, but she knew what was beneath the fastidiousness and gloss. Fear. Fear of failure.

She'd built her confidence stone by meticulous stone, until most of the time she believed in it herself. But at moments like this, when she was alone, a little weary, a little discouraged, the woman inside crept out, and with her, all the tiny doubts and fears behind that laboriously built wall.

She'd been trained from birth to be little more than an intelligent, attractive ornament. Well-spoken, well-groomed, well-disciplined. It was all her family expected of her. No, Lee corrected. It was *what* had been expected of her. In that respect, she'd already failed.

What trick of fate had made it so impossible for her to fit the mold she'd been fashioned for? Since childhood she'd known she needed more, yet it had taken her until after college to store up enough courage to break away from the road that would have led her from proper debutante to proper matron.

When she'd told her parents she wasn't going to be Mrs. Jonathan T. Willoby, but was leaving Palm Springs to live and work in Los Angeles, she'd been quaking inside. Not until later did she realize it had been their training that had seen her through the very difficult meeting. She'd been taught to remain cool and composed, never to raise her voice, never to show any vulgar signs of temper. When she'd spoken to them, she'd seemed perfectly sure of her own mind, while in truth she'd been terrified of leaving that comfortable gilt cage they'd been fashioning for her since before she was born.

Five years later, the fear had dulled, but it remained. Part of her drive to reach the top in her profession came from the very basic need to prove herself to her parents.

Foolish, she told herself, turning away from the vulnerability of the woman in the glass. She had nothing to prove to anyone, unless it was to herself. She'd come for a story, and that was her first, her only priority. The story was going to gel for her if she had to dog Hunter Brown's footsteps like a bloodhound.

Lee looked down at her notebook again, and at the notes that filled less than a page. She'd have more before the day was over, she promised herself. Much more. He wouldn't get the upper hand again, nor would he distract her from her purpose. As soon as she'd dressed and had her morning coffee, she'd look for Hunter. This time, she'd stay firmly behind the wheel.

When she heard the knock, Lee glanced at the clock beside her bed and gave a little sigh of frustration. She was running behind schedule, something she never permitted herself to do. She'd deliberately requested coffee and rolls for nine o'clock so that she could be dressed and ready to go when they were delivered. Now she'd have to rush to make certain she had a couple of solid hours with Hunter before check-out time. She wasn't going to miss an opportunity twice.

Impatient with herself, she went to the door, drew off the chain and pulled it open.

"You might as well eat nothing if you think you can subsist on a couple of pieces of bread and some jam." Before she could recover, Hunter swooped by her, carrying her breakfast tray. "And an intelligent woman never answers the door without asking who's on the other side." Setting the tray on the table, he turned to pin her with one of his long, intrusive stares.

She looked younger without the gloss of makeup and careful style. The traces of fragility he'd already sensed had no patina of sophistication over them now, though her robe was silk and the sapphire color flattering. He felt a flare of desire and a simultaneous protective twinge. Neither could completely deaden his anger.

She wasn't about to let him know how stunned she was to see him, or how disturbed she was that he was here alone with her when she was all but naked. "First a chauffeur, now a waiter," she said coolly, unsmiling. "You're a man of many talents, Hunter."

"I could return the compliment." Because he knew just how volatile his temper could be, he poured a cup of coffee. "Since one of the first requirements of a fiction writer is that he be a good liar, you're well on your way." He gestured to a chair, putting Lee uncomfortably in the position of visitor. As though she weren't the least concerned, she crossed the room and seated herself at the table.

"I'd ask you to join me, but there's only one cup." She broke a croissant in two and nibbled on it, unbuttered. "You're welcome to a roll." With a steady hand, she added cream to the coffee. "Perhaps you'd like to explain what you mean about my being a good liar."

"I suppose it's a requirement of a reporter as well." Hunter saw her fingers tense on the flaky bit of bread then relax, one by one.

"No." Lee took another bite of her roll as if her stomach hadn't just sunk to her knees. "Reporters deal in fact, not fiction." He said nothing, but the silent look demanded more of her than a dozen words would have. Taking her time, determined not to fumble again, she sipped at her coffee. "I don't remember mentioning that I was a reporter."

"No, you didn't mention it." He caught her wrist as she set down the cup. The grip of his fingers told her immediately just how angry he was. "You quite deliberately didn't mention it."

With a jerk of her head, she tossed the hair out of her eyes. If she'd lost, she wouldn't go down groveling. "It wasn't required that I tell you." Ignoring the fact that he held one of her hands prisoner, Lee picked up her croissant with the other and took a bite. "I paid my registration fee."

"And pretended to be something you're not."

She met his gaze without flinching. "Apparently, we both pretended to be something we weren't, right from the start."

He tilted his head at her reference to their initial meeting. "I didn't want anything from you. You, on the other hand, went beyond the harmless in your deception."

She didn't like the way it sounded when he said it— so petty, so dirty. And so true. If his fingers hadn't been biting into her wrist, she might have found herself apologizing. Instead, Lee held her ground. "I have a perfect right to be here and a perfect right to try to sell an article on any facet of this conference."

"And I," he said, so mildly her flesh chilled, "have a perfect right to my privacy, to the choice of speaking to a reporter or refusing to speak to one."

"If I'd told you that I was on staff at *Celebrity,*" she threw back, making her first attempt to free her arm, "would you have spoken to me at all?"

He still held her wrist; he still held her eyes. For several long seconds, he said nothing. "That's something neither of us will ever know now." He released her wrist so abruptly, her arm dropped to the table, clattering the cup. Lee found that she'd squeezed the flaky pastry into an unpalatable ball.

He frightened her. There was no use denying it even to herself. The force of his anger, so finely restrained, had tiny shocks of cold moving up and down her back. She didn't know him or understand him, nor did she have any way of being certain of what he might do. There was violence in his books; therefore, there was violence in his mind. Clinging to her composure, she lifted her coffee again, drank and tasted absolutely nothing.

"I'm curious to know how you found out." Good, her voice was calm, unhurried. She took the cup in both hands to cover the one quick tremor she couldn't control.

She looked like a kitten backed into a corner, Hunter observed. Ready to spit and scratch, even though her heart was pounding hard enough to be almost audible. He didn't want to respect her for it when he'd rather strangle her. He didn't want to feel a strong urge to touch the pale skin of her cheek. Being deceived by a woman was perhaps the only thing that still had the power to bring him to this degree of rage.

"Oddly enough, I took an interest in you, Lenore. Last night—" He saw her stiffen and felt a certain satisfaction. No, he wasn't going to let her forget that, any more than he could forget it himself. "Last night," he repeated slowly, waiting until her gaze lifted to his again, "I wanted to make love with you. I wanted to get beneath the careful layer of polish and discover you. When I had, you'd have looked as you do now. Soft, fragile, with your mouth naked and your eyes clouded."

Her bones were already melting, her skin already heating, and it was only words. He didn't touch her, didn't attempt to, but the sound of his voice flowed over her skin like the gentlest of caresses. "I don't— I had no intention of letting you make love to me."

"I don't believe in making love to a woman, only with." His eyes never left hers. She could feel her head begin to swim with passion, her breath tremble with it. "Only with," Hunter repeated. "When you left, I turned to the next best way of discovering you."

Lee gripped her hands together in her lap, knowing she had to control the shudders. How could a man have such power? And how could she fight it? Why did she feel as though they were already lovers? Was it just the sense of inevitability that they would be, no matter what her choice? "I don't know what you mean." Her voice was no longer calm.

"Your manuscript."

Uncomprehending, she stared. She'd completely forgotten it the night before in her fear of him, and of herself. Anger and frustration had prevented her from remembering it that morning. Now, on top of a dazed desire, she felt the helplessness of a novice confronted by the master. "I never intended for you to read it," she began. Without thinking, she was shredding her napkin in her lap. "I don't have any aspirations toward being a novelist."

"Then you're a fool as well as a liar."

All sense of helplessness fled. No one, no one in all of her memory, had ever spoken to her like that. "I'm neither a fool nor a liar, Hunter. What I am is an excellent reporter. I want to write an exclusive, in-depth and accurate article on you for our readers."

"Why do you waste your time writing gossip when you've got a novel to finish?"

She went rigid. The eyes that had been clouded with confused desire became frosty. "I don't write gossip."

"You can gloss over it, you can write it with style and intelligence, but it's still gossip." Before Lee could retort, he rose up so quickly, so furiously, her own words were swallowed. "You've no right working forty hours a week on anything but the novel you have inside you. Talent's a two-headed coin, Lenore, and the other side's obligation."

"I don't know what you're talking about." She rose, too, and found she could shout just as effectively as he. "I know my obligations, and one of them's to write a story on you for my magazine."

"And what about the novel?"

Flinging up her hands, she whirled away from him. "What about it?"

"When do you intend to finish it?"

Finish it? She should never have started it. Hadn't

she told herself that a dozen times? "Damn it, Hunter, it's a pipe dream."

"It's good."

She turned back, her brows still drawn together with anger but the eyes beneath them suddenly wary. "What?"

"If it hadn't been, your camouflage would have worked very well." He drew out a cigarette while she stared at him. How could he be so patient, move so slowly, when she was ready to jump at every word? "I nearly called you last night to see if you had any more with you, but decided it would keep. I called my editor instead." Still calm, he blew out smoke. "When I gave the chapters to her to read, she recognized your name. Apparently she's quite a fan of *Celebrity*."

"You gave her…" Astonished, Lee dropped into the chair again. "You had no right to show anyone."

"At the time, I fully believed you were precisely what you'd led me to believe you were."

She stood again, then gripped the back of her chair. "I'm a reporter, not a novelist. I'd like you to get the manuscript from her and return it to me."

He tapped his cigarette in an ashtray, only then noticing her neatly written notes. As he skimmed them, Hunter felt twin surges of amusement and annoyance. So, she was trying to put him into a few tidy little slots. She'd find it more difficult than she'd imagined. "Why should I do that?"

"Because it belongs to me. You had no right to give it to anyone else."

"What are you afraid of?" he demanded.

Of failure. The words were almost out before Lee managed to bite them back. "I'm not afraid of anything.

I do what I'm best at, and I intend to continue doing it. What are you afraid of?" she retorted. "What are you hiding from?"

She didn't like the look in his eyes when he turned his head toward her again. It wasn't anger she saw there, nor was it arrogance, but something beyond both. "I do what I do best, Lenore." When he'd come into the room, he hadn't planned to do any more than rake her to the bone for her deception and berate her for wasting her talent. Now, as he watched her, Hunter began to think there was a better way to do that and at the same time learn more about her for his own purposes. He was a long way from finished with Lenore Radcliffe. "Just how important is doing a story on me to you?"

Alerted by the change in tone, Lee studied him cautiously. She'd tried everything else, she decided abruptly, perhaps she could appeal to his ego. "It's very important. I've been trying to learn something about you for over three months. You're one of the most popular and critically acclaimed writers of the decade. If you—"

He cut her off by merely lifting a hand. "If I decided to give you an interview, we'd have to spend a great deal of time together, and under my terms."

Lee heard the little warning bell, but ignored it. She could almost taste success. "We can hash out the terms beforehand. I keep my word, Hunter."

"I don't doubt that, once it's given." Crushing out his cigarette, Hunter considered the angles. Perhaps he was asking for trouble. Then again, he hadn't asked for any in quite some time. He was due. "How much more of the manuscript do you have completed?"

"That has nothing to do with this." When he merely

lifted a brow and stared, she clenched her teeth. *Humor him,* Lee told herself. *You're too close now.* "About two hundred pages."

"Send the rest to my editor." He gave her a mild look. "I'm sure you have her name by now."

"What does that have to do with the interview?"

"It's one of the terms," Hunter told her easily. "I've plans for the week after next," he continued. "You can join me—with another copy of your manuscript."

"Join you? Where?"

"For two weeks I'll be camping in Oak Creek Canyon. You'd better buy some sturdy shoes."

"Camping?" She had visions of tents and mosquitoes. "If you're not leaving for your vacation right away, why can't we set up the interview a day or two before?"

"Terms," he reminded her. "My terms."

"You're trying to make this difficult."

"Yes." He smiled then, just a hint of amusement around his sculpted mouth. "You'll work for your exclusive, Lenore."

"All right." Her chin came up. "Where should I meet you and when?"

Now he smiled fully, appreciating determination when he saw it. "In Sedona. I'll contact you when I'm certain of the date—and when my editor's let me know she's received the rest of your manuscript."

"I hardly see why you're using that to blackmail me."

He crossed to her then, unexpectedly combing his fingers through her hair. It was casual, friendly and uncannily intimate. "Perhaps one of the first things you should know about me is I'm eccentric. If people accept their own eccentricities, they can justify anything they do. Anything at all." He ended the words by clos-ing his mouth over hers.

He heard her suck in her breath, felt her stiffen. But she didn't struggle away. Perhaps she was testing her-self, though he didn't think she could know she tested him, too. He wanted to carry her to the rumpled bed, slip off that thin swirl of silk and fit his body to hers. It would fit; somehow he already knew. She'd move with him, for him, as if they'd always been lovers. He knew, though he couldn't explain.

He could feel her melting into him, her lips grow-ing warm and moist from his. They were alone and the need was like iron. Yet he knew, without understand-ing, that if they made love now, sated that need, he'd never see her again. They both had fears to face before they became lovers, and after.

Hunter gave himself the pleasure of one long, last kiss, drawing her taste into him, allowing himself to be overwhelmed, just for a moment, by the feel of her against him. Then he forced himself to level, forced himself to remember that they each wanted something from the other—secrets and an intimacy both would put into words in their own ways.

Drawing back, he let his hands linger only a moment on the curve of her cheek, the softness of her hair, while she said nothing. "If you can get through two weeks in the canyon, you'll have your story."

Leaving her with that, he turned and strolled out the door.

"If I can make it through two weeks," Lee muttered, pulling a heavy sweater out of her drawer. "I tell you, Bryan, I've never met anyone who says as little who can irritate me as much." Ten days back in L.A. hadn't dulled her fury.

Bryan fingered the soft wool of the sweater. "Lee, don't you have *any* grub-around clothes?"

"I bought some sweatshirts," she said under her breath. "I haven't spent a great deal of my time in a tent."

"Advice." Before another pair of the trim slacks could be packed into the knapsack Lee had borrowed from her, Bryan took her hand.

Lee lifted one thin coppery brow. "You know I detest advice."

Grinning, Bryan dropped down on the bed. "I know. That's why I can never resist dishing it out. Lee, really, I know you have a pair of jeans. I've *seen* you wear them." She brushed at the hair that escaped her braid. "Designer or not, take jeans, not seventy-five-dollar slacks. Invest in another pair or two," she went on while Lee frowned down at the clothes still in her free hand. "Put that gorgeous wool sweater back in your drawer and pick up a couple of flannel shirts. That'll take care of the nights if it turns cool. Now…"

Because Lee was listening with a frown of concentration, she continued. "Put in some T-shirts—blouses are for the office, not for hiking. Take at least one pair of shorts and invest in some good thick socks. If you had more time, I'd tell you to break in those new hiking boots, because they're going to make you suffer."

"The salesman said—"

"There's nothing wrong with them, Lee, except they've never been out of the box. Face it." She stretched back among Lee's collection of pillows. "You've been too concerned about packing enough paper and pencils to worry about gear. If you don't want to make an ass of yourself, listen to momma."

With a quick hiss of breath, Lee replaced the sweater. "I've already made an ass of myself, several times." She slammed one of her dresser drawers. "He's not going to get the best of me during these next two weeks, Bryan. If I have to sleep out in a tent and climb rocks to get this story, then I'll do it."

"If you tried real hard, you could have fun at the same time."

"I'm not looking for fun. I'm looking for an exclusive."

"We're friends."

Though it was a statement, not a question, Lee glanced over. "Yes." For the first time since she'd begun packing, she smiled. "We're friends."

"Then tell me what it is that bothers you about this guy. You've been ready to chew your nails for over a week." Though she spoke lightly, the concern leaked through. "You wanted to interview Hunter Brown, and you're going to interview Hunter Brown. How come you look like you're preparing for war?"

"Because that's how I feel." With anyone else, Lee would have evaded the question or turned cold. Because it was Bryan, she sat on the edge of the bed, twisting a newly purchased sweatshirt in her hands. "He makes me want what I don't want to want, feel what I don't want to feel. Bryan, I don't have room in my life for complications."

"Who does?"

"I know exactly where I'm going," Lee insisted, a bit too vehemently. "I know exactly how to get there. Somehow I have a feeling that Hunter's a detour."

"Sometimes a detour is more interesting than a planned route, and you get to the same place eventually."

"He looks at me as though he knows what I'm thinking. More, as if he knows what I thought yesterday, or last year. It's not comfortable."

"You've never looked for the comfortable," Bryan stated, pillowing her head on her folded arms. "You've always looked for a challenge. You've just never found one in a man before."

"I don't want one in a man." Violently, Lee stuffed the sweatshirt into the knapsack. "I want them in my work."

"You don't have to go."

Lee lifted her head. "I'm going."

"Then don't go with your teeth gritted." Crossing her legs under her, Bryan sat up. She was as rumpled as Lee was tidy but seemed oddly suited to the luxurious pile of pillows around her. "This is a tremendous opportunity for you, professionally and personally. Oak Creek's one of the most beautiful canyons in the country. You'll have two weeks to be part of it. There's a man who doesn't bore or cater to you." She grinned at Lee's arch look. "You know damn well they do one or the other and you can't abide it. Enjoy the change of scene."

"I'm going to work," Lee reminded her. "Not to pick wildflowers."

"Pick a few anyway. You'll still get your story."

"And make Hunter Brown squirm."

Bryan gave her throaty laugh, tossing a pillow into the air. "If that's what you're set on doing, you'll do it. I'd feel sorry for the guy if he hadn't given me nightmares." After a quick grimace, her look softened into one of affection. "And, Lee..." She laid her hand over her friend's. "If he makes you want something, take it. Life isn't crowded with offers. Give yourself a present."

Lee sat silently for a moment, then sighed. "I'm not sure if I'd be giving myself a present or a curse." Rising, she went to her dresser. "How many pairs of socks?"

"But is she pretty?" Sarah sat in the middle of the rug, one leg bent toward her while she tried valiantly to hook the other behind her neck. "*Really* pretty?"

Hunter dug into the basket of laundry. Sarah had scrupulously reminded him it was his turn to sort and fold. "I wouldn't use the word *pretty*. A carefully arranged basket of fruit's pretty."

Sarah giggled, then rolled and arched into a back bend. She liked nothing better than talking with her father, because no one else talked like him. "What word would you use, then?"

Hunter folded a T-shirt with the name of a popular rock band glittered across it. "She has a rare, classic beauty that a lot of women wouldn't know precisely what to do with."

"But she does?"

He remembered. He wanted. "She does."

Sarah lay down on her back to snuggle with the dog that stretched out beside her. She liked the soft, warm feel of Santanas's fur, in much the same way she liked to close her eyes and listen to her father's voice. "She tried to fool you," Sarah reminded him. "You don't like it when people try to fool you."

"To her way of thinking, she was doing her job."

With one hand on the dog's neck, Sarah looked up

at her father with big, dark eyes so much like his own. "You never talk to reporters."

"They don't interest me." Hunter came upon a pair of jeans with a widening hole in the knee. "Aren't these new?"

"Sort of. So why are you taking her camping with you?"

"Sort of new shouldn't have holes already, and I'm not taking her, she's coming with me."

Digging in her pocket, she came up with a stick of gum. She wasn't supposed to chew any because of her braces, so she fondled the wrapped piece instead. In six months, Sarah thought, she was going to chew a dozen pieces, all at once. "Because she's a reporter or because she has a rare, classic beauty?"

Hunter glanced down to see his daughter's eyes laughing at him. She was entirely too clever, he decided, and threw a pair of rolled socks at her. "Both, but mostly because I find her interesting and talented. I want to see how much I can find out about her, while she's trying to find out about me."

"You'll find out more," Sarah declared, idly tossing the socks up in the air. "You always do. I think it's a good idea," she added after a moment. "Aunt Bonnie says you don't see enough women, especially women who challenge your mind."

"Aunt Bonnie thinks in couples."

"Maybe she'll incite your simmering passion."

Hunter's hand paused on its way to the basket. "What?"

"I read it in a book." Expertly, she rolled so that her feet touched the floor behind her head. "This man met this woman, and they didn't like each other at first, but

there was this strong physical attraction and this growing desire, and—"

"I get the picture." Hunter looked down at the slim,
dark-haired girl on the floor. She was his daughter, he
thought. She was ten. How in God's name had they
gotten involved in the subject of passion? "You of all
people should know that things don't often happen in
real life the way they do in books."

"Fiction's based on reality." Sarah grinned, pleased
to throw one of his own quotes back at him. "But before
you do fall in love with her, or have too much simmering passion, I want to meet her."

"I'll keep that in mind." Still watching her, Hunter
held up three unmatched socks. "Just how does this
happen every week?"

Sarah considered the socks a moment, then sat up.
"I think there's a parallel universe in the dryer. On the
other side of the door, at this very minute, someone else
is holding up three unmatched socks."

"An interesting theory." Reaching down, Hunter
grabbed her. As Sarah's laughter bounced off the lofted
ceiling, he dropped her, bottom first, into the basket.

Chapter 5

It was like every Western she'd ever seen. With the sun bright in her eyes, Lee could almost see outlaws outrunning posses and Indians hiding in wait behind rocks and buttes. If she let her imagination go, she could almost hear the hoofbeats ring against the rock-hard ground. Because she was alone in the car, she could let her imagination go.

The rich red mountains rose up into a painfully blue sky. There was a vastness that was almost outrageous in scope, with no lushness, with no need for any, with no patience for any. It made her throat dry and her heart thud.

There was green—the silvery-green of sage clinging to the red, rocky soil and the deeper hue of junipers, which would give way to a sudden, seemingly planned sparseness. Yet the sparseness was rich in itself. The space, the overwhelming space, left her stunned and humble and oddly hungry for more. Everywhere there were more rocky ridges, more color, more... Lee shook her head. Just more.

Even when she came closer to town, the houses and buildings couldn't compete with the openness. Stop signs, streetlights, flower gardens were inconsequential. Her car joined more cars, but five times the number would still have been insignificant. It was a view you drank in, she thought, but its taste was hot and packed a punch.

She liked Sedona immediately. Its tidy Western flavor suited the fabulous backdrop instead of marring it. She hadn't been sure anything could.

The main street was lined with shops with neat signs and clean plate glass. She noticed lots of wood, lots of bargains and absolutely no sense of urgency. Sedona clung to the aura of town rather than city. It seemed comfortable with itself and with the spectacular spread of sky. Perhaps, Lee mused as she followed the directions to the rental-car drop-off, just perhaps, she'd enjoy the next two weeks after all.

Since she was early for her arranged meeting time with Hunter even after dealing with the paperwork on her rental car, Lee decided she could afford to indulge herself playing tourist. She had nearly an hour to vacation before work began again.

The liquid silver necklaces and turquoise earrings in the shop windows tempted her, but she moved past them. There'd be plenty of opportunities after this little adventure for something frivolous—as a reward for success. For now, she was only passing time.

But the scent of fudge drew her. Slipping inside the

little shop that claimed to sell the world's best, Lee bought a half pound. For energy, she told herself as the sample melted in her mouth. There was no telling what kind of food she'd get over the next two weeks. Hunter had very specifically told her when he contacted her by phone that he'd handle the supplies. The fudge, Lee told herself, would be emergency rations.

Besides, some of Bryan's advice had been valid enough. There was no use going into this thing thinking she'd be miserable and uncomfortable. There wasn't any harm getting into the spirit a bit, Lee decided as she strolled into a Western-wear shop. If she viewed the next two weeks as a working vacation, she'd be much better off.

Though she toyed with conch belts for a few minutes, Lee rejected them. They wouldn't suit her, any more than the fringed or sequined shirts would. Perhaps she'd pick one up for Bryan before heading back to L.A. Anything Bryan put on suited her, Lee mused with something closer to a sigh than to envy. Bryan never had to feel restricted to the tailored, the simple or the proper.

Was it a matter of suitability, Lee wondered, or a matter of image? With a shrug, she ran a fingertip down the shoulder of a short suede jacket. Image or not, she'd locked herself into it for too long to change now. She didn't want to change, in any case, Lee reminded herself as she wandered through rows and rows of hats. She understood Lee Radcliffe just as she was.

Telling herself she'd stay only another minute, she set her knapsack at her feet. She wasn't particularly athletic. Lee tried on a dung-colored Stetson with a curved brim. She wasn't flighty. She exchanged the first hat for a smaller one with a spray of feathers in the band.

What she was, was businesslike and down-to-earth. She dropped a black flat-brimmed hat on her head and studied the result. Sedate, she decided, smiling a little. Practical. Yes, if she were in the market for—

"You're wearing it all wrong."

Before Lee could react, two strong hands were tilting the hat farther down on her head. Critically, Hunter angled it slightly, then stepped away. "Yes, it's the perfect choice for you. The contrast with your hair and skin, that practical sort of dash." Taking her shoulders, her turned her toward the mirror, where both his image and hers looked back at her.

She saw the way his fingers held her shoulders, long and confident. She could see how small she looked pressing against him. In no more than an instant, Lee could feel the pleasure she wanted to ignore and the annoyance she had to concentrate on.

"I've no intention of buying it." Embarrassed, she drew the hat off and returned it to the shelf.

"Why not?"

"I've no need for it."

"A woman who buys only what she needs?" Amusement crossed his face even as anger crossed hers. "A sexist remark if I've ever heard one," Hunter continued before she could speak. "Still, it's a pity you won't buy it. It gives you a breezy air of confidence."

Ignoring that, Lee bent down and picked up her knapsack again. "I hope I haven't kept you waiting long. I got into town early and decided to kill some time."

"I saw you wander in here when I drove in. Even in jeans you walk as though you were wearing a three-piece suit." While she tried to work out if that had been a compliment, he smiled. "What kind did you buy?"

"What?" She was still frowning over his comment.

"Fudge." He glanced down at the bag. "What kind did you buy?"

Caught again, Lee thought, nearly resigned to it. "Some milk chocolate and some rocky road."

"Good choice." Taking her arm, he led her through the shop. "If you're determined to resist the hat, we may as well get started."

She noted the Jeep parked at the curb and narrowed her eyes. This was certainly the same one he'd had in Flagstaff. "Have you been staying in Arizona?"

He circled the hood, leaving her to climb in on her own. "I've had some business to take care of."

Her reporter's sense sharpened. "Research?"

He gave her that odd ghost of a smile. "A writer's always researching." He wouldn't tell her—yet—that his research on Lenore Radcliffe had led him to some intriguing conclusions. "You brought a copy of the rest of your manuscript?"

Unable to prevent herself, Lee shot him a look of intense dislike. "That was one of the conditions."

"So it was." Easily he backed up, then pulled into the thin stream of traffic. "What's your impression of Sedona?"

"I can see that the weather and the atmosphere would draw the tourist trade." She found it necessary to sit very erect and to look straight ahead.

"The same might be said of Maui or the South of France."

She couldn't stop her lips from curving, but turned to look out the side window. "It has the air of having been here forever, with very little change. The sense of space is fierce, not at all soothing, but it pulls you in. I suppose it makes me think of the people who first saw it from horseback or the seat of a wagon. I imagine some of them would have been compelled to build right away, to set up a community so that the vastness didn't overwhelm them."

"And others would have been drawn to the desert or the mountains so that the buildings wouldn't close them in."

As she nodded, it occurred to her that she might fit into the first group, and he into the second.

The road he took narrowed and twisted down. He didn't drive sedately, but with the air of a man who knew he could negotiate whatever curve was thrown at him. Lee gripped the door handle, determined not to comment on his speed. It was like taking the downhill rush of a roller coaster without having had the preparatory uphill climb. They whooshed down, a rock wall on one side, a spiraling drop on the other.

"Do you camp often?" Her knuckles were whitening on the handle, but though she had to shout to be heard she was satisfied that her voice was calm enough.

"Now and again."

"I'm curious…" She stopped and cleared her throat as Hunter whipped around a snaking turn. "Why camping?" Did the rocks in the sheer wall beside them ever loosen and tumble onto the road? She decided it was best not to think about it. "A man in your position could go anywhere and do anything he chose."

"This is what I chose," he pointed out.

"All right. Why?"

"There are times when everyone needs simplicity."

Her foot pressed down on the floorboard as if it were

a brake pedal. "Isn't this just one more way you have of avoiding people?"

"Yes." His easy agreement had her turning her head to stare at him. He was amused to note that her hand loosened on the handle and that her concentration was on him now rather than the road. "It's also a way of getting away from my work. You never get away from writing, but there are times you need to get away from the trappings of writing."

Her gaze sharpened. Though her fingers itched for her notebook, Lee had faith in her own powers of retention. "You don't like trappings."

"We don't always like what's necessary."

Oblivious to the speed and the curves now, Lee tucked one leg under her and turned toward him. That attracted him, Hunter reflected. The way she'd unconsciously drop that careful shield whenever something challenged her mind. That attracted him every bit as much as her cool, nineteenth-century beauty.

"What do you consider trappings as regards your profession?"

"The confinement of an office, the hum of a machine, the paperwork that's unavoidable but interferes with the story flow."

Odd, but that was precisely what she needed in order to maintain discipline. "If you could change it, what would you do?"

He smiled again. Hunter had never known anyone who thought in more basic terms or straighter lines. "I'd go back a few centuries to when I could simply travel and tell the story."

She believed him. Though he had wealth and fame and critical acclaim, Lee believed him. "None of the rest means anything to you, does it? The glory, the admiration?"

"Whose admiration?"

"Your readers and the critics."

He pulled off the road next to a small wooden building that served as a trading post. "I'm not indifferent to my readership, Lenore."

"But to the critics."

"I admire the orderliness of your mind," he said and stepped from the Jeep.

It was a good beginning, Lee thought, pleased, as she climbed out the passenger side. He'd already told her more than anyone else knew, and the two weeks had barely begun. If she could just keep him talking, learn enough generalities, then she could pin him down on specifics. But she'd have to pace herself. When you were dealing with a master of evasion, you had to tread carefully. She couldn't afford to relax.

"Do we have to check in?"

From behind her back Hunter grinned, while Lee struggled to pull out her knapsack. "I've already taken care of the paperwork."

"I see." Her pack was heavy, but she told herself she'd refuse any offer of assistance and carry it herself. A moment later, she saw it wouldn't be an issue. Hunter merely stood aside, watching as she wriggled into the shoulder straps. So much for chivalry, she thought, annoyed that he hadn't given her the opportunity to assert her independence. She caught the gleam in his eye. He read her mind much too easily.

"Want me to carry the fudge?"

She closed her fingers firmly over the bag. "I'll manage."

With his own gear on his back, Hunter started down

a path, leaving her no choice but to follow. He moved as though he'd been walking dirt paths all his life—as if perhaps he'd cut a few of his own. Though she felt out of place in her hiking boots, Lee was determined to keep up and to make it look easy.

"You've camped here before?"

"Mmm-hmm."

"Why?"

He stopped, turning to fix her with that dark, intense stare that always took her breath away. "You only have to look."

She did and saw that the walls and peaks of the canyon rose up as if they'd never stop. They were a color and texture unique to themselves, enhanced by the snatches of green from rough, hardy trees and shrubs that seemed to grow out of the rock. As she had from the air, Lee thought of castles and fortresses, but without the distance the plane had given her, she couldn't be sure whether she was storming the walls or being enveloped by them.

She was warm. The sun was strong, even with the shade of trees that grew thickly at this elevation. Though she saw other people—children, adults, babies carried papoose-style—she felt no sense of crowding.

It's like a painting, she realized all at once. *It's as though we're walking into a canvas.* The feeling it gave her was both eerie and irresistible. She shifted the pack on her back as she kept pace with Hunter.

"I noticed some houses," she began. "I didn't realize people actually lived in the canyon."

"Apparently."

Sensing his mind was elsewhere, Lee lapsed into silence. She'd done too well to start pushing. For now, she'd follow Hunter, since he obviously knew where he was going.

It surprised her that she found the walk pleasant. For years her life had been directed by deadlines, rush and self-imposed demands. If someone had asked her where she'd choose to spend two weeks relaxing, her mind would have gone blank. But when ideas had begun to come, roughing it in a canyon in Arizona wouldn't have made the top ten. She'd never have considered that the purity of air and the unimpeded arch of sky would be so appealing to her.

She heard a quiet, musical tinkle that took her several moments to identify. The creek, Lee realized. She could smell the water. The new sensation gave her a quick thrill. Her guide, and her project, continued to move at a steady pace in front of her. Lee banked down the urge to share her discovery with him. He'd only think her foolish.

Did she realize how totally out of her element she looked? Hunter wondered. It had taken him only one glance to see that the jeans and the boots she wore were straight out of the box. Even the T-shirt that fit softly over her torso was obviously boutiqueware rather than a department-store purchase. She looked like a model posing as a camper. She smelled expensive, exclusive. Wonderful. What kind of woman carried a worn knapsack and wore sapphire studs in her ears?

As her scent wafted toward him again, carried on the breeze, Hunter reminded himself that he had two weeks to find out. Whatever notes she would make on him, he'd be making an equal number on her. Perhaps both of them would have what they wanted before the time was up. Perhaps both of them would have cause to regret it.

He wanted her. It had been a long time since he'd wanted anything, anyone, that he didn't already have. Over the past days he'd thought often of her response to that long, lingering kiss. He'd thought of his own response. They'd learn about each other over the next two weeks, though they each had their own purposes. But nothing was free. They'd both pay for it.

The quiet soothed him. The towering walls of the canyon soothed him. Lee saw their ferocity, he their tranquillity. Perhaps they both saw what they needed to see.

"For a woman, and a reporter, you have an amazing capacity for silence."

The weight of her pack was beginning to take precedence over the novelty of the scenery. Not once had he asked if she wanted to stop and rest, not once had he even bothered to look back to see if she was still behind him. She wondered why he didn't feel the hole her eyes were boring into his back.

"You have an amazing capacity for the insulting compliment."

Hunter turned to look at her for the first time since they'd started out. There was a thin sheen of perspiration on her brow and her breath came quickly. It didn't detract an iota from her cool, innate beauty. "Sorry," he said, but didn't appear to be. "Have I been walking too fast? You don't look out of shape."

Despite the ache that ran down the length of her back, Lee straightened. "I'm *not* out of shape." Her feet were killing her.

"The site's not much farther." Reaching down to

his hip, he lifted the canteen and unscrewed the top. "It's perfect weather for hiking," he said mildly. "Mid-seventies, and there's a breeze."

Lee managed to suppress a scowl as she eyed the canteen. "Don't you have a cup?"

It took Hunter a moment to realize she was perfectly serious. Wisely, he decided to swallow the chuckle. "Packed away with the china," he told her soberly enough.

"I'll wait." She hooked her hands in the front straps of her knapsack to ease some of the weight.

"Suit yourself." While Lee looked on, Hunter drank deeply. If he sensed her resentment, he gave no sign as he capped the canteen again and resumed the walk.

Her throat was all the drier at the thought of water. He'd done it on purpose, she thought while she gritted her teeth. Did he think she'd missed that quick flash of humor in his eyes? It was just one more thing to pay him back for when the time came. Oh, she couldn't wait to write the article and expose Hunter Brown for the arrogant, coldhearted demigod he'd set himself up to be.

She wouldn't be surprised if he was walking her in circles, just to make her suffer. Bryan had been all too right about the boots. Lee had lost count of the number of campsites they'd passed, some occupied and some empty. If this was his way of punishing her for not revealing from the start that she worked for *Celebrity,* he was certainly doing an elaborate job.

Disgusted, exhausted, with her legs feeling less like flesh and more like rubber, she reached out and grabbed his arm. "Just why, when you obviously have a dislike for women and for reporters, did you agree to spend two weeks with me?"

"Dislike women?" His brows arched. "My likes and dislikes aren't as generalized as that, Lenore." Her skin was warm and slightly damp when he curled his fingers around the back of her neck. "Have I given you the impression I dislike you?"

She had to fight the urge to stretch like a cat under his hand. "I don't care what your personal feelings are toward me. This is business."

"For you." His fingers squeezed gently, bringing her an inch closer. "I'm on vacation. Do you know, your mouth's every bit as appealing now as it was the first time I saw it."

"I don't want to appeal to you." But her voice was breathy. "I want you to think of me only as a reporter."

The smile hovered at the edges of his mouth, around the corners of his eyes. "All right," he agreed. "In a minute."

Then he touched his lips to hers, as gently as he had the first time, and as devastatingly. She stood still, amazed to feel as intense a swirl of sensation as she had before. When he touched her, hardly touching her, it was as if she'd never been kissed before. A new discovery, a fresh beginning—how could it be?

The weight on her back seemed to vanish. The ache in her muscles turned into a deeper, richer ache that penetrated to the bone. Her lips parted, though she knew what she invited. Then his tongue joined with hers, slipping into the moistness, drinking up her flavor.

Lee felt the urgency scream through her body, but he was patient. So patient, she couldn't know what the patience cost him. He hadn't expected pain. No woman had ever brought him pain with desire. He hadn't expected the need to flame through him like brushfire, fast and out of control. Hunter had a vision, with perfect clarity, of what it would be like to take her there, on the ground, under the blazing sun with the canyon circling like castle walls around them and the sky like a cathedral dome.

But there was too much fear in her. He could sense it. Perhaps there was too much fear in him. When they came together, it might have the power to topple both their worlds.

"Your lips melt against mine, Lenore," he whispered. "It's all but impossible to resist."

She drew back, aroused, alarmed and all too aware of how helpless she'd been. "I don't want to repeat myself, Hunter," she managed. "And I don't want to amuse you with clichés, but this is business. I'm a reporter on assignment. If we're to make it through the next two weeks peacefully, it'd be wise to remember that."

"I don't know about the peace," he countered, "but we'll try your rules first."

Suspicious, but finding no room to argue, Lee followed him again. They walked out of the sunlight into the dim coolness of a stand of trees. The creek was distant but still audible. From somewhere to the left came the tinny sound of music from a portable radio. Closer at hand was the rustling of small animals. With a nervous look around, Lee convinced herself they were nothing more than squirrels and rabbits.

With the trees closing around them, they might have been anywhere. The sun filtered through, but softly, on the rough, uneven ground. There was a clearing, small and snug, with a circle of stones surrounding a long-dead campfire. Lee glanced around, fighting off the uneasiness. Somehow, she hadn't thought it would be this remote, this quiet, this…alone.

"There're shower and bathroom facilities a few hundred yards east," Hunter began as he slipped off his pack. "Primitive but adequate. The metal can's for trash. Be sure the lid's tightly closed or it'll attract animals. How's your sense of direction?"

Gratefully, she slipped out of her own pack and let it drop. "It's fine." Now, if she could just take off the boots and rest her feet.

"Good. Then you can gather some firewood while I set up the tent."

Annoyed with the order, she opened her mouth, then firmly shut it again with only a slight hiss. He wouldn't have any cause to complain about her. But as she started to stalk off, the rest of his sentence hit home.

"What do you mean *the* tent?"

He was already unfastening the straps of his pack. "I prefer sleeping in something in case it rains."

"*The* tent," Lee repeated, closing in on him. "As in singular?"

He didn't even spare her a look. "One tent, two sleeping bags."

She wasn't going to explode; she wasn't going to make a scene. After taking a deep breath, she spoke precisely. "I don't consider those adequate arrangements."

He didn't speak for a minute, not because he was choosing his words but because the unpacking occupied him more than the conversation. "If you want to sleep in the open, it's up to you." Hunter drew out a slim, folded piece of material that looked more like a bedsheet than a tent. "But when we decide to become lovers, the arrangements won't make any difference."

"We didn't come here to be lovers," Lee snapped back furiously.

"A reporter and an assignment," Hunter replied mildly. "Two sexless terms. They shouldn't have any problem sharing a tent."

Caught in her own logic, Lee turned and stalked away. She wouldn't give him the satisfaction of seeing her behave like a woman.

Hunter lifted his head and watched her storm off through the trees. She'd make the first move, he promised himself, suddenly angry. By God, he wouldn't touch her until she came to him.

While he set up camp, he tried to convince himself it was as easy as it sounded.

Chapter 6

Two sexless terms, Lee repeated silently as she scooped up some twigs. *Bastard,* she thought with grim satisfaction, was also a sexless term. It suited Hunter Brown to perfection. He had no business treating her like a fool just because she'd made a fool of herself already.

She wasn't going to give an inch. She'd sleep in the damn sleeping bag in the damn tent for the next thirteen nights without saying another word about it.

Thirteen, she thought, sending a malicious look over her shoulder. He'd probably planned that, too. If he thought she was going to make a scene, or curl up outside the tent to sleep in the open to spite him, he'd be disappointed. She'd be scrupulously professional, unspeakably cooperative and utterly sexless. Before it was over, he'd think he'd been sharing his tent with a robot.

But she'd know better. Lee let out one long, frustrated breath as she scouted for more sticks. She'd know there was a man beside her in the night. A powerfully sexy, impossibly attractive man who could make her blood swim with no more than a look.

It wouldn't be easy to forget she was a woman over the next two weeks, when she'd be spending every night with a man who already had her nerves jumping.

Her job wasn't to make herself forget, Lee reminded herself, but to make certain *he* forgot. A challenge. That was the best way to look at it. It was a challenge she promised herself she'd succeed at.

With her arms full of sticks and twigs, Lee lifted her chin. She felt hot, dirty and tired. It wasn't an auspicious way to begin a war. Ignoring the ache, she squared her shoulders. She might have to sacrifice a round or two, but she'd win the battle. With a dangerous light in her eyes, she headed toward camp.

She had to be grateful his back was to her when she walked into the clearing. The tent was smaller, much, much smaller, than she'd imagined. It was fashioned from tough, lightweight material that looked nearly transparent. It arched, rounded rather than pointed at the peak, and low to the ground. So low, Lee noted, that she'd have to crawl to get inside. Once in, they'd be forced to sleep nearly elbow to elbow. Then and there, she determined to sleep like a rock. Unmoving.

The size of the tent preoccupied her, so that she didn't notice what Hunter was doing until she was almost beside him. Fresh rage broke out as she dropped her load of wood on the ground. "Just what the hell do you think you're doing?"

Unperturbed by the fury in her voice, Hunter glanced up. In one hand he held a large clear-plastic bag filled with makeup, in the other a flimsy piece of peach-colored material trimmed with ivory lace. "You did know we were going camping," he said mildly, "not to the Beverly Wilshire?"

The color she considered the curse of fair skin flooded her cheeks. "You have no right to go digging around in my things." She snatched the teddy out of his hand, then balled it in her fist.

"I was unpacking." Idly, he turned the makeup bag over to study it from both sides. "I thought you knew to bring only necessities. While I'll admit you have a very subtle, experienced way with this sort of thing—" he gestured with the bag "—eye shadow and lip gloss are excess baggage around a campfire." His voice was infuriatingly friendly, his eyes were only lightly amused. "I've seen you without any of it and had no cause to complain. You certainly don't have to bother with this on my account."

"You conceited jerk." Lee snatched the bag out of his hand. "I don't care if I look like a hag on your account." Taking the knapsack, she stuffed her belongings back inside. "It's *my* baggage, and I'll carry it."

"You certainly will."

"You officious sonofa—" She broke off, barely. "Just don't tell me how to run my life."

"Now, now, name-calling's no way to promote goodwill." Rising, Hunter held out a friendly hand. "Truce?"

Lee eyed him warily. "On what terms?"

He grinned. "That's what I like about you, Lenore, no easy capitulations. A truce with as little interference as possible on both sides. An amiable business arrangement." He saw her relax slightly and couldn't resist the temptation to ruffle her feathers again. "You won't complain about my coffee, and I won't complain when you wear that little scrap of lace to bed."

She gave him a cool smile as she took his hand. "I'm sleeping in my clothes."

"Fair enough." He gave her hand a quick squeeze. "I'm not. Let's see about that coffee."

As he often did, he left her torn between frustration and amusement.

When he put his mind to it, Lee was to discover, Hunter could make things easier. Without fuss, he had the campfire burning and the coffee brewing. Its scent alone was enough to soothe her temper. The economical way he went about it made her think more kindly of him.

There was no point in being at each other's throats for the next two weeks, she decided as she found a convenient rock to sit on. Relaxing might be out of the question, she mused, watching him take clever, compact cooking utensils out of the pack, but animosity wouldn't help, not with a man like Hunter. He was playing games with her. As long as she knew that and avoided the pitfalls, she'd get what she'd come for. So far, she'd allowed him to set the rules and change them at his whim. That would have to change. Lee hooked her hands around a raised knee.

"Do you go camping to get away from the pressure?"

Hunter didn't look back at her, but checked the lantern. So, they were going to start playing word games already. "What pressure?"

Lee might have sighed if she weren't so determined to be pleasantly professional. "There must be pressures from all sides in your line of work. Demands from your publisher, disagreements with your editor, a story that just won't gel the way you want it to, deadlines."

"I don't believe in deadlines."

There was something, Lee thought, and reached for her notepad. "But doesn't every writer face deadlines from time to time? And can't they be an enormous pressure when the story isn't flowing or you're blocked?"

"Writer's block?" Hunter poured coffee into a metal cup. "There's no such thing."

She glanced over for only a second, brow raised. "Oh, come on, Hunter, some very successful writers have suffered from it, even sought professional help. There must have been a time in your career when you found yourself up against a wall."

"You push the wall out of the way."

Frowning, she accepted the cup he handed her. "How?"

"By working through it." He had a jar of powdered milk, which she refused. "If you don't believe in something, refuse to believe it exists, it doesn't, not for you."

"But you write about things that couldn't possibly exist."

"Why not?"

She stared at him, a dark, attractive man sitting on the ground drinking coffee from a metal cup. He looked so at ease with himself, so relaxed, that for a moment she found it difficult to connect him to the man who created stark terror out of words. "Because there aren't monsters under the bed or demons in the closet."

"There's demons in every closet," he disagreed mildly, "some better hidden than others."

"You're saying you believe in what you write about."

"Every writer believes in what he writes. There'd be no purpose in it otherwise."

"You think some—" She didn't want to use the word *demon* again, and her hand moved in frustration as she sought the right phrase. "Some evil force," Lee chose, "can actually manipulate people?"

"It's more accurate to say I don't believe in anything. Possibilities." Did his eyes become darker, or was it her imagination? "There's no limit to possibilities, Lenore."

His eyes were too dark to read. If he was playing with her, baiting her, she couldn't tell. Uncomfortable, she shifted the topic. "When you sit down to write a story, you craft it, spending hours, days, on the angles and the edges, the same way a carpenter builds a cabinet."

He liked her analogy. Hunter sipped at the strong black coffee, enjoying the taste, enjoying the mingled scents of burning wood, summer and Lee's quiet perfume. "Telling a story's an art, writing's a craft."

Lee felt a quick kick of excitement. That was exactly what she was after, those concise little quotes that gave an insight into his character. "Do you consider yourself an artist, then, or a craftsman?"

He drank without hurry, noting that Lee had barely touched her coffee. The eagerness was with her again, her pen poised, her eyes fixed on his. He found he wanted her more when she was like this. He wanted to see that eager look on her face for him, for the man, not the writer. He wanted to sense the ripe anticipation, lover to lover, arms reaching, mouth softening.

If he were writing the script, he'd keep these two people from fulfilling each other's needs for some time yet. It was necessary to flesh them out a bit first, but the ache told him what he needed. Carefully he arranged another piece of wood on the fire.

"An artist by birth," he said at length, "a craftsman by choice."

"I know it's a standard question," she began, with a brisk professionalism that made him smile, "but where do you get your ideas?"

"From life."

She looked over again as he lit a cigarette. "Hunter, you can't convince me that the plot for *Devil's Due* came out of the everyday."

"If you take the everyday, twist it, add a few maybes, you can come up with anything."

"So you take the ordinary, twist it and come up with the extraordinary." Understanding this a bit better, she nodded, satisfied. "How much of yourself goes into your characters?"

"As much as they need."

Again it was so simply, so easily said, she knew he meant it exactly. "Do you ever base one of your characters on someone you know?"

"From time to time." He smiled at her, a smile she neither trusted nor understood. "When I find someone intriguing enough. Do you ever get tired of writing about other people when you've got a world of characters in your own head?"

"It's my job."

"That's not an answer."

"I'm not here to answer questions."

"Why are you here?"

He was closer. Lee hadn't realized he'd moved. He was sitting just below her, obviously relaxed, slightly curious, in charge. "To do an interview with a success-ful, award-winning author."

"An award-winning author wouldn't make you ner-vous."

The pencil was growing damp in her hand. She could have cursed in frustration. "You don't."

"You lie too quickly, and not easily at all." His hands rested loosely on his knees as he watched her. The odd ring he wore glinted dully, gold and silver. "If I were to touch you, just touch you, right now, you'd tremble."

"You think too much of yourself," she told him, but rose.

"I think of you," he said, so quietly the pad slipped out of her hand, unnoticed. "You make me want, I make you nervous." He was looking into her again; she could almost feel it. "It should be an interesting combination over the next couple of weeks."

He wasn't going to intimidate her. He *wasn't* going to make her tremble. "The sooner you remember I'm going to be working for the next two weeks, the simpler things will be." Trying to sound haughty nearly worked. Lee wondered if he heard the slight catch in her voice.

"Since you're resigned to working," he said easily, "you can give me a hand starting dinner. After tonight, we'll take turns making meals."

She wasn't going to give him the satisfaction of tell-ing him she knew nothing about cooking over a fire. He already knew. Neither would she give the satisfaction of being confused by his mercurial mood changes. Instead, Lee brushed at her bangs. "I'm going to wash up first."

Hunter watched her start off in the wrong direction, but said nothing. She'd find the shower facilities sooner or later, he figured. Things would be more interesting if neither of them gave the other an inch.

He wasn't sure, but Hunter thought he heard Lee swear from somewhere behind him. Smiling a little, he leaned back against the rock and finished his cigarette.

Groggy, stiff and sniffing the scent of coffee in the air, Lee woke. She knew exactly where she was—as far over on her side of the tent as she could get, deep into the sleeping bag Hunter had provided for her. And alone. It took her only seconds to sense that Hunter no longer shared the tent with her. Just as it had taken her hours the night before to convince herself it didn't matter that he was only inches away.

Dinner had been surprisingly easy. Easy, Lee realized as she stared at the ceiling of the tent, because Hunter's mood had shifted again when she'd returned to help him fix it. Amiable? No, she decided, cautiously stretching her cramped muscles. *Amiable* was too free a word when applied to Hunter. *Moderately friendly* was more suitable. Cooperative he hadn't been at all. He'd spent the evening hours reading by the light of his lamp, while she'd taken out a fresh notepad and begun what would be a journal on her two weeks in Oak Creek Canyon.

She found it helpful to write down her feelings. Lee had often used her manuscript in much the same fashion. She could say what she wanted, feel what she wanted, without ever taking the risk that anyone would read her words. Perhaps it hadn't worked out precisely that way with her book, since Hunter had read more of her neat double-spaced typing under the steady lamplight, but the journal would be for no one's eyes but her own.

In any case, she thought, it was to her advantage that he'd been occupied with her manuscript. She hadn't had to talk to him as the night had grown later, the darkness deeper. While he'd still been reading, she'd been able to crawl into the tent and squeeze herself into a corner. When he'd joined her, much later, it hadn't been necessary to exchange words in the intimacy of the tent. She'd made certain he'd thought her asleep—though sleep hadn't come for hours.

In the quiet, she'd listened to him breathe beside her. Quiet, steady. That was the kind of man he was. Lee had lain still, telling herself the closeness meant nothing. But this morning, she saw that her nails, which had begun to grow again, had been gnawed down.

The first night was bound to be the hardest, she told herself and sat up, dragging a hand through her hair. She'd survived it. Her problem now was how to get by him and to the showers, where she could change out of the clothes she'd slept in and fix her hair and face. Cautiously, she crept forward to peek through the tent flap.

He knew she was awake. Hunter had sensed it almost the moment she'd opened her eyes. He'd gotten up early to start coffee, knowing that if he'd had trouble sleeping beside her, he'd never have been able to handle waking with her.

He'd seen little more than the coppery mass of hair above the sleeping bag in the dim morning light of the tent. Because he'd wanted to touch it, draw her to him, wake her, he'd given himself some distance. Today he'd walk for miles and fish for hours. Lee could stick to her role of reporter, and by answering her questions he'd

learn as much about her as she believed she was learning about him. That was his plan, Hunter reminded himself, and poured a second cup of coffee. He was better
off remembering it.

"Coffee's hot," Hunter commented without turning
around. Though she'd taken great care to be quiet, he'd
heard Lee push the tent flap aside.

Biting back an oath, Lee scooped up her pack. The
man had ears like a wolf. "I want to shower first," she
mumbled.

"I told you that you didn't have to fix up your face
for me." He began to arrange strips of bacon in a skillet. "I like it fine the way it is."

Infuriated, Lee scrambled to her feet. "I'm not fix-
ing anything for you. Sleeping all night in my clothes
tends to make me feel dirty."

"Probably sleep better without them," Hunter agreed
mildly. "Breakfast's in fifteen minutes, so I'd move
along if I wanted to eat."

Clutching her bag and her dignity, Lee strode off
through the trees.

He wouldn't get to her so easily if she wasn't stiff and
grubby and half-starved, she thought, making her way
along the path to the showers. God knows how he could
be so cheerful after spending the night sleeping on the
ground. Maybe Bryan had been right all along. The man
was weird. Lee took her shampoo and her plastic case
of French-milled soap and stepped into a shower stall.

The spot he'd chosen might be magnificent, the air
might smell clean and pure, but a sleeping bag wasn't a
feather bed. Lee stripped and hung her clothes over the
door. She heard the water running in the stall next to

hers and sighed. For the next two weeks she'd be sharing bathroom facilities. She might as well get used to it.

The water came out in a steady gush, lukewarm. Gritting her teeth, she stepped under. Today, she was going to begin to dig out a few more personal facts on Hunter Brown.

Was he married? She frowned, then deliberately relaxed her features. The question was for the article, not for herself. His marital status meant nothing to her.

He probably wasn't. She soaped her hair vigorously. What woman would put up with him? Besides, wouldn't a wife come along on camping trips even if she detested them? Would that kind of man marry anyone who didn't like precisely what he did?

What did he do for relaxation? Besides playing Daniel Boone in the woods, she added with a grim smile. Where did he live? Where had he grown up? What sort of childhood had he had?

The water streamed over her, sluicing away soap and shampoo. The curiosity she felt was purely professional. Lee found she had to remind herself of that a bit too often. She needed the whole man to do an incisive article. She needed the whole man…

Alarmed at her own thoughts, she opened her eyes wide, then swore when shampoo stung them. Damn the whole man! she thought fiercely. She'd take whatever pieces of him she could get and write an article that would pay him back, in spades, for all the trouble he'd caused her.

Clean, fragrant and shivering, she turned off the water. It wasn't until that moment that Lee remembered she hadn't brought a towel. Campground showers didn't lay in their own linen supply. Damn it, how was she supposed to remember everything?

Dripping, her chilled skin covered with gooseflesh, she stood in the middle of the stall and swore silently and pungently. For as long as she could stand it, Lee let the air dry her while she squeezed water out of her hair. Revenge, she thought, placing the blame squarely on Hunter's shoulders. Sooner or later, she'd have it.

She reached under the stall door for her pack and pulled out a fresh sweatshirt. Resigned, she dabbed at her wet face with the soft outside. Once she'd dragged it over her damp shoulders, she hunted up underwear. Though her clothes clung to her, her skin warmed. In front of the line of sinks and mirrors, she plugged in her blow-dryer and set to work on her hair.

In spite of him, Lee thought, not because of him, she spent more than her usual time perfecting her makeup. Satisfied, she repacked her portable hairdryer and left the showers, smelling lightly of jasmine.

Her scent was the first thing he sensed when she stepped back into the clearing. Hunter's stomach muscles tightened. As if he were unaffected, he finished off another cup of coffee, but he didn't taste it.

Calmer and much more at ease now, Lee stowed her pack before she walked toward the low-burning campfire. On a small shelf of rocks beside it sat the skillet with the remainder of the bacon and eggs. She didn't have to taste them to know they were cold.

"Feel better?" Hunter asked conversationally.

"I feel fine." She wouldn't say one word about the food being cold and, Lee told herself as she scooped her breakfast onto a plate, she'd eat every bite. She'd give him no more cause to smirk at her.

While she nibbled on the bacon, Lee glanced over at him. He'd obviously showered earlier. His hair glinted in the sun and he smelled cleanly of soap without the interference of cologne or aftershave. A man didn't use aftershave if he didn't bother with a razor, Lee concluded, studying the shadow of stubble over his chin. It should've made him look unkempt, but somehow he managed to look oddly dashing. She concentrated on her cold eggs.

"Sleep well?"

"I slept fine," she lied, and gratefully washed down her breakfast with strong, hot coffee. "You?"

"Very well," he lied, and lit a cigarette. She was getting on nerves he hadn't known he had.

"Have you been up long?"

Since dawn, Hunter thought. "Long enough." He glanced down at her barely scuffed hiking boots and wondered how long it would take before her feet just gave out. "I plan to do some hiking today."

She wanted to groan but put on a bright smile. "Fine, I'd like to see some of the canyon while I'm here." Preferably in a Jeep, she thought, swallowing the last crumb of bacon. If there was one cliché she could now attest to, it was that the open air increased the appetite.

It took Lee perhaps half again as long to wash up the breakfast dishes with the plastic water container as it would've taken Hunter, but she already understood the unstated rule. One cooks, the other cleans.

By the time she was finished, he was standing impatiently, binocular and canteen straps crisscrossed over his chest and a light pack in one hand. This he shoved at her. Lee resisted the urge to shove it back at him.

"I want my camera." Without giving him a chance

to complain, she dug it out of her own gear and slipped the small rectangle in the back pocket of her jeans. "What's in here?" she asked, adjusting the strap of the pack over her shoulder.

"Lunch."

Lee lengthened her stride to keep up with Hunter as he headed out of the clearing. If he'd packed a lunch, she'd have to resign herself to a very long day on her feet. "How do you know where you're going and how to get back?"

For the first time since she'd returned to camp smelling like fragility and flowers, Hunter smiled. "Landmarks, the sun."

"Do you mean moss growing on one side of a tree?" She looked around, hoping to find some point of reference for herself. "I've never trusted that sort of thing."

She wouldn't know east from west, either, he mused, unless they were discussing L.A. and New York. "I've got a compass, if that makes you feel better."

It did—a little. When you hadn't the faintest idea how something worked, you had to take it on faith. Lee was far from comfortable putting her faith in Hunter.

But as they walked, she forgot to worry about losing her way. The sun was a white flash of light, and though it was still shy of 9:00 a.m., the air was warm. She liked the way the light hit the red walls of the canyon and deepened the colors. The path inclined upward, narrow, pebbled with loose stones. She heard people laugh, and the sound carried so cleanly over the air, they might have been standing beside her.

Green became sparser as they climbed. What she saw now was scrubby bushes, dusty and faded, that forced their way out of thin ribbons of dirt in the rock. Curious, she broke off a spray of leaves. Their scent was strong, tangy and fresh. Then she found she had to dash to catch up with Hunter. It had been his idea to hike, but he didn't appear to be enjoying it. More, he looked like a man who had some urgent, unpleasant appointment to keep.

It might be a good time, Lee considered, to start a casual conversation that could lead to the kind of personal information she was shooting for. As the path became steadily steeper, she decided she'd better talk while she had the breath to do it. The sweatshirt had been a mistake, too. Her back was damp again, this time from sweat.

"Have you always preferred the outdoors?"

"For hiking."

Undaunted, she scowled at his back. "I suppose you were a Boy Scout."

"No."

"Your interest in camping and hiking is fairly new, then."

"No."

She had to grit her teeth to hold back a groan. "Did you go off and pitch a tent in the woods with your father when you were a boy?"

She'd have been interested in the amused expression on his face if she could have seen it. "No."

"You lived in the city, then."

She was clever, Hunter reflected. And persistent. He shrugged. "Yes."

At last, Lee thought. "What city?"

"L.A."

She tripped over a rock and nearly stumbled headlong into his back. Hunter never slackened his pace. "L.A.?" she repeated. "You live in Los Angeles and still manage to bury yourself so that no one knows you're there?"

"I grew up in L.A.," he said mildly. "In a part of the city you'd have little occasion for visiting. Socially, Lenore Radcliffe, formerly of Palm Springs, wouldn't even know such neighborhoods existed."

That pulled her up short. Again, she had to dash to catch him, but this time she grabbed his arm and made him stop. "How do you know I came from Palm Springs?"

He watched her with the tolerant amusement she found both infuriating and irresistible. "I did my research. You graduated from U.C.L.A. with honors, after three years in a very classy Swiss boarding school. Your engagement to Jonathan Willoby, up-and-coming plastic surgeon, was broken when you accepted a position in *Celebrity*'s Los Angeles office."

"I was never engaged to Jonathan," she began furiously, then decisively bit her tongue. "You have no business probing into my life, Hunter. I'm doing the article, not you."

"I make it a habit to find out everything I can about anyone I do business with. We do have a business arrangement, don't we, Lenore?"

He was clever with words, she thought grimly. But so was she. "Yes, and it consists of my interviewing you, not the other way around."

"On my terms," Hunter reminded her. "I don't talk to anyone unless I know who they are." He reached out, touching the ends of her hair as he'd done once before. "I think I know who you are."

"You don't," she corrected, struggling against the need to back away from a touch that was barely a touch. "And you don't have to. But the more honest and open you are with me, the more honest the article I write will be."

He uncapped the canteen. When she refused his offer with a shake of her head, Hunter drank. "I am being honest with you." He secured the cap. "If I made it easier for you, you wouldn't get a true picture of who I am." His eyes were suddenly dark, intense and piercing. Without warning, he reached out. The power in his eyes made her believe he could quite easily sweep her off the path. Yet his hand skimmed down her cheek, light as rain. "You wouldn't understand what I am," he said quietly. "Perhaps, for my own reasons, I want you to."

She'd have been less frightened if he'd shouted at her, raged at her, grabbed at her. The sound of her own heartbeat vibrated in her head. Instinctively, she stepped back, escape her first and only thought. Her foot met empty space.

In an instant, she was caught against him, pressed body to body, so that the warmth from his seeped right into hers. The fear tripled so that she arched back, raising both hands to his chest.

"Idiot," he said, with an edge to his voice that made her head snap up. "Take a look behind you before you tell me to let you go."

Automatically, she turned her head to look over her shoulder. Her stomach rose up to her throat, then plummeted. The hands that had been poised to push him away grabbed his shoulders until the fingers dug into his flesh. The view behind her was magnificent, sweeping and straight down.

"We—we walked farther up than I'd thought," she managed. And if she didn't sit down, very, very soon, she was going to disgrace herself.

"The trick is to watch where you're going." Hunter didn't move her away from the edge, but took her chin in his hand until their eyes met and held. "Always watch exactly where you're going, then you'll know how to fall."

He kissed her, just as unexpectedly as before, but not so gently. Not nearly so gently. This time, she felt the full force of the strength that had been only an undercurrent each other time his mouth had touched hers. If she'd pitched back and taken that dizzying fall, she'd have been no more helpless than she was at this moment, molded to him, supported by him, wrapped around him. The edge was close—inside her, behind her. Lee couldn't tell which would be more fatal. But she knew, helplessly, that either could break her.

He hadn't meant to touch her just then, but the demanding climb up the path hadn't deadened the need he'd woken with. He'd take this much, her taste, her softness, and make it last until she willingly turned to him. He wanted the sweetness she tried to gloss over, the fragility she tried to deny. And he wanted the strength that kept her pushing for more. Yes, he thought he knew her and was very close to understanding her. He knew he wanted her.

Slowly, very slowly, for lingering mouth-to-mouth both soothed and excited him, Hunter drew her away. Her eyes were as clouded as his thoughts, her pulse as rapid as his. He shifted her until she was close to the cliff wall and away from the drop.

"Never step back unless you've looked over your

shoulder first," he said quietly. "And don't step forward until you've tested the ground."

Turning, he continued up the path, leaving her to wonder if he'd been speaking of hiking or something entirely different.

Chapter 7

Lee wrote in her journal:

On the eighth day of this odd on-again, off-again interview, I know more about Hunter and understand less. By turns, he's friendly, then distant. There's an aloof streak in him, bound so tightly around his private life that I've found no way through it. When I ask about his preference in books, he can go on indefinitely—apparently he has no real preference except for the written word itself. When I ask about his family, he just smiles and changes the subject or gives me one of those intense stares and says nothing. In either case, he keeps a cloak of mystery around his privacy.

He's possibly the most efficient man I've ever met. There's no waste of time, no extra movements and, infuriating to me, never a mistake, when it comes to starting a campfire or cooking a meal—such as they are. Yet, he's content to do absolutely nothing for hours at a time.

He's fastidious—the camp looks as if we've been here no more than a half hour rather than a week—yet he hasn't shaved in that amount of time. The beard should look scruffy, but somehow it looks so natural I find myself wondering if he didn't always have one.

Always, I've been able to find a category to slip an assignment into. An acquaintance into. Not with Hunter. In all this time, I've found no easy file for him.

Last night we had a heated discussion on Sylvia Plath, and this morning I found him paging through a comic book over coffee. When I questioned him on it, his answer was that he respected all forms of literature. I believed him. One of the problems I'm having on this assignment is that I find myself believing everything he says, no matter how contradictory the statement might be to another he makes. Can a total lack of consistency make someone consistent?

He's the most complex, frustrating, fascinating man I've ever known. I've yet to find a way of controlling the attraction he holds for me, or even the proper label for it. Is it physical? Hunter's very compelling physically. Is it intellectual? His mind has such odd twists and turns, it takes all my effort to follow them.

Either of these I believe I could handle successfully enough. Over the years, I've had to deal professionally with attractive, intelligent, charismatic men. It's a challenge, certainly, but here I have the uncomfortable feeling that I'm caught in the middle of a silent chess game and have already lost my queen.

My greatest fear at this moment is that I'm going to find myself emotionally involved.

Since the first day we walked up the canyon, he hasn't touched me. I can still remember exactly how I felt, exactly what the air smelled like at that moment. It's foolish, overly romantic and absolutely true.

Each night we sleep together in the same tent, so close I can feel his breath. Each morning I wake alone. I should be grateful that he isn't making this assignment any more difficult than it already is, and yet I find myself waiting to be held by him.

For over a week I've thought of little else but him. The more I learn, the more I want to know—for myself. Too much for myself.

Twice, I've woken in the middle of the night, aching, and nearly turned to him. Now, I wonder what would happen if I did. If I believed in the spells and forces Hunter writes of, I'd think one was on me. No one's ever made me want so much, feel so much. Fear so much. Every night, I wonder.

Sometimes Lee wrote of the scenery and her feelings about it. Sometimes, she wrote a play-by-play description of the day. But most of the time, more of the time, she wrote of Hunter. What she put down in her journal had nothing to do with her organized, precisely written notes for the article. She wouldn't permit it. What she didn't understand, and what she wouldn't write down in either space, was that she was losing sleep. And she was having fun.

Though he was cannily evasive on personal details, she was gathering information. Even now, barely halfway through the allotted time, Lee had enough for a solid, successful article—more, she knew, than she'd expected to gather. But she wanted even more, for her readers and, undeniably, for herself.

"I don't see how any self-respecting fish could be

fooled by something like this." Lee fiddled with the small rubbery fly Hunter attached to her line.

"Myopic," Hunter countered, bending to choose his own lure. "Fish are notoriously nearsighted."

"I don't believe you." Clumsily, she cast off. "But this time *I'm* going to catch one."

"You'll need to get your fly in the water first." He glanced down at the line tangled on the bank of the creek before expertly casting his own.

He wouldn't even offer to help. After a week in his company, Lee had learned not to expect it. She'd also learned that if she wanted to compete with him in this, or in a discussion of eighteenth-century English literature, she had to get into the spirit of things.

It wasn't simple and it wasn't quick, but kneeling, Lee worked on the tangles until she was back to square one. She shot a look at Hunter, who appeared much too engrossed with the surface of the creek to notice her progress. By now, Lee knew better. He saw everything that went on around him, whether he looked or not.

Standing a few feet away, Lee tried again. This time, her lure landed with a quiet plop.

Hunter saw the rare, quick grin break out, but said nothing. She was, he'd learned, a woman who generally took herself too seriously. Yet he saw the sweetness beneath, and the warmth Lee tried to be so frugal with.

She had a low, smoky laugh she didn't use often enough. It only made him want to urge it out of her.

The past week hadn't been easy for her. Hunter hadn't intended it to be. You learned more about people by observing them in difficult situations than at a catered cocktail party. He was adding to the layers of the first impression he'd had, at the airport in Flagstaff. But he had layers still to go.

She could, unlike most people he knew, be comfortable with long spells of silence. It appealed to him. The more careless he became in his attire and appearance, the more meticulous she became in hers. It amused him to see her go off every morning and return with her makeup perfected and her hair carefully groomed. Hunter made sure they'd been mussed a bit by the end of the day.

Hiking, fishing. Hunter had seen to it that her jeans and boots were thoroughly broken in. Often, in the evening, he'd caught her rubbing her tired feet. When she was back in Los Angeles, sitting in her cozy office, she wouldn't forget the two weeks she'd spent in Oak Creek Canyon.

Now, Lee stood near the edge of the creek, a fishing rod held in both hands, a look of smug concentration on her face. He liked her for it—for her innate need to compete and for the vulnerability beneath the confidence. She'd stand there, holding the rod, until he called a halt to the venture. Back in camp, he knew she'd rub her hands with cream and they would smell lightly of jasmine and stay temptingly soft.

Since it was her turn to cook, she'd do it, though she still fumbled a bit with the utensils and managed to singe almost anything she put on the fire. He liked her for that, too—for the fact that she never gave up on anything.

Her curiosity remained unflagging. She'd question him, and he'd evade or answer as he chose. Then she'd grant him silence to read, while she wrote. Comfortable. Hunter found that she was an unusually comfortable woman in the quiet light of a campfire. Whether she knew it or not, she relaxed then, writing in the journal, which intrigued him, or going over her daily notes for the article, which didn't.

He'd expected to learn about her during the two weeks together, knowing he'd have to give some information on himself in return. That, he considered, was an even enough exchange. But he hadn't expected to enjoy her companionship.

The sun was strong, the air almost still, with an early-morning taste to it. But the sky wasn't clear. Hunter wondered if she'd noticed the bank of clouds to the east and if she realized there'd be a storm by nightfall. The clouds held lightning. He simply sat crosslegged on the ground. It'd be more interesting if Lee found out for herself.

The morning passed in silence, but for the occasional voice from around them or the rustle of leaves. Twice Hunter pulled a trout out of the creek, throwing the second back because of size. He said nothing. Lee said nothing, but barely prevented herself from grinding her teeth. On every jaunt, he'd gone back to camp with fish. She'd gone back with a sore neck.

"I begin to wonder," she said, at length, "if you've put something on that lure that chases fish away."

He'd been smoking lazily and now he stirred himself to crush out the cigarette. "Want to change rods?"

She slanted him a look, taking in the slight amusement in his arresting face. When her muscles quivered, Lee stiffened them. Would she never become completely accustomed to the way her body reacted when they looked at each other? "No," she said coolly. "I'll keep this one. You're rather good at this sort of thing, for a boy who didn't go fishing."

"I've always been a quick study."

"What did your father do in L.A.?" Lee asked, knowing he would either answer in the most offhand way or evade completely.

"He sold shoes."

It took a moment, as she'd been expecting the latter. "Sold shoes?"

"That's right. In the shoe department of a moderately successful department store downtown. My mother sold stationery on the third floor." He didn't have to look at her to know she was frowning, her brows drawn together. "Surprised?"

"Yes," she admitted. "A bit. I suppose I imagined you'd been influenced by your parents to some extent and that they'd had some unusual career or interests."

Hunter cast off again with an agile flick of his wrist. "Before my father sold shoes, he sold tickets at the local theater. Before that, it was linoleum, I think." His shoulders moved slightly before he turned to her. "He was a man trapped by financial circumstances into working, when he'd been born to dream. If he'd been born into affluence, he might've been a painter or a poet. As it was, he sold things and regularly lost his job because he wasn't suited to selling anything, not even himself."

Though he spoke casually, Lee had to struggle to distance herself emotionally. "You speak as though he's not living."

"I've always believed my mother died from overwork, and my father from lack of interest in life without her."

Sympathy welled up in her throat. She couldn't swallow at all. "When did you lose them?"

"I was eighteen. They died within six months of each other."

"Too old for the state to care for you," she murmured, "too young to be alone."

Touched, Hunter studied her profile. "Don't feel sorry for me, Lenore. I managed very well."

"But you weren't a man yet." No, she mused, perhaps he had been. "You had college to face."

"I had some help, and I waited tables for a while."

Lee remembered the wallet full of credit cards she'd carried through college. Anything she'd wanted had always been at her fingertips. "It couldn't have been easy."

"It didn't have to be." He lit a cigarette, watching the clouds move slowly closer. "By the time I was finished with college, I knew I was a writer."

"What happened from the time you graduated from college to when your first book was published?"

He smiled through the smoke that drifted between them. "I lived, I wrote, I went fishing when I could."

She wasn't about to be put off so easily. Hardly realizing she did it, Lee sat down on the ground beside him. "You must've worked."

"Writing, though many disagree, is work." He had a talent for making the sharpest sarcasm sound mildly droll.

Another time, she might have smiled. "You know that's not what I mean. You had to have an income, and your first book wasn't published until nearly six years ago."

"I wasn't starving in a garret, Lenore." He ran a finger down the hand she held on the rod and felt a flash of pleasure at the quick skip of her pulse. "You'd just have been starting at *Celebrity* when *The Devil's Due* hit the stands. One might say our stars were on the rise at the same time."

"I suppose." She turned from him to look back at the surface of the creek again.

"You're happy there?"

Unconsciously, she lifted her chin. "I've worked my way up from gofer to staff reporter in five years."

"That's not an answer."

"Neither are most of yours," she mumbled.

"True enough. What're you looking for there?"

"Success," she said immediately. "Security."

"One doesn't always equal the other."

Her voice was as defiant as the look she aimed at him. "You have both."

"A writer's never secure," Hunter disagreed. "Only a foolish one expects to be. I've read all of the manuscript you brought."

Lee said nothing. She'd known he'd bring it up before the two weeks were over, but she'd hoped to put it off a bit longer. The faintest of breezes played with the ends of her hair while she sat, staring at the moving waters of the creek. Some of the pebbles looked like gems. Such were illusions.

"You know you have to finish it," he told her calmly. "You can't make me believe you're content to leave your characters in limbo, when you've drawn them so carefully. Your story's two-thirds told, Lenore."

"I don't have time," she began.

"Not good enough."

Frustrated, she turned to him again. "Easy for you

to say from your little pinnacle of fame. I have a demanding full-time job. If I give it my time and my talent, there's no place I can go but up at *Celebrity*."

"Your novel needs your time and talent."

She didn't like the way he said it—as if she had no real choice. "Hunter, I didn't come here to discuss my work, but you and yours. I'm flattered that you think my novel has some merit, but I have a job to do."

"Flattered?" he countered. The deep, black gaze pinned her again, and his hand closed over hers. "No, you're not. You wish I'd never seen your novel and you don't want to discuss it. Even if you were convinced it was worthwhile, you'd still be afraid to put it all on the line."

The truth grated on her nerves and on her temper. "My job is my first priority. Whether that suits you or not doesn't matter. It's none of your business."

"No, perhaps not," he said slowly, watching her. "You've got a fish on your line."

"I don't want you to—" Eyes narrowing, she broke off. "What?"

"There's a fish on your line," he repeated. "You'd better reel it in."

"I've got one?" Stunned, Lee felt the rod jerk in her hands. "I've got one! Oh, God." She gripped the rod in both hands again and watched the line jiggle. "I've really caught one. What do I do now?"

"Reel it in," Hunter suggested again, leaning back on the grass.

"Aren't you going to help?" Her hands felt foolishly clumsy as she started to crank the reel. Hoping leverage would give her some advantage, she scrambled to her feet. "Hunter, I don't know what I'm doing. I might lose it."

"Your fish," he pointed out. Grinning, he watched her. Would she look any more exuberant if she'd been given an interview with the president? Somehow, Hunter didn't think so, though he was sure Lee would disagree. But then, she couldn't see herself at that moment, hair mussed, cheeks glowing, eyes wide and her tongue caught firmly between her teeth. The late-morning sunlight did exquisite things to her skin, and the quick laugh she gave when she pulled the struggling fish from the water ran over the back of his neck like soft fingers.

Desire moved lazily through him as he took his gaze up the long length of leg flattered by brief shorts, then over the subtle curves accented by the shifting of muscle under her shirt as she continued to fight with the fish, to her face, still flushed with surprise.

"Hunter!" She laughed as she held the still-wriggling fish high over the grass. "I did it."

It was nearly as big as the largest one he'd caught that week. He pursed his lips as he sized it up. It was tempting to compliment her, but he decided she looked smug enough already. "Gotta get it off the hook," he reminded her, shifting only slightly on his elbows.

"Off the hook?" Lee shot him an astonished look. "I don't want to touch it."

"You have to touch it to take it off the hook."

Lee lifted a brow. "I'll just toss it back in."

With a shrug, Hunter shut his eyes and enjoyed the faint breeze. The hell she would. "Your fish, not mine."

Torn between an abhorrence of touching the still-flopping fish and pride at having caught it, Lee stared down at Hunter. He wasn't going to help; that was painfully obvious. If she threw the fish back into the water, he'd smirk at her for the rest of the evening. Intolerable. And, she reasoned logically, wouldn't she still have to touch it to get rid of it? Setting her teeth, Lee reached out a hand for the catch of the day.

It was wet, slippery and cold. She pulled her hand back. Then, out of the corner of her eye, she saw Hunter grinning up at her. Holding her breath, Lee took the trout firmly in one hand and wiggled the hook out with the other. If he hadn't been looking at her, challenging her, she never would've managed it. With the haughtiest air at her disposal, she dropped the trout into the small cooler Hunter brought along on fishing trips.

"Very good." He closed the lid on the cooler before he reeled in his line. "That looks like enough for tonight's dinner. You caught a good-sized one, Lenore."

"Thank you." The words were icily polite and self-satisfied.

"It'll nearly be enough for both of us, even after you've cleaned it."

"It's as big as…" He was already walking back toward camp, so that she had to run to catch up with him and his statement. "*I* clean it?"

"Rule is, you catch, you clean."

She planted her feet, but he wasn't paying attention. "I'm not cleaning any fish."

"Then you don't eat any fish." His words were as offhand and careless as a shrug.

Abandoning pride, Lee caught at his arm. "Hunter, you'll have to change the rule." She sighed, but convinced herself she wouldn't choke on the word. At least not very much. "Please."

He stopped, considering. "If I clean it, you've got to balance the scales—" the smile flickered over his face "—no pun intended, by doing me a favor."

"I can cook two nights in a row."

"I said a favor."

Her head turned sharply, but one look at his face had her laughing. "All right, what's the deal?"

"Why don't we leave it open-ended?" he suggested. "I don't have anything in mind at the moment."

This time, she considered. "It'll be negotiable?"

"Naturally."

"Deal." Turning her palms up, Lee wrinkled her nose. "Now I'm going to wash my hands."

She hadn't realized she could get such a kick out of catching a fish or out of cooking it herself over an open fire. There were other things Lee hadn't realized. She hadn't looked at the trim gold watch on her wrist in days. If she hadn't kept a journal, she probably wouldn't know what day it was. It was true that her muscles still revolted after a night in the tent and the shower facilities were an inconvenience at best, purgatory at worst, but despite herself she was relaxing.

For the first time in her memory, her day wasn't regimented, by herself or by anyone else. She got up when she woke, slept when she was tired and ate when she was hungry. For the moment, the word *deadline* didn't exist. That was something she hadn't allowed herself since the day she'd walked out of her parents' home in Palm Springs.

No matter how rapid Hunter could make her pulse by one of those unexpected looks, or how much desire for him simmered under the surface, she found him comfortable to be with. Because it was so unlikely, Lee didn't try to find the reasons. On this late afternoon, in the hour before dusk, she was content to sit by the fire and tend supper.

"I never knew anything could smell so good."

Hunter continued to pour a cup of coffee before he glanced over at her. "We cooked fish two days ago."

"Your fish," Lee pointed out, carefully turning the trout. "This one's mine."

He grinned, wondering if she remembered just how horrified she'd been the first time he'd suggested she pick up a rod and reel. "Beginner's luck."

Lee opened her mouth, ready with a biting retort, then saw the way he smiled at her. Not only did her retort vanish, but so did much of her defensive wall. She let out a long, quiet breath as she turned back to the skillet. The man became only more dangerous with familiarity. "If fishing depends on luck," she managed, "you've had more than your share."

"Everything depends on luck." He held out two plates. Lee slipped the sizzling trout onto them, then sat back to enjoy.

"If you believe that, what about fate? You've said more than once that we can fight against our fate, but we can't win."

He lifted a brow. That consistently sharp, consistently logical mind of hers never failed to impress him. "One works with the other." He tasted a bit of trout, noting that she'd been careful enough not to singe her own catch. "It's your fate to be here, with me. You were lucky enough to catch a fish for dinner."

"It sounds to me as though you twist things to your own point of view."

"Yes. Doesn't everyone?"

"I suppose." Lee ate, thoughtfully studying the view over his shoulder. Had anything ever tasted this wonderful? Would anything ever again? "But not everyone makes it work as well as you." Reluctantly, she accepted some of the dried fruit he offered. He seemed to have an unending supply, but Lee had yet to grow used to the taste or texture.

"If you could change one thing about your life, what would it be?"

Perhaps because he'd asked without preamble, perhaps because she was so unexpectedly relaxed, Lee answered without thinking. "I'd have more."

He didn't, as her parents had done, ask more what. Hunter only nodded. "We could say it's your fate to want it, and your luck to have it or not."

Nibbling on an apricot, she studied him. The lowering light and flickering fire cast his face in shadows. They suited him. The short, rough beard surrounded the poet's mouth, making it all the more compelling. He was a man a woman would never be able to ignore, never be able to forget. Lee wondered if he knew it. Then she nearly laughed. Of course he did. He knew entirely too much.

"What about you?" She leaned forward a bit, as she did whenever the answer was important. "What would you change?"

He smiled in the way that made her blood heat. "I'd take more," he said quietly.

She felt the shiver race up her spine, was all but certain Hunter could see it. Lee found she was compelled to remind herself of her job. "You know," she began easily enough, "you've told me quite a bit over this week, more in some ways than I'd expected, but much less in others." Steady again, she took another bite of trout. "I might understand you quite a bit better if you'd give me a run-through of a typical day."

He ate, enjoying the tender, open-air flavor. The clouds were rolling in, the breeze picking up. He wondered if she noticed. "There's no such thing as a typical day."

"You're evading again."

"Yeah."

"It's my job to pin you down."

He watched her over the rim of his coffee cup. "I like watching you do your job."

She laughed. It seemed he could always frustrate and amuse her at the same time. "Hunter, why do I have the feeling you're doing your best to make this difficult for me?"

"You're very perceptive." Setting his plate aside, he began to toy with the ends of her hair in a habit she could never take casually. "I have an image of a woman with a romantic kind of beauty and an orderly, logical mind."

"Hunter—"

"Wait, I'm just fleshing her out. She's ambitious, full of nerves, highly sensuous without being fully aware of it." He could see her eyes change, growing as dark as the sky above them. "She's caught in the middle of something she can't explain or understand. Things happen around her and she's finding it more and more difficult to distance herself from it. And there's a man, a man she desires but can't quite trust. He doesn't offer her the logical explanations she wants, but the illogic he offers seems terrifyingly close to the truth. If she puts her trust in him, she has to turn her back on most of what she believes is fact. If she doesn't, she'll be alone."

He was talking to her, about her, for her. Lee knew her throat was dry and her palms were damp, but she didn't know if it was from his words or the light touch on the ends of her hair. "You're trying to frighten me by weaving a plot around me."

"I'm weaving a plot around you," Hunter agreed. "Whether I frighten you or not depends on how successful I am with that plot. Shadows and storms are my business." As if on cue, lightning snaked out in the sky overhead. "But all writers need a foil. Smooth, pale skin—" He stroked the back of his hand up her cheek. "Soft hair with touches of gold and fire. Against that I have darkness, wind, voices that speak from shadows. Logic against the impossible. The unspeakable against cool, polished beauty."

She swallowed to relieve the dryness in her throat and tried to speak casually. "I suppose I should be flattered, but I'm not sure I want to see myself molded into a character in a horror story."

"That comes back to fate again, doesn't it?" Lightning ripped through the early dusk as their eyes met again. "I need you, Lenore," he murmured. "For the tale I have to tell—and more."

Nerves prickled along her skin, all the more frantically because of the relaxed hours. "It's going to rain." But her voice wasn't calm and even. Her senses were already swimming. When she started to rise, she found that her hand was caught in his and that he stood with her. The wind blew around her, stirring leaves, stirring desire. The light dimmed to shadow. Thunder rumbled.

What she saw in his eyes chilled her, then heated her

blood so quickly she had no way to keep up with the change. The grip on her hand was light. Lee could've broken the hold if she'd had the will to do so. It was his look that drained the will from her. They stood there, hands touching, eyes locked, while the storm swirled like madness around them.

Perhaps life was made up of the choices Hunter had once spoken of. Perhaps luck swayed the balance. But at that moment, for hardly more than a heartbeat, Lee believed that fate ruled everything. She was meant to go to him, to give to him, with no more choice than one of the characters his imagination formed.

Then the sky opened. The rain poured out. The shock of the sudden drenching had Lee jolting back, breaking contact. Yet for several long seconds she stood still while water ran over her and lightning flashed in wicked bolts.

"Damn it!" But he knew she spoke to him, not the storm. "Now what am I supposed to do?"

Hunter smiled, barely resisting the urge to cup her face in his hands and kiss her until her legs gave way. "Head for drier land." He continued to smile despite the rain, the wind, the lightning.

Wet, edgy and angry, Lee crawled inside the tent. He's enjoying this, she thought, tugging on the sodden laces of her boots. There's nothing he likes better than to see me at my worst. It would probably take a week for the boots to dry out, she thought grimly as she managed to pry the first one off.

When Hunter slipped into the tent beside her, she said nothing. Concentrating on anger seemed the best solution. The pounding of the rain on the sides of the tent made the space inside seem to shrink. She'd never been more aware of him, or of herself. Water dripped uncomfortably down her neck as she leaned forward to pull off her socks.

"I don't suppose this'll last long."

Hunter pulled the sodden shirt over his head. "I wouldn't count on it stopping much before morning."

"Terrific." She shivered and wondered how the hell she was supposed to get out of the wet clothes and into dry ones.

Hunter turned the lantern he'd carried in with him down to a dim glow. "Relax and listen to it. It's different from rain in the city. There's no swish of tires on wet asphalt, no horns, no feet running on the sidewalk." He took a towel out of his pack and began to dry her hair.

"I can do it." She reached up, but his hands continued to massage.

"I like to do it. Wet fire," he murmured. "That's what your hair looks like now."

He was so close she could smell the rain on him. The heat from his body called subtly, temptingly, to hers. Was the rain suddenly louder, or were her senses more acute? For a moment, she thought she could hear each individual drop as it hit the tent. The light was dim, a smoky gray that held touches of unreality. Lee felt as though she'd been running away from this one isolated spot all her life. Or perhaps she'd been running toward it.

"You need to shave," she murmured, and found that her hand was already reaching out to touch the untrimmed growth of beard on his face. "This hides too much. You're already difficult to know."

"Am I?" He moved the towel over her hair, soothing and arousing by turns.

"You know you are." She didn't want to turn away now, from the look that could infuse such warmth through her chilled, damp skin. Lightning flashed, illuminating the tent brilliantly before plunging it back into gloom. Yet, through the gloom she could see all she needed to, perhaps more than she wanted to. "It's my job to find out more, to find out everything."

"And my right to tell you only what I want to."

"We just don't look at things the same way."

"No."

She took the towel and, half dreaming, began to dry his hair. "We have no business being together like this."

He hadn't known desire with claws. If he didn't touch her soon, he'd be ripped through. "Why?"

"We're too different. You look for the unexplainable, I look for the logical." But his mouth was so near hers, and his eyes held such power. "Hunter..." She knew what was going to happen, recognized the impossibility of it and the pain that was bound to follow. "I don't want this to happen."

He didn't touch her, though he was certain he'd soon be mad from the lack of it. "You have a choice."

"No." It was said quietly, almost on a sigh. "I don't think I do." She let the towel fall. She saw the flicker of lightning and waited, six long heartbeats, for the answering thunder. "Maybe neither one of us has a choice."

Her breath was already unsteady as she let her hands curl over his bare shoulders. There was strength there. She wanted to feel it, but had been afraid to. His eyes never left hers as she touched him. Though the force of need curled tight in his stomach, he'd let her set the pace this first time, this most important time.

Her fingers were long and smooth on his skin, cool, not so much hesitant as cautious. They ran down his arms, moving slowly over his chest and back until desire was taut as a bow poised for firing. The sound of the rain drummed in his head. Her face was pale and elegant in the gloomy light. The tent was suddenly too big. He wanted her in a space that was too small to move in unless they moved together.

She could hardly believe she could touch him this way, freely, openly, so that his skin quivered under the trace of her fingers. All the while, he watched her with a passion so fierce it would have terrified her if she hadn't been so dazed with her own need. Carefully, afraid to make the wrong move and break the mood for both of them, she touched her mouth to his.

The rough brush of beard was a stunning contrast to the softness of his lips. He gave back to her such feelings, such warmth, with no pressure. She'd never known anyone who could give without taking. This generosity was, to her, the ultimate seduction. In that moment, any reserve she'd clung to was washed away. Her arms went around his neck, her cheek pressed to his.

"Make love to me, Hunter."

He drew her away, only far enough so that they could see each other again. Wet hair curled around her face. Her eyes were as the sky had been an hour before. Dusky and clouded. "With."

Her lips curved. Her heart opened. He poured inside. "Make love with me."

Then his hands were framing her face, and the kiss was so gentle it drugged every cell of her body. She felt him tug the wet shirt from her, and shivered once before he warmed her. His body felt so strong against hers, so solid, yet his hands played over her with the care of a jeweler polishing a rare gem. He sighed when she touched him, so she touched once again, wanting to give pleasure as it was given to her.

She'd thought the panic would return, or at least the need to rush. But they'd been given all the time in the world. The rain could fall, the thunder bellow. It didn't involve them. She tasted hunger on his lips, but he held it in check. He'd sup slowly. Pleasure bubbled up inside her and came softly through her lips.

His mouth on her breast had the need leaping up to the next plane. Yet he didn't hurry, even when she arched against him. His tongue flicked, his teeth nibbled, until he could feel the crazed desire vibrating through her. She thought only of him now, Hunter knew it even as he struggled to hold the reins of his own passion. She'd have more. She'd take all. And so, by God, would he.

When she struggled with the snap of his jeans, he let her have her way. He wanted to be flesh-to-flesh with her, body-to-body, without barriers. In his mind, he'd already had her bare, like this, a dozen times. Her hair was cool and wet, her skin smooth and fragrant. Spring flowers and summer rain. The scents raced through him as her hands became more urgent.

Her breathing was ragged as she tugged the wet denim down his legs. She recognized strength, power and control. It was only the last she needed to break so that she could have what she ached for.

Wherever she could reach, she touched, she tasted, wallowing in pleasure each time she heard his breath tremble. Her shorts were drawn slowly down her body by strong, clever hands, until she wore nothing but the lacy triangle riding low on her hips. With his lips, he journeyed down, down her body, slowly, so that the bristle of beard awakened every pore. His tongue slid under the lace, making her gasp. Then, as abruptly as the storm had broken, Lee was lost in a morass of sensation too dark, too deep, to understand.

He felt her explode, and the power sang through him. He heard her call his name, and the greed to hear it again almost overwhelmed him. Bracing himself over her, Hunter held back that final, desperate need until she opened her eyes. She'd look at him when they came together. He'd promised himself that.

Dazed, trembling, frenzied, Lee stared at him. He looked invincible. "What do you want from me?"

His mouth swooped down on hers, and for the first time the kiss was hard, urgent, almost brutal with the force of passion finally unleashed. "Everything." He plunged into her, catapulting them both closer to the crest. "Everything."

Chapter 8

Dawn was clear as glass. Lee woke to it slowly, naked, warm and, for the first time in over a week, comfortable. And for the first time in over a week, she woke not precisely sure where she was.

Her head was pillowed in the curve of Hunter's shoulder, her body turned toward his of its own volition and by the weight of the arm held firmly around her. There was a drowsy feeling that was a mix of security and excitement. In all of her memory, she couldn't recall experiencing anything quite like it.

Before she was fully awake, she smelled the lingering fragrance of rain on his skin and remembered. In remembering, she took a deep, drinking breath of the scent.

It was like a dream, like something in some subliminal fantasy, or a scene that had come straight from the imagination. She'd never offered herself to anyone so freely before, or so completely. Never. Lee knew there'd never been anyone who'd tempted her to.

She could still remember the sensation of her lips touching his, and all doubt, all fear, melting away with the gentle contact.

Should she feel so content now that the rain had stopped and dawn was breaking? Fantasies were for that private hour of the night, not for the daylight. After all, it hadn't been a dream, and there'd be no pretending it had been. Perhaps she should be appalled that she'd given him exactly what he'd demanded: everything.

She couldn't. No, it was more than that, she realized. She wouldn't. Nothing, no one, would spoil what had happened, not even she herself.

Still, it might be best if he didn't realize quite yet how completely victorious he'd been. Lee let her eyes close and wrapped the sensation of closeness around her. For the next few days, there was no desk, no typewriter, no phone ringing with more demands. There'd be no self-imposed schedule. For the next few days, she was alone with her lover. Maybe the time had come to pick those wildflowers.

She tilted her head, wanting to look at him, trying not to wake him. Over the week they'd spent in such intimate quarters, she'd never seen him sleep. Every other morning he'd been up, already making coffee. She wanted the luxury of absorbing him when he was unaware.

Lee knew that most people looked more vulnerable in sleep, more innocent, perhaps. Hunter looked just as dangerous, just as compelling, as ever. True, those dark, intense eyes were hidden, but knowing the lids could lift at any moment, and the eyes spear you with that peculiar power, didn't add innocence to his face, only more mystery.

Lee discovered she didn't want it to. She was glad he was more dangerous than the other men she'd known. In an odd way, she was glad he was more difficult. She hadn't fallen in love with the ordinary, the everyday, but with the unique.

Fallen in love. She ran the phrase around in her head, taking it apart and putting it back together again with the caution she was prone to. It triggered a trickle of unease. The phrase itself connoted bruises. Hadn't Hunter himself warned her to test the ground before she started forward? Even warned, she hadn't. Even seeing the pit, she hadn't checked her step. The tumble she'd taken had a soft fall. This time. Lee knew it was all too possible to stumble and be destroyed.

She wasn't going to think about it. Lee allowed herself the luxury of cuddling closer. She was going to find those wildflowers and enjoy each individual petal. The dream would end soon enough, and she'd be back to the reality of her life. It was, of course, what she wanted. For a while, she lay still, just listening to the silence.

The clever thing to do, she thought lazily, would be to hang their wet clothes out in the sun. Her boots certainly needed drying out, but in the meantime, she had her sneakers. She yawned, thinking she wanted a few moments to write in her journal as well. Hunter's breathing was slow and even. A smile curved her lips. She could do all that, then come back and wake him. Waking him, in whatever way she chose, was a lover's privilege.

Lover. Skimming her gaze over his face again, she

wondered why she didn't feel any particular surprise at the word. Was it possible she'd recognized it from the beginning? Foolish, she told herself, and shook her head.

Slowly, she shifted away from him, then crawled to the front of the tent to peek out. Even as she reached for the flap, a hand closed around her ankle. Hunter pillowed his other hand under his head as he watched her.

"If you're going out like that, we won't keep everyone away from the campsite for long."

As she was naked, the haughty look she sent him lost something. "I was just looking out. I thought you were asleep."

He smiled, thinking she was the only woman who could make a viable stab at dignity while on her hands and knees in a tent, without a stitch on. The finger around her ankle stroked absently. "You're up early."

"I thought I'd hang these clothes out to dry."

"Very practical." Because he sensed she was feeling awkward, Hunter sat up and grabbed her arm, tugging until she tumbled back, sprawled over him. Content, he held her against him and sighed. "We'll do it later."

Unsure whether to laugh or complain, Lee blew the hair out of her eyes as she propped herself on one elbow. "I'm not tired."

"You don't have to be tired to lie down." Then he rolled on top of her. "It's called relaxing."

As the planes of his body fit against the curves of hers, Lee felt the warmth seep in. A hundred tiny pulse points began to drum. "I don't think this has a lot to do with relaxing."

"No?" He'd wanted to see her like this, in the thin light of dawn with her hair mussed from his hands, her skin flushed from sleep, her limbs heavy from a night of loving and alert for more. He ran a hand down her with a surge of possession that wasn't quite comfortable, wasn't quite expected. "Then we'll relax later, too." He saw her lips form a gentle smile just before he brushed his over them.

Hunter didn't question that he wanted her just as urgently now as he had all the days and nights before. He rarely questioned feelings, because he trusted them. Her arms went around him, her lips parted. The completeness of her giving shot a shaft of heat through him that turned to a unified warmth. Lifting his head, Hunter looked down at her.

Milkmaid skin over a duchess's cheekbones, eyes like the sky at dusk and hair like copper shot with gold. Hunter gave himself the pleasure of looking at all of her, slowly.

She was small and sleek and smooth. He ran a fingertip along the curve of her shoulder and studied the contrast of his skin against hers. Fragile, delicate—but he remembered how much strength there was inside her.

"You always look at me as if you know everything there is to know about me."

The intensity in his eyes remained, as he caught her hand in his. "Not enough. Not nearly enough." With the lightest of touches, he kissed her shoulder, her temple, then her lips.

"Hunter…" She wanted to tell him that no one had ever made her feel this way before. She wanted to tell him that no one had ever made her want so badly to believe in magic and fairy tales and the simplicity of love. But as she started to speak, courage deserted her. She was afraid to risk, afraid to fail. Instead she touched a hand to his cheek. "Kiss me again."

He understood there was something more, something he needed to know. But he understood, too, that when something fragile was handled clumsily, it broke. He did as she asked and savored the warm, dark taste of her mouth.

Soft...sweet...silky. It was how he could make her feel with only a kiss. The ground was hard and unyielding under the thin tent mattress, but it might have been a luxurious pile of feathers. It was so easy to forget where she was, when he was with her this way, to forget a world existed outside that small space two bodies required. He could make her float, and she'd never known she'd wanted to. He could make her ache, and she'd never known there could be pleasure from it. He spoke against her mouth words she didn't need to understand. She wanted and was wanted, needed and was needed. She loved...

With an inarticulate murmur of acceptance for whatever he could give, Lee drew him closer. Closer. The moment was all that mattered.

Deep, intoxicating, tender, the kiss went on and on and on.

Even an imagination as fluid as his hadn't fantasized anything so sweet, anything so soft. It was as though she melted into him, giving everything before he could ask. Once, only once, only briefly, it sped through his mind that he was as vulnerable as she. The unease came, flicking at the corner of his mind. Then her hands ran over him, stroking, and he accepted the weakness.

Only one other person had ever had the power to reach inside him and hold his heart. Now there were two. The time to deal with it was tomorrow. Today was for them alone.

Without hurry, he whispered kisses over her face. Perhaps it was an homage to beauty, perhaps it was much, much more. He didn't question his motives as he traced the slope of her cheek. There was an immediacy he'd never experienced before, but it didn't carry the urgency he'd expected. She was there for him as long as he needed. He understood that, without words.

"You smell of spring and rain," he murmured against her ear. "Why should that drive me mad?"

The words vibrated through her, as arousing as the most intimate caress. Heavy-lidded, clouded, her eyes met his. "Just show me. Show me again."

He loved her with such generosity. Each touch was a separate pleasure, each kiss a luxurious taste. Patience—there was more patience in him than in her. Her body was tossed between utter contentment and urgency, until reason was something too vague to grasp.

"Here—" He nibbled lightly at her breast, listening to and allured by her unsteady breaths. "You're small and soft. Here—" He took his hand over her hip to her thigh. "You're taut and lean. I can't seem to touch enough, taste enough." He drew the peak of her breast into his mouth, so that she arched against him, center to center.

"Hunter." His name was barely audible, but the sound of it was enough to bring him to desperation. "I need you."

God, had he wanted to hear that so badly? Struggling to understand what those three simple words had triggered, he buried his mouth against her skin. But he couldn't think, only feel. Only want. "You have me."

With his hands and lips alone, he took her spiraling over the first peak.

Her movements beneath him grew wild, her murmurs frenzied, but she was unaware. All Lee knew was that they were flesh-to-flesh. This was the storm he'd gentled the night before, the power unleashed, the demands unsoftened. The tenderness became passion so quickly, she could only ride with it, blind to her own power and her own demands. She was spinning too fast in the world they'd created to know how hungrily her mouth sought him, how sure were her own hands. She drew from him everything he drew from her. Again and again she took him to the edge, and again and again he clung, wanting more. And still more.

Greed. He'd never known this degree of greed. With the blood pounding in his head, singing in his veins, he molded his open mouth to hers. With his hands gripping her hips, he rolled until she lay over him. They were still mouth-to-mouth when they joined, and her gasp of pleasure rocketed through him.

Strength seemed to build, impossibly. She thought she could feel each individual muscle of her body coil and release as they moved together. Power called to power. Lee remembered the lightning, remembered the thunder, and lived it again. When the storm broke, she was clasped against him, as if the heat had fused them.

Minutes, hours, days. Lee couldn't have measured the time. Slowly, her body settled. Gradually, her heartbeat leveled. With her body pressed close to his, she could feel each breath he took and found a foolish satisfaction that the rhythm matched her own.

"A pity we wasted a week." Finding the effort to open his eyes too great, Hunter kept them closed as he combed his fingers through her hair.

She smiled a little, because he couldn't see. "Wasted?"

"If we'd started out this way, I'd've slept a lot better."

"Really?" Schooling her features, Lee lifted her head. "Have you had trouble sleeping?"

His eyelids opened lazily. "I've rarely found it necessary to get up at dawn, unless it's to write."

The surge of pleasure made her voice smug. She traced a fingertip over his shoulder. "Is that so?"

"You insisted on wearing that perfume to make me crazy."

"To make you crazy?" Folding her arms on his chest, she arched a brow. "It's a very subtle scent."

"Subtle." He ran a casual hand over her bottom. "Like a hammer in the solar plexus."

The laugh nearly escaped. "You were the one who insisted we share a tent."

"Insisted?" He gave her a mildly amused glance. "I told you I had no objection if you chose to sleep outside."

"Knowing I wouldn't."

"True, but I didn't expect you to resist me for so long."

Her head came up off her folded arms. "Resist you?" she repeated. "Are you saying you plotted this out like a scene in a book?"

Grinning, he pillowed his arms behind his head. God, he couldn't remember a time he'd felt so clean, so…complete. "It worked."

"Typical," she said, wishing she were insulted and trying her best to act as though she were. "I'm surprised

there was room in here for the two of us and your inflated ego."

"And your stubbornness."

She sat up at the word, both brows disappearing
under her tousled bangs. "I suppose you thought I'd
just—" her hand gestured in a quick circle "—fall at
your feet."

Hunter considered this a moment, while he gave himself the pleasure of memorizing every curve of her body.
"It might've been nice, but I'd figured a few detours
into the scenario."

"Oh, had you?" She wondered if he realized he was
steadily digging himself into a hole. "I bet we can come
up with a great many more." Searching in her pack, Lee
found a fresh T-shirt. "Starting now."

As she started to drag the shirt over her head, Hunter
grabbed the hem and yanked. Lee tumbled down on top
of him again, to find her mouth captured. When he let
her surface, she narrowed her eyes. "You think you're
pretty clever, don't you?"

"Yeah." He caught her chin in his hand and kissed
her again. "Let's have breakfast."

She swallowed a laugh, but her eyes gave her away.
"Bastard."

"Okay, but I'm still hungry." He tugged her shirt
down her torso before he started to dress.

Lying back, Lee strugggled into a pair of jeans. "I
don't suppose, now that the point's been made, we could
finish out this week at a nice resort?"

Hunter dug out a fresh pair of socks. "A resort? Don't
tell me you're having problems roughing it, Lenore."

"I wouldn't say problems." She stuck a hand in one
boot and found the inside damp. Resigned, she hunted

for her sneakers. "But there is the matter of having fantasies about a hot tub and a soft bed." She pressed a hand to her lower back. "Wonderful fantasies."

"Camping does take a certain amount of strength and endurance," he said easily. "I suppose if you've reached your limit and want to quit—"

"I didn't say anything about quitting," she retorted. She set her teeth, knowing whichever way she went, she lost. "We'll finish out the damn two weeks," she mumbled, and crawled out of the tent.

Lee couldn't deny that the quality of the air was exquisite and the clarity of the sky more perfect than any she'd ever seen. Nor, if he'd asked, would she have told Hunter that she wanted to be back in Los Angeles. It was a matter of basic creature comforts, she thought. Like soaking in hot, fragrant water and stretching out on a firm, linen-covered mattress. Certainly, it wasn't more than most people wanted in their day-to-day lives. But then, she reflected, Hunter Brown wasn't most people.

"Fabulous, isn't it?" His arms came around her waist, drawing her back to his chest. He wanted her to see what he saw, feel what he felt. Perhaps he wanted it too much.

"It's a beautiful spot. It hardly seems real." Then she sighed, not entirely sure why. Would Los Angeles seem more real to her when this final week was up? At the very least, she understood the tall buildings and crowded streets. Here—here she seemed so small, and that top rung of the ladder seemed so vague and unimportant.

Abruptly, she turned and clung to him. "I hate to admit it, but I'm glad you brought me." She found she wanted to continue clinging, continue holding, so that there wouldn't be a time when she had to let go. Pushing away all thoughts of tomorrow, Lee told herself to remember the wildflowers. "I'm starving," she said, able to smile when she drew away. "It's your turn to cook."

"A small blessing."

Lee gave him a quick jab before they cleaned up the dishes they'd left out in the rain.

In his quick, efficient manner, Hunter had the campfire burning and bacon sizzling. Lee sat back, absorbing the scents while she watched him break eggs into the pan.

"We've been through a lot of eggs," she commented idly. "How do you manage to keep them fresh out here?"

Because she was watching his hands, she missed the quick smile. "Just one of the many mysteries of life. You'd better pass me a plate."

"Yes, but— Oh, look." The movement that had caught her eye turned out to be two rabbits, curious enough to bound to the edge of the clearing and watch. The mystery of the eggs was forgotten in the simple fascination of something she'd just begun to appreciate. "Every time I see one, I want to touch."

"If you managed to get close enough to touch, they'd show you they have very sharp teeth."

Shrugging, she dropped her chin to her knees and continued to stare back at the visitors. "The bunnies I think about don't bite."

Hunter reached for a plate himself. "Bunnies, fuzzy little squirrels and cute raccoons are nice to look at but foolish to handle. I remember having a long, heated argument with Sarah on the subject a couple of years ago."

"Sarah?" Lee accepted the plate he offered, but her attention was fully on him.

Until that moment, Hunter hadn't realized how completely he'd forgotten who she was and why she was there. To have mentioned Sarah so casually showed him he needed to keep personal feelings separate from professional agreements. "Someone very special," he told her as he scooped the remaining eggs onto his plate. He remembered his daughter's comment about simmering passion and falling in love. The smile couldn't be prevented. "I imagine she'd like to meet you."

Lee felt something cold squeeze her heart and fought to ignore it. They'd said nothing about commitment, nothing about exclusivity. They were adults. She was responsible for her own emotions and their consequences. "Would she?" Taking the first bite of eggs, she tasted nothing. Her eyes were drawn to the ring on his finger. It wasn't a wedding band, but… She had to ask, she had to know before things went any further.

"The ring you wear," she began, satisfied her voice was even. "It's very unusual. I've never seen another quite like it."

"You shouldn't." He ate with the ease of a man completely content. "My sister made it."

"Sister?" If her name was Sarah…

"Bonnie raises children and makes jewelry," Hunter went on. "I'm not sure which comes first."

"Bonnie." Nodding, she forced herself to continue eating. "Is she your only sister?"

"There were just the two of us. For some odd reason, we got along very well." He remembered those early years when he was struggling to learn how to be both father and mother to Sarah. He smiled. "We still do."

"How does she feel about what you do?"

"Bonnie's a firm believer that everyone should do

exactly what suits them. As long as they're married, with a half-dozen children." He grinned, recognizing the unspoken question in Lee's eyes. "In that area, I've disappointed her." He paused for a moment, the grin fading. "Do you think I could make love with you if I had a wife waiting for me at home?"

She dropped her gaze to her plate. Why could he always read her when she couldn't read him? "I still don't know very much about you."

He didn't know if he consciously made the decision at that moment or if he'd been ready to make it all along. "Ask," he said simply.

Lee looked up at him. It no longer mattered if she needed to know for herself or for her job. She just needed to know. "You've never been married?"

"No."

"Is that an outgrowth of your need for privacy?"

"No, it's an outgrowth of not finding anyone who could deal with the way I live and my obligations."

Lee mulled this over, thinking it a rather odd way to phrase it. "Your writing?"

"Yes, there's that."

She started to press further, then decided to change directions. Personal questions could be reciprocated with personal questions. "You said you hadn't always wanted to be a writer, but were born to be one. What made you realize it?"

"I don't think it was a matter of realizing, but of accepting." Understanding that she wanted something specific, he drew out a cigarette, studying the tip. He was no more certain why he was answering than Lee was why she was asking. "It must've been in my first year of college. I'd written stories ever since I could remember, but I was dead set on a career as an athlete. Then I wrote something that seemed to trigger it. It was nothing fabulous," he added thoughtfully. "A very basic plot, simple background, but the characters pulled me in. I knew them as well as I knew anyone. There was nothing else for me to do."

"It must've been difficult. Publishing isn't an easy field. Even when you break in, it isn't particularly lucrative unless you write bestsellers. With your parents gone, you had to support yourself."

"I had experience waiting tables." He smiled, a bit more easily now. "And detested it. Sometimes you have to put it all on the line, Lenore. So I did."

"How did you support yourself from the time you graduated from college until you broke through with *The Devil's Due?*"

"I wrote."

Lee shook her head, forgetting the half-full plate on her lap. "The articles and short stories couldn't have brought in very much. And that was your first book."

"No, I'd had a dozen others before it." Blowing out a stream of smoke, he reached for the coffeepot. "Want some?"

She leaned forward a bit, her brows drawing together. "Look, Hunter, I've been researching you for months. I might not have gotten much, but I know every book, every article and every short story you've written, including the majority of your college work. There's no way I'd've missed a dozen books."

"You know everything Hunter Brown's written," he corrected and poured himself coffee.

"That's precisely what I said."

"You didn't research Laura Miles."

"Who?"

He sipped, enjoying the coffee and the conversation more than he'd anticipated. "A great many writers use pseudonyms. Laura Miles was mine."

"A woman's name?" Confused on one level, reporter's instincts humming on another, she frowned at him. "You wrote a dozen books before *The Devil's Due* under a woman's name?"

"Yeah. One of the problems with writing is that the name alone can project a certain perception of the author." He offered her the last piece of bacon. "Hunter Brown wasn't right for what I was doing at the time."

Lee let out a frustrated breath. "What were you doing?"

"Writing romance novels." He flicked his cigarette into the fire.

"Writing... *You?*"

He studied her incredulous face before he leaned back. He was used to criticism of genre fiction and, more often than not, amused by it. "Do you object to the genre in general, or to my writing in it?"

"I don't—" Confused, she broke off to try to gather her thoughts. "I just can't picture you writing happy-ever-after love stories. Hunter, I just finished *Silent Scream*. I kept my bedroom door locked for a week." She dragged a hand through her hair as he quietly watched her. "Romances?"

"Most novels have some kind of relationship with them. A romance simply focuses on it, rather than using it as a subplot or a device."

"But didn't you feel you were wasting your talent?" Lee knew his skill in drawing the reader in from the first page, from the first sentence. "I understand there being a matter of putting food on the table, but—"

"No." He cut her off. "I never wrote for the money, Lenore, any more than the novel you're writing is done for financial gain. As far as wasting my talent, you shouldn't look down your nose at something you don't understand."

"I'm sorry, I don't mean to be condescending. I'm just—" Helplessly, she shrugged. "I'm just surprised. No, I'm astonished. I see those colorful little paperbacks everywhere, but—"

"You never considered reading one," he finished. "You should, they're good for you."

"I suppose, for simple entertainment."

He liked the way she said it, as though it were something to be enjoyed in secret, like a child's lollipop. "If a novel doesn't entertain, it isn't a novel and it's wasted your time. I imagine you've read *Jane Eyre, Rebecca, Gone with the Wind, Ivanhoe.*"

"Yes, of course."

"Romances. A lot of the same ingredients are in those colorful little paperbacks."

He was perfectly serious. At that moment, Lee would've given up half the books in her personal library for the chance to read one Laura Miles story. "Hunter, I want to print this."

"Go ahead."

Her mouth was already open for the argument she'd expected. "Go ahead?" she repeated. "You don't care?"

"Why should I? I'm not ashamed of the work I did as Laura Miles. In fact..." He smiled, thinking back. "I'm rather pleased with most of it."

"Then why—" She shook her head as she began to

absently nibble on cold bacon. "Damn it, Hunter, why haven't you ever said so before? Laura Miles is as much a deep, dark secret as everything else about you."

"I never met a reporter I chose to tell before." He rose, stretching, and enjoyed the wide blue expanse of sky. Just as he'd never met a woman he'd have chosen to live with before. Hunter was beginning to wonder if one had very much to do with the other. "Don't complicate the simple, Lenore," he told her, thinking aloud. "It usually manages to complicate itself."

Setting her plate aside, she stood in front of him. "One more question, then."

He brought his gaze back down to hers. She hadn't bothered to fuss with her hair or makeup that morning, as she had from the first morning of the trip. For a moment, he wondered if the reporter was too anxious for the story or the woman was too involved with the man. He wished he knew. "All right," he agreed. "One more question."

"Why me?"

How did he answer what he didn't know? How did he answer what he was hesitant to ask himself? Framing her face, he brought his lips to hers. Long, lingering and very, very new. "I see something in you," Hunter murmured, holding her face still so that he could study it. "I want something from you. I don't know what either one is yet, and maybe I never will. Is that answer enough?"

She put her hands on his wrists and felt his life pump through them. It was almost possible to believe hers pumped through them, too. "It has to be."

Chapter 9

Standing high on the bluff, Lee could see down the canyon, over the peaks and pinnacles, beyond the rich red buttes to the sheer-faced walls. There were pictures in them. People, creatures, stories. They pleased her all the more because she hadn't realized she could find them.

She hadn't known land could be so demanding, or so compelling. Not knowing that, how could she have known she would feel at home so far away from the world she knew or the life she'd made?

Perhaps it was the mystery, the awesomeness—the centuries of work nature had done to form beauty out of rock, the centuries it had yet to work. Weather had landscaped, carved and created without pampering. It might have been the quiet she'd learned to listen to, the quiet she'd learned to hear more than she'd ever heard sound before. Or it might have been the man she'd discovered in the canyon, who was slowly, inevitably dominating every aspect of her life in much the same way wind, water and sun dominated the shape of everything around her. He wouldn't pamper, either.

They'd been lovers only a matter of days, yet he seemed to know just where her strengths lay, and her weaknesses. She learned about him, step by gradual step, always amazed that each new discovery came so naturally, as though she'd always known. Perhaps the intensity came from the briefness. Lee could almost accept that theory, but for the timelessness of the hours they spent together.

In two days, she'd leave the canyon, and the man, and go back to being the Lee Radcliffe she'd molded herself into over the years. She'd step back into the rhythm, write her article and go on to the next stage of her career.

What choice was there? Lee asked herself as she stood with the afternoon sun beating down on her. In L.A., her life had direction, it had purpose. There, she had one goal: to succeed. That goal didn't seem so important here and now, where just being, just breathing, was enough, but this world wasn't the one she would live in day after day. Even if Hunter had asked, even if she'd wanted to, Lee couldn't go on indefinitely in this unscheduled, unplanned existence. Purpose, she wondered. What would her purpose be here? She couldn't dream by the campfire forever.

But two days. She closed her eyes, telling herself that everything she'd done and everything she'd seen would be forever implanted in her memory. Did the time left have to be so short? And the time ahead of her loomed so long.

"Here." Hunter came up alongside her, holding out a pair of binoculars. "You should always see as far as you can."

She took them, with a smile for the way he had of putting things. The canyon zoomed closer, abruptly becoming more personal. She could see the water rushing by in the creek, rushing with a sound too distant to be heard. Why had she never noticed how unique each leaf on a tree could be? She could see other campers loitering near their sites or mingling with the day tourists on paths. Lee let the binoculars drop. They brought intrusion too close.

"Will you come back next year?" She wanted to be able to picture him there, looking out over the endless space, remembering.

"If I can."

"It won't have changed," she murmured. If she came back, five, ten years from then, the creek would still snake by, the buttes would still stand. But she couldn't come back. With an effort, she shook off the mood and smiled at him. "It must be nearly lunchtime."

"It's too hot to eat up here." Hunter wiped at the sweat on his brow. "We'll go down and find some shade."

"All right." She could see the dust plume up from his boots as he walked. "Someplace near the creek." She glanced to the right. "Let's go this way, Hunter. We haven't walked down there yet."

He hesitated only a moment. "Fine." Holding her hand, he took the path she'd chosen.

The walk down was always easier than the walk up.

That was another invaluable fact Lee had filed away during the last couple of weeks. And Hunter, though he held her hand, didn't guide or lead. He simply walked his own way. Just as he'd walk his own way in forty-eight hours, she mused, and stretched her stride to keep pace with him.

"Will you start on your next book as soon as you get back?"

Questions, he thought. He'd never known anyone with such an endless supply of questions. "Yes."

"Are you ever afraid you'll, well, dry up?"

"Always."

Interested, she stopped a moment. "Really?" She'd considered him a man without any fear at all. "I'd have thought that the more success you achieved, the more confident you'd become."

"Success is a deity that's never satisfied." She frowned, a bit uncomfortable with his description. "Every time I face that first blank page, I wonder how I'll ever get through a beginning, middle and end."

"How do you?"

He began to walk again, so that she had to keep up or be left behind. "I tell the story. It's as simple and as miserably complex as that."

So was he, she reflected, that simple, that complex. Lee thought over his words as she felt the temperature gradually change with the decrease in elevation.

It seemed tidier in this section of the canyon. Once she thought she heard the purr of a car's engine, a sound she hadn't heard in days. The trees grew thicker, the shade more generous. How strange, she reflected, to have those sheer, unforgiving walls at her back and a cozy little forest in front of her. More unreality? Then, glancing down, she saw a patch of small white flowers. Lee picked three, leaving the rest for someone else. She hadn't come for them, she remembered as she tucked them in her hair, but she was glad, so very glad, to have found them.

"How's this?" He turned to see her secure the last flower in her hair. The need for her, the complete her, rose inside him so swiftly it took his breath away. Lenore. He had no trouble understanding why the man in Poe's verse had mourned the loss of her to the point of madness. "You grow lovelier. Impossible." Hunter touched a fingertip to her cheek. Would he, too, grow mad from mourning the loss of her?

Her face, lifted to the sun, needed nothing more than the luminescence of her skin to make it exquisite. But how long, he wondered, how long would she be content to shun the polish? How long would it be before she craved the life she'd begun to carve out for herself?

Lee didn't smile, because his eyes prevented her. He was looking into her again, for something… Something. She wasn't certain, even if she'd known what it was, that she could give him the answer he wanted. Instead, she did what he'd once done. Placing her hands on his shoulders, she touched her mouth to his. With her eyes squeezed shut, she dropped her head onto his chest.

How could she leave? How could she not? There seemed to be no direction she could go and not lose something essential. "I don't believe in magic," she murmured, "but if I did, I'd say this was a magic place. Now, in the day, it's quiet. Sleeping, perhaps. But at night, the air would be alive with spirits."

He held her closer as he rested his neck on top of her head. Did she realize how romantic she was? he wondered. Or just how hard she fought not to be? A week ago, she might have had such a thought, but she'd never have said it aloud. A week from now... Hunter bit back a sigh. A week from now, she'd give no more thought to magic.

"I want to make love with you here," he said quietly. "With the sunlight streaming through the leaves and onto your skin. In the evening, just before the dew falls. At dawn, when the light's caught somewhere between rose and gray."

Moved, ruled by love, she smiled up at him. "And at midnight, when the moon's high and anything's possible."

"Anything's always possible." He kissed one cheek, then the other. "You only have to believe it."

She laughed, a bit shakily. "You almost make me believe it. You make my knees weak."

His grin flashed as he swept her up in his arms. "Better?"

Would she ever feel this free again? Throwing her arms around his neck, Lee kissed him with all the feeling that welled inside her. "Yes. And if you don't put me down, I'll want you to carry me back to camp."

The half smile touched his lips. "Decided you aren't hungry after all?"

"Since I doubt you've got anything in that bag but dried fruit and sunflower seeds, I don't have any illusions about lunch."

"I've still got a couple pieces of fudge."

"Let's eat."

Hunter dropped her unceremoniously on the ground. "It shows the woman's basic lust centers around food."

"Just chocolate," Lee disagreed. "You can have my share of the sunflower seeds."

"They're good for you." Digging into the pack, he pulled out some small clear plastic bags.

"I can handle the raisins," Lee said unenthusiastically. "But I can do without the seeds."

Shrugging, Hunter popped two in his mouth. "You'll be hungry before dinner."

"I've been hungry before dinner for two weeks," she tossed back, and began to root through the pack herself for the fudge. "No matter how good seeds and nuts and little dried pieces of apricot are for you, they don't take the place of red meat—" she found a small square of fudge "—or chocolate."

Hunter watched her close her eyes in pure pleasure as she chewed the candy. "Hedonist."

"Absolutely." Her eyes were laughing when she opened them. "I like silk blouses, French champagne and lobster with warm butter sauce." She sighed as she sat back, wondering if Hunter had any emotional attachment to the last piece of fudge. "I especially enjoy them after I've worked all week to justify having them."

He understood that, perhaps too well. She wasn't a woman who wanted to be taken care of, nor was he a man who believed anyone should have a free ride. But what future was there in a relationship when two people couldn't acclimate to each other's lifestyle? He'd never imposed his on anyone else, nor would be permit anyone to sway him from his own. And yet, now that he felt the clock ticking the hours away, the days away, he wondered if it would be as simple to go back, alone, as he'd once expected it to be.

"You enjoy living in the city?" he asked casually.

"Of course." It wasn't possible to tell him that she hated the thought of going back, alone, to what she'd always thought was perfect for her. "My apartment's twenty minutes from the magazine."

"Convenient." And practical, he mused. It seemed she would always choose the practical, even if she had a whim for the fanciful. He opened the canteen and drank. When he passed it to Lee, she accepted. She'd learned to make a number of adjustments.

"I suppose you work at home."

"Yes."

She touched a hand absently to one of the flowers in her hair. "That takes discipline. I think most people need the structure of an office away from their living space to accomplish anything."

"You wouldn't."

She looked over then, wishing they could talk about more personal things without bringing on that quiet sense of panic. Better that they talked of work or the weather, or of nothing at all. "No?"

"You'd drive yourself harder than any supervisor or time clock." He bit into an apple slice. "If you put your mind to it, you'd have that manuscript finished within a month."

Restlessly, she moved her shoulders. "If I worked eight hours a day, without any other obligations."

"The story's your only obligation."

She held back a sigh. She didn't want to argue or even debate, not when they had so little time left together. Yet if they didn't discuss her work, she might not be able to prevent herself from talking about her feelings. That was a circle without any meeting point.

"Hunter, as a writer, you can feel that way about a

book. I suppose you have to. I have a job, a career that demands blocks of time and a great deal of my attention. I can't simply put that into hiatus while I speculate on my chances of getting a manuscript published."

"You're afraid to risk it."

It was a direct hit to her most sensitive area. Both of them knew her anger was a defense. "What if I am? I've worked hard for my position at *Celebrity*. Everything I've done there, and every benefit I've received, I've earned on my own. I've already taken enough risks."

"By not marrying Jonathan Willoby?"

The fury leaped into her eyes quickly, interesting him. So, it was still a sore point, Hunter realized. A very sore point.

"Do you find that amusing?" Lee demanded. "Does the fact that I reneged on an unspoken agreement appeal to your sense of humor?"

"Not particularly. But it intrigues me that you'd consider it possible to renege on something unspoken."

From the meticulous way she recapped the canteen, he gauged just how angry she was. Her voice was cool and detached, as he hadn't heard it for days. "My family and the Willobys have been personally and professionally involved for years. The marriage was expected of me and I knew it from the time I was sixteen."

Hunter leaned back against the trunk of a tree until he was comfortable. "And at sixteen you didn't consider that sort of expectation antiquated?"

"How could you possibly understand?" Fuming, she rose. The nerves that had been dormant for days began to jump again. Hunter could almost see them spring to life. "You said your father was a dreamer who made his living as a salesman. My father was a realist who made his living socializing and delegating. He social-ized with the Willobys. He delegated me to complete the social and professional merger with them by mar-rying Jonathan." Even now, the tidy, unemotional plans gave her a twinge of distaste. "Jonathan was attractive, intelligent, already successful. My father never consid-ered that I'd object."

"But you did," Hunter pointed out. "Why do you continue to insist on paying for something that was your right?"

Lee whirled to him. It was no longer possible for her to answer coolly, to rebuff with aloofness. "Do you know what it cost me not to do what was expected of me? Everything I did, all my life, was ultimately for their approval."

"Then you did something for yourself." Without hurry, he rose to face her. "Is your career for yourself, Lenore, or are you still trying to win their approval?"

He had no right to ask, no right to make her search for the answer. Pale, she turned away from him. "I don't want to discuss this with you. It's none of your concern."

"Isn't it?" Abruptly as angry as she, Hunter spun her around again. "Isn't it?" he repeated.

Her hands curled around his arms—whether in pro-test or for support, she wasn't certain. Now, she thought, now perhaps she'd reached that edge where she had to make a stand, no matter how unsteady the ground under her feet. "My life and the way I live it are my business, Hunter."

"Not anymore."

"You're being ridiculous." She threw back her head, the better to meet his eyes. "This argument doesn't even have a point."

Something was building inside him so quickly he didn't have a chance to fight it or reason it through. "You're wrong."

She was beginning to tremble without knowing why. Along with the anger came the quick panic she recognized too well. "I don't know what you want."

"You." She was crushed against him before she understood her own reaction. "All of you."

His mouth closed over hers with none of the gentle patience he usually showed. Lee felt a lick of fear that was almost immediately swallowed by raging need.

He'd made her feel passion before, but not so swiftly. Desire had burst inside her before, but not so painfully. Everything was as it always was whenever he touched her, and yet everything was so different.

Was it anger she felt from him? Frustration? Passion? She only knew that the control he mastered so finely was gone. Something strained inside him, something more primitive than he'd let free before. This time, they both knew it could break loose. Her blood swam with the panicked excitement of anticipation.

Then they were on the ground, with the scent of sun-warmed leaves and cool water. She felt his beard scrape over her cheek before he buried his mouth in her throat. Whatever drove him left her no choice but to race with him to the end that waited for both of them.

He didn't question his own desperation. He couldn't. If she held off sharing certain pieces of herself with him, she still shared her body willingly. He wanted more, all, though he told himself it wasn't reasonable. Even now, as he felt her body heat and melt for him, he knew he wouldn't be satisfied. When would she give her feelings to him as freely? For the first time in his life, he wanted too much.

He struggled back to the edge of reason, resisting the wave after wave of need that raged through him. This wasn't the time, the place or the way. In his mind, he knew it, but emotion battled to betray him. Still holding her close, he buried his face in her hair and waited for the madness to pass.

Stunned, as much by his outburst of passion as by her unquestioning response, Lee lay still. Instinctively, she stroked a hand down his back to soothe. She knew him well enough to understand that his temper was rarely unguarded. Now she knew why.

Hunter lifted his head to look at her, seeing on a surge of self-disgust that her eyes were wary again. The flowers had fallen from her hair. Taking one, he pressed it into her hand. "You're much too fragile to be handled so clumsily."

His eyes were so intense, so dark, it was impossible for her to relax again. Against his back, her fingers curled and uncurled. There was a warning somewhere in her brain that he wanted more than she'd expected him to want, more than she knew how to give. Play it light, Lee ordered herself, and deliberately stilled the movement of her fingers. She smiled, though her eyes remained cautious.

"I should've waited until we were back in the tent before I made you angry."

Understanding what she was trying to do, Hunter lifted a brow. Under his voice, and hers, was a strain both of them pretended not to hear. "We can go back now. I can toss you around a bit more."

As the panic subsided, she sent him a mild glance. "I'm stronger than I look."

"Yeah?" He sent her a smile of his own. He had the long hours of night to think about what had happened and what he was going to do about it. "Show me."

More confident than she should've been, Lee pushed against him, intent on rolling him off her. He didn't budge. The look of calm amusement on his face had her doubling her efforts. Breathless, unsuccessful, she lay back and frowned at him. "You're heavier than you look," she complained. "It must be all those sunflower seeds."

"Your muscles are full of chocolate," he corrected.

"I only had one piece," she began.

"Today. By my count, you've polished off—"

"Never mind." Her brow arched elegantly. The nerves in her stomach hadn't completely subsided. "If you want to talk about unhealthy habits, you're the one who smokes too much."

He shrugged, accepting the truth. "Everyone's entitled to one vice."

Her grin became wicked, then sultry. "Is that your only one?"

If she'd planned to make her mouth irresistible, she'd succeeded. Hunter lowered his to nibble at the sweetness. "I've never been one to consider pleasures vices."

Sighing, she linked her arms around his neck. They didn't have enough time left to waste it arguing, or even thinking. "Why don't we go back to the tent so you can show me what you mean?"

He laughed softly and shifted to kiss the curve of her shoulder. Her laugh echoed his, then Lee's smile froze when she glanced down the length of his body to what stood at their feet.

Fear ripped through her. She couldn't have screamed. Her short, unpainted nails dug into Hunter's back.

"What—" He lifted his head. Her face was ice-white and still. Though her body was rigid beneath his, there was lively fear in the hands that dug into his back. Muscles tense, he turned to look in the direction she was staring. "Damn." The word was hardly out of his mouth before a hundred pounds of fur and muscle leaped on him. This time, Lee's scream tore free.

Adrenaline born of panic gave her the strength to send the three of them rolling to the edge of the bank. As she struck out blindly, Lee heard Hunter issue a sharp command. A whimper followed it.

"Lenore." Her shoulders were gripped before she could spring to her feet. In her mind, the only thought was to find a weapon to defend them. "It's all right." Without giving her a choice, Hunter held her close. "It's all right, I promise. He won't hurt you."

"My God, Hunter, it's a wolf!" Every nightmare she'd ever read or heard about fangs and claws spun in her mind. With her arms wrapped around him to protect him, as much as for protection for herself, Lee turned her head. Silver eyes stared back at her from a silver coat.

"No." He felt the fresh fear jump through her and continued to soothe. "He's only half wolf."

"We've got to do something." Should they run? Should they sit perfectly still? "He attacked—"

"Greeted," Hunter corrected. "Trust me, Lenore. He's not vicious." Annoyed and resigned, Hunter held out a hand. "Here, Santanas."

A bit embarrassed at having lost control of himself, the dog crawled forward, head down. Speechless, Lee watched Hunter stroke the thick silver-gray fur.

"He's usually better behaved," Hunter said mildly. "But he hasn't seen me for nearly two weeks."

"Seen you?" She pressed herself closer to Hunter. "But…" Logic began to seep through her panic as she saw the dog lick Hunter's extended hand. "You called him by name," she said shakily. "What did you call him?"

Before Hunter could answer, there was a rustling in the trees behind them. Lee had nearly mustered the breath to scream again when another voice, young and high, shouted out. "Santanas! You come back here. I'm going to get in trouble."

"Damn right," Hunter mumbled under his breath.

Lee drew back far enough to look into Hunter's face. "Just what the hell's going on?"

"A reunion," he said simply.

Puzzled, with her heart still pounding in her ears, Lee watched the girl break through the trees. The dog's tail began to thump the ground.

"Santanas!" She stopped, her dark braids whipping back and forth. Smiling, she uninhibitedly showed her braces. "Whoops." The quick exclamation trailed off as Lee was treated to a long intense stare that was hauntingly familiar. The girl stuck her hands in the pockets of cutoff jeans, scuffing the ground with battered sneakers. "Well, hi." Her gaze shifted to Hunter briefly before it focused on Lee again. "I guess you wonder what I'm doing here."

"We'll get into that later," Hunter said in a tone both females recognized as basic male annoyance.

"Hunter—" Lee drew farther away, traces of anger and anxiety working their way through the confusion. She couldn't bring herself to look away from the dark, dark eyes of the girl who stared at her. "What's going on here?"

"Apparently a lesson in manners should be," he returned easily. "Lenore, the creature currently sniffing at your hand is Santanas, my dog." At the gesture of his hand, the large, lean animal sat and lifted a friendly paw. Dazed, Lee found herself taking it while she turned to watch the dog's master. She saw Hunter's gaze travel beyond her with a smile that held both irony and pride. "The girl rudely staring at you is Sarah. My daughter."

Chapter 10

Daughter...Sarah...

Lee turned her head to meet the dark, direct eyes that were a duplicate of Hunter's. Yes, they were a duplicate. It struck her like a blast of air. He had a child? This lovely, slender girl with a tender mouth and braids secured by mismatched rubber bands was Hunter's daughter? So many opposing emotions moved through her that she said nothing. Nothing at all.

"Sarah." Hunter spoke into the drumming silence. "This is Ms. Radcliffe."

"Sure, I know, the reporter. Hi."

Still sitting on the ground, with the dog now sniffing around her shoulder, Lee felt like a complete fool. "Hello." She hoped the word wasn't as ridiculously formal as it sounded to her.

"Dad said I shouldn't call you pretty because pretty

was like a bowl of fruit." Sarah didn't tilt her head as one might to study from a new angle, but Lee had the impression she was being weighed and dissected like a still life. "I like your hair," Sarah declared. "Is it a real color?"

"A definite lesson in manners," Hunter put in, more amused than annoyed. "I'm afraid Sarah's a bit of a brat."

"He always says that." Sarah moved thin, expressive shoulders. "He doesn't mean it, though."

"Until today." He ruffled the dog's fur, wondering just how he would handle the situation. Lee was still silent, and Sarah's eyes were all curiosity. "Take Santanas back to the house. I assume Bonnie's there."

"Yeah. We came back yesterday because I remembered I had a soccer game and she had an inspiration and couldn't do anything with it in Phoenix with all the kids running around like monkeys."

"I see." And though he did, perfectly, Lee was left floundering in the dark. "Go ahead, then, we'll be right along."

"Okay. Come on, Santanas." Then she shot Lee a quick grin. "He looks pretty ferocious, but he doesn't bite." As the girl darted away, Lee wondered if she'd been speaking of the dog or her father. When she was once again alone with Hunter, Lee remained still and silent.

"I'll apologize for the rudeness of my family, if you'd like."

Family. The word struck her, a dose of reality that flung her out of the dream. Rising, Lee meticulously dusted off her jeans. "There's no need." Her voice was cool, almost chill. Her muscles were wire-taut. "Since the game's over, I'd like you to drive me into Sedona so I can arrange for transportation back to L.A."

"Game?" In one long, easy motion, he came to his feet, then took her hand, stopping its nervous movement. It was a gesture that had become so much of a habit, neither of them noticed. "There's no game, Lenore."

"Oh, you played it very well." The hurt she wouldn't permit in her voice showed clearly in her eyes. Her hand remained cold and rigid in his. "So well, in fact, I completely forgot we were playing."

Patience deserted him abruptly and without warning. Anger he could handle, with more anger or with amusement. But hurt left him with no defense, no attack. "Don't be an idiot. Whatever game there was ended a few nights ago in the tent."

"Ended." Tears sprang to her eyes, stunning her. Furiously she blinked them back, filled with self-disgust, but not before he'd seen them. "No, it never ended. You're an excellent strategist, Hunter. You seemed to be so open with me that I didn't think you were holding anything back." She jerked her hand from his, longing for the luxury of dissolving into those hot, cleansing tears. "How could you?" she demanded. "How could you touch me that way and lie?"

"I never lied to you." His voice was as calm as hers, his eyes were as full of passion.

"You have a child." Something snapped inside her, so that she had to grip her hands together to prevent herself from wringing them. "You have a half-grown daughter you never mentioned to me. You told me you'd never been married."

"I haven't been," he said simply, and waited for the inevitable questions.

They leaped into her mind, but Lee found she couldn't ask them. She didn't want to know. If she was to put him out of her life immediately and completely, she couldn't ask. "You said her name once, and when I asked, you avoided answering."

"Who asked?" he countered. "You or the reporter?"

She paled, and her step away from him said more than a dozen words.

"If that was an unfair question," he said, feeling his way carefully, "I'm sorry."

Lee stifled a bitter answer. He'd just said it all. "I want to go back to Sedona. Will you drive me, or do I have to arrange for a car?"

"Stop this." He gripped her shoulders before she could back farther away. "You've been a part of my life for a few days. Sarah's been my life for ten years. I take no risks with her." She saw the fury come and go in his eyes as he fought against it. "She's off the record, do you understand? She stays off the record. I won't have her childhood disturbed by photographers dogging her at soccer games or hanging from trees at school picnics. Sarah's not an item for the glossy pages of any magazine."

"Is that what you think of me?" she whispered. "We've come no further than that?" She swallowed a mixture of pain and betrayal. "Your daughter won't be mentioned in any article I write. You have my word. Now let me go."

She wasn't speaking only of the hands that held her there, and they both knew it. He felt a bubble of panic he'd never expected, a twist of guilt that left him baffled. Frustrated, he stared down at her. He'd never realized she could be a complication. "I can't." It was said with such simplicity her skin iced. "I want you to understand, and I need time for that."

"You've had nearly two weeks to make me understand, Hunter."

"Damn it, you came here as a reporter." He paused, as if waiting for her to confirm or deny, but she said nothing. "What happened between us wasn't planned or expected by either one of us. I want you to come back with me to my home."

Somehow she met his eyes levelly. "I'm still a reporter."

"We have two days left in our agreement." His voice softened, his hands gentled. "Lenore, spend those two days with me at home, with my daughter."

"You have no problem asking for everything, do you?"

"No." She was still holding herself away from him. No matter how badly he wanted to, Hunter knew better than to try to draw her closer. Not yet. "It's important to me that you understand. Give me two days."

She wanted to say no. She wanted to believe she could deny him even that and turn away, go away, without regrets. But there'd be regrets, Lee realized, if she went back to L.A. without taking whatever was left. "I can't promise to understand, but I'll stay two more days."

Though she was reluctant, he held her hand to his lips. "Thank you. It's important to me."

"Don't thank me," she murmured. The anger had slipped away so quietly, she couldn't recall it. "Things have changed."

"Things changed days ago." Still holding her hand, he drew her in the direction Sarah had gone. "I'll come back for the gear."

Now that the first shock had passed, the second occurred to her. "But you live here in the canyon."

"That's right."

"You mean to tell me you have a house, with hot and cold running water and a normal bed, but you chose to spend two weeks in a tent?"

"It relaxes me."

"That's just dandy," she muttered. "You've had me showering with lukewarm water and waking up with aching muscles, when you knew I'd've given a week's pay for one tub bath."

"Builds character," he claimed, more comfortable with her annoyance.

"The hell it does. You did it deliberately." She stopped, turning to him as the sun dappled light through the trees. "You did it all deliberately to see just how much I could tolerate."

"You were very impressive." He smiled infuriatingly. "I admit I never expected you to last out a week, much less two."

"You sonofa—"

"Don't get cranky now," he said easily. "You can take as many baths as you like over the next couple of days." He swung a friendly arm over her shoulder before she could prevent it. And he'd have time, he thought, to explain to her about Sarah. Time, he hoped, to make her understand. "I'll even see to it that you have that red meat you've been craving."

Fury threatened. Control strained. "Don't you dare patronize me."

"I'm not. You're not a woman a man could patronize." Though she mistrusted his answer, his voice was bland with sincerity and he wasn't smiling. "I'm enjoying you and, I suppose, the foul-up of my own plans. Believe me, I hadn't intended for you to find out I lived a couple miles from the campsite in quite this way."

"Just how did you intend for me to find out?"

"By offering you a quiet candlelight dinner on our last night. I'd hoped you'd see the—ah—humor in the situation."

"You'd've been wrong," she said precisely, then caught sight of the house cocooned in the trees.

It was smaller than she'd expected, but with the large areas of glass in the wood, it seemed to extend into the land. It made her think of dolls' houses and fairy tales, though she didn't know why. Dolls' houses were tidy and formal and laced with gingerbread. Hunter's house was made up of odd angles and unexpected peaks. A porch ran across the front, where the roof arched to a high pitch. Plants spilled over the banister—bloodred geraniums in jade-green pots. The roof sloped down again, then ran flat over a parallelogram with floor-to-ceiling windows. On the patio that jutted out from it, a white wicker chair lay overturned next to a battered soccer ball.

The trees closed in around it. Closed it in, Lee thought. Protected, sheltered, hid. It was like a house out of a play, or… Stopping, she narrowed her eyes and studied it again. "This is Jonas Thorpe's house in *Silent Scream*."

Hunter smiled, rather pleased she'd seen it so quickly. "More or less. I wanted to put him in isolation, miles away from what would normally be considered civilized, but in reality, the only safe place left."

"Is that how you look at it?" she wondered aloud. "As the only safe place left?"

"Often." Then a shriek, which after a heart-stopping moment Lee identified as laughter, ripped through the silence. It was followed by an excited bout of barking and a woman's frazzled voice. "Then there're other times," Hunter murmured as he led Lee toward the front door.

Even as he opened it, Sarah came bounding out. Unsure of her own feelings, Lee watched the girl throw her arms around her father's waist. She saw Hunter stroke a hand over the dark hair at the crown of Sarah's head.

"Oh, Dad, it's so funny! Aunt Bonnie was making a bracelet out of glazed dough and Santanas ate it—or he chewed on it until he found out it tasted awful."

"I'm sure Bonnie thinks it's a riot."

Her eyes, so like her father's, lit with a wicked amusement that would've made a veteran fifth-grade teacher nervous. "She said she had to take that sort of thing from art critics, but not from half-breed wolves. She said she'd make some tea for Lenore, but there aren't any cookies because we ate them yesterday. And she said—"

"Never mind, we'll find out for ourselves." He stepped back so that Lee could walk into the house ahead of him. She hesitated for a moment, wondering just what she was walking into, and his eyes lit with the same wicked amusement as Sarah's. They were quite a pair, Lee decided, and stepped forward.

She hadn't expected anything so, well, normal in Hunter Brown's home. The living room was airy, sunny in the afternoon light. *Cheerful.* Yes, Lee realized, that was precisely the word that came to mind. No shadowy corners or locked doors. There were wildflowers in an enameled vase and plump pillows on the sofa.

"Were you expecting witches' brooms and a satin-lined coffin?" he murmured in her ear.

Annoyed, she stepped away from him. "Of course not. I suppose I didn't expect you to have something quite so...domesticated."

He arched a brow at the word. "I am domesticated."

Lee looked at him, at the face that was half rugged, half aristocratic. On one level, perhaps, she mused. But only on one.

"I guess Aunt Bonnie's got the mess in the kitchen pretty well cleaned up." Sarah kept one arm around her father as she gave Lee another thorough going-over. "She'd like to meet you because Dad doesn't see nearly enough women and never talks to reporters. So maybe you're special because he decided to talk to you."

While she spoke, she watched Lee steadily. She was only ten, but already she'd sensed there was something between her father and this woman with the dark blue eyes and nifty hair. What she didn't know was exactly how she felt about it yet. In the manner of her father, Sarah decided to wait and see.

Equally unsure of her own feelings, Lee went with them into the kitchen. She had an impression of sunny walls, white trim and confusion.

"Hunter, if you're going to keep a wolf in the house, you should at least teach him to appreciate art. Hi, I'm Bonnie."

Lee saw a tall, thin woman with dark brown shoulder-length hair streaked liberally with blond. She wore

a purple T-shirt with faded pink printing over cutoffs
as ragged as her niece's. Her bare feet were tipped at
the toes with hot-pink polish. Studying her thin model's face, Lee couldn't be sure if she was years older
than Hunter or years younger. Automatically she held
out her hand in response to Bonnie's outstretched one.

"How do you do?"

"I'd be doing a lot better if Santanas hadn't tried
to make a snack of my latest creation." She held up a
golden-brown half circle with ragged ends. "Just lucky
for him it was a dreadful idea. Anyway, sit." She gestured to a table piled with bowls and canisters and
dusted with flour. "I'm making tea."

"You didn't turn the kettle on," Sarah pointed out,
and did so herself.

"Hunter, the child's always picking on details. I
worry about her."

With a shrug of acceptance, he picked up what
looked like a small doughnut and might, with imagination, have been an earring. "You're finding gold and
silver too traditional to work with these days?"

"I thought I might start a trend." When Bonnie
smiled, she became abruptly and briefly stunning. "In
any case, it was a small failure. Probably cost you less
than three dollars in flour. Sit," she repeated as she
began to transfer the mess from the table to the counter
behind her. "So, how was the camping trip?"

"Enlightening. Wouldn't you say, Lenore?"

"Educational," she corrected, but thought the last half
hour had been the most educational of all.

"So, you work for *Celebrity*." Bonnie's long, twisted
gold earrings swung when she walked, much like Sarah's braids. "I'm a faithful reader."

"That's because she's had a couple of embarrassingly flattering write-ups."

"Write-ups?" Lee watched Bonnie dust her flour-covered hands on her cutoffs.

Hunter smiled as he watched his sister reach for a tin of tea and send others clattering to the counter. "Professionally she's known as B. B. Smithers."

The name rang a bell. For years, B. B. Smithers had been considered the queen of avant-garde jewelry. The elite, the wealthy and the trendy flocked to her for personal designs. They paid, and paid well, for her talent, her creativity, and the tiny *B*s etched into the finished product. Lee stared at the thin, somewhat clumsy woman with something close to wonder. "I've admired your work."

"But you wouldn't wear it," Bonnie put in with a smile as she shoved tumbled boxes and tins out of her way. "No, it's the classics for you. What a fabulous face. Do you want lemon in your tea? Do we have any lemons, Hunter?"

"Probably not."

Taking this in stride, Bonnie set the teapot on the table to let the tea steep. "Tell me, Lenore, how did you talk the hermit into coming out of his cave?"

"By making him furious, I believe."

"That might work." She sat down across from Lee as Sarah walked to her father's side. Her eyes were softer than her brother's, less intense, but not, Lee thought, less perceptive. "Did the two weeks playing pioneer in the canyon give you the insight to write an article on him?"

"Yes." Lee smiled, because there was humor in Bonnie's eyes. "Plus I gained a growing affection for box springs and mattresses."

The quick, stunning smile flashed again. "My husband takes the children camping once a year. That's when I go to Elizabeth Arden's for the works. When we come home, both of us feel we've accomplished several small miracles."

"Camping's not so bad," Sarah commented in her father's defense.

"Is that so?" He patted her bottom as he drew her closer. "Why is it that you always have this all-consuming desire to visit Bonnie in Phoenix whenever I start packing gear?"

She giggled, and her arm went easily around his shoulder. "Must be coincidence," she said in a dry tone that echoed his. "Did he make you go fishing?" Sarah wanted to know. "And sit around for just *hours?*"

Lee watched Hunter's brow lift before she answered. "Actually, he did, ah, suggest fishing several days running."

"Ugh" was Sarah's only comment.

"But I caught a bigger fish than he did."

Unimpressed, Sarah shook her head. "It's awfully boring." She sent her father an apologetic glance. "I guess somebody's got to do it." Leaning her head against her father's, she smiled at Lee. "Mostly he's never boring, he just likes some weird stuff. Like fishing and beer."

"Sarah doesn't consider Hunter's shrunken-head collection at all unusual." Bonnie picked up the teapot. "Are you having some?" she asked her brother.

"I'll pass. Sarah and I'll go and break camp."

"Take your wolf with you," Bonnie told him as she

poured tea into Lee's cup. "He's still on my hit list. By the way, a couple of calls from New York came in for you yesterday."

"They'll keep." As he rose, he ran a careless hand down Lee's hair, a gesture not lost on either of the other females in the room. "I'll be back shortly."

She started to offer her help, but it was so comfortable in the sunny, cluttered kitchen, and the tea smelled like heaven. "All right." She saw the proprietary hand Sarah put on her father's arm and thought it just as well to stay where she was.

Together, father and daughter walked to the back door. Hunter whistled for the dog, then they were gone.

Bonnie stirred her tea. "Sarah adores her father."

"Yes." Lee thought of the way they'd looked, side by side.

"And so do you."

Lee had started to lift her cup; now it only rattled in the saucer. "I beg your pardon?"

"You're in love with Hunter," Bonnie said mildly. "I think it's marvelous."

She could've denied it—vehemently, icily, laughingly, but hearing it said aloud seemed to put her in some kind of trance. "I don't—that is, it doesn't…" Lee stopped, realizing she was running the spoon handle through her hands. "I'm not sure how I feel."

"A definite symptom. Does being in love worry you?"

"I didn't say I was." Again, Lee stopped. Could anyone make evasions with those soft doe eyes watching? "Yes, it worries me a lot."

"Only natural. I used to fall in and out of love like some people change clothes. Then I met Fred." Bonnie laughed into her tea before she sipped. "I went around with a queasy stomach for weeks."

Lee pressed a hand to her own before she rose. Tea wasn't going to help. She had to move. "I have no illusions about Hunter and myself," she said, more firmly than she'd expected to. "We have different priorities, different tastes." She looked through the kitchen window to the high red walls far beyond the clustering trees. "Different lives. I have to get back to L.A."

Bonnie calmly continued to drink tea. "Of course." If Lee heard the irony, she didn't respond to it. "There are people who have it fixed in their heads that in order to have a relationship, the two parties involved must be on the same wavelength. If one adores sixteenth-century French poetry and the other detests it, there's no hope." She noticed Lee's frown but continued, lightly. "Fred's an accountant who gets a primal thrill out of interest rates." She wiped absently at a smudge of flour on the table. "Statistically, I suppose we should've divorced years ago."

Lee turned back, unable to be angry, unable to smile. "You're a great deal like Hunter, aren't you?"

"I suppose. Is your mother Adreanne Radcliffe?"

Though she no longer wanted it, Lee came back to the table for her tea. "Yes."

"I met her at a party in Palm Springs two, no, must've been three years ago. Yes, three," Bonnie said decisively, "because I was still nursing Carter, my youngest, and he's currently terrorizing everyone at nursery school. Just last week he tried to cook a goldfish in a toy oven. You're not at all like your mother, are you?"

It took a moment for Lee to catch up. She set down her tea again, untasted. "Aren't I?"

"Do you think you are?" Bonnie tossed her tousled, streaked hair behind her shoulder. "I don't mean any offense, but she wouldn't know what to say to anyone not born to the blue, so to speak. I'd've considered her a very sheltered woman. She's very lovely—you certainly appear to've inherited her looks. But that seems to be all."

Lee stared down at her tea. How could she explain that, because of the strong physical resemblance between her and her mother, she'd always figured there were other resemblances. Hadn't she spent her childhood and adolescence trying to find them, and all of her adult life trying to repress them? A sheltered woman. She found it a terrifying phrase, and too close to what she herself could have become.

"My mother has standards," she answered, at length. "She never seems to have any trouble living up to them."

"Oh, well, everyone should do what they do best." Bonnie propped her elbows on the table, lacing her fingers so that the three rings on her right hand gleamed and winked. "According to Hunter, the thing you do best is write. He mentioned your novel to me."

The irritation came so quickly Lee hadn't the chance to mask it. "He's the kind of man who can't admit when he's made a mistake. I'm a reporter, not a novelist."

"I see." Still smiling blandly, Bonnie dropped her chin onto her laced fingers. "So, what are you going to report about Hunter?"

Was there a challenge under the smile? A trace of mockery? Whatever there was at the edges, Lee couldn't help but respond to it. Yes, she thought again, Bonnie Smithers was a great deal like her brother.

"That he's a man who considers writing both a sacred duty and a skilled profession. That he has a sense of humor that's often so subtle it takes you hours to catch up. That he believes in choices and luck with the same stubbornness that he believes in fate." Pausing, she lifted her cup. "He values the written word, whether it's in comic books or Chaucer, and he works desperately hard to do what he considers his job—to tell the story."

"I like you."

Cautiously, Lee smiled. "Thank you."

"I love my brother," Bonnie went on easily. "More than that, I admire him, for personal and professional reasons. You understand him. Not everyone would."

"Understand him?" Lee shook her head. "It seems to me that the more I find out about him, the less I understand. He's shown me more beauty in a pile of rocks than I'd ever have found for myself, yet he writes about horror and fears."

"And you consider that a contradiction?" Bonnie shrugged as she leaned back in her chair. "It's just that Hunter sees both sides of life very clearly. He writes about the dark side because it's the most intriguing."

"Yet he lives..." Lee gestured as she glanced around the kitchen.

"In a cozy little house nestled in the woods."

The laugh came naturally. "I wouldn't precisely call it cozy, but it's certainly not what you'd expect from the country's leading author of horror and occult fiction."

"The country's leading author of horror and occult fiction has a child to raise."

"Yes." Lee's smile faded. "Yes, Sarah. She's lovely."

"Will she be in your article?"

"No." Again, she lifted her gaze to Bonnie's. "No, Hunter made it clear he objected to that."

"She's the focal point of his life. If he seems a bit overprotective in certain ways, believe me, it's a completely unselfish act." When Lee merely nodded, Bonnie felt a stirring of sympathy. "He hasn't told you about her?"

"No, nothing."

There were times Bonnie's love and admiration for Hunter became clouded with frustration. A great many times. This woman was in love with him, was one step away from being irrevocably committed to him. Any fool could see it, Bonnie mused. Any fool except Hunter. "As I said, there are times he's overly protective. He has his reasons, Lenore."

"And will you tell me what they are?"

She was tempted. It was time Hunter opened that part of his life, and she was certain this was the woman he should open it to. "The story's Hunter's," Bonnie said at length. "You should hear it from him." She glanced around idly as she heard the Jeep pull up in the drive. "They're back."

"I guess I'm glad you brought her back," Sarah commented as they drove the last mile toward home.

"You guess?" Hunter turned his head, to see his daughter looking pensively through the windshield.

"She's beautiful, like a princess." For the first time in months, Sarah worried her braces with her tongue. "You like her a lot, I can tell."

"Yes, I like her a lot." He knew every nuance of his daughter's voice, every expression, every gesture. "That doesn't mean I like you any less."

Sarah gave him one long look. She needed no other words from him to reaffirm love. "I guess you have to like me," she decided, half teasing, "'cause we're stuck with each other. But I don't think she does."

"Why shouldn't Lenore like you?" Hunter countered, able to follow her winding statement without any trouble.

"She doesn't smile much."

Not enough, he silently agreed, but more each day. "When she relaxes, she does."

Sarah shrugged, unconvinced. "Well, she looked at me awful funny."

"Your grammar's deteriorating."

"She did."

Hunter frowned a bit as he turned into the dirt drive to their house. "It's only that she was surprised. I hadn't mentioned you to her."

Sarah stared at him a moment, then put her scuffed sneakers on the dash. "That wasn't very nice of you."

"Maybe not."

"You'd better apologize."

He sent his daughter a mild glance. "Really?"

She patted Santanas's head when he leaned over the back of her seat and dropped it on her shoulder. "Really. You always make me apologize when I'm rude."

"I didn't consider that you were any of her business." At first, Hunter amended silently. Things changed. Everything changed.

"You always make me apologize, even when I make up excuses," Sarah pointed out unmercifully. When they pulled up by the house, she grinned at him. "And even when I hate apologizing."

"Brat," he mumbled, setting the brake.

With a squeal of laughter, Sarah launched herself at him. "I'm glad you're home."

He held her close a moment, absorbing her scent—youthful sweat, grass and flowery shampoo. It seemed impossible that ten years had passed since he'd first held her. Then she'd smelled of powder and fragility and fresh linen. It seemed impossible that she was half-grown and the time had been so short.

"I love you, Sarah."

Content, she cuddled against him a moment, then, lifting her head, she grinned. "Enough to make pizza for dinner?"

He pinched her subtly pointed chin. "Maybe just enough for that."

Chapter 11

Whemember Lee thought of family dinners, she thought of quiet meals at a glossy mahogany table laid with heavy Georgian silver, meals where conversation was subdued and polite. It had always been that way for her.

Not this dinner.

The already confused kitchen became chaotic while Sarah dashed around, half dancing, half bobbing, as she filled her father in on every detail of the past two weeks. Oblivious to the noise, Bonnie used the kitchen phone to call home and check in with her husband and children. Santanas, forgiven, lay sprawled on the floor, dozing. Hunter stood at the counter, preparing what Sarah claimed was the best pizza in the stratosphere. Somehow he managed to keep up with his daughter's disjointed conversation, answer the questions Bonnie tossed at him and cook at the same time.

Feeling like oil poured heedlessly on a rub of churning water, Lee began to clear the table. If she didn't do something, she decided, she'd end up standing in the middle of the room with her head swiveling back and forth, like a fan at a tennis match.

"I'm supposed to do that."

Awkwardly, Lee set down the teapot she'd just lifted and looked at Sarah. "Oh." *Stupid,* she berated herself. *Haven't you any conversation for a child?*

"You can help, I guess," Sarah said after a moment. "But if I don't do my chores, I don't get my allowance." Her gaze slid to her father, then back again. "There's this album I want to buy. You know, the Total Wrecks."

"I see." Lee searched her mind for even a wispy knowledge of the group but came up blank.

"They're actually not as bad as the name makes them sound," Bonnie commented on her way out to the kitchen. "Anyway, Hunter won't dock your pay if you take on an assistant, Sarah. It's considered good business sense."

Turning his head, Hunter caught his sister's quick grin before she waltzed out of the room. "I suppose Lee should earn her supper as well," he said easily. "Even if it isn't red meat."

The smile made it difficult for her to casually lift the teapot again.

"You'll like the pizza better," Sarah stated confidently. "He puts *everything* on it. Anytime I have friends over for dinner, they always want Dad's pizza." As she continued to clear the table, Lee tried to imagine Hunter competently preparing meals for several young, chattering girls. She simply couldn't. "I think he was a cook in another life."

Good Lord, Lee thought, did the child already have views on reincarnation?

"The same way you were a gladiator," Hunter said dryly.

Sarah laughed, childlike again. "Aunt Bonnie was a slave sold at an Arabian auction for thousands and thousands of drachmas."

"Bonnie has a very fluid ego."

With a clatter, Sarah set the cups in the sink. "I think Lenore must've been a princess."

With a damp cloth in her hands, Lee looked up, not certain if she should smile.

"A medieval princess," Sarah went on. "Like with King Arthur."

Hunter seemed to consider the idea a moment, while he studied his daughter and the woman under discussion. "It's a possibility. One of those delicate jeweled crowns and filmy veils would suit her."

"And dragons." Obviously enjoying the game, Sarah leaned back against the counter, the better to imagine Lee in a flowing pastel gown. "A knight would have to kill at least one full-grown male dragon before he could ask for her hand."

"True enough," Hunter murmured, thinking that dragons came in many forms.

"Dragons aren't easy to kill." Though she spoke lightly, Lee wondered why her stomach was quivering. It was entirely too easy to imagine herself in a great torchlit hall, with jewels winking from her hair and from the bodice of a rich silk gown.

"It's the best way to prove valor," Sarah told her, nibbling on a slice of green pepper she'd snitched from her father. "A princess can't marry just anyone, you know.

The king would either give her to a worthy knight, or marry her off to a neighboring prince so he could have more land with peace and prosperity."

Incredibly, Lee pictured her father, staff in hand, decreeing that she would marry Jonathan of Willoby.

"I bet you never had to wear braces."

Cast from one century to another in the blink of an eye, Lee merely stared. Sarah was frowning at her with the absorbed, absorbing concentration she could have inherited only from Hunter. It was all so foolish, Lee thought. Knights, princesses, dragons. For the first time, she was able to smile naturally at the slim, dark girl who was a part of the man she loved.

"Two years."

"You did?" Interest sprang into Sarah's solemn face. She stepped forward, obviously to get a better look at Lee's teeth. "It worked good," she decided. "Did you hate them?"

"Every minute."

Sarah giggled, so that the silver flashed. "I don't mind too much, 'cept I can't chew gum." She sent a sulky look over her shoulder in Hunter's direction. "Not even one stick."

"Neither could I." Ever, she thought, but didn't add it. Gum chewing was not permitted in the Radcliffe household.

Sarah studied her another moment, then nodded. "I guess you can help me set the table, too."

Acceptance, Lee was to discover, was just that simple.

The sun was streaming into the kitchen while they ate. It was rich and golden, without those harsh, stunning flashes of white she remembered from the cliffs of the canyon. She found it peaceful, despite all the talk and laughter and arguments swimming around her.

Her fantasies had run to eating a thick, rare steak and a crisp chef's salad in a dimly lit, quiet restaurant where the hovering waiter saw that your glass of Bordeaux was never empty. She found herself in a bright, noisy kitchen, eating pizza stringy with cheese, chunky with slices of green pepper and mushroom, spiced with pepperoni and hot sausage. And while she did, she found herself agreeing with Sarah's accolade. The best in the stratosphere.

"If only Fred could learn how to make one of these." Bonnie cut into her second slice with the same dedication she'd cut into her first. "On a good day he makes a superior egg salad, but it's not the same."

"With a family the size of yours," Hunter commented, "you'd need to set up an assembly line. Five hungry children could keep a pizzeria hopping."

"And do," Bonnie agreed. "In a bit less than seven months, it'll be six."

She grinned as Hunter's knife paused. "Another?"

"Another." Bonnie winked across the table at her niece. "I always said I'd have half a dozen kids," she said casually to Lee. "People should do what they do best."

Hunter reached over to take her hand. Lee saw the fingers interlock. "Some might call it overachievement."

"Or sibling rivalry," she tossed back. "I'll have as many kids as you do bestsellers." With a laugh, she squeezed her brother's hand. "It takes us about the same length of time to produce."

"When you bring the baby to visit, she should sleep in my room." Sarah bit off another mouthful of pizza.

"She?" Hunter ruffled her hair before he started to eat again.

"It'll be a girl." With the confidence of youth, Sarah nodded. "Aunt Bonnie already has three boys, so another girl makes it even."

"I'll see what I can do," Bonnie told her. "Anyway, I'll be heading back in the morning. Cassandra, she's my oldest," she put in for Lee's benefit, "has decided she wants a tattoo." She closed her eyes as she leaned back. "Ah, it's nice to be needed."

"A tattoo?" Sarah wrinkled her nose. "That's gross. Cassie's nuts."

"Fred and I are forced to agree."

Interested, Hunter lifted his wine. "Where does she want it?"

"On the curve of her right shoulder. She insists it'll be very tasteful."

"Dumb." Sarah handed out the decree with a shrug. "Cassie's thirteen," she added, rolling her eyes. "Boy, is she a case."

Lee choked back a laugh at both the facial and verbal expressions. "How will you handle it?"

Bonnie only smiled. "Oh, I think I'll take her to the tattoo parlor."

"But you wouldn't—" Lee broke off, seeing Bonnie's liberally streaked hair and shoulder-length earrings. Perhaps she would.

With a laugh, Bonnie patted Lee's hand. "No, I wouldn't. But it'll be a lot more effective if Cassie makes the decision herself—which she will, the minute she gets a good look at all those nasty little needles."

"Sneaky," Sarah approved with a grin.

"Clever," Bonnie corrected.

"Same thing." With her mouth half-full, she turned to Lee. "There's always a crisis at Aunt Bonnie's house," she said confidentially. "Did you have brothers and sisters?"

"No." Was that wistfulness she saw in the child's eyes? She'd often had the same wish herself. "There was only me."

"I think it's better to have them, even though it gets crowded." She slanted her father a guileless smile. "Can I have another piece?"

The rest of the evening passed, not quietly but, for all the noise, peacefully. Sarah dragged her father outside for soccer practice, which Bonnie declined, grinning. Her condition, she claimed, was too delicate. Lee, over her protests, found herself drafted. She learned, though her aim was never very accurate, to kick a ball with the side of her foot and bounce it off her head. She enjoyed it, which surprised her, and didn't feel like a fool, which surprised her more.

Dusk came quickly, then a dark that flickered with fireflies. Though her eyes were heavy, Sarah groaned about going to bed until Hunter agreed to carry her up on his back. Lee didn't have to be told it was a nightly ritual; she only had to see them together.

He'd said Sarah was his life, and though she'd only seen them together for a matter of hours, Lee believed it.

She'd never have expected the man whose books she'd read to be a devoted father, content to spend his time with a ten-year-old girl. She'd never have imagined him here, in a house so far away from the excitement of the city. Even the man she'd grown to know over the past two weeks didn't quite fit the structure of being parent, disciplinarian and mentor to a ten-year-old. Yet he was.

If she superimposed the image of Sarah's father over

those of her lover and the author of *Silent Scream,* they all seemed to meld into one. The problem was dealing with it.

Righting the overturned chair on the patio, Lee sat. She could hear Sarah's sleepy laughter drift through the open window above her. Hunter's voice, low and indistinct, followed it. It was an odd way to spend her last hours with Hunter, here in his home, only a few miles from the campsite where they'd become lovers. And yes, she realized as she stared up at the stars, friends. She very much wanted to be his friend.

Now, when she wrote the article, she'd be able to do so with knowledge of both sides of him. It was what she'd come for. Lee closed her eyes because the stars were suddenly too bright. She was going back with much more and, because of it, much less.

"Tired?"

Opening her eyes, she looked up at Hunter. This was how she'd always remember him, cloaked in shadows, coming out of the darkness. "No. Is Sarah asleep?"

He nodded, coming around behind her to put his hands on her shoulders. This was where he wanted her. Here, when night was closing in. "Bonnie, too."

"You'd work now," she guessed. "When the house was quiet and the windows dark."

"Yes, most of the time. I finished my last book on a night like this." He hadn't been lonely then, but now... "Let's walk. The moon's full.

"Afraid? I'll give you a talisman." He slipped his ring off his pinky, sliding it onto her finger.

"I'm not superstitious," she said loftily, but curled her fingers into her palm to hold the ring in place.

"Of course you are." He drew her against his side as they walked. "I like the night sounds."

Lee listened to them—the faintest breeze through the trees, the murmur of water, the singsong of insects. "You've lived here a long time." As the day had passed, it had become less feasible to think of his living anywhere else.

"Yes. I moved here the year Sarah was born."

"It's a lovely spot."

He turned her into his arms. Moonlight spilled over her, silver, jewel-like in her hair, marbling her skin, darkening her eyes. "It suits you," he murmured. He ran a hand through her hair, then watched it fall back into place. "The princess and the dragon."

Her heart had already begun to flutter. Like a teenager's, Lee thought. He made her feel like a girl on her first date. "These days women have to kill their own dragons."

"These days—" his mouth brushed over hers "—there's less romance. If these were the Dark Ages, and I came upon you in a moonlit wood, I'd take you because it was my right. I'd woo you because I'd have no choice." His voice darkened like the shadows in the trees surrounding them. "Let me love you now, Lenore, as if it were the first time."

Or the last, she thought dimly as his lips urged her to soften, to yield, to demand. With his arms around her, she could let her consciousness go. Imagine and feel. Lovemaking consisted of nothing more. Even as her head tilted back in submission, her arms strengthened around him, challenging him to take whatever he wanted, to give whatever she asked.

Then his hands were on her face, gently, as gently

as they'd ever been, memorizing the slope and angle of her bones, the softness of her skin. His lips followed, tasting, drinking in each separate flavor. The pleasure that could come so quickly ran liquid through her. Bonelessly, she slid with him to the ground.

He'd wanted to love her like this, in the open, with the moon silvering the trees and casting purple shadows. He'd wanted to feel her muscles coil and go fluid under the touch of his hand. What she gave to him now was something out of his own dreams and much, much more real than anything he'd ever had. Slowly, he undressed her, while his lips and the tips of his fingers both pleasured and revered her. This would be the night when he gave her all of him and when he asked for all of her.

Moonlight and shadows washed over her, making his heart pound in his ears. He heard the creek bubble nearby to mix with her quiet sighs. The woods smelled of night. And so, as she buried his face against her neck, did she.

She felt the surging excitement in him, the growing, straining need that swept her up. Willingly, she went into the whirlpool he created. There the air was soft to the touch and streaked with color. There she would stay, endlessly possessed.

His skin was warm against hers. She tasted, her head swimming from pleasure, power and newly awakened dizzying speed. Ravenous for more, she raced over him, acutely aware of every masculine tremble beneath her, every drawn breath, every murmur of her name.

Silver and shadows. Lee felt them every bit as tangibly as she saw them flickering around her. The silver streak of power. The dark shadow of desire. With them, she could take him to that trembling precipice.

When he swore, breathlessly, she laughed. Their needs were tangled together, twining tighter. She felt it. She celebrated it.

The air seemed to still, the breeze pause. The sounds that had grown to one long din around them seemed to hush. The fingers tangled in her hair tightened desperately. In the silence, their eyes met and held, moment after moment.

Her lips curved as she opened for him.

She could have slept there, effortlessly, with the bare ground beneath her, the sky overhead and his body pressed to hers. She might have slept there, endlessly, like a princess under a spell, if he hadn't drawn her up into his arms.

"You fall asleep like a child," he murmured. "You should be in bed. My bed."

Lee sighed, content to stay where she was. "Too far."

With a low laugh, he kissed the hollow between her neck and shoulder. "Should I carry you?"

"Mmm." She nestled against him. "'Kay."

"Not that I object, but you might be a bit disconcerted if Bonnie happened to walk downstairs while I was carrying you in, naked."

She opened her eyes, so that her irises were dusky blue slits under her lashes. Reality was returning. "I guess we have to get dressed."

"It might be advisable." His gaze skimmed over her, then back to her face. "Should I help you?"

She smiled. "I think that we might have the same result with you dressing me as we do with you undressing me."

"An interesting theory." Hunter reached over her for the brief strip of ivory lace.

"But this isn't the time to test it out." Lee plucked her panties out of his hand and wiggled into them. "How long have we been out here?"

"Centuries."

She shot him a look just before her head disappeared into her shirt. She wasn't completely certain he was exaggerating. "The least I deserve after these past two weeks is a real mattress."

He took her hand, pressing her palm to his lips. "You're welcome to share mine."

Lee curled her fingers around his briefly, then released them. "I don't think that's wise."

"You're worried about Sarah."

It wasn't a question. Lee took her time, making certain all the clouds of romance were out of her head before she spoke. "I don't know a great deal about children, but I imagine she's unprepared for someone sharing her father's bed."

Silence lay for a moment, like the eye of a storm. "I've never brought a woman to our home before."

The statement caused her to look at him quickly, then, just as quickly, look away. "All the more reason."

"All the more reason for many things." He dressed without speaking while Lee stared out into the trees. So beautiful, she thought. And more and more distant.

"You wanted to ask me about Sarah, but you didn't."

She moistened her lips. "It's not my business."

Her chin was captured quickly, not so gently. "Isn't it?" he demanded.

"Hunter—"

"This time you'll have the answer without asking."

He dropped his hand, but his gaze never faltered. She needed nothing else to tell her the calm was over. "I met a woman, almost a dozen years ago. I was writing as Laura Miles by then, so that I could afford a few luxuries. Dinner out occasionally, the theater now and then. I was still living in L.A., alone, enjoying my work and the benefits it brought me. She was a student in her last year. Brains and ambition she had in abundance, money she didn't have at all. She was on scholarship and determined to be the hottest young attorney on the West Coast."

"Hunter, what happened between you and another woman all those years ago isn't my business."

"Not just another woman. Sarah's mother."

Lee began to pull at the tuft of grass by her side. "All right, if it's important for you to tell me, I'll listen."

"I cared about her," he continued. "She was bright, lovely and full of dreams. Neither of us had ever considered becoming too serious. She still had law school to finish, the bar to pass. I had stories to tell. But then, no matter how much we plan, fate has a way of taking over."

He drew out a cigarette, thinking back, remembering each detail. His tiny, cramped apartment with the leaky plumbing, the battered typewriter with its hiccuping carriage, the laughter from the couple next door that would often seep through the thin walls.

"She came by one afternoon. I knew something was wrong because she had afternoon classes. She was much too dedicated to skip classes. It was hot, one of those sultry, breathless days. The windows were up, and I had a little portable fan that stirred the air around without doing much to cool it. She'd come to tell me she was pregnant."

He could remember the way she'd looked if he concentrated. But he never chose to. But whether he chose to or not, he'd always be able to remember the tone of her voice when she'd told him. Despair, laced with fury and accusation.

"I said I cared about her, and that was true. I didn't love her. Still, our parents' values do trickle down. I offered to marry her." He laughed then, not humorously, but not, Lee reflected, bitterly. It was the laugh of a man who'd accepted the joke life had played on him. "She refused, almost as angry with the solution I'd offered as she was with the pregnancy. She had no intention of taking on a husband and a child when she had a career to carve out. It might be difficult to understand, but she wasn't being cold, simply practical, when she asked me to pay for the abortion."

Lee felt all of her muscles contract. "But, Sarah—"

"That's not the end of the story." Hunter blew out a stream of smoke and watched it fade into darkness. "We had a memorable fight, threats, accusations, blame-casting. At the time, I couldn't see her end of it, only the fact that she had part of me inside her that she wanted to dispose of. We parted then, both of us furious, both of us desperate enough to know we each needed time to think."

She didn't know what to say, or how to say it. "You were young," she began.

"I was twenty-four," Hunter corrected. "I'd long since stopped being a boy. I was—we were—responsible for our own actions. I didn't sleep for two days. I thought of a dozen answers and rejected them all, over and over. Only one thing stuck with me in that whole sweaty, terrified time. I wanted the child. It's not something I can explain, because I did enjoy my life, the lack of responsibilities, the possibility of becoming really successful. I simply knew I had to have the child. I called her and asked her to come back.

"We were both calmer the second time, and both more frightened than either of us had ever been in our lives. Marriage couldn't be considered, so we set it aside. She didn't want the child, so we dealt with that. I did. That was something a bit more complex to deal with. She needed freedom from the responsibility we'd made together, and she needed money. In the end, we resolved it all."

Dry-mouthed, Lee turned to him. "You paid her."

He saw, as he'd expected to see, the horror in her eyes. When he continued, his voice was calm, but it took a great deal of effort to make it so. "I paid all the medical expenses, her living expenses up until she delivered, and I gave her ten thousand dollars for my daughter."

Stunned, heartsick, Lee stared at the ground. "How could she—"

"We each wanted something. In the only way open, we gave it to each other. I've never resented that young law student for what she did. It was her choice, and she could've taken another without consulting me."

"Yes." She tried to understand, but all Lee could see was that slim, dark little girl. "She chose, but she lost."

It meant everything just to hear her say it. "Sarah's been mine, only mine, from the first moment she breathed. The woman who carried her gave me a priceless gift. I only gave her money."

"Does Sarah know?"

"Only that her mother had choices to make."

"I see." She let out a long breath. "The reason you're

so careful about keeping publicity away from her is to keep speculation away."

"One of them. The other is simply that I want her to have the uncomplicated life every child's entitled to."

"You didn't have to tell me." She reached a hand for his. "I'm glad you did. It can't have been easy for you, raising a baby by yourself."

There was nothing but understanding in her eyes now. Every taut muscle in his body relaxed as if she'd stroked them. He knew now, with utter certainty, that she was what he'd been waiting for. "No, not easy, but always a pleasure." His fingers tightened on hers. "Share it with me, Lenore."

Her thoughts froze. "I don't know what you mean."

"I want you here, with me, with Sarah. I want you here with the other children we'll have together." He looked down at the ring he'd put on her hand. When his eyes came back to hers, she felt them reach inside her. "Marry me."

Marry? She could only stare at him blankly while the panic quietly built and built. "You don't—you don't know what you're asking."

"I do," he corrected, holding her hand more firmly when she tried to draw it away. "I've asked only one other woman, and that out of obligation. I'm asking you because you're the first and only woman I've ever loved. I want to share your life. I want you to share mine."

Panic steadily turned into fear. He was asking her to change everything she'd aimed for. To risk everything. "Our lives are too far apart," she managed. "I have to go back. I have my job."

"A job you know you weren't made for." Urgency slipped into his voice as he took her shoulders. "You know you were made to write about the images you have in your head, not about other people's social lives and tomorrow's trends."

"It's what I know!" Trembling, she jerked away from him. "It's what I've been working for."

"To prove a point. Damn it, Lenore, do something for yourself. For yourself."

"It is for myself," she said desperately. *You love him,* a voice shouted inside her. *Why are you pushing away what you need, what you want?* Lee shook her head, as if to block the voice out. Love wasn't enough, needs weren't enough. She knew that. She had to remember it. "You're asking me to give it all up, every hard inch I've climbed in five years. I have a life in L.A., I know who I am, where I'm going. I can't live here and risk—"

"Finding out who you really are?" he finished. He wouldn't allow despair. He barely controlled anger. "If it was only myself, I'd go anywhere you liked, live anywhere that suited you, even if I knew it was a mistake. But there's Sarah. I can't take her away from the only home she's ever known."

"You're asking for everything again." Her voice was hardly a whisper, but he'd never heard anything more clearly. "You're asking me to risk everything, and I can't. I won't."

He rose, so that shadows shifted around him. "I'm asking you to risk everything," he agreed. "Do you love me?" And by asking, he'd already risked it all.

Torn by emotions, pushed by fear, she stared at him. "Yes. Damn you, Hunter, leave me alone."

She streaked back toward the house until the darkness closed in between them.

Chapter 12

"If you're not going to break for lunch, at least take this." Bryan held out one of her inexhaustible supply of candy bars.

"I'll eat when I've finished the article." Lee kept her eyes on the typewriter and continued to pound at the keys, lightly, rhythmically.

"Lee, you've been back for two days and I haven't seen you so much as nibble on a Danish." And her photographer's eye had seen beneath the subtle use of cosmetics to the pale bruises under Lee's eyes. That must've been some interview, she thought, as the brisk, even clickity-click of the typewriter keys went on.

"Not hungry." No, she wasn't hungry any more than she was tired. She'd been working steadily on Hunter's article for the better part of forty-eight hours. It was going to be perfect, she promised herself. It was going to be polished like a fine piece of glass. And oh, God, when she finished it, *finished it,* she'd have purged her system of him.

She'd gripped that thought so tightly, it often skidded away.

If she'd stayed… If she went back…

The oath came quickly, under her breath, as her fingers faltered. Meticulously, Lee reversed the carriage to make the correction. She couldn't go back. Hadn't she made that clear to Hunter? She couldn't just toss everything over her shoulder and go. But the longer she stayed away, the larger the hole in her life became. In the life, Lee was ruthlessly reminded, that she'd so carefully carved out for herself.

So she'd work in a nervous kind of fury until the article was finished. Until, she told herself, it was all finished. Then it would be time to take the next step. When she tried to think of that next step, her mind went stunningly, desperately blank. Lee dropped her hands into her lap and stared at the paper in front of her.

Without a word, Bryan bumped the door with her hip so that it closed and muffled the noise. Dropping down into the chair across from Lee, she folded her hands and waited a beat. "Okay, now why don't you tell me the story that's not for publication?"

Lee wanted to be able to shrug and say she didn't have time to talk. She was under a deadline, after all. The article was under a deadline. But then, so was her life. Drawing a breath, she turned in her chair. She didn't want to see the neat, clever little words she'd typed. Not now.

"Bryan, if you'd taken a picture, one that required a great deal of your time and all of your skill to set up, then once you'd developed it, it had come out in a completely different way than you'd planned, what would you do?"

"I'd take a good hard look at the way it had come out," she said immediately. "There'd be a good possibility I should've planned it that way in the first place."

"But wouldn't you be tempted to go back to your original plans? After all, you'd worked very, very hard to set it up in a certain way, wanting certain specific results."

"Maybe, maybe not. It'd depend on just what I'd seen when I looked at the picture." Bryan sat back, crossing long, jeans-clad legs. "What's in your picture, Lee?"

"Hunter." Her troubled gaze shifted, and locked on Bryan's. "You know me."

"As well as you let anyone know you."

With a short laugh, Lee began to push at a paper clip on her desk. "Am I as difficult as all that?"

"Yeah." Bryan smiled a bit to soften the quick answer. "And, I've always thought, as interesting. Apparently, Hunter Brown thinks the same thing."

"He asked me to marry him." The words came out in a jolt that left both women staring.

"Marry?" Bryan leaned forward. "As in 'till death do us part'?"

"Yes."

"Oh." The word came out like a breath of air as Bryan leaned back again. "Fast work." Then she saw Lee's unhappy expression. Just because Bryan didn't smell orange blossoms when the word *marriage* came up was no reason to be flippant. "Well, how do you feel? About Hunter, I mean."

The paper clip twisted in Lee's fingers. "I'm in love with him."

"Really?" Then she smiled, because it sounded nice when said so simply. "Did all this happen in the canyon?"

"Yes." Lee's fingers moved restlessly. "Maybe it started to happen before, when we were in Flagstaff. I don't know anymore."

"Why aren't you happy?" Bryan narrowed her eyes as she did when checking the light and angle. "When the man you love, really love, wants to build a life with you, you should be ecstatic."

"How do two people build a life together when they've both already built separate ones, completely different ones?" Lee demanded. "It isn't just a matter of making more room in the closet or shifting furniture around." The end of the paper clip broke off in her fingers as she rose. "Bryan, he lives in Arizona, in the canyon. I live in L.A."

Lifting booted feet, Bryan rested them on Lee's polished desk, crossing her ankles. "You're not going to tell me it's all a matter of geography."

"It just shows how impossible it all is!" Angry, Lee whirled around. "We couldn't be more different, almost opposites. I do things step-by-step, Hunter goes in leaps and bounds. Damn it, you should see his house. It's like something out of a sophisticated fairy tale. His sister's B. B. Smithers—" Before Bryan could fully register that, Lee was blurting out, "He has a daughter."

"A daughter?" Her attention fully caught, Bryan dropped her feet again. "Hunter Brown has a child?"

Lee pressed her fingers to her eyes and waited for calm. True, it wouldn't have come out if she hadn't been so agitated, and she'd never discuss such personal agitations with anyone but Bryan, but now she had to deal with it. "Yes, a ten-year-old girl. It's important that it not be publicized."

"All right."

Lee needed no promises from Bryan. Trying to calm herself, she took a quiet breath. "She's bright, lovely and quite obviously the center of his life. I saw something in him when they were together, something incredibly beautiful. It scared the hell out of me."

"Why?"

"Bryan, he's capable of so much talent, brilliance, emotion. He's put them together to make a complete success of himself, in all ways."

"That bothers you?"

"I don't know what I'm capable of. I only know I'm afraid I'd never be able to balance it all out, make it all work."

Bryan said something short, quick and rude. "You won't marry him because you don't think you can juggle? You should know yourself better."

"I thought I did." Shaking her head, she took her seat again. "It's ridiculous, in the first place," she said more briskly. "Our lives are miles apart."

Bryan glanced out the window at the tall, sleek building that was part of Lee's view of the city. "So, he can move to L.A. and close the distance."

"He won't." Swallowing, Lee looked at the pages on her desk. The article was finished, she knew it, just as she knew that if she didn't let it go, she'd polish it to death. "He belongs there. He wants to raise his daughter there. I understand that."

"So, you move to the canyon. Great scenery."

Why did it always sound so simple, so plausible, when spoken aloud? The little trickle of fear returned, and her voice firmed. "My job's here."

"I guess it comes down to priorities, doesn't it?" Bryan knew she wasn't being sympathetic, just as she knew it wasn't sympathy that Lee needed. Because she cared a great deal, she spoke without any compassion. "You can keep your job and your apartment in L.A. and be miserable. Or you can take a few chances."

Chances. Lee ran a finger down the slick surface of her desk. But you were supposed to test the ground before you stepped forward. Even Hunter had said that. But… She looked at the mangled paper clip in the center of her spotless blotter. How long did you test it before you took the jump?

It was barely two weeks later that Lee sat in her apartment in the middle of the day. She was so rarely there during the day, during the week, that she somehow expected everything to look different. Everything looked precisely the same. Even, she was forced to admit, herself. Yet nothing was.

Quit. She tried to digest the word as she dealt with the panic she'd held off the past few days. There was a leafy, blooming African violet on the table in front of her. It was well-tended, as every area of her life had been well-tended. She'd always water it when the soil was dry and feed it when it required nourishing. As she stared at the plant, Lee knew she would never be capable of pulling it ruthlessly out by the roots. But wasn't that what she'd done to herself?

Quit, she thought again, and the word reverberated in her brain. She'd actually handed in her resignation, served her two weeks' notice and summarily turned her back on her steadily thriving career—ripped out its roots.

For what? she demanded of herself as panic trickled through. To follow some crazy dream that had planted itself in her mind years ago. To write a book that would probably never be published. To take a ridiculous risk and plunge headlong into the unknown.

Because Hunter had said she was good. Because he'd fed that dream, just as she fed the violet. More than that, Lee thought, he'd made it impossible for her to stop thinking about the "what ifs" in her life. And he was one of them. The most important one of them.

Now that the step was taken and she was here, alone in her impossibly quiet midweek, midmorning apartment, Lee wanted to run. Out there were people, noise, distractions. Here, she'd have to face those "what-ifs." Hunter would be the first.

He hadn't tried to stop her when she left the morning after he'd asked her to marry him. He'd said nothing when she'd made her goodbyes to Sarah. Nothing at all. Perhaps they'd both known that he'd said all there was to say the night before. He'd looked at her once, and she'd nearly wavered. Then Lee had climbed into the car with Bonnie, who'd driven her to the airport that was one step closer to L.A.

He hadn't phoned her since she'd returned. Had she expected him to? Lee wondered. Maybe she had, but she'd hoped he wouldn't. She didn't know how long it would take before she'd be able to hear his voice without going to pieces.

Glancing down, she stared at the twisted gold-and-silver ring on her hand. Why had she kept it? It wasn't hers. It should've been left behind. It was easy to tell herself she'd simply forgotten to take it off in the confusion, but it wasn't the truth. She'd known the ring was still on her finger as she packed, as she walked out of Hunter's house, as she stepped into the car. She just hadn't been capable of taking it off.

She needed time, and it was time, Lee realized, that she now had. She had to prove something again, but not to her parents, not to Hunter. Now there was only herself. If she could finish the book. If she could give it her very best and really finish it...

Rising, Lee went to her desk, sat down at the typewriter and faced the fear of the blank page.

Lee had known pressure in her work on *Celebrity*. The minutes ticking away while deadlines drew closer and closer. There was the pressure of making not-so-fascinating seem fascinating, in a limited space, and of having to do it week after week. And yet, after nearly a month of being away from it, and having only herself and the story to account for, Lee had learned the full meaning of pressure. And of delight.

She hadn't believed—truly believed—that it would be possible for her to sit down, hour after hour, and finish a book she'd begun on a whim so long ago. And it was true that for the first few days she'd met with nothing but frustration and failure. There'd been a ring of terror in her head. Why had she left a job where she was respected and knowledgeable to stumble in the dark this way?

Time after time, she was tempted to push it all aside and go back, even if it would mean starting over at *Celebrity*. But each time, she could see Hunter's face—lightly mocking, challenging and somehow encouraging.

"It takes a certain amount of stamina and endurance. If you've reached your limit and want to quit..."

The answer was no, just as grimly, just as determinedly as it had been in that little tent. Perhaps she'd fail. She shut her eyes as she struggled to deal with the thought. Perhaps she'd fail miserably, but she wouldn't quit. Whatever happened, she'd made her own choice, and she'd live with it.

The longer she worked, the more of a symbol those typewritten pages became. If she could do this, and do it well, she could do anything. The rest of her life balanced on it.

By the end of the second week, Lee was so absorbed she rarely noticed the twelve- and fourteen-hour days she was putting in. She plugged in her phone machine and forgot to return the calls as often as she forgot to eat.

It was as Hunter had once said. The characters absorbed her, drove her, frustrated and delighted her. As time passed, Lee discovered she wanted to finish the story, not only for her sake but for theirs. She wanted, as she'd never wanted before, for these words to be read. The excitement of that, and the dread, kept her going.

She felt a queer little thrill when the last word was typed, a euphoria mixed with an odd depression. She'd finished. She'd poured her heart into her story. Lee wanted to celebrate. She wanted to weep. It was over. As she pressed her fingers against her tired eyes, she realized abruptly that she didn't even know what day it was.

* * *

He'd never had a book race so frantically, so quickly. Hunter could barely keep up with his own zooming thoughts. He knew why, and flowed with it because he had no choice. The main character of this story was Lenore, though her name would be changed to Jennifer. She was Lenore, physically, emotionally, from the elegantly groomed red-gold hair to the nervously bitten fingernails. It was the only way he had of keeping her.

It had cost him more than she'd ever know to let her go. When he'd watched her climb into the car, he'd told himself she wouldn't stay away. She couldn't. If he was wrong about her feelings for him, then he'd been wrong about everything in his life.

Two women had crashed into his life with importance. The first, Sarah's mother, he hadn't loved, yet she'd changed everything. After that, she'd gone away, unable to find it possible to mix her ambition with a life that included children and commitment.

Lee, he loved, and she'd changed everything again. She, too, had gone away. Would she stay away, for the same reasons? Was he fated to bind himself to women who wouldn't share the tie? He wouldn't believe it.

So he'd let her go, aches and fury under the calm. She'd be back.

But a month had passed, and she hadn't come. He wondered how long a man could live when he was starving.

Call her. Go after her. You were a fool to ever let her go. Drag her back if necessary. You need her. You need...

His thoughts ran this way like clockwork. Every day at dusk. Every day at dusk, Hunter fought the urge to follow through on them. He needed; God, he needed. But if she didn't come to him willingly, he'd never have what he needed, only the shell of it. He looked down at his naked finger. She hadn't left everything behind. It was more, much more, than a piece of metal that she'd taken with her.

He'd given her a talisman, and she'd kept it. As long as she had it, she didn't sever the bond. Hunter was a man who believed in fate, omens and magic.

"Dinner's ready." Sarah stood in the doorway, her hair pulled back in a ponytail, her narrow face streaked with a bit of flour.

He didn't want to eat. He wanted to go on writing. As long as the story moved through him, he had a part of Lenore with him. Just as, whenever he stopped, the need to have all of her tore him apart. But Sarah smiled at him.

"Nearly ready," she amended. She came into the room, barefoot. "I made this meat loaf, but it looks more like a pancake. And the biscuits." She grinned, shrugging. "They're pretty hard, but we can put some jam or something on them." Sensing his mood, she wrapped her arms around his neck, resting her cheek against his. "I like it better when you cook."

"Who turned her nose up at the broccoli last night?"

"It looks like little trees that got sick." She wrinkled her nose, but when she drew back from him, her face was serious. "You really miss her a lot, huh?"

He could've evaded with anyone else. But this was Sarah. She was ten. She knew him inside out. "Yeah, I miss her a lot."

Thinking, Sarah fiddled with the hair that fell over his forehead. "I guess maybe you wanted her to marry you."

"She turned me down."

Her brows lowered, not so much from annoyance that anyone could say no to her father, but in concentration. Donna's father hardly had any hair at all, she thought, touching Hunter's again, and Kelly's dad's stomach bounced over his belt. Shelley's mother never got jokes. She didn't know anybody who was as neat to look at or as neat to be with as her dad. Anybody would want to marry him. When she'd been little, she'd wanted to marry him herself. But of course, she knew now that was just silly stuff.

Her brows were still drawn together when she brought her gaze to his. "I guess she didn't like me."

He heard everything just as clearly as if she'd spoken her thoughts aloud. He was greatly touched, and not a little impressed. "Couldn't stand you."

Her eyes widened, then brightened with laughter. "Because I'm such a brat."

"Right. I can barely stand you myself."

"Well." Sarah huffed a moment. "She didn't look stupid, but I guess she is if she wouldn't marry you." She cuddled against him, and knowing it was to comfort, Hunter warmed with love. "I liked her," Sarah murmured. "She was nice, kinda quiet, but really nice when she smiled. I guess you love her."

"Yes, I do." He didn't offer her any words of reassurance—it's different from the way I love you, you'll always be my little girl. Hunter simply held her, and it was enough. "She loves me, too, but she has to make her own life."

Sarah didn't understand that, and personally thought it was foolish, but decided not to say so. "I guess I wouldn't mind if she decided to marry you after all.

It might be nice to have somebody who'd be like a mother."

He lifted a brow. She never asked about her own mother, knowing with a child's intuition, he supposed, that there was nothing to ask about. "Aren't I?"

"You're pretty good," she told him graciously. "But you don't know a whole lot about lady stuff." Sarah sniffed the air, then grinned. "Meat loaf's done."

"Overdone, from the smell of it."

"Picky, picky." She jumped off his lap before he could retaliate. "I hear a car coming. You can ask them to dinner so we can get rid of all the biscuits."

He didn't want company, Hunter thought as he watched his daughter dash out of the room. An evening with Sarah was enough, then he'd go back to work. After switching off his machine, he rose to go to the door. It was probably one of her friends, who'd talked her parents into dropping by on their way home from town. He'd brush them off, as politely as he could manage, then see if anything could be done about Sarah's meat loaf.

When he opened the door, she was standing there, her hair caught in the light of a late summer's evening. He was, quite literally, knocked breathless.

"Hello, Hunter." How calm a voice could sound, Lee thought, even when a heart's hammering against ribs. "I'd've called, but your number's unlisted." When he said nothing, Lee felt her heart move from her ribs to her throat. Somehow, she managed to speak over it. "May I come in?"

Silently, he stepped back. Perhaps he was dreaming, like the character in "The Raven." All he needed was a bust of Pallas and a dying fire.

She'd used up nearly all of her courage just coming back. If he didn't speak soon, they'd end up simply staring at each other. Like a nervous speaker about to lecture on a subject she hadn't researched, Lee cleared her throat. "Hunter..."

"Hey, I think we'd better just give the biscuits to Santanas because—" Sarah stopped her headlong flight into the room. "Well, gee."

"Sarah, hello." Lee was able to smile now. The child looked so comically surprised, not cool and distant like her father.

"Hi." Sarah glanced uncertainly from one adult to the other. She supposed they were going to make a mess of things. Aunt Bonnie said that people who loved each other usually made a mess of things, for at least a little while. "Dinner's ready. I made meat loaf. It's probably not too bad."

Understanding the invitation, Lee grasped at it. At least it would give her more time before Hunter tossed her out again. "It smells wonderful."

"Okay, come on." Imperiously, Sarah held out her hand, waiting until Lee took it. "It doesn't look very good," she went on, as she led Lee into the kitchen. "But I did everything I was supposed to."

Lee looked at the flattened meat loaf and smiled. "Better than I could do."

"Really?" Sarah digested this with a nod. "Well, Dad and I take turns." And if they got married, Sarah figured, she'd only have to cook every third day. "You'd better set another place," she said lightly to her father. "The biscuits didn't work, but we've got potatoes."

The three of them sat down, very much as if it were the natural thing to do. Sarah served, carrying on a babbling conversation that alleviated the need for either adult to speak to the other. They each answered her, smiled, ate, while their thoughts were in a frenzy.

He doesn't want me anymore.

Why did she come?

He hasn't even spoken to me.

What does she want? She looks lovely. So lovely.

What can I do? He looks wonderful. So wonderful.

Sarah lifted the casserole containing the rest of the meat loaf. "I'll give this to Santanas." Like most children, she detested leftovers—unless it was spaghetti. "Dad has to do the dishes," she explained to Lee. "You can help him if you like." After she'd dumped Santanas's dinner in his bowl, she danced out of the room. "See you later."

Then they were alone, and Lee found she was gripping her hands together so tightly they were numb. Deliberately, she unlaced her fingers. He saw the ring, still on her finger, and felt something twist, loosen, then tighten again in his chest.

"You're angry," she said in that same calm, even voice. "I'm sorry, I shouldn't have come this way."

Hunter rose and began to stack dishes. "No, I'm not angry." Anger was possibly the only emotion he hadn't experienced in the last hour. "Why did you?"

"I…" Lee looked down helplessly at her hands. She should help him with the dishes, keep busy, stay natural. She didn't think her legs would hold her just yet. "I finished the book," she blurted out.

He stopped and turned. For the first time since she'd opened the door, she saw that hint of a smile around his mouth. "Congratulations."

"I wanted you to read it. I know I could've mailed

it—I sent a copy on to your editor—but..." She lifted her eyes to his again. "I didn't want to mail it. I wanted to give it to you. Needed to."

Hunter put the dishes in the sink and came back to the table, but he didn't sit. He had to stand. If this was what she'd come for, all she'd come for, he wasn't certain he could face it. "You know I want to read it. I expect you to autograph the first copy for me."

She managed a smile. "I'm not as optimistic as that, but you were right. I had to finish it. I wanted to thank you for showing me." Her lips remained curved, but the smile left her eyes. "I quit my job."

He hadn't moved, but it seemed that he suddenly became very still. "Why?"

"I had to try to finish the book. For me." If only he'd touch her, just her hand, she wouldn't feel so cold. "I knew if I could do that, I could do anything. I needed to prove that to myself before I..." Lee trailed off, not able to say it all. "I've been reading your work, your earlier work as Laura Miles."

If he could just touch her... But once he did, he'd never let her go again. "Did you enjoy it?"

"Yes." There was enough lingering surprise in her voice to make him smile. "I'd never have believed there could be a similarity of styles between a romance novel and a horror story, but there was. Atmosphere, tension, emotion." Taking a deep breath, she stood so that she could face him. It was perhaps the most difficult step she'd taken so far. "You understand how a woman feels. It shows in your work."

"*Writer*'s a word without gender."

"Still, it's a rare gift, I think, for a man to be able to understand and appreciate the kinds of emotions and insecurities that go on inside a woman." Her eyes met his again, and this time held. "I'm hoping you can do the same with me."

He was looking into her again. She could feel it.

"It's more difficult when your own emotions are involved."

She gripped her fingers together, tightly. "Are they?"

He didn't touch her, not yet, but she thought she could almost feel his hand against her cheek. "Do you need me to tell you I love you?"

"Yes, I—"

"You've finished your book, quit your job. You've taken a lot of risks, Lenore." He waited. "But you've yet to put it all on the line."

Her breath trembled out. No, he'd never make things easy for her. There'd always be demands, expectations. He'd never pamper. "You terrified me when you asked me to marry you. I thought about it a great deal, like the small child thinks about a dark closet. I don't know what's in there—it might be dream or nightmare. You understand that."

"Yes." Though it hadn't been a question. "I understand that."

She breathed a bit easier. "I used what I had in L.A. as an excuse because it was logical, but it wasn't the real reason. I was just afraid to walk into that closet."

"And are you still?"

"A little." It took more effort than she'd imagined to relax her fingers. She wondered if he knew it was the final step. She held out her hand. "But I want to try. I want to go there with you."

His fingers laced with hers, and she felt the nerves

melt away. Of course he knew. "It won't be dream or nightmare, Lenore. Every minute of it will be real."

She laughed then, because his hand was in hers. "Now you're really trying to scare me." Stepping closer, she kissed him softly, until desire built to a quiet roar. It was so easy, like sliding into a warm, clear stream. "You won't scare me off," she whispered.

The arms around her were tight, but she barely noticed. "No, I won't scare you off." He breathed in the scent of her hair, wallowed in the texture of it. She'd come to him. Completely. "I won't let you go, either. I've waited too long for you to come back."

"You knew I would," she murmured.

"I had to, I'd've gone mad otherwise."

She closed her eyes, content, but with a thrill of excitement underneath. "Hunter, if Sarah doesn't, that is, if she isn't able to adjust…"

"Worried already." He drew her back. "Sarah gave me a pep talk just this evening. You do, I assume, know quite a bit about lady stuff?"

"Lady stuff?"

He drew her back just a bit farther, to look her up and down. "Every inch the lady. You'll do, Lenore, for me, and for Sarah."

"Okay." She let out a long breath, because as usual, she believed him. "I'd like to be with you when you tell her."

"Lenore." Framing her face, he kissed both cheeks, gently, with a hint of a laugh beneath. "She already knows."

A brow lifted. "Her father's daughter."

"Exactly." He grabbed her, swinging her around once in a moment of pure, irrepressible joy. "The lady's going to find it interesting living in a house with real and imaginary monsters."

"The lady can handle that," she tossed back. "And anything else you dream up."

"Is that so?" He shot her a wicked look—amusement, desire, knowledge—as he released her. "Then let's get these dishes done and I'll see what I can do."

* * * * *

SUMMER DESSERTS

To Marianne Shock,
for the cheerful and clever last-minute help.

Chapter 1

Her name was Summer. It was a name that conjured visions of hot petaled flowers, sudden storms and long, restless nights. It also brought images of sun-warmed meadows and naps in the shade. It suited her.

As she stood, hands poised, body tensed, eyes alert, there wasn't a sound in the room. No one, absolutely no one, took their eyes off her. She might move slowly, but there wasn't a person there who wanted to chance missing a gesture, a motion. All attention, all concentration, was riveted upon that one slim, solitary figure. Strains of Chopin floated romantically through the air. The light slanted and shot through her neatly bound hair—rich, warm brown with hints and tints of gold. Two emerald studs winked at her ears.

Her skin was a bit flushed so that a rose tinge accented already prominent cheekbones and the elegant bone structure that comes only from breeding. Excitement, intense concentration, deepened the amber flecks that were sprinkled in the hazel of her eyes. The same excitement and concentration had her soft, molded lips forming a pout.

She was all in white, plain, unadorned white, but she drew the eye as irresistibly as a butterfly in full, dazzling flight. She wouldn't speak, yet everyone in the room strained forward as if to catch the slightest sound.

The room was warm, the smells exotic, the atmosphere taut with anticipation.

Summer might have been alone for all the attention she paid to those around her. There was only one goal, one end. Perfection. She'd never settled for less.

With infinite care she lifted the final diamond-shape and pressed the angelica onto the Savarin to complete the design she'd created. The hours she'd already spent preparing and baking the huge, elaborate dessert were forgotten, as was the heat, the tired leg muscles, the aching arms. The final touch, the *appearance* of a Summer Lyndon creation, was of the utmost importance. Yes, it would taste perfect, smell perfect, even slice perfectly. But if it didn't look perfect, none of that mattered.

With the care of an artist completing a masterpiece, she lifted her brush to give the fruits and almonds a light, delicate coating of apricot glaze.

Still, no one spoke.

Asking no assistance—indeed, she wouldn't have tolerated any—Summer began to fill the center of the Savarin with the rich cream whose recipe she guarded jealously.

Hands steady, head erect, Summer stepped back to give her creation one last critical study. This was the ultimate test, for her eye was keener than any other's when it came to her own work. She folded her arms across her body. Her face was without expression. In the huge kitchen, the ping of a pin dropped on the tile would have reverberated like a gunshot.

Slowly her lips curved, her eyes glittered. Success. Summer lifted one arm and gestured rather dramatically. "Take it away," she ordered.

As two assistants began to roll the glittering concoction from the room, applause broke out.

Summer accepted the accolade as her due. There was a place for modesty, she knew, and she knew it didn't apply to her Savarin. It was, to put it mildly, magnificent. Magnificence was what the Italian duke had wanted for his daughter's engagement party, and magnificence was what he'd paid for. Summer had simply delivered.

"Mademoiselle." Foulfount, the Frenchman whose specialty was shellfish, took Summer by both shoulders. His eyes were round and damp with appreciation. *"Incroyable."* Enthusiastically, he kissed both her cheeks while his thick, clever fingers squeezed her skin as they might a fresh-baked loaf of bread. Summer broke out in her first grin in hours.

"Merci." Someone had opened a celebratory bottle of wine. Summer took two glasses, handing one to the French chef. "To the next time we work together, *mon ami.*"

She tossed back the wine, took off her chef's hat, then breezed out of the kitchen. In the enormous marble-floored, chandeliered dining room, her Savarin was even now being served and admired. Her last thought before leaving was—thank God someone else had to clean up the mess.

Two hours later, she had her shoes off and her eyes closed. A gruesome murder mystery lay open on her lap as her plane cruised over the Atlantic. She was going home. She'd spent almost three full days in Milan for the sole purpose of creating that one dish. It wasn't an unusual experience for her. Summer had baked *Charlotte Malakoff* in Madrid, flamed *Crêpes Fourée* in Athens and molded *île Flottante* in Istanbul. For her expenses, and a stunning fee, Summer Lyndon would create a dessert that would live in the memory long after the last bite, drop or crumb was consumed.

Have wisk, will travel, she thought vaguely and smiled through a yawn.

She considered herself a specialist, not unlike a skilled surgeon. Indeed, she'd studied, apprenticed and practiced as long as many respected members of the medical profession. Five years after passing the stringent requirements to become a Cordon Bleu chef in Paris, the city where cooking is its own art, Summer had a reputation for being as temperamental as any artist, for having the mind of a computer when it came to remembering recipes and for having the hands of an angel.

Summer half dozed in her first-class seat and fought off a desperate craving for a slice of pepperoni pizza.

She knew the flight time would go faster if she could read or sleep her way through it. She decided to mix the two, taking the light nap first. Summer was a woman who prized her sleep almost as highly as she prized her recipe for chocolate mousse.

On her return to Philadelphia, her schedule would be hectic at best. There was the bombe to prepare for the governor's charity banquet, the annual meeting of the Gourmet Society, the demonstration she'd agreed to do for public television...and that meeting, she remembered drowsily.

What had that bird-voiced woman said over the phone? Summer wondered. Drake—no, Blake—Cocharan. Blake Cocharan III of the Cocharan hotel chain. Excellent hotels, Summer thought without any real interest. She'd patronized a number of them in various corners of the world. Mr. Cocharan the Third had a business proposition for her.

Summer assumed that he wanted her to create some special dessert exclusively for his chain of hotels, something they could attach the Cocharan name to. She wasn't averse to the notion—under the proper circumstances. And for the proper fee. Naturally she'd have to investigate the entire Cocharan enterprise carefully before she agreed to involve her skill or her name with it. If any one of their hotels was of inferior quality...

With a yawn, Summer decided to think about it later—after she'd met with The Third personality. Blake Cocharan III, she thought again with a sleepily amused smile. Plump, balding, probably dyspeptic. Italian shoes, Swiss watch, French shirts, German car—and no doubt he'd consider himself unflaggingly American. The image she created hung in her mind a moment, and, bored with it, she yawned again—then sighed as the idea of pizza once again invaded her thoughts. Summer tilted her seat back farther and determinedly willed herself to sleep.

Blake Cocharan III sat in the plush rear seat of the gunmetal-gray limo and meticulously went over the report on the newest Cocharan House being constructed in Saint Croix. He was a man who could scoop us a mess of scattered details and align them in perfect, systematic order. Chaos was simply a form of order waiting to be unjumbled with logic. Blake was a very logical man. Point A invariably led to point B, and from there to C. No matter how confused the maze, with patience and logic, one could find the route.

Because of his talent for doing just that, Blake, at thirty-five, had almost complete control of the Cocharan empire. He'd inherited his wealth and, as a result, rarely thought of it. But he'd earned his position, and valued it. Quality was a Cocharan tradition. Nothing but the finest would do for any Cocharan House, from the linen on the beds to the mortar in the foundations.

His report on Summer Lyndon told him she was the best.

Setting aside the Saint Croix packet, Blake slipped another file from the slim briefcase by his feet. A single ring, oval-faced, gold and scrolled, gleamed dully on his hand. Summer Lyndon, he mused, flipping the file open....

Twenty-eight, graduate Sorbonne, certified Cordon Bleu chef. Father, Rothschild Lyndon, respected member of British Parliament. Mother, Monique Dubois Lyndon, former star of the French cinema. Parents amicably divorced for twenty-three years. Summer Lyndon had spent her formative years between London and Paris before her mother had married an American hardware tycoon, based in Philadelphia. Summer had then returned to Paris to complete her education and currently had living quarters both there and in Philadelphia. Her mother had since married a third time, a paper baron on this round, and her father was separated from his second wife, a successful barrister.

All of Blake's probing had produced the same basic answer. Summer Lyndon was the best dessert chef on either side of the Atlantic. She was also a superb all-around chef with an instinctive knowledge of quality, a flair for creativity and the ability to improvise in a crisis. On the other hand, she was reputed to be dictatorial, temperamental and brutally frank. These qualities, however, hadn't alienated her from heads of state, aristocracy or celebrities.

She might insist on having Chopin piped into the kitchen while she cooked, or summarily refuse to work at all if the lighting wasn't to her liking, but her mousse alone was enough to make a strong man beg to grant her slightest wish.

Blake wasn't a man to beg for anything…but he wanted Summer Lyndon for Cocharan House. He never doubted he could persuade her to agree to precisely what he had in mind.

A formidable woman, he imagined, respecting that. He had no patience with weak wills or soft brains—particularly in people who worked for him. Not many women had risen to the position, or the reputation, that Summer Lyndon held. Women might traditionally be cooks, but men were traditionally chefs.

He imagined her thick waisted from sampling her own creations. Strong hands, he thought idly. Her skin was probably a bit pasty from all those hours indoors in kitchens. A no-nonsense woman, he was sure, with an uncompromising view on what was edible and why. Organized, logical and cultured—perhaps a bit plain due to her preoccupation with food rather than fashion.

Blake imagined that they would deal with each other
very well. With a glance at his watch, Blake noted with
satisfaction that he was right on time for the meeting.

The limo cruised to a halt beside the curb. "I'll be no
more than an hour," Blake told the driver as he climbed
out.

"Yes, sir." The driver checked his watch. When Mr.
Cocharan said an hour, you could depend on it.

Blake glanced up at the fourth floor as he crossed
to the well-kept old building. The windows were open,
he noted. Warm spring air poured in, while music—a
melody he couldn't quite catch over the sounds of traffic—poured out. When Blake went in, he learned that
the single elevator was out of order. He walked up four
flights.

After Blake knocked, the door was opened by a small
woman with a stunning face who was dressed in a T-
shirt and slim black jeans. The maid on her way out for
a day off? Blake wondered idly. She didn't look strong
enough to scrub a floor. And if she was going out, she
was going out without her shoes.

After the brief, objective glance, his gaze was drawn
irresistibly back to her face. Classic, naked and undeniably sensuous. The mouth alone would make a man's
blood move. Blake ignored what he considered an au-
tomatic sexual pull.

"Blake Cocharan to see Ms. Lyndon."

Summer's left brow rose—a sign of surprise. Then
her lips curved slightly—a sign of pleasure.

Plump, he wasn't, she observed. Hard and lean—
racketball, tennis, swimming. He was obviously a
man more prone to these than lingering over executive
lunches. Balding, no. His hair was rich black and thick.

It was styled well, with slight natural waves that added to the attractiveness of a cool, sensual face. A sweep of cheekbones, a firm line of chin. She liked the look of the former that spoke of strength, and the latter, just barely cleft, that spoke of charm. Black brows were almost straight over clear, water-blue eyes. His mouth was a bit long but beautifully shaped. His nose was very straight—the sort she'd always thought was made to be looked down. Perhaps she'd been right about the outward trimmings—the Italian shoes, and so forth— but, Summer admitted, she'd been off the mark with the man.

The assessment didn't take her long—three, perhaps four, seconds. But her mouth curved more. Blake couldn't take his eyes off it. It was a mouth a man, if he breathed, wanted to taste. "Please come in, Mr. Cocharan." Summer stepped back, swinging the door wider in invitation. "It's very considerate of you to agree to meet here. Please have a seat. I'm afraid I'm in the middle of something in the kitchen." She smiled, gestured and disappeared.

Blake opened his mouth—he wasn't used to being brushed off by servants—then closed it again. He had enough time to be tolerant. As he set down his briefcase he glanced around the room. There were fringed lamps, a curved sofa in plush blue velvet, a fussily carved cherrywood table. Aubusson carpets—two—softly faded in blues and grays—were spread over the floors. A Ming vase. Potpourri in what was certainly a Dresden compote.

The room had no order; it was a mix of European periods and styles that should never have suited, but was instantly attractive. He saw that a pedestal table at the far end of the room was covered with jumbled typewritten pages and handwritten notes. Street sounds drifted in through the window. Chopin floated from the stereo.

As he stood there, drawing it in, he was abruptly certain there was no one in the apartment but himself and the woman who had opened the door. Summer Lyndon? Fascinated with the idea, and with the aroma creeping from the kitchen, Blake crossed the room.

Six pastry shells, just touched with gold and moisture, sat on a rack. One by one Summer filled them to overflowing with what appeared to be some rich white cream. When Blake glanced at her face he saw the concentration, the seriousness and intensity he might have associated with a brain surgeon. It should have amused him. Yet somehow, with the strains of Chopin pouring through the kitchen speakers, with those delicate, slim-fingered hands arranging the cream in mounds, he was fascinated.

She dipped a fork in a pan and dribbled what he guessed was warmed caramel over the cream. It ran lavishly down the sides and gelled. He doubted that it was humanly possible not to lust after just one taste. Again, one by one, she scooped up the tarts and placed them on a plate lined with a lacy paper doily. When the last one was arranged, she looked up at Blake.

"Would you like some coffee?" She smiled and the line of concentration between her brows disappeared. The intensity that had seemed to darken her irises lightened.

Blake glanced at the dessert plate and wondered how her waist could be hand-spannable. "Yes, I would."

"It's hot," she told him as she lifted the plate. "Help yourself. I have to run these next door." She was past him and to the doorway of the kitchen before she turned around. "Oh, there're some cookies in the jar, if you like. I'll be right back."

She was gone, and the pastries with her. With a shrug, he turned back to the kitchen, which was a shambles. Summer Lyndon might be a great cook, but she was obviously not a neat one. Still if the scent and look of the pastries had been any indication...

He started to root in the cupboards for a cup, then gave in to temptation. Standing in his Saville Row suit, Blake ran his finger along the edge of the bowl that had held the cream. He laid it on his tongue. With a sigh, his eyes closed. Rich, thick and very French.

He'd dined in the most exclusive restaurants, in some of the wealthiest homes, in dozens of countries all over the world. Logically, practically, honestly, he couldn't say he'd ever tasted better than what he now scooped from the bowl in this woman's kitchen. In deciding to specialize in desserts and pastries, Summer Lyndon had chosen well, he concluded. He felt a momentary regret that she'd taken those rich, fat tarts to someone else. This time when Blake started his search for a cup, he spotted the ceramic cookie jar shaped like a panda.

Normally he wouldn't have been interested. He wasn't a man with a particularly active sweet tooth. But the flavor of the cream lingered on his tongue. What sort of cookie did a woman who created the finest of haute cuisine make? With a cup of English bone china in one hand, Blake lifted off the top of the panda's head. Setting it down, he pulled out a cookie and stared in simple wonder.

No American could mistake that particular munchie. A classic? he mused. A tradition? An Oreo. Blake continued to stare at the chocolate sandwich cookie with its double dose of white center. He turned it over in his hand. The brand was unmistakably stamped into both sides. This from a woman who baked and whipped and glazed for royalty?

A laugh broke from him as he dropped the Oreo back into the panda. Throughout his career he'd had to deal with more than his share of eccentrics. Running a chain of hotels wasn't just a matter of who checked in and who checked out. There were designers, artists, architects, decorators, chefs, musicians, union representatives. Blake considered himself knowledgeable of people. It wouldn't take him long to learn what made Summer tick.

She dashed back into the kitchen just as he was finally pouring the coffee. "I'm sorry to have kept you waiting, Mr. Cocharan. I know it was rude." She smiled, as if she had no doubt she'd be forgiven, as she poured her own coffee. "I had to get those pastries finished for my neighbor. She's having a small engagement tea this afternoon—with prospective in-laws." Her smile turned to a grin and, sipping her black coffee, she plucked the top from the panda. "Did you want a cookie?"

"No. Please, you go ahead."

Taking him at his word, Summer chose one and nibbled. "You know," she said thoughtfully, "these are uniformly excellent for their kind." She gestured with the half cookie she had left. "Shall we go sit down and discuss your proposition?"

She moved fast, he mused with approval. Perhaps he'd at least been on the mark about the no-nonsense attitude. With a nod of acknowledgment, Blake followed her. He was successful in his profession, not because he was a third-generation Cocharan, but because he had a quick and analytical mind. Problems were systematically solved. At the moment, he had to decide just how to approach a woman like Summer Lyndon.

She had a face that belonged in the shade of a tree on the Bois de Boulogne. Very French, very elegant. Her voice had the round, clear tones that spoke unmistakably of European education and upbringing—a wisp of France again but with the discipline of Britain. Her hair was pinned up, a concession to the heat and humidity, he imagined—though she had the windows open, ignoring the available air-conditioning. The studs in her ears were emeralds, round and flawless. There was a good-sized tear in the sleeve of her T-shirt.

Sitting on the couch, she folded her legs under her. Her bare toes were painted with a wild rose enamel, but her fingernails were short and unvarnished. He caught the allure of her scent—a touch of the caramel from the pastries, but under it something unmistakably French, unapologetically sexual.

How did one approach such a woman? Blake reflected. Did he use charm, flattery or figures? She was reputed to be a perfectionist and occasionally a firebrand. She'd refused to cook for an important political figure because he wouldn't fly her personal kitchen equipment to his country. She'd charged a Hollywood celebrity a small fortune to create a twenty-tiered wedding cake extravaganza. And she'd just hand-baked and hand-delivered a plate of pastries to a neighbor for a tea. Blake would much prefer to have the key to her before he made his offer. He knew the advantages of taking a circular route. Indeed some might call it stalking.

"I'm acquainted with your mother," Blake began easily as he continued to gauge the woman beside him.

"Really?" He caught both amusement and affection in the word. "I shouldn't be surprised," she said as she nibbled on the cookie again. "My mother always patronized a Cocharan House when we traveled. I believe I had dinner with your grandfather when I was six or seven." The amusement didn't fade as she sipped at her coffee. "Small world."

An excellent suit, Summer decided, relaxing against the back of the sofa. It was well cut and conservative enough to have gained her father's approval. The form it was molded to was well built and lean enough to have gained her mother's. It was perhaps the combination of the two that drew her interest.

Good God, he is attractive, she thought as she took another considering survey of his face. Not quite smooth, not quite rugged, his power sat well on him. That was something she recognized—in herself and in others. She respected someone who sought and got his own way, as she judged Blake did. She respected herself for the same reason. Attractive, she thought again—but she felt that a man like Blake would be so, regardless of physical appearance.

Her mother would have called him *séduisant,* and accurately so. Summer would have called him dangerous. A difficult combination to resist. She shifted, perhaps unconsciously, to put more distance between them. Business, after all, was business.

"You're familiar then with the standards of a Cocharan House," Blake began. Quite suddenly he wished her scent weren't so alluring or her mouth so tempting. He didn't care to have business muddled with attraction, no matter how pleasant.

"Of course." Summer set down her coffee because drinking it only seemed to accentuate the odd little flutter in her stomach. "I invariably stay at them myself."

"I've been told your standards of quality are equally high."

This time when Summer smiled there was a hint of arrogance to it. "I'm the very best at what I do because I have no intention of being otherwise."

The first key, Blake decided with satisfaction. Professional vanity. "So my information tells me, Ms. Lyndon. The very best is all that interests me."

"So." Summer propped an elbow on the back of the sofa then rested her head on the palm. "How exactly do I interest you, Mr. Cocharan?" She knew the question was loaded, but couldn't resist. When a woman was constantly taking risks and making experiments in her professional life, the habit often leaked through.

Six separate answers skimmed through his mind, none of which had any bearing on his purpose for being there. Blake set down his coffee. "The restaurants at the Cocharan Houses are renowned for their quality and service. However, recently the restaurant here in our Philadelphia complex seems to be suffering from a lack of both. Frankly, Ms. Lyndon, it's my opinion that the food has become too pedestrian—too boring. I plan to do some remodeling, both in physical structure and in staff."

"Wise. Restaurants, like people, often become too complacent."

"I want the best head chef available." He aimed a level look. "My research tells me that's you."

Summer lifted a brow, not in surprise this time but in consideration. "That's flattering, but I freelance, Mr. Cocharan. And I specialize."

"Specialize, yes, but you do have both experience and knowledge in all areas of haute cuisine. As for the freelancing, you'd be free to continue that to a large extent, at least after the first few months. You'd need to establish your own staff and create your own menu. I don't believe in hiring an expert, then interfering."

She was frowning again—concentration, not annoyance. It was tempting, very tempting. Perhaps it was just the travel weariness from her trip back from Italy, but she'd begun to grow a bit tired—bored? —with the constant demands of flying to any given country to make that one dish. It seemed he'd hit her at the right moment to stir her interest in concentrating on one place, and one kitchen, for a span of time.

It would be interesting work—if he were being truthful about the free hand she'd have—redoing a kitchen and the menu in an old, established and respected hotel. It would take her perhaps six months of intense effort, and then... It was the "and then" that made her hesitate again. If she gave that much time and effort to a full-time job, would she still retain her flair for the spectacular? That, too, was something to consider.

She'd always had a firm policy against committing herself to any one establishment—a wariness of commitments ribboned through all areas of her life. If you locked yourself into something, to someone, you opened yourself to all manner of complications.

Besides, Summer reasoned, if she wanted to affiliate herself with a restaurant, she could open and run her own. She hadn't done it yet because it would tie her too long to one place, attach her too closely to one project. She preferred traveling, creating one superb dish at a time, then moving on. The next country, the next dish. That was her style. Why should she consider altering it now?

"A very flattering offer, Mr. Cocharan—"

"A mutually advantageous one," he interrupted, perceptive enough to catch the beginning of a refusal. With deliberate ease, he tossed out a six-digit annual salary that rendered Summer momentarily speechless—not a simple task.

"And generous," she said when she found her voice again.

"One doesn't get the best unless one's willing to pay for it. I'd like you to think about this, Ms. Lyndon." He reached in his briefcase and pulled out a sheaf of papers. "This is a draft of an agreement. You might like to have your attorney look it over, and of course, points can be negotiated."

She didn't want to look at the damn contract because she could feel, quite tangibly, that she was being maneuvered into a corner—a very plush one. "Mr. Cocharan, I do appreciate your interest, but—"

"After you've thought it over, I'd like to discuss it with you again, perhaps over dinner. Say, Friday?"

Summer narrowed her eyes. The man was a steamroller, she decided. A very attractive, very sleek steamroller. No matter how elegant the machinery, you still got flattened if you were in the path. Haughtiness emanated from her. "I'm sorry, I'm working Friday evening—the governor's charity affair."

"Ah, yes." He smiled, though his stomach had tightened. He had a suddenly vivid, completely wild image of making love to her on the ground of some moist, shadowy forest. That alone nearly made him consider accepting her refusal. And that alone made him all the more determined not to. "I can pick you up there. We can have a late supper."

"Mr. Cocharan," Summer said in a frigid voice, "you're going to have to learn to take no for an answer."

Like hell, he thought grimly, but gave her a rather rueful, rather charming smile. "My apologies, Ms. Lyndon, if I seem to be pressuring you. You were my first choice, you see, and I tend to go with my instincts. However…" Seemingly reluctant, he rose. The knot of tension and anger in Summer's stomach began to loosen. "If your mind's made up…" He plucked the contract from the table and started to slip it into his briefcase. "Perhaps you can give me your opinion on Louis LaPointe."

"LaPointe?" The word whispered through Summer's lips like venom. Very slowly she uncurled from the sofa, then rose, her whole body stiff. "You ask me of LaPointe?" In anger, her French ancestry became more pronounced in her speech.

"I'd appreciate anything you could tell me," Blake went on amiably, knowing full well he'd scored his first real point off her. "Seeing that you and he are associates and—"

With a toss of her head, Summer said something short, rude and to the point in her mother's tongue. The gold flecks in her eyes glimmered. Sherlock Holmes had Professor Moriarty. Superman had Lex Luthor. Summer Lyndon had Louis LaPointe.

"Slimy pig," she grated, reverting to English. "He

has the mind of a peanut and the hands of a lumberjack. You want to know about LaPointe?" She snatched a cigarette from the case on the table, lighting it as she did only when extremely agitated. "He's a peasant. What else is there to know?"

"According to my information, he's one of the five top chefs in Paris." Blake pressed because a good pressure point was an invaluable weapon. "His *Canard en Croûte* is said to be unsurpassable."

"Shoe leather." She all but spat out the words, and Blake had to school every facial muscle to prevent the grin. Professional vanity, he thought again. She had her share. Then as she drew in a deep breath, he had to school the rest of his muscles to hold off a fierce surge of desire. Sensuality—perhaps she had more than her share. "Why are you asking me about LaPointe?"

"I'm flying to Paris next week to meet with him. Since you're refusing my offer—"

"You'll offer this—" she wagged a finger at the contract still in Blake's hand "—to him?"

"Admittedly he's my second choice, but there are those on the board who feel Louis LaPointe is more qualified for the position."

"Is that so?" Her eyes were slits now behind a screen of smoke. She plucked the contract from his hand, then dropped it beside her cooling coffee. "The members of your board are perhaps ignorant?"

"They are," he managed, "perhaps mistaken."

"Indeed." Summer took a drag of her cigarette, then released smoke in a quick stream. She detested the taste. "You can pick me up at nine o'clock on Friday at the governor's kitchen, Mr. Cocharan. We'll discuss this matter further."

"My pleasure, Ms. Lyndon." He inclined his head, careful to keep his face expressionless until he'd closed the front door behind him. He laughed his way down four flights of steps.

Chapter 2

Making a good dessert from scratch isn't a simple matter. Creating a masterpiece from flour, eggs and sugar is something else again. Whenever Summer picked up a bowl or a whisk or beater, she felt it her duty to create a masterpiece. Adequate, as an adjective in conjunction with her work, was the ultimate insult. Adequate, to Summer, was the result achieved by a newlywed with a cookbook first opened the day after the honeymoon. She didn't simply bake, mix or freeze—she conceived, developed and achieved. An architect, an engineer, a scientist did no more, no less. When she'd chosen to study the art of haute cuisine, she hadn't done so lightly, and she hadn't done so without the goal of perfection in mind. Perfection was still what she sought whenever she lifted a spoon.

She'd already spent the better part of her day in the

kitchen of the governor's mansion. Other chefs fussed with soups and sauces—or each other. All of Summer's talent was focused on the creation of the finale, the exquisite mix of tastes and textures, the overall aesthetic beauty of the bombe.

The mold was already lined with the moist cake she'd baked, then systematically sliced into a pattern. This had been done with templates as meticulously as when an engineer designs a bridge. The mousse, a paradise of chocolate and cream, was already inside the dessert's dome. This deceptively simple element had been chilling since early morning. Between the preparations, the mixing, making and building, Summer had been on her feet essentially that long.

Now, she had the beginnings of her bombe on a waist-high table, with a large stainless steel bowl of crushed berries at her elbow. At her firm instructions, Chopin drifted through the kitchen speakers. The first course was already being enjoyed in the dining room. She could ignore the confusion reigning around her. She could shrug off the pressure of having her part of the meal complete and perfect at precisely the right moment. That was all routine. But as she stood there, prepared to begin the next step, her concentration was scattered.

LaPointe, she thought with gritted teeth. Naturally it was anger that had kept her attention from being fully focused all day, the idea of having Louis LaPointe tossed in her face. It hadn't taken Summer long to realize that Blake Cocharan had used the name on purpose. Knowing it, however, didn't make the least bit of difference to her reaction…except perhaps that her venom was spread over two men rather than one.

Oh, he thinks he's very clever, Summer decided, thinking of Blake—as she had too often that week. She took three cleansing breaths as she studied the golden dome in front of her. Asking me, *me,* to give LaPointe a reference. Despicable French swine, she muttered silently, referring to LaPointe. As she scooped up the first berries she decided that Blake must be an equal swine even to be considering dealing with the Frenchman.

She could remember every frustrating, annoying contact she'd had with the beady-eyed, undersized LaPointe. As she carefully coated the outside of the cake with crushed berries, Summer considered giving him a glowing recommendation. It would teach that sneaky American a lesson to find himself stuck with a pompous ass like LaPointe. While her thoughts raged, her hands were delicately smoothing the berries, rounding out and firming the shape.

Behind her one of the assistants dropped a pan with a clatter and a bang and suffered a torrent of abuse. Neither Summer's thoughts nor her hands faltered.

Smug, self-assured jerk, she thought grimly of Blake. In a steady flow, she began layering rich French cream over the berries. Her face, though set in concentration, betrayed anger in the flash in her eyes. A man like him delighted in maneuvering and outmaneuvering. It showed, she thought, in that oh-so-smooth delivery, in that gloss of sophistication. She gave a disdainful little snort as she began to smooth out the cream.

She'd rather have a man with a few rough edges than one so polished that he gleamed. She'd rather have a man who knew how to sweat and bend his back than one with manicured nails and five-hundred-dollar suits. She'd rather have a man who...

Summer stopped smoothing the cream while her thoughts caught up with her consciousness. Since when had she considered having any man, and why, for God's sake, was she using Blake for comparisons? Ridiculous.

The bombe was now a smooth white dome waiting for its coating of rich chocolate. Summer frowned at it as an assistant whisked empty bowls out of her way. She began to blend the frosting in a large mixer as two cooks argued over the thickness of the sauce for the entrée.

For that matter, her thoughts ran on, it was ridiculous how often she'd thought of him the past few days, remembering foolish details.... His eyes were almost precisely the shade of the water in the lake on her grandfather's estate in Devon. How pleasant his voice was, deep, with that faint but unmistakable inflection of the American Northeast. How his mouth curved in one fashion when he was amused, and another when he smiled politely.

It was difficult to explain why she'd noticed those things, much less why she'd continued to think of them days afterward. As a rule, she didn't think of a man unless she was with him—and even then she only allowed him a carefully regulated portion of her concentration.

Now, Summer reminded herself as she began to layer on frosting, wasn't the time to think of anything but the bombe. She'd think of Blake when her job was finished, and she'd deal with him over the late supper she'd agreed to. Oh, yes—her mouth set—she'd deal with him.

Blake arrived early deliberately. He wanted to see her work. That was reasonable, even logical. After all, if he were to contract Summer to Cocharan House for a year, he should see firsthand what she was capable of, and how she went about it. It wasn't at all unusual for him to check out potential employees or associates on their own turf. If anything, it was characteristic of him. Good business sense.

He continued to tell himself so, over and over, because there was a lingering doubt as to his own motivations. Perhaps he had left her apartment in high good spirits knowing he'd outmaneuvered her in the first round. Her face, at the mention of her rival LaPointe, had been priceless. And it was her face that he hadn't been able to push out of his mind for nearly a week.

Uncomfortable, he decided as he stepped into the huge, echoing kitchen. The woman made him uncomfortable. He'd like to know the reason why. Knowing the reasons and motivations was essential to him. With them neatly listed, the answer to any problem would eventually follow.

He appreciated beauty—in art, in architecture and certainly in the female form. Summer Lyndon was beautiful. That shouldn't have made him uncomfortable. Intelligence was something he not only appreciated but invariably demanded in anyone he associated with. She was undoubtedly intelligent. No reason for discomfort there. Style was something else he looked for—he'd certainly found it in her.

What was it about her…the eyes? he wondered as he passed two cooks in a heated argument over pressed duck. That odd hazel that wasn't precisely a definable color—those gold flecks that deepened or lightened according to her mood. Very direct, very frank eyes, he mused. Blake respected that. Yet the contrast of moody color that wasn't really a color intrigued him. Perhaps too much.

Sexuality? It was a foolish man who was wary because of a natural feminine sexuality and he'd never considered himself a foolish man. Nor a particularly susceptible one. Yet the first time he'd seen her he'd felt that instant curl of desire, that immediate pull of man for woman. Unusual, he thought dispassionately. Something he'd have to consider carefully—then dispose of. There wasn't room for desire between business associates.

And they would be that, he thought as his lips curved. Blake counted on his own powers of persuasion, and his casual mention of LaPointe to turn Summer Lyndon his way. She was already turning that way, and after tonight, he reflected, then stopped dead. For a moment it felt as though someone had delivered him a very quick, very stunning blow to the base of the spine. He'd only had to look at her.

She was half-hidden by the dessert she worked on. Her face was set, intent. He saw the faint line that might've been temper or concentration run down between her brows. Her eyes were narrowed, the lashes swept down so that the expression was unreadable. Her mouth, that soft, molded mouth that she seemed never to paint, was forming a pout. It was utterly kissable.

She should have looked plain and efficient, all in white. The chef's hat over her neatly bound hair could have given an almost comic touch. Instead she looked outrageously beautiful. Standing there, Blake could hear the Chopin that was her trademark, smell the exotic pungent scents of cooking, feel the tension in the air as temperamental cooks fussed and labored over their creations. All he could think, and think quite clearly, was how she would look naked, in his bed, with only candles to vie with the dark.

Catching himself, Blake shook his head. *Stop it,* he thought with grim amusement. *When you mix business and pleasure, one or both suffers.* That was something Blake invariably avoided without effort. He held the position he did because he could recognize, weigh and dismiss errors before they were ever made. And he could do so with a cold-blooded ruthlessness that was as clean as his looks.

The woman might be as delectable as the concoction she was creating, but that wasn't what he wanted—correction, what he could afford to want—from her. He needed her skill, her name and her brain. That was all. For now, he comforted himself with that thought as he fought back waves of a more insistent and much more basic need.

As he stood, as far outside of the melee as possible, Blake watched her patiently, methodically apply and smooth on layer after layer. There was no hesitation in her hands—something he noticed with approval even as he noted the fine-boned elegant shape of them. There was no lack of confidence in her stance. Looking on, Blake realized that she might have been alone for all the noise and confusion around her mattered.

The woman, he decided, could build her spectacular bombe on the Ben Franklin Parkway at rush hour and never miss a step. Good. He couldn't use some hysterical female who folded under pressure.

Patiently he waited as she completed her work. By the time Summer had the pastry bag filled with white icing and had begun the final decorating, most of the kitchen staff were on hand to watch. The rest of the meal was a fait accompli. There was only the finale now.

On the last swirl, she stepped back. There was a communal sigh of appreciation. Still, she didn't smile as she walked completely around the bombe, checking, rechecking. Perfection. Nothing less was acceptable.

Then Blake saw her eyes clear, her lips curve. At the scattered applause, she grinned and was more than beautiful—she was approachable. He found that disturbed him even more.

"Take it in." With a laugh, she stretched her arms high to work out a dozen stiffened muscles. She decided she could sleep for a week.

"Very impressive."

Arms still high, Summer turned slowly to find herself facing Blake. "Thank you." Her voice was very cool, her eyes wary. Sometime between the berries and the frosting, she'd decided to be very, very careful with Blake Cocharan III. "It's meant to be."

"In looks," he agreed. Glancing down, he saw the large bowl of chocolate frosting that had yet to be removed. He ran his finger around the edge, then licked it off. The taste was enough to melt the hardest hearts. "Fantastic."

She couldn't have prevented the smile—a little boy's trick from a man in an exquisite suit and silk tie. "Naturally," she told him with a little toss of her head. "I only make the fantastic. Which is why you want me—correct, Mr. Cocharan?"

"Mmm." The sound might have been agreement, or it might have been something else. Wisely, both left it at that. "You must be tired, after being on your feet for so long."

"A perceptive man," she murmured, pulling off the chef's hat.

"If you'd like, we'll have supper at my penthouse. It's private, quiet. You'd be comfortable."

She lifted a brow, then sent a quick, distrustful look over his face. Intimate suppers were something to be considered carefully. She might be tired, Summer mused, but she could still hold her own with any man—particularly an American businessman. With a shrug, she pulled off her stained apron. "That's fine. It'll only take me a minute to change."

She left him without a backward glance, but as he watched, she was waylaid by a small man with a dark moustache who grabbed her hand and pressed it dramatically to his lips. Blake didn't have to overhear the words to gauge the intent. He felt a twist of annoyance that, with some effort, he forced into amusement.

The man was speaking rapidly while working his way up Summer's arm. She laughed, shook her head and gently nudged him away. Blake watched the man gaze after her like a forlorn puppy before he clutched his own chef's hat to his heart.

Quite an effect she has on the male of the species, Blake mused. Again dispassionately, he reflected that there was a certain type of woman who drew men without any visible effort. It was an innate…skill, he supposed was the correct term. A skill he didn't admire or condemn, but simply mistrusted. A woman like that could manipulate with the flick of the wrist. On a personal level, he preferred women who were more obvious in their gifts.

He positioned himself well out of the way while the cacophony and confusion of cleaning up began. It was a skill he figured wouldn't hurt in her position as head chef of his Philadelphia Cocharan House.

In nine more than the minute she'd claimed she'd be, Summer strolled back into the kitchen. She'd chosen the thin poppy-colored silk because it was perfectly simple—so simple it had a tendency to cling to every curve and draw every eye. Her arms were bare but for one ornately carved gold bracelet she wore just above the elbow. Drop spiral earrings fell almost to her shoulders. Unbound now, her hair curled a bit around her face from the heat and humidity of the kitchen.

She knew the result was part eccentric, part exotic. Just as she knew it transmitted a primal sexuality. She dressed as she did—from jeans to silks—for her own pleasure and at her own whim. But when she saw the fire, quickly banked, in Blake's eyes she was perversely satisfied.

No iceman, she mused—of course she wasn't interested in him in any personal way. She simply wanted to establish herself as a person, an individual, rather than a name he wanted neatly signed on a contract. Her work clothes were jumbled into a canvas tote she carried in one hand, while over her other shoulder hung a tiny exquisitely beaded purse. In a rather regal gesture, she offered Blake her hand.

"Ready?"

"Of course." Her hand was cool, small and smooth. He thought of streaming sunlight and wet, fragrant grass. Because of it, his voice became cool and pragmatic. "You're lovely."

She couldn't resist. Humor leaped into her eyes. "Of course." For the first time she saw him grin—fast, appealing. Dangerous. In that moment she wasn't quite certain who held the upper hand.

"My driver's waiting outside," Blake told her smoothly. Together they walked from the brightly lit, noisy kitchen out into the moonlit street. "I take it you were satisified with your part of the governor's meal. You didn't choose to stay for the criticism or compliments."

As she stepped into the back of the limo, Summer sent him an incredulous look. "Criticism? The bombe is my specialty, Mr. Cocharan. It's always superb. I need no one to tell me that." She got in the car, smoothed her skirt and crossed her legs.

"Of course," Blake murmured, sliding beside her, "it's a complicated dish." He went on conversationally, "If my memory serves me, it takes hours to prepare properly."

She watched him remove a bottle of champagne from ice and open it with only a muffled pop. "There's very little that can be superb in a short amount of time."

"Very true." Blake poured champagne into two tulip glasses and, handing Summer one, smiled. "To a lengthy association."

Summer gave him a frank look as the streetlights flickered into the car and over his face. A bit Scottish warrior, a bit English aristocrat, she decided. Not a simple combination. Then again, simplicity wasn't always what she looked for. With only a brief hesitation, she touched her glass to his. "Perhaps," she said. "You enjoy your work, Mr. Cocharan?" She sipped, and without looking at the label, identified the vintage of the wine she drank.

"Very much." He watched her as he drank, noting

that she'd done no more than sweep some mascara over her lashes when she'd changed. For an instant he was distracted by the speculation of what her skin would feel like under his fingers. "It's obvious by what I caught of that session in there that you enjoy yours."

"Yes." She smiled, appreciating him and what she thought would be an interesting struggle for power. "I make it a policy to do only what I enjoy. Unless I'm very much mistaken, you have the same policy."

He nodded, knowing he was being baited. "You're very perceptive, Ms. Lyndon."

"Yes." She held her glass out for a refill. "You have excellent taste in wines. Does that extend to other areas?"

His eyes locked on hers as he filled her glass. "All other areas?"

Her mouth curved slowly as she brought the champagne to it. Summer enjoyed the effervescence she could feel just before she tasted it. "Of course. Would it be accurate to say that you're a discriminating man?"

What the hell was she getting at? "If you like," Blake returned smoothly.

"A businessman," she went on. "An executive. Tell me, don't executives…delegate?"

"Often."

"And you? Don't you delegate?"

"That depends."

"I wondered why Blake Cocharan III himself would take the time and trouble to woo a chef into his organization."

He was certain she was laughing at him. More, he was certain she wanted him to know it. With an effort, he suppressed his annoyance. "This project is a personal pet of mine. Since I want only the best for it, I take the time and trouble to acquire the best personally."

"I see." The limo glided smoothly to the curb. Summer handed Blake her empty glass as the driver opened her door. "Then how strange that you would even mention LaPointe if only the best will serve you." With the haughty grace a woman can only be born with, Summer alighted. That, she thought smugly, should poke a few holes in his arrogance.

The Cocharan House of Philadelphia stood only twelve stories and had a weathered brick facade. It had been built to blend and accent the colonial architecture that was the heart of the city. Other buildings might zoom higher, might gleam with modernity, but Blake Cocharan had known what he'd wanted. Elegance, style and discretion. That was Cocharan House. Summer was forced to approve. In a great many things, she preferred the old world to the new.

The lobby was quiet, and if the gold was a bit dull, the rugs a bit soft and faded looking, it was a deliberate and canny choice. Old, established wealth was the ambience. No amount of gloss, gleam or gilt would have been more effective.

Taking Summer's arm, Blake passed through with only a nod here and there to the many "Good evening, Mr. Cocharans" he received. After inserting a key into a private elevator, he led her inside. They were enveloped by silence and smoked glass.

"A lovely place," Summer commented. "It's been years since I've been inside. I'd forgotten." She glanced around the elevator and saw their reflections trapped deep in gray glass. "But don't you find it confining to live in a hotel—to live, that is, where you work?"

"No. Convenient."

A pity, Summer mused. When she wasn't working, she wanted to remove herself from the kitchens and timers. She'd never been one—as her mother and father had been—to bring her work home with her.

The elevator stopped so smoothly that the change was hardly noticeable. The doors slid open silently. "Do you have the entire floor to yourself?"

"There're three guest suites as well as my penthouse," Blake explained as they walked down the hall. "None of them are occupied at the moment." He inserted a key into a single panel of a double oak door then gestured her inside.

The lights were already dimmed. He'd chosen his colors well, she thought as she stepped onto the thick pewter-toned carpet. Grays from silvery pale to smoky dominated in the low, spreading sofa, the chairs, the walls. With the lights low it had a dreamlike effect that was both sensuous and soothing.

It might have been dull, even bland, but there were splashes of color cleverly interspersed. The deep midnight blue of the drapes, the pearl-like tones of the army of cushions lining the sofa, the rich, primal green of an ivy tangling down the rungs of a breakfront. Then there were the glowing colors of the one painting, a French Impressionist that dominated one wall.

There was none of the clutter she would have chosen for herself, but a sense of style she admired immediately. "Unusual, Mr. Cochran," Summer complimented as she automatically stepped out of her shoes. "And effective."

"Thank you. Another drink, Ms. Lyndon? The bar's fully stocked, or there's champagne if you prefer."

Still determined to come out of the evening on top, Summer strolled to the sofa and sat. She sent him a cool, easy smile. "I always prefer champagne."

While Blake dealt with the bottle and cork, she took an extra moment to study the room again. Not an ordinary man, she decided. Too often ordinary was synonymous with boring. Summer was forced to admit that because she'd associated herself with the bohemian, the eccentric, the creative for most of her life, she'd always thought of people in business as innately boring.

No, Blake Cocharan wouldn't be dull. She almost regretted it. A dull man, no matter how attractive, could be handled with the minimum of effort. Blake was going to be difficult. Particularly since she'd yet to come to a firm decision on his proposition.

"Your champagne, Ms. Lyndon." When she lifted her eyes to his, Blake had to fight back a frown. The look was too measuring, too damn calculating. Just what was the woman up to now? And why in God's name did she look so right, so temptingly right, curled on his sofa with pillows at her back? "You must be hungry," he said, astonished that he needed the defense of words. "If you'd tell me what you'd like, the kitchen will prepare it. Or I can get you a menu, if you'd prefer."

"A menu won't be necessary." She sipped more cold, frothy French champagne. "I'd like a cheeseburger."

Blake watched the silk shift as she nestled into the corner of the sofa. "A what?"

"Cheeseburger," Summer repeated. "With a side order of fries, shoestring." She lifted her glass to examine the color of the liquid. "Do you know, this was a truly exceptional year."

"Ms. Lyndon…" With strained patience, Blake

dipped his hands in his pockets and kept his voice even. "Exactly what game are you playing?"

She sipped slowly, savoring. "Game?"

"Do you seriously want me to believe that you, a gourmet, a Cordon Bleu chef, want to eat a cheeseburger and shoestring fries?"

"I wouldn't have said so otherwise." When her glass was empty, Summer rose to refill it herself. She moved, he noted, lazily, with none of that sharp, almost military motion she'd used when cooking. "Your kitchen does have lean prime beef, doesn't it?"

"Of course." Certain she was trying to annoy him, or make a fool of him, Blake took her arm and turned her to face him. "Why do you want a cheeseburger?"

"Because I like them," she said simply. "I also like tacos and pizza and fried chicken—particularly when someone else is cooking them. That sort of thing is quick, tasty and convenient." She grinned, relaxed by the wine, amused by his reaction. "Do you have a moral objection to junk food, Mr. Cocharan?"

"No, but I'd think you would."

"Ah, I've shattered your image of a gastronomic snob." She laughed, a very appealing, purely feminine sound. "As a chef, I can tell you that rich sauces and heavy creams aren't easy on the digestion either. Besides that, I cook professionally. For long periods of time I'm surrounded by the finest of haute cuisine. Delicacies, foods that have to be prepared with absolute perfection, split-second timing. When I'm not working, I like to relax." She drank champagne again. "I'd prefer a cheeseburger, medium rare, to *Filet aux Champignons* at the moment, if you don't mind."

"Your choice," he muttered and moved the phone to

order. Her explanation had been reasonable, even logical. There was nothing that annoyed him more than having his own style of manuevering used against him.

With her glass in hand, Summer wandered to the window. She liked the looks of a city at night. The buildings rose and spread in the distance and traffic wound its way silently on the intersecting roads. Lights, darkness, shadows.

She couldn't have counted the number of cities she'd been in or viewed from a similar spot, but her favorite remained Paris. Yet she'd chosen to live for long lengths of time in the States—she liked the contrast of people and cultures and attitudes. She liked the ambition and enthusiasm of Americans, which she saw typified in her mother's second husband.

Ambition was something she understood. She had a lot of her own. She understood this to be the reason she looked for men with more creative ability than ambition in her personal relationships. Two competitive, career-oriented people made an uneasy couple. She'd learned that early on watching her own parents with each other, and their subsequent spouses. When she chose permanence in a relationship—something Summer considered was at least a decade away—she wanted someone who understood that her career came first. Any cook, from a child making a peanut butter sandwich to a master chef, had to understand priorities. Summer had understood her own all of her life.

"You like the view?" Blake stood behind her, where he'd been studying her for a full five minutes. Why should she seem different from any other woman he'd ever brought to his home? Why should she seem more elusive, more alluring? And why should her presence alone make it so difficult for him to keep his mind on the business he'd brought her there for?

"Yes." She didn't turn because she realized abruptly just how close he was. It was something she should have sensed before, Summer thought with a slight frown. If she turned, they'd be face-to-face. There'd be a brush of bodies, a meeting of eyes. The quick scramble of nerves made her sip the champagne again. Ridiculous, she told herself. No man made her nervous.

"You've lived here long enough to recognize the points of interest," Blake said easily, while his thoughts centered on how the curve of her neck would taste, would feel under the brush of his lips.

"Of course. I consider myself a Philadelphian when I'm in Philadelphia. I'm told by some of my associates that I've become quite Americanized."

Blake listened to the flow of the European accented voice, drew in the subtle, sexy scent of Paris that was her perfume. The dim light touched on the gold scattered through her hair. Like her eyes, he thought. He had only to turn her around and look at her face to see her sculptured, exotic look. And he wanted, overwhelmingly, to see that face.

"Americanized," Blake murmured. His hands were on her shoulders before he could stop them. The silk slid cool under his palms as he turned her. "No…" His gaze flicked down, over her hair and eyes, and lingered on her mouth. "I think your associates are very much mistaken."

"Do you?" Her fingers had tightened on the stem of her glass, her mouth had heated. Willpower alone kept her voice steady. Her body brushed his once, then twice as he began to draw her closer. Needs, tightly controlled, began to smolder. While her mind raced with the possibilities, Summer tilted her head back and spoke calmly. "What about the business we're here to discuss, Mr. Cocharan?"

"We haven't started on business yet." His mouth hovered over hers for a moment before he shifted to whisper a kiss just under one eyebrow. "And before we do, it might be wise to settle this one point."

Her breathing was clogging, backing up in her lungs. Drawing away was still possible, but she began to wonder why she should consider it. "Point?"

"Your lips—will they taste as exciting as they look?"

Her lashes were fluttering down, her body softening. "Interesting point," she murmured, then tilted her head back in invitation.

Their lips were only a breath apart when the sharp knock sounded at the door. Something cleared in Summer's brain—reason—while her body continued to hum. She smiled, concentrating hard on that one slice of sanity.

"The service in a Cocharan House is invariably excellent."

"Tomorrow," Blake said as he drew reluctantly away, "I'm going to fire my room service manager."

Summer laughed, but took a shaky sip of wine when he left her to answer the door. Close, she thought, letting out a long, steadying breath. Much too close. It was time to steer the evening into business channels and keep it there. She gave herself a moment while the waiter set up the meal on the table.

"Smells wonderful," Summer commented, crossing the room as Blake tipped and dismissed the waiter. Before sitting, she glanced at his meal. Steak, rare, a steaming potato popping out of its skin, buttered asparagus. "Very sensible." She shot him a teasing grin over her shoulder as he held out her chair.

"We can order dessert later."

"Never touch them," she said, tongue in cheek. With a generous hand she spread mustard over her bun. "I read over your contract."

"Did you?" He watched as she cut the burger neatly in two then lifted a half. It shouldn't surprise him, Blake mused. She did, after all, keep Oreos in her cookie jar.

"So did my attorney."

Blake added some ground pepper to his steak before cutting into it. "And?"

"And it seems to be very much in order. Except..." She allowed the word to hang while she took the first bite. Closing her eyes, Summer simply enjoyed.

"Except?" Blake prompted.

"*If* I were to consider such an offer, I'd need considerably more room."

Blake ignored the *if*. She was considering it, and they both knew it. "In what area?"

"Certainly you're aware that I do quite a bit of traveling." Summer dashed salt on the French fries, tasted and approved. "Often it's a matter of two or three days when I go to, say, Venice and prepare a *Gâteau St. Honoré*. Some of my clients book me months in advance. On the other hand, there are some that deal more spontaneously. A few of these—" Summer bit into the cheeseburger again "—I'll accommodate because of personal affection or professional challenge."

"In other words you'd want to fly to Venice or wherever when you felt it necessary." However incongruous he felt the combination was, Blake poured more champagne into her glass while she ate.

"Precisely. Though your offer does have some slight interest for me, it would be impossible, even, I feel, unethical, to turn my back on established clients."

"Understood." She was crafty, Blake thought, but so was he. "I should think a reasonable arrangement could be worked out. You and I could go over your current schedule."

Summer nibbled on a fry, then dusted her fingers on a white linen napkin. "You and I?"

"That would keep it simpler. Then if we agreed to discuss whatever other occasions might crop up during the year on an individual basis..." He smiled as she picked up the second half of her cheeseburger. "I like to think I'm a reasonable man, Ms. Lyndon. And, to be frank, I personally would prefer signing you with my hotel. At the moment, the board's leaning toward LaPointe, but—"

"Why?" The word was a demand and an accusation. Nothing could have pleased Blake more.

"Characteristically, the great chefs are men." She cursed, bluntly and brutally in French. Blake merely nodded. "Yes, exactly. And, through some discreet questioning, we've learned that Monsieur LaPointe is very interested in the position."

"The swine would scramble at a chance to roast chestnuts on a street corner if only to have his picture in the paper." Tossing down her napkin, she rose. "You think perhaps I don't understand your strategy, Mr. Cocharan." The regal lifting of her head accentuated her long, slender neck. Blake remembered quite vividly how that skin had felt under his fingers. "You throw

LaPointe in my face thinking that I'll grab your offer as a matter of ego, of pride."

He grinned because she looked magnificent. "Did it work?"

Her eyes narrowed, but her lips wanted badly to curve. "LaPointe is a philistine. *I* am an artist."

"And?"

She knew better than to agree to anything in anger. Knew better, but... "You accommodate my schedule, Mr. Cocharan the Third, and I'll make your restaurant the finest establishment of its kind on the East Coast." And damn it, she could do it. She found she wanted to do it to prove it to both of them.

Blake rose, lifting both glasses. "To your art, mademoiselle." He handed her a glass. "And to my business. May it be a profitable union for both of us."

"To success," she amended, clinking glass to glass. "Which, in the end, is what we both look for."

Chapter 3

Well, I've done it, Summer thought, scowling. She swept back her hair and secured it with two mother-of-pearl combs. Critically she studied her face in the mirror to check her makeup. She'd learned the trick of accenting her best features from her mother. When the occasion called for it, and she was in the mood, Summer exploited the art. Although she felt the face that was reflected at her would do, she frowned anyway.

Whether it had been anger or ego or just plain cussedness, she'd agreed to tie herself to the Cocharan House, and Blake, for the next year. Maybe she did want the challenge of it, but already she was uncomfortable with the long-term commitment and the obligations that went with it.

Three hundred sixty-five days. No, that was too overwhelming, she decided. Fifty-two weeks was hardly a better image. Twelve months. Well, she'd just have to live with it. No, she'd have to do better than that, Summer decided as she wandered back into the studio where she'd be taping a demonstration for public TV. She had to live up to her vow to give the Philadelphia Cocharan House the finest restaurant on the East Coast.

And so she would, she told herself with a flick of her hair over her shoulder. So she damn well would. Then she'd thumb her nose at Blake Cocharan III. The sneak.

He'd manipulated her. Twice, he'd manipulated her. Even though she'd been perfectly aware of it the second time, she'd strolled down the garden path anyway. Why? Summer ran her tongue over her teeth and watched the television crew set up for the taping.

The challenge, she decided, twisting her braided gold chain around one slim finger. It would be a challenge to work with him and stay on top. Competing was her greatest weakness, after all. That was one reason she'd chosen to excel in a career that was characteristically male-dominated. Oh, yes, she liked to compete. Best of all, she liked to win.

Then there was that ripe masculinity of his. Polished manners couldn't hide it. Tailored clothes couldn't cloak it. If she were honest—and she decided she would be for the moment—Summer had to admit she'd enjoy exploring it.

She knew her effect on men. A genetic gift, she'd always thought, from her mother. It was rare that she paid much attention to her own sexuality. Her life was too full of the pressures of her work and the complete relaxation she demanded between clients. But it might be time, Summer mused now, to alter things a bit.

Blake Cocharan III represented a definite challenge.

And how she'd love to shake up that smug male arrogance. How she'd like to pay him back for maneuvering her to precisely where he'd wanted her. As she considered varied ways and means to do just that, Summer idly watched the studio audience file in.

They had the capacity for about fifty, and apparently they'd have a full house this morning. People were talking in undertones, the mumbles and shuffles associated with theaters and churches. The director, a small, excitable man whom Summer had worked with before, hustled from grip to gaffer, light to camera, tossing his arms in gestures that signaled pleasure or dread. Only extremes. When he came over to her, Summer listened to his quick nervous instructions with half an ear. She wasn't thinking of him, nor was she thinking of the vacherin she was to prepare on camera. She was still thinking of the best way to handle Blake Cocharan.

Perhaps she should pursue him, subtly—but not so subtly that he wouldn't notice. Then when his ego was inflated, she'd...she'd totally ignore him. A fascinating idea.

"The first baked shell is in the center storage cabinet."

"Yes, Simon, I know." Summer patted the director's hand while she went over the plan for flaws. It had a big one. She could remember all too clearly that giddy sensation that had swept over her when he'd nearly—just barely—kissed her a few evenings before. If she played the game that way, she just might find herself muddling the rules. So...

"The second is right beneath it."

"Yes, I know." Hadn't she put it there herself to cool after baking? Summer gave the frantic director an absent smile. She could ignore Blake right from the start. Treat him—not with contempt, but with disinterest. The smile became a bit menacing. Her eyes glinted. That should drive him crazy.

"All the ingredients and equipment are exactly where you put them."

"Simon," Summer began kindly, "stop worrying. I can build a vacherin in my sleep."

"We roll tape in five minutes—"

"Where is she!"

Both Summer and Simon looked around at the bellowing voice. Her grin was already forming before she saw its owner. "Carlo!"

"Aha." Dark and wiry and as supple as a snake, Carlo Franconi wound his way around people and over cable to grab Summer and pull her jarringly against his chest. "My little French pastry." Fondly he patted her bottom.

Laughing, she returned the favor. "Carlo, what're you doing in downtown Philadelphia on a Wednesday morning?"

"I was in New York promoting my new book, *Pasta by the Master*." He drew back enough to wiggle his eyebrows at her. "And I said, Carlo, you are just around the corner from the sexiest woman who ever held a pastry bag. So I come."

"Just around the corner," Summer repeated. It was typical of him. If he'd been in Los Angeles, he'd have done the same thing. They'd studied together, cooked together, and perhaps if their friendship had not become so solid and important, they might have slept together. "Let me look at you."

Obligingly, Carlo stepped back to pose. He wore straight, tight jeans that flattered narrow hips, a salmon-

colored silk shirt and a cloth fedora that was tilted rak-
ishly over his dark, almond-shaped eyes. An outrageous
diamond glinted on his finger. As always, he was beautiful, male and aware of it.

"You look fantastic, Carlo. *Fantastico.*"

"But of course." He ran a finger down the brim of his
hat. "And you, my delectable puff pastry—" he took her
hands and pressed each palm to his lips "—*esquisita.*"

"But of course." Laughing again, she kissed him
full on the mouth. She knew hundreds of people, professionally, socially, but if she'd been asked to name a
friend, it would have been Carlo Franconi who'd have
come to her mind. "It's good to see you, Carlo. What's
it been? Four months? Five? You were in Belgium the
last time I was in Italy?"

"Four months and twelve days," he said easily. "But
who counts? It's only that I lusted for your Napoleons,
your eclairs, your—" he grabbed her again and nibbled
on her fingers "—chocolate cake."

"It's vacherin this morning," she said dryly, "and
you're welcome to some when the show's over."

"Ah, your meringue. To die for." He grinned wickedly. "I will sit in the front row and cross my eyes at
you."

Summer pinched his cheek. "Try to lighten up, Carlo.
You're so stuffy."

"Ms. Lyndon, please."

Summer glanced at Simon, whose breathing was
becoming shallower as the countdown began. "It's all
right, Simon, I'm ready. Get your seat, Carlo, and watch
carefully. You might learn something this time."

He said something short and rude and easily trans-
lated as they went their separate ways. Relaxed, Sum-

mer stood behind her work surface and watched the floor director count off the seconds. Easily ignoring the face Carlo made at her, Summer began the show, talking directly to the camera.

She took this part of her profession as seriously as she took creating the royal wedding cake for a European princess. If she were to teach the average person how to make something elaborate and exciting, she would do it well.

She did look exquisite, Carlo thought. Then she always did. And confident, competent, cool. On one hand, he was glad to find it true, for he was a man who disliked things or people who changed too quickly—particularly if he had nothing to do with it. On the other hand, he worried about her.

As long as he'd known Summer—good God, had it been ten years?—she'd never allowed herself a personal involvement. It was difficult for a volatile, emotional man like himself to fully understand her quality of reserve, her apparent disinterest in romantic encounters. She had passion. He'd seen it explode in temper, in joy, but never had he seen it directed toward a man.

A pity, he thought as he watched her build the meringue rings. A woman, he felt, was wasted without a man—just as a man was wasted without a woman. He'd shared himself with many.

Once over kirsch cake and Chablis, she'd loosened up enough to tell him that she didn't think that men and women were meant for permanent relationships. Marriage was an institution too easily dissolved and, therefore, not an institution at all but a hypocrisy perpetuated by people who wanted to pretend they could make commitments. Love was a fickle emotion and, therefore, untrustworthy. It was something exploited by people as an excuse to act foolishly or unwisely. If she wanted to act foolish, she'd do so without excuses.

At the time, because he'd been on the down end of an affair with a Greek heiress, Carlo had agreed with her. Later, he'd realized that while his agreement had been the temporary result of sour grapes, Summer had meant precisely what she'd said.

A pity, he thought again as Summer took out the previously baked rings from beneath the counter and began to build the shell. If he didn't feel about her as he would about a sister, it would be a pleasure to show her the…appealing side of the man/woman mystique. Ah, well—he settled back—that was for someone else.

Keeping an easy monologue with the camera and the studio audience, Summer went through the stages of the dessert. The completed shell, decorated with strips of more meringue and dotted with candied violets, was popped into an oven. The one that she'd baked and cooled earlier was brought out to complete the final stage. She filled it, arranged the fruit, covered it all with rich raspberry sauce and whipped cream to the murmured approval of her audience. The camera came in for a close-up.

"Brava!" Carlo stood, applauding as the dessert sat tempting and complete on the counter. *"Bravissima!"*

Summer grinned and, pastry bag in hand, took a deep bow as the camera clicked off.

"Brilliant, Ms. Lyndon." Simon rushed up to her, whipping off his earphones as he came. "Just brilliant. And, as always, perfect."

"Thank you, Simon. Shall we serve this to the audience and crew?"

"Yes, yes, good idea." He snapped his fingers at his assistant. "Get some plates and pass this out before we have to clear for the next show. Aerobic dancing," he muttered and dashed off again.

"Beautiful, *cara*," Carlo told her as he dipped a finger into the whipped cream. "A masterpiece." He took a spoon from the counter and took a hefty serving directly from the vacherin. "Now, I will take you to lunch and you can fill me in on your life. Mine—" he shrugged, still eating "—is so exciting it would take days. Maybe weeks."

"We can grab a slice of pizza around the corner." Summer pulled off her apron and tossed it on the counter. "As it happens, there's something I'd like your advice about."

"Advice?" Though the idea of Summer's asking advice of him, of anyone, stunned him, Carlo only lifted a brow. "Naturally," he said with a silky smile as he drew her along. "Who else would an intelligent woman come to for advice—or for anything—but Carlo?"

"You're such a pig, darling."

"Careful." He slipped on dark glasses and adjusted his hat. "Or you pay for the pizza."

Within moments, Summer was taking her first bite and bracing herself as Carlo zoomed his rented Ferrari into Philadelphia traffic. Carlo managed to steer and eat and shift gears with maniacal skill. "So tell me," he shouted over the boom of the radio, "what's on your mind?"

"I've taken a job," Summer yelled back at him. Her hair whipped across her face and she tossed it back again.

"A job? So, you take lots of jobs?"

"This is different." She shifted, crossing her legs beneath her and turning sideways as she took the next bite. "I've agreed to revamp and manage a hotel restaurant for the next year."

"Hotel restaurant?" Carlo frowned over his slice of pizza as he cut off a station wagon. "What hotel?"

She took a deep sip of soda through a straw. "The Cocharan House here in Philadelphia."

"Ah." His expression cleared. "First class, *cara*. I should never have doubted you."

"A year, Carlo."

"Goes quickly when one has one's health," he finished blithely.

She let the grin come first. "Damn it, Carlo, I painted myself into a corner because, well, I just couldn't resist the idea of trying it and this—this American steamroller tossed LaPointe in my face."

"LaPointe?" Carlo snarled as only an Italian can. "What does that Gallic slug have to do with this?"

Summer licked sauce from her thumb. "I was going to turn down the offer at first, then Blake—that's the steamroller—asked me for my opinion on LaPointe, since he was also being considered for the position."

"And did you give it to him?" Carlo asked with relish.

"I did, and I kept the contract to look it over. The next hitch was that it was a tremendous offer. With the budget I have, I could turn a two-room slum into a gourmet palace." She frowned, not noticing when Carlo zoomed around a compact with little more than wind between metal. "In addition to that, there's Blake himself."

"The steamroller."

"Yes. I can't control the need to get the best of him. He's smart, he's smug and, damn it, he's sexy as hell."

"Oh, yes?"

"I have this tremendous urge to put him in his place."

Carlo breezed through a yellow light as it was turning red. "Which is?"

"Under my thumb." With a laugh, Summer polished off her pizza. "So because of those things, I've locked myself into a year-long commitment. Are you going to eat the rest of that?"

Carlo glanced down to the remains of his pizza, then took a healthy bite. "Yes. And the advice you wanted?"

After drawing through the straw again, Summer discovered she'd hit bottom. "If I'm going to stay sane while locked into a project for a year, I need a diversion." Grinning, she stretched her arms to the sky. "What's the most foolproof way to make Blake Cocharan III crawl?"

"Heartless woman," Carlo said with a smirk. "You don't need my advice for that. You already have men crawling in twenty countries."

"No, I don't."

"You simply don't look behind you, *cara mia*."

Summer frowned, not certain she liked the idea after all. "Turn left at the corner, Carlo, we'll drop in on my new kitchen."

The sights and smells were familiar enough, but within moments, Summer saw a dozen changes she'd make. The lighting was good, she mused as she walked arm-in-arm with Carlo. And the space. But they'd need an eye-level wall-oven there—brick lined. A replacement for the electric oven, and certainly more kitchen help. She glanced around, checking the corners of the ceiling for speakers. None. That, too, would change.

"Not bad, my love." Carlo took down a large chef's

knife and checked it for weight and balance. "You have the rudiments here. It's a bit like getting a new toy for Christmas and having to assemble it, *si?*"

"Hmmm." Absently she picked up a skillet. Stainless steel, she noted and set it down again. The pans would have to be replaced with copper washed with tin. She turned and thudded firmly into Blake's chest.

There was a fraction of a second when she softened, enjoying the sensation of body against body. His scent, sophisticated, slightly aloof, pleased her. Then came the annoyance that she hadn't sensed him behind her as she felt she should have. "Mr. Cocharan." She drew away, masking both the attraction and the annoyance with a polite smile. "Somehow I didn't think to find you here."

"My staff keeps me well informed, Ms. Lyndon. I was told you were here."

The idea of being reported on might have grated, but Summer only nodded. "This is Carlo Franconi," she began. "One of the finest chefs in Italy."

"*The* finest chef in Italy," Carlo corrected, extending his hand. "A pleasure to meet you, Mr. Cocharan. I've often enjoyed the hospitality of your hotels. Your restaurant in Milan makes a very passable linguini."

"Very passable is a great compliment from Carlo," Summer explained. "He doesn't think anyone can make an Italian dish but himself."

"Not think, know." Carlo lifted the lid on a steaming pot and sniffed. "Summer tells me she'll be associated with your restaurant here. You're a fortunate man."

Blake looked down at Summer, glancing at the lean, tanned hand Carlo had placed on her shoulder. Jealousy is a sensation that can be recognized even if it has never been experienced before. Blake didn't care for it, or the cause. "Yes, I am. Since you're here, Ms. Lyndon, you might like to sign the final contract. It would save us both a meeting later."

"All right. Carlo?"

"Go, do your business. They do a rack of lamb over there—it interests me." Without a backward glance, he went to add his two cents.

"Well, he's happy," Summer commented as she walked through the kitchen with Blake.

"Is he in town on business?"

"No, he just wanted to see me."

It was said carelessly, and truthfully, and had the effect of knotting Blake's stomach muscles. So she liked slick Italians, he thought grimly, and slipped a proprietary hand over her arm without being aware of it. That was certainly her business. His was to get her into the kitchens as quickly as possible.

In silence he led her though the lobby and into the hotel offices. Quiet and efficient. Those were brief impressions before she was led into a large, private room that was obviously Blake's.

The colors were bones and creams and browns, the decor a bit more modern than his apartment, but she could recognize his stamp on it. Without being asked, Summer walked over and took a chair. It was hardly past noon, but it occurred to her that she'd been on her feet for almost six consecutive hours.

"Handy that I happened to drop by when you were around," she began, sliding her toes out of her shoes. "It simplifies this contract business. Since I've agreed to do it, we might as well get started." *Then there will be only three hundred and sixty-four days,* she added silently, and sighed.

He didn't like her careless attitude about the contract any more than he liked her careless affection toward the Italian. Blake walked over to his desk and lifted a packet of papers. When he looked back at her, some of his anger drained. "You look tired, Summer."

The lids she allowed to droop lifted again. His first, his only, use of her given name intrigued her. He said it as though he was thinking of the heat and the storms. She felt her chest tighten and blamed it on fatigue. "I am. I was baking meringue at seven o'clock this morning."

"Coffee?"

"No, thanks. I'm afraid I've overdone that already today." She glanced at the papers he held, then smiled with a trace of self-satisfaction. "Before I sign those, I should warn you I'm going to order some extensive changes in the kitchen."

"One of the essential reasons you're to sign them."

She nodded and held out her hand. "You might not be so amiable when you get the bill."

Taking a pen from a holder on his desk, Blake gave it to her. "I think we're both after the same thing, and would both agree cost is secondary."

"I might think so." With a flourish, she looped her name on the line. "But I'm not signing the checks. So—" she passed the contract back to him "—it's official."

"Yes." He didn't even glance at her signature before he dropped the paper on his desk. "I'd like to take you to dinner tonight."

She rose, though she found her legs a bit reluctant to hold weight again. "We'll have to put the seal on our bargain another time. I'll be entertaining Carlo." Smiling, she held out her hand. "Of course, you're welcome to join us."

"It has nothing to do with business." Blake took her hand, then surprised them both by taking her other one. "And I want to see you alone."

She wasn't ready for this, Summer realized. She was supposed to begin the maneuvers, in her own time, on her own turf. Now she was forced to realign her strategy and to deal with the blood warming just under her skin. Determined not to be outflanked this time, she tilted her head and smiled. "We are alone."

His brow lifted. Was that a challenge, or was she plainly mocking him? Either way, this time, he wasn't going to let it go. Deliberately he drew her into his arms. She fit there smoothly. It was something each of them noticed, something they both found disturbing.

Her eyes were level on his, but he saw, fascinated, that the gold flecks had deepened. Amber now, they seemed to glow against the cloudy, changeable hazel of her irises. Hardly aware of what he did, Blake brushed the hair away from her cheek in a gesture that was as sweet and as intimate as it was uncharacteristic.

Summer fought not to be affected by something so casual. A hundred men had touched her, in greeting, in friendship, in anger and in longing. There was no reason why the mere brush of a fingertip over her skin should have her head spinning. An effort of will kept her from melting into his arms or from jerking away. She remained still, watching him. Waiting.

When his mouth lowered toward hers, she knew she was prepared. The kiss would be different, naturally, because he was different. It would be new because he was new. But that was all. It was still a basic form of communication between man and woman. A touch of lips, a pressure, a testing of another's taste; it was no different from the kiss of the first couple, and so it went through culture and time.

And the moment she experienced that touch of lips, that pressure, that taste, she knew she was mistaken. Different? New? Those words were much too mild. The brush of lips, for it was no more at first, changed the fabric of everything. Her thoughts veered off into a chaos that seemed somehow right. Her body grew hot, from within and without, in the space of a heartbeat. The woman who'd thought she knew exactly what to expect, sighed with the unexpected. And reached out.

"Again," she murmured when his lips hovered a breath from hers. With her hands on either side of his face, she drew him to her, through the smoke and into the fire.

He'd thought she'd be cool and smooth and fragrant. He'd been so sure of it. Perhaps that was why the flare of heat had knocked him back on his heels. Smooth she was. Her skin was like silk when he ran his hands up her back to cup her neck. Fragrant. She had a scent that he would, from that moment on, always associate with woman. But not cool. There was nothing cool about the mouth that clung to his, or the breath that mixed with his as two pairs of lips parted. There was something mindless here. He couldn't grip it, couldn't analyze it, could only experience it.

With a deep, almost feline sound of pleasure, she ran her hands through his hair. God, she'd thought there wasn't a taste she hadn't already known, a texture she hadn't already felt. But his, his was beyond her scope and now, just now, within her reach. Summer wallowed in it and let her lips and tongue draw in the sweetness.

More. She'd never known greed. She'd grown up in a world of affluence where enough was always available. For the first time in her life, Summer knew true hunger, true need. Those things brought pain, she discovered. A deep well of it that spread from the core. *More.* The thought ran through her mind again with the knowledge that the more she took, the more she would ache for.

Blake felt her stiffen. Not knowing the cause, he tightened his hold. He wanted her now, at once, more than he'd ever wanted or had conceived of wanting any woman. She shifted in his arms, resisting for the first time since he'd drawn her here. Throwing her head back, she looked up into the passion and impatience of Blake's eyes.

"Enough."

"No." His hand was still tangled possessively in her hair. "No, it's not."

"No," she agreed on an unsteady breath. "That's why you have to let me go."

He released her, but didn't back away. "You'll have to explain that."

She had more control now—barely, Summer realized shakily, but it was better than none. It was time to establish the rules—her rules—quickly and precisely. "Blake, you're a businessman, I'm an artist. Each of us has priorities. This—" she took a step back and stood straight "—can't be one of them."

"Want to bet?"

Her eyes narrowed more in surprise than annoyance. Odd that she'd missed the ruthlessness in him. It would be best if she considered that later, when there was some distance between them. "We'll be working together for a specific purpose," she went on smoothly. "But we're two different people with two very different outlooks. You're interested in a profit, naturally, and in the reputation of your company. I'm interested in creating the proper showcase for my art, and my own reputation. We both want to be successful. Let's not cloud the issue."

"That issue's perfectly clear," Blake countered. "So's this one. I want you."

"Ah." The sound came out slowly. Deliberately she reached for her neglected purse. "Straight and to the point."

"It would be a bit ridiculous to take a more circular route at the moment." Amusement was overtaking frustration. He was grateful for that because it would give him the edge he'd begun to lose the minute he'd tasted her. "You'd have to be unconscious not to realize it."

"And I'm not." Still, she backed away, relying on poise to get her out before she lost whatever slim advantage she had. "But it's your kitchen—and it'll be *my* kitchen—that's my main concern right now. With the amount of money you're paying me, you should be grateful I understand the priorities. I'll have a tentative list of changes and new equipment you'll have to order on Monday."

"Fine. We'll go to dinner Saturday."

Summer paused at the door, turned and shook her head. "No."

"I'll pick you up at eight."

It was rare that anyone ignored a statement she'd made. Rather than temper, Summer tried the patient tone she remembered from her governess. It was bound to infuriate. "Blake, I said no."

If he was infuriated, he concealed it well. Blake merely smiled at her—as one might smile at a fussy child. Two, it seemed, could play the same game with equal skill. "Eight," he repeated and sat on the corner of his desk. "We can even have tacos if you like."

"You're very stubborn."

"Yes, I am."

"So am I."

"Yes, you are. I'll see you Saturday."

She had to put a lot of effort into the glare because she wanted to laugh. In the end, Summer found satisfaction by slamming the door, quite loudly.

Chapter 4

"Incredible nerve," Summer mumbled. She took another bite of her hot dog, scowled and swallowed. "The man has incredible nerve."

"You shouldn't let it affect your appetite, *cara*." Carlo patted her shoulder as they strolled along the sidewalk toward the proud, weathered bricks of Independence Hall.

Summer bit into the hot dog again. When she tossed her head, the sun caught at the ends of her hair and flicked them with gold. "Shut up, Carlo. He's so *arrogant*." With her free hand, she gestured wildly while continuing to munch, almost vengefully, on the dog and bun. "Carlo, I don't take orders from anyone, especially some tailored, polished, American executive with dictatorial tendencies and incredible blue eyes."

Carlo lifted a brow at her description, then shot an

approving look at a leggy blonde in a short pink skirt who passed them. "Of course not, *mi amore*," he said absently, craning his neck to follow the blonde's progress down the street. "This Philadelphia of yours has the most fascinating tourist attractions, *sì?*"

"I make my own decisions, run my own life," Summer grumbled, jerking his arm when she saw where his attention had wandered. "I take requests, Franconi, not orders."

"It's always been so." Carlo gave a last wistful look over his shoulder. Perhaps he could talk Summer into stopping somewhere, a park bench, an outdoor café, where he could get a more…complete view of Philadelphia's attractions. "You must be tired of walking, love," he began.

"I'm definitely not having dinner with him tonight."

"That should teach him to push Summer Lyndon around." The park, Carlo thought, might have the most interesting of possibilities.

She gave him a dangerous stare. "You're amused because you're a man."

"*You're* amused," Carlo corrected, grinning. "And interested."

"I am not."

"Oh, yes, *cara mia,* you are. Why don't we sit so I can take in the…beauty and attractions of your adopted city? After all—" he tipped the brim of his hat at a strolling brunette in brief shorts "—I'm a tourist, *sì?*"

She caught the gleam in his eyes, and the reason for it. After letting out a huff of breath, Summer turned a sharp right. "I'll show you tourist attractions, *amico.*"

"But Summer…" Carlo caught sight of a redhead in

snug jeans walking a poodle. "The view from out here is very educational and uplifting."

"I'll lift you up," she promised and ruthlessly dragged him inside. "The Second Continental Congress met here in 1775, when the building was known as the Pennsylvania State House."

There was an echoing of feet, of voices. A group of schoolchildren flocked by led by a prim, stern-faced teacher wearing practical shoes. "Fascinating," Carlo muttered. "Why don't we go to the park, Summer. It's a beautiful day." For female joggers in tiny shorts and tiny shirts.

"I'd consider myself a poor friend if I didn't give you a brief history lesson before you leave this evening, Carlo." She linked her arm more firmly through his. "It was actually July 8, not July 4, 1776, that the Declaration of Independence was read to the crowd in the yard outside this building."

"Incredible." Hadn't that brunette been heading for the park? "I can't tell you how interesting I find this American history, but some fresh air perhaps—"

"You can't leave Philadelphia without seeing the Liberty Bell." Taking him by the hand, Summer dragged him along. "A symbol of freedom is international, Carlo." She didn't even hear his muttered assent as her thoughts began to swing back to Blake again. "Just what was he trying to prove with that gloss and machismo?" she demanded. "Telling me he'd pick me up at eight after I'd refused to go." Gritting her teeth, she put her hands on her hips and glared at Carlo. "Men—you're all basically the same, aren't you?"

"But no, *carissima*." Amused, he gave her a charming smile and ran his fingers down her cheek. "We are all unique, especially Franconi. There are women in every city of the world who can attest to that."

"Pig," she said bluntly, refusing to be swayed with humor. She sidled closer to him, unconcerned that there was a group of three female college students hanging on every word. "Don't throw your women up to me, you Italian lecher."

"Ah, but, Summer…" He brought her palm to his lips, watching the three young women over it. "The word is…connoisseur."

Her comment was an unladylike snort. "You—men," she corrected, jerking her hand from his, "think of women as something to toy with, enjoy for a while, then disregard. No one's ever going to play that game with me."

Grinning from ear to ear, Carlo took both her hands and kissed them. "Ah, no, no, *cara mia*. A woman, she is like the most exquisite of meals."

Summer's eyes narrowed. As the three girls edged closer she struggled with a grin of her own. "A meal? You dare to compare a woman with a meal?"

"An exquisite one," Carlo reminded her. "One you anticipate with great excitement, one you linger over, savor, even worship."

Her brows arched. "And when your plate's clean, Carlo?"

"It stays in your memory." Touching his thumb and forefinger together, he kissed them dramatically. "Returns in your dreams and keeps you forever searching for an equally sensual experience."

"Very poetic," she said dryly. "But I'm not going to be anyone's entrée."

"No, my Summer, you are the most forbidden of desserts, and therefore, the most desirable." Irrepressible, he winked at the trio of girls. "This Cocharan, do you not think his mouth waters whenever he looks at you?"

Summer gave a short laugh, took two steps away, then stopped. The image had an odd, primitive appeal. Intrigued, she looked back over her shoulder. "Does it?"

Because he knew he'd distracted her, Carlo slipped an arm around her waist and began to lead her from the building. There was still time for fresh air and leggy joggers in the park. Behind them, the three girls muttered in disappointment. "*Cara,* I am a man who has made a study of *amore.* I know what I see in another man's eyes."

Summer fought off a surge of pleasure and shrugged. "You Italians insist on giving a pretty label to basic lust."

With a huge sigh, Carlo led her outside. "Summer, for a woman with French blood, you have no romance."

"Romance belongs in books and movies."

"Romance," Carlo corrected, "belongs everywhere." Though she'd spoken lightly, Carlo understood that she was being perfectly frank. It worried him and, in the way of friend for friend, disappointed him. "You should try candlelight and wine and soft music, Summer. Let yourself experience it. It won't hurt you."

She gave him a strange sidelong smile as they walked. "Won't it?"

"You can trust Carlo like you trust no one else."

"Oh, I do." Laughing again, she swung an arm around his shoulders. "I trust no one else, Franconi."

That too, was the unvarnished truth. Carlo sighed again but spoke with equal lightness. "Then trust yourself, *cara.* Be guided by your own instincts."

"But I do trust myself."

"Do you?" This time it was Carlo who slanted a look at her. "I think you don't trust yourself to be alone with the American."

"With Blake?" He could feel her stiffen with outrage under the arm he still held around her waist. "That's absurd."

"Then why are you so upset about the idea of having a simple dinner with him?"

"Your English is suffering, Carlo. Upset's the wrong word. I'm annoyed." She made herself relax under his arm again, then tilted her chin. "I'm annoyed because he assumed I'd have dinner with him, then continued to assume I would even after I'd refused. It's a normal reaction."

"I believe your reaction to him is very normal. One might say even—ah—basic." He took out his dark glasses and adjusted them meticulously. Perhaps squint lines added character to a face, but he wanted none on his. "I saw what was in your eyes as well that day in the kitchen."

Summer scowled at him, then lifted her chin a bit higher. "You don't know what you're talking about."

"I'm a gourmet," Carlo corrected with a sweep of his free arm. "Of food, yes, but also of love."

"Just stick to your pasta, Franconi."

He only grinned and patted her flank. "*Carissima,* my pasta never sticks."

She uttered a single French word in the most dulcet tones. It was one most commonly seen scrawled in Parisian alleyways. In tune with each other, they walked on, but both were speculating about what would happen that evening at eight.

* * *

It was quite deliberate, well thought out and very satisfying. Summer put on her shabbiest jeans and a faded T-shirt that was unraveled at the hem on one sleeve. She didn't bother with even a pretense of makeup. After seeing Carlo off at the airport, she'd gone through the drive-in window at a local fast-food restaurant and had picked up a cardboard container of fried chicken, complete with French fries and a tiny plastic bowl of coleslaw.

She opened a can of diet soda and flicked the television on to a syndicated rerun of a situation comedy.

Picking up a drumstick, Summer began to nibble. She'd considered dressing to kill, then breezing by him when he came to the door with the careless comment that she had a date. Very self-satisfying. But this way, Summer decided as she propped up her feet, she could be comfortable and insult him at the same time. After a day spent walking around the city while Carlo ogled and flirted with every female between six and sixty, comfort was every bit as important as the insult.

Satisfied with her strategy, Summer settled back and waited for the knock. It wouldn't be long, she mused. If she was any judge of character, she'd peg Blake as a man who was obsessively prompt. And fastidious, she added, taking a pleased survey of her cluttered, comfortably disorganized apartment.

Let's not forget smug, she reminded herself as she polished off the drumstick. He'd arrive in a sleek, tailored suit with the shirt crisp and monogrammed on the cuffs. There wouldn't be a smudge on the Italian leather of his shoes. Not a hair out of place. Pleased, she glanced down at the tattered hem on her oldest jeans. A pity they didn't have a few good holes in them.

Grinning gleefully, she reached for her soda. Holes or not, she certainly didn't look like a woman waiting anxiously to impress a man. And that, Summer concluded, was what a man like Blake expected. Surprising him would give her a great deal of pleasure. Infuriating him would give her even more.

When the knock came, Summer glanced around idly before unfolding her legs. Taking her time, she rose, stretched, then moved to the door.

For the second time, Blake wished he'd had a camera to catch the look of blank astonishment on her face. She said nothing, only stared. With a hint of a smile on his lips, Blake tucked his hands into the pockets of his snug, faded jeans. There was no one, he reflected, whom he'd ever gotten more pleasure out of outwitting. So much so, it was tempting to make a career out of it.

"Dinner ready?" He took an appreciative sniff of the air. "Smells good."

Damn his arrogance—and his perception, Summer thought. How did he always manage to stay one step ahead of her? Except for the fact that he wore tennis shoes—tattered ones—he was dressed almost identically to her. It was only more annoying that he looked every bit as natural, and every bit as attractive, in jeans and a T-shirt as he did in an elegant business suit. With an effort, Summer controlled her temper, and twin surges of humor and desire. The rules might have changed, but the game wasn't over.

"*My* dinner's ready," she told him coolly. "I don't recall inviting you."

"I did say eight."

"I did say no."

"Since you objected to going out—" he took both her hands before breezing inside "—I thought we'd just eat in."

With her hands caught in his, Summer stood in the open doorway. She could order him to leave, she considered. Demand it... And he might. Although she didn't mind being rude, she didn't see much satisfaction in winning a battle so directly. She'd have to find another, more devious, more gratifying method to come out on top.

"You're very persistent, Blake. One might even say pigheaded."

"One might. What's for dinner?"

"Very little." Freeing one hand, Summer gestured toward the take-out box.

Blake lifted a brow. "Your penchant for fast food's very intriguing. Ever thought of opening your own chain—Minute Croissants? Drive Through Pastries?"

She wouldn't be amused. "You're the businessman," she reminded him. "I'm an artist."

"With a teenager's appetite." Strolling over, Blake plucked a drumstick from the box. He settled on the couch, then propped his feet on the coffee table. "Not bad," he decided after the first bite. "No wine?"

No, she didn't want to be amused, was determined not to be, but watching him make himself at home with her dinner, Summer fought off a grin. Maybe her plan to insult him hadn't worked, but there was no telling what the evening might bring. She only needed one opening to give him a good, solid jab. "Diet soda." She sat down and lifted the can. "There's more in the kitchen."

"This is fine." Blake took the drink from her and

sipped. "Is this how one of the greatest dessert chefs spends her evenings?"

Lifting a brow, Summer took the can back from him. "*The* greatest dessert chef spends her evenings as she pleases."

Blake crossed one ankle over the other and studied her. The flecks in her eyes were more subtle this evening—perhaps because she was relaxed. He liked to think he could make them glow again before the night was over. "Yes, I'm sure you do. Does that extend to other areas?"

"Yes." Summer took another piece of chicken before handing Blake a paper napkin. "I've decided your company's tolerable—for the moment."

Watching her, he took another bite. "Have you?"

"That's why you're here eating half my meal." She ignored his chuckle and propped her own feet on the table beside his. There was something cozy about the setting that appealed to her—something intimate that made her wary. She was too cautious a woman to allow herself to forget the effect that one kiss had had on her. She was too stubborn a woman to back down.

"I'm curious about why you insisted on seeing me tonight." A commercial on floor wax flicked across the television screen. Summer glanced at it before turning to Blake. "Why don't you explain?"

He took a plastic fork and sampled the coleslaw. "The professional reason or the personal one?"

He answered a question with a question too often, she decided. It was time to pin him down. "Why don't you take it one at a time?"

How did she eat this stuff? he wondered as he dropped the fork back into the box. When you looked at her you could see her in the most elegant of restaurants—flowers, French wine, starchily correct waiters. She'd be wearing silk and toying with some exotic dessert.

Summer rubbed the bottom of one bare foot over the top of the other while she took another bite of chicken. Blake smiled even as he asked himself why she attracted him.

"Business first then. We'll be working together closely for several months at least. I think it's wise if we get to know each other—find out how the other works so we can make the proper adjustments when necessary."

"Logical." Summer plucked out a couple of French fries before offering the box to Blake. "It's just as well that you find out up front that I don't make adjustments at all. I work only one way—my way. So…personal?"

He enjoyed her confidence and the complete lack of compromise. He planned to explore the first and undo the second. "Personally, I find you a beautiful, interesting woman." Dipping his hand into the box, he watched her. "I want to take you to bed." When she said nothing, he nibbled on a fry. "And I think we should get to know each other first." Her stare was direct and unblinking. He smiled. "Logical?"

"Yes, and egotistical. You seem to have your share of both qualities. But—" she wiped her fingers on the napkin before she picked up the soda again "—you're honest. I admire honesty in other people." Rising, she looked down at him. "Finished?"

His gaze remained as cool as hers while he handed her the box. "Yeah."

"I happen to have a couple of éclairs in the fridge, if you're interested."

"Supermarket special?"

Her lips curved, slowly, slightly. "No. I do have some standards. They're mine."

"Then I could hardly insult you by turning them down."

This time she laughed. "I'm sure diplomacy's your only motive."

"That, and basic gluttony," he added as she walked away. *She's a cool one,* Blake reflected, thinking back to her reaction, or lack of one, to his statement about taking her to bed. The coolness, the control, intrigued him. Or perhaps more accurately, challenged him.

Was it a veneer? If it was, he'd like the opportunity to strip off the layers. Slowly, he decided, even lazily, until he found the passion beneath. It would be there— he imagined it would be like one of her desserts—dark and forbidden beneath a cool white icing. Before too much time had passed, Blake intended to taste it.

Her hands weren't steady. Summer cursed herself as she opened the refrigerator. He'd shaken her—just as he'd meant to. She only hoped he hadn't been able to see through her off-hand response. Yes, he'd intended to shake her, but he'd said precisely what he'd meant. That she understood. At the moment, she didn't have the time to absorb and dissect her feelings. There was only her first reaction—not shock, not outrage, but a kind of nervous excitement she hadn't experienced in years.

Silly, Summer told herself while she arranged éclairs on two Meissen plates. She wasn't a teenager who delighted in fluttery feelings. Nor would she tolerate being informed she was about to become someone's lover.

Affairs, she knew, were dangerous, time-consuming and distracting. And there always seemed to be one party who was more involved, therefore, more vulnerable, than the other. She wouldn't allow herself to be in that position.

But the little twinges of nervous excitement remained.

She was going to have to do something about Blake Cocharan, Summer decided as she poured out two cups of coffee. And she was going to have to do it quickly. The problem was—what?

As Summer arranged cups and plates on a tray, she decided to do what she did best under pressure. She'd wing it.

"You're about to have a memorable, sensuous experience."

Blake glanced up at the announcement and watched her come into the room, tray in hand. Desire hit him surprisingly hard, surprisingly fast. It warned him that if he wanted to stay in control, he'd have to play the game with skill.

"My éclairs aren't to be taken lightly," Summer continued. "Nor are they to be eaten with anything less than reverence."

He waited until she sat beside him again before he took a plate. Very skillfully done, he thought again as her scent drifted to him. "I'll do my best."

"Actually—" she brought down the side of her fork and broke off the first bite "—no effort's required. Just taste buds." Unable to resist, Summer brought the fork to his lips.

He watched her, and she him, as she fed him. The light slanted through the window behind them and caught in her eyes. More green now, Blake thought, almost feline. A man, any man, could lose himself trying to define that color, read that expression. The rich cream and flaky pastry melted in his mouth. Exotic, unique, desirable—like its creator. The first taste, like the first kiss, demanded more.

"Incredible," he murmured, and as her lips curved, he wanted them under his.

"Naturally." As she broke off another portion, Blake's hand closed over her wrist. Her pulse scrambled briefly, he could feel it, but her eyes remained cool and level.

"I'll return the favor." He said it quietly, and his fingers stayed lightly on her wrist as he took the fork in his other hand. He moved slowly, deliberately, keeping his eyes on hers, bringing the pastry to her lips, then pausing. He watched them part, saw the tip of her tongue. It would have been so easy to close his mouth over hers just then—from the rapid beat of her pulse under his fingers, he knew there'd be no resistance. Instead, he fed her the éclair, his stomach muscles tightening as he imagined the taste that was even now lying delicately on her tongue.

She'd never felt anything like this. She'd sampled her own cooking countless times, but had never had her senses so heightened. The flavor seemed to fill her mouth. Summer wanted to keep it there, exploring the sensation that had become so unexpectedly, so intensely, sexual. It took a conscious effort to swallow, and another to speak.

"More?" she asked.

His gaze flicked down from her eyes to her mouth then back again. "Always."

A dangerous game. She knew it, but opted to play.

And to win. Taking her time, she fed him the next bite. Was the color of his eyes deeper? She didn't think she was imagining it, nor the waves of desire that seemed to pound over her. Did they come from her, or from him?

On the television, someone broke into raucous laughter. Neither of them noticed. It would be wise to step back now, cautiously. Even as the thought passed through her mind, she opened her mouth for the next taste.

Some things exploded on the tongue, others heated it or tantalized. This was a cool, elegant experience, no less sensual than champagne, no less primitive than ripened fruit. Her nerves began to calm, but her awareness intensified. He was wearing some subtle cologne that made her think of the woods in autumn. His eyes were the deep blue of an evening sky. When his knee brushed hers, she felt a warmth that seeped through two layers of material and touched flesh. Moment after moment passed without her being aware that they weren't speaking, only slowly, luxuriously, feeding each other. The intimacy wrapped around her, no less intense, no less exciting than lovemaking. The coffee sat cooling. Shadows spread through the room as the sun went down.

"The last bite," Summer murmured, offering it. "You approve?"

He caught the ends of her hair between his thumb and finger. "Completely."

Her skin tingled, much too pleasantly. Although she didn't shift away, Summer set the fork down with great care. She was feeling soft—too soft. And too vulnerable. "One of my clients has a secret passion for éclairs. Four times a year I go to Brittany and make him two dozen. Last fall he gave me an emerald necklace."

Blake lifted a brow as he twined a strand of her hair around his finger. "Is that a hint?"

"I'm fond of presents," she said easily. "But then, that sort of thing isn't quite ethical between business associates."

As she leaned forward for her coffee, Blake tightened his fingers in her hair and held her still. In the moment her eyes met his, he saw mild surprise and mild annoyance. She didn't like to be held down by anyone. "Our business association is only one level. We're both acutely aware of that by this time."

"Business is the first level, and the first priority."

"Maybe." It was difficult to admit, even to himself, that he was beginning to have doubts about that. "In any case, I haven't any intention of staying at level one."

If she were ever going to handle him, it would have to be now. Summer draped her arm negligently across the back of the sofa and wished her stomach would unknot. "I'm attracted to you. And I think it should be difficult, and interesting, to work around that for the next few months. You said you wanted to understand me. I rarely explain myself, but I'll make an exception." Leaning forward again, she plucked a cigarette from its holder. "Have you a light?"

It was strange how easily she drew feelings from him without warning. Now it was annoyance. Blake took out his lighter and flicked it on. He watched her pull in smoke, then blow it out quickly in a gesture he realized came more from habit than pleasure. "Go on."

"You said you knew my mother," Summer began. "You'd know of her in any case. She's a beautiful, talented, intelligent woman. I love her very much, both as a mother, and as a person who's full of the joy of life. If she has one weakness, it is men."

Summer folded her legs under her and concentrated on relaxing. "She's had three husbands, and innumerable lovers. She's always certain each relationship is forever. When she's involved with a man, she's blissfully happy. His interests are her interests, his dislikes her dislikes. Naturally, when it ends, she's crushed."

Again, Summer drew on her cigarette. She'd expected him to make some passing comment. When instead, he only listened, only watched, she went further than she'd intended. "My father is a more practical man, and yet he's been through two wives and quite a few discreet affairs. Unlike my mother, who accepts flaws—even enjoys them for a short time—he looks for perfection. Since there is no perfection in people, only in what people create, he's continually disappointed. My mother looks for elation and romance, my father looks for the perfect companion. I don't look for either of those."

"Why don't you tell me what you look for then?"

"Success," she said simply. "Romance has a beginning, so it follows it has an end. A companion demands compromise and patience. I give all my patience to my work, and I have no talent for compromise."

It should have satisfied him, even relieved him. After all, he wanted nothing more than a casual affair, no strings, no commitments. He didn't understand why he wanted to shake the words back down her throat, only knew that he did. "No romance," he said with a nod. "No companionship. That doesn't rule out the fact that you want me, and I want you."

"No." The smoke was leaving a bitter taste in her

mouth. As Summer crushed out her cigarette she thought how much their discussion sounded like a negotiation. Yet wasn't that how she preferred things? "I said it would be difficult to work around, but it's also necessary. You want a service from me, Blake, and I agreed to give you that, because I want the experience and the publicity I'll get out of it. But changing the tone and face of your restaurant is going to be a long, complicated process. Combining that with my other commitments, I won't have time for any personal distractions."

"Distractions?" Why should that one word have infuriated him? It did, just as her businesslike dismissal of desire infuriated him. Perhaps she hadn't meant it as a challenge, but he couldn't take it as anything less. "Does this distract you?" He ran his finger down the side of her throat before he cupped the back of her neck.

She could feel the firm pressure of each of his fingers against her skin. And in his eyes, she could see the temper, the need. Both pulled at her. "You're paying me a great deal of money, to do a job, Blake." Her voice was steady. Good. Her heartbeat wasn't. "As a businessman, you should want the complications left to a minimum."

"Complications," he repeated. He drew his other hand through her hair so that her face was tilted back. Summer felt a jolt of excitement shoot down her spine. "Is this—" he brushed his lips over her cheek "—a complication?"

"Yes." Her brain sent out the signal to pull away, but her body refused the command.

"And a distraction?"

He took his mouth on a slow journey to hers, but only nibbled. There was no pressure but the slight grip he kept on the base of her neck with fingers moving slowly, rhythmically over her skin. Summer didn't move away, though she told herself she still could. She'd never permitted herself to be seduced, and tonight was no different.

Just a sample, she thought. She knew how to taste and judge, then step away from even the most tempting of flavors. Just as she knew how to absorb every drop of pleasure from that one tiny test.

"Yes," she murmured and let her eyes flutter closed. She needed no visual image now, but only the sensations. Warm, soft, moist—his mouth against hers. Firm, strong, persuasive—the fingers against her skin. Subtle, male, intriguing—the scent that clung to him. When he spoke her name, his voice flowed over her like a breeze, one that carried a trace of heat and the hint of a storm.

"How simple do you want it to be, Summer?" It was happening again, he realized. That total involvement he neither looked for nor wanted—the total involvement he couldn't resist. "There's only you and me."

"There's nothing simple about that." Even as she disagreed, her arms were going around him, her mouth was seeking his again.

It was only a kiss. She told herself that as his lips slanted lightly over hers. She could still end it, she was still in control. But first, she wanted just one more taste. Without thinking, she touched the tip of his tongue with hers, to fully explore the flavor. Her own moan sounded softly in her ears as she drew him closer. Body against body, firm and somehow right. This new thought drifted to her even as the sensation concentrated on the play of mouth to mouth.

Why had kisses seemed so basic, so simplistic before

this? There were hundreds of pulse points in her body she'd remained unaware of until this moment. There were pleasures deeper, richer than she'd ever imagined that could be drawn out and exploited by the most elemental gesture between a man and a woman. She'd thought she'd known the limits of her own needs, the depth of her own passions…until now. Barely touching her, Blake was tearing something from her that wasn't calm, ordered and disciplined. And when it was totally free, what then?

She found herself at the verge of something she'd never come to before—where emotions commanded her mind completely. A step further and he would have all of her. Not just her body, not just her thoughts, but that most private, most well guarded possession, her heart.

She felt a greed for him and pulled away from it. If she were greedy, if she took, then he would too. He still held her, lightly enough for her to draw back, firmly enough to keep her close. She was breathless, moved. As she struggled to think clearly, Summer decided it would be foolish to try to deny either.

"I think I proved my point," she managed.

"Yours?" Blake countered as he ran a hand up her back. "Or mine?"

She took a deep breath, expelling it slowly. That one small show of emotion had desire clawing at him again. "I've mixed enough ingredients to know that business affairs and personal affairs aren't palatable. On Monday, I go to work for Cocharan. I intend to give you your money's worth. There can't be anything else."

"There's quite a bit else already." He cupped her chin in his hand so that their eyes held steady. Inside he was a mass of aching needs and confusion. With that kiss, that long, slow kiss, he'd all but forgotten his strictest rule. *Keep the emotions harnessed, both in business and in pleasure. Otherwise, you make mistakes that aren't easily rectified.* He needed time, and he realized he needed distance. "We know each other better now," he said after a moment. "When we make love, we'll understand each other."

Summer remained seated when he rose. She wasn't completely sure she could stand. "On Monday," she said in a firmer voice, "we'll be working together. That's all there is between us from this point on."

"When you deal with as many contracts as I do, Summer, you learn that paper is just that: paper. It's not going to make any difference."

He walked to the door thinking he needed some fresh air to clear his head, a drink to settle his nerves. And distance, a great deal of distance, before he forgot everything except the raging need to have her.

With his hand on the knob, Blake turned around for one last look at her. There was something in the way she frowned at him, with her eyes focused and serious, her lips soft in a half pout that made him smile.

"Monday," he told her, and was gone.

Chapter 5

Why in hell couldn't he stop thinking of her? Blake sat at his desk examining the details of a twenty-page contract in preparation for what promised to be a long, tense meeting in the boardroom. He wasn't taking in a single word. Uncharacteristic. He knew it, resented it and could do nothing about it.

For days Summer had been slipping into his mind and crowding out everything else. For a man who took order and self-control for granted, it was nerve-racking.

Logically, there was no reason for his obsession with her. Blake called it obsession, for lack of a better term, but it didn't please him. She was beautiful, he mused as his thoughts drifted further away from clauses and terms. He'd known hundreds of beautiful women. She was intelligent, but intelligent women had been in his life before. Desirable—even now in his neat, quiet office he could feel the first stirrings of need. But he was no stranger to desire.

He enjoyed women, as friends and as lovers. Enjoyment, Blake reflected, was perhaps the key word—he'd never looked for anything deeper in a relationship with a woman. But he wasn't certain it was the proper word to describe what was already between himself and Summer. She moved him—too strongly, too quickly—to the point where his innate control was shaken. No, he didn't enjoy that, but it didn't stop him from wanting more. Why?

Utilizing his customary method of working through a problem, Blake leaned back and, picking up a pen, began to list the possibilities.

Perhaps part of the consistent attraction was the fact that he liked outmaneuvering her. It wasn't easily done, and took quick thinking and careful planning. Up till this point, he'd countered her at every turn. Blake was realistic enough to know that that wouldn't last, but he was human enough to want to try. Just where would they clash next? he wondered. Over business…or over something more personal? In either case he wanted to go head to head with her just as much—well, almost as much—as he wanted to make love with her.

And perhaps another reason was that he knew the attraction was just as strong on her part—yet she continued to refuse it. He admired that strength of will in her. She mistrusted intimacy, he mused. Because of her parents' track record? Yes, partially, he decided. But he didn't think that was all of it. He'd just have to dig a bit deeper to get the whole picture.

He wanted to dig, he realized. For the first time in

his life Blake wanted to know a woman completely. Her thought process, her eccentricities, what made her laugh, what annoyed, what she really wanted for and in her life. Once he knew all there was to know… He couldn't see past that. But he wanted to know her, understand her. And he wanted her as a lover as he'd never wanted anything else.

When the buzzer on his desk sounded, Blake answered it automatically with his thoughts still centering on Summer Lyndon.

"Your father's on his way back, Mr. Cocharan."

Blake glanced down at the contract on his desk and mentally filed it. He still needed an hour with it before the board meeting. "Thanks." Even as he released the intercom button, the door swung open. Blake Cocharan II strolled into the room and took it over.

In build and coloring, he was similar to his son. Exercise and athletics had kept him trim and hard over the years. There were threads of gray in the dark hair that was covered by a white sea captain's hat. But his eyes were young and vibrant. He walked with the easy rolling gait of a man more accustomed to decks than floors. He wore canvas on his sockless feet, and a Swiss watch on his wrist. When he grinned, the lines etched by time and squinting at the sun fanned out from his eyes and mouth. As he stood to greet him, Blake caught the salty, sea-breezy scent he always associated with his father.

"B.C." Their hands clasped, one older and rougher than the other, both firm. "Just passing through?"

"On my way to Tahiti, going to do some sailing." B.C. grinned again, appealingly, as he ran a finger along the brim of his cap. "Want to play hookey and crew for me?"

"Can't. I'm booked solid for the next two weeks."

"You work too hard, boy." In an old habit, B.C. walked over to the bar at the west side of the room and poured himself bourbon, neat.

Blake grinned at his father's back as B.C. tossed down three fingers of liquor. It was still shy of noon. "I came by it honestly."

With a chuckle, B.C. poured a second drink. When it had been his office, he'd stocked only the best bourbon. He was glad his son carried on the tradition. "Maybe— but I learned to play just as hard."

"You paid your dues, B.C."

"Yeah." Twenty-five years of ten-hour days, he reflected. Of hotel rooms, airports and board meetings. "So did the old man—so've you." He turned back to his son. Like looking into a mirror that's twenty years past, he thought, and smiled rather than sighed. "I've told you before, you can't wrap your life up in hotels." He sipped appreciatively at the bourbon this time, then swirled it. "Gives you ulcers."

"Not so far." Sitting again, Blake steepled his fingers, watching his father over them. He knew him too well, had apprenticed under him, watched him wheel and deal. Tahiti might be his destination, but he hadn't stopped off in Philadelphia without a reason. "You came in for the board meeting."

B.C. nodded before he found some salted almonds under the bar. "Have to put in my two cents worth now and again." He popped two nuts in his mouth and bit down with relish. He was always grateful that the teeth were still his and his eyesight was keen. If a man had those, and a forty-foot sloop, he needed little else. "If we buy the Hamilton chain, it's going to mean twenty more hotels, over two thousand more employees. A big step."

Blake lifted a brow. "Too big?"

With a laugh, B.C. dropped down into a chair across from the desk. "I didn't say that, don't think that—and apparently you don't think so either."

"No, I don't." Blake waved away his father's offering of almonds. "Hamilton's an excellent chain, simply mismanaged at this point. The buildings themselves are worth the outlay." He gave his father a mild, knowledgeable look. "You might check out the Hamilton Tahiti while you're there."

Grinning, B.C. leaned back. The boy was sharp, he thought, pleased. But then he came by that honestly, too. "Thought crossed my mind. By the way, your mother sends her love."

"How is she?"

"Up to her neck in a campaign to save another crumbling ruin." The grin widened. "Keeps her off the streets. Going to meet me on the island next week. Hell of a first mate, your mother." He nibbled on another almond, pleased to think of having some time alone with his wife in the tropics. "So, Blake, how's your sex life?"

Too used to his father to be anything but amused, Blake inclined his head. "Adequate, thanks."

With a short laugh, B.C. downed the rest of his drink. "Adequate's a disgrace to the Cocharan name. We do everything in superlatives."

Blake drew out a cigarette. "I've heard stories."

"All true," his father told him, gesturing with the empty glass. "One day I'll have to tell you about this dancer in Bangkok in '39. In the meantime, I've heard you plan to do some face-lifting right here."

"The restaurant." Blake nodded and thought of Summer. "It promises to be...fascinating work."

B.C. caught the tone and began to gently probe. "I can't disagree that the place needs a little glitzing up. So you hired on a French chef to oversee the operation."

"Half French."

"A woman?"

"That's right." Blake blew out smoke, aware which path his father was trying to lead him down.

B.C. stretched out his legs. "Knows her business, does she?"

"I wouldn't have hired her otherwise."

"Young?"

Blake drew on his cigarette and suppressed a smile. "Moderately, I suppose."

"Attractive?"

"That depends on your definition—I wouldn't call her attractive." Too tame a word, Blake thought, much, much too tame. Exotic, alluring—those suited her more. "I can tell you that she's dedicated to her profession, an ambitious perfectionist and that her éclairs..." His thoughts drifted back to that intoxicating interlude. "Her éclairs are an experience not to be missed."

"Her éclairs," B.C. repeated.

"Fantastic." Blake leaned back in his chair. "Absolutely fantastic." He kept the grin under control as his buzzer sounded again.

"Ms. Lyndon is here, Mr. Cocharan."

Monday morning, he thought. Business as usual. "Send her in."

"Lyndon." B.C. set down his glass. "That's the cook, isn't it?"

"Chef," Blake corrected. "I'm not sure if she answers to the term 'cook.'"

The knock was brief before Summer walked in. She carried a slim leather folder in one hand. Her hair was braided and rolled at the nape of her neck so that the hints of gold threaded through the brown. Her suit in a deep plum color was Chanel, simple and exquisite over a high-necked lace blouse that rose to frame her face. The strict professionalism of her attire made Blake instantly speculate on what she wore beneath—something brief, silky and sexy, the same color as her skin.

"Blake." Following her own self-lecture on priorities, Summer held out her hand. Impersonal, business-like and formal. She wasn't going to think about what happened when his mouth touched hers. "I've brought you the list of changes of equipment and suggestions we spoke about."

"Fine." He saw her turn her head as B.C. rose from his chair. And he saw the gleam light his father's eyes as it always did when he was in the company of a beautiful woman. "Summer Lyndon, Blake Cocharan II. B.C., Ms. Lyndon will be managing the kitchen here at the Philadelphia Cocharan House."

"Mr. Cocharan." Summer found her hand enveloped in a large, calloused one. He looks, she realized with a jolt, exactly as Blake will in thirty years. Distinguished, weathered, with that perennial touch of polish. Then B.C. grinned, and she understood that Blake would still be dangerous in three decades.

"B.C.," he corrected, lifting her fingers to his lips. "Welcome to the family."

Summer shot Blake a quick look. "Family?"

"We consider anyone associated with Cocharan House part of the family." B.C. gestured to the chair he'd vacated. "Please, sit down. Let me get you a drink."

"Thank you. Perhaps some Perrier." She watched B.C. cross the room before she sat and laid the folder on her lap. "I believe you're acquainted with my mother, Monique Dubois."

That stopped him. B.C. turned, the bottle of Perrier still in his hand, the glass in the other still empty. "Monique? You're Monique's girl? I'll be damned."

And so he might be, B.C. thought. Years before— was it nearly twenty now?—during a period of marital upheaval on both sides, he'd had a brief, searing affair with the French actress. They'd parted on amicable terms and he'd reconciled with his wife. But the two weeks with Monique had been...memorable. Now he was in his son's office pouring Perrier for her daughter. Fate, he thought wryly, was a tricky sonofabitch.

If Summer had suspected before that her mother and Blake's father had once been lovers, she was now certain of it. Her thoughts on fate directly mirrored his as she crossed her legs. Like mother, like daughter? she wondered. Oh, no, not in this case. B.C. was still staring at her. For a reason she didn't completely understand, she decided to make it easy for him.

"Mother is a loyal client of Cocharan Houses; she'll stay nowhere else. I've already mentioned to Blake that we once had dinner with your father. He was very gracious."

"When it suits him," B.C. returned, relieved. She knows, he concluded before his gaze strayed to Blake's. There he saw a frown of concentration that was all too familiar. *And so will he if I don't watch my step,* B.C. decided. *Hot water,* he mused. *After twenty years I could still be in hot water.* His wife was the love of his life, his best friend, but twenty years wasn't long enough to be safe from a transgression.

"So—" he finished pouring the Perrier, then brought it to her "—you decided against following in your mother's footsteps and became a chef instead."

"I'm sure Blake would agree that following in a parent's footsteps is often treacherous."

Instinct told Blake that it wasn't business she spoke of now. A look passed between his father and Summer that he couldn't comprehend. "It depends where the path leads," Blake countered. "In my case I preferred to look at it as a challenge."

"Blake takes after his grandfather," B.C. put in. "He has that cagey kind of logic."

"Yes," Summer murmured. "I've seen it in action."

"Apparently you made the right choice," B.C. went on. "Blake told me about your éclairs."

Slowly, Summer turned her head until she was facing Blake again. The muscles in her stomach, in her thighs, tightened with the memory. Her voice remained calm and cool. "Did he? Actually, my specialty is the bombe."

Blake met her gaze directly. "A pity you didn't have one available the other night."

There were vibrations there, B.C. thought, that didn't need to bounce off a third party. "Well, I'll let you two get on with your business. I've some people to see before the board meeting. A pleasure meeting you, Summer." He took her hand again and held it as his eyes held hers. "Please, give my best to your mother."

She saw his eyes were like Blake's, in color, in shape, in appeal. Her lips curved. "I will."

"Blake, I'll see you this afternoon."

He only murmured an assent, watching Summer rather than his father. The door closed before he spoke. "Why do I feel as though there were messages being passed in front of me?"

"I have no idea," Summer said coolly as she lifted the folder. "I'd like you to glance over these papers while I'm here, if you have time." Zipping open the folder, she pulled them out. "That way, if there are any questions or any disagreements, we can get through them now before I begin downstairs."

"All right." Blake picked up the first sheet but studied her over it. "Is that suit supposed to keep me at a distance?"

She sent him a haughty look. "I have no idea what you're talking about."

"Yes, you do. And another time I'd like to peel it off you, layer by layer. But at the moment, we'll play it your way." Without another word, he lowered his gaze to the paper and started to read.

"Arrogant swine," Summer said distinctly. When he didn't even bother to look up she folded her arms over her chest. She wanted a cigarette to give her something to do with her hands, but refused herself the luxury. She would sit like a stone, and when the time came, she would argue for every one of the changes she'd listed. And win every one of them. On that level *she* was in complete control.

She wanted to hate him for realizing she'd worn the elegant, career-oriented suit to set a certain tone. Instead, she had to respect him for being perceptive enough to pick up on small details. She wanted to hate him for making her want so badly with only a look and a few words. It wasn't possible when she'd spent the remainder of the weekend alternately wishing she'd never met him and wishing he'd come back and bring her that excitement again. He was a problem; there was no denying it. She understood that you solved problems one step at a time. Step one, her kitchen—accent on the personal pronoun.

"Two new gas ovens," he murmured as he scanned the sheet. "One electric oven and two more ranges of each kind." Without lowering it, he glanced at her over the top of the page.

"I believe I explained to you before the need for both gas and electric ovens. First, yours are antiquated. Second, in a restaurant of this size the need for two gas ovens is imperative."

"You specify brands."

"Of course, I know what I like to work with."

He only lifted a brow, thinking that procurement was going to grumble. "All new pots and pans?"

"Definitely."

"Perhaps we should have a yard sale," Blake mumbled as he went back to the sheet. He hadn't the vaguest idea what a *sautoir* was or why she required three of them. "And this particular heavy-duty mixer?"

"Essential. The one you have is adequate. I don't accept adequate."

He smothered a laugh as he recalled his father's view on adequate in relation to love lives. "Did you list so much of this in French to confuse me?"

"I listed in French," Summer countered, "because French is correct."

He made an indefinable sound as he passed over the next sheet. "In any case, I've no intention of quibbling over equipment in French or English."

"Good. Because I've no intention of working with any less than the best." She smiled at him and settled back. First point taken.

Blake flipped over the second sheet and went on to the third. "You intend to rip out the existing counters, have the new ranges built in, add an island and an additional six feet of counter space."

"More efficient," Summer said easily.

"And time-consuming."

"In a hurry? You hired me, Blake, not Minute Chef." His quick grin made her eyes narrow. "My function is to organize your kitchen, which means making it as efficient and creative as I know how. Once the nuts and bolts of that are done, I'll beef up your menu."

"And this—" he flipped through the five typed sheets "—is all necessary for that?"

"I don't bother with anything that isn't necessary when it comes to business. If you don't agree," she said as she rose, "we can terminate the agreement. Hire LaPointe," she suggested, firing up. "You'll have an ostentatious, overpriced, second-rate kitchen that produces equally ostentatious, overpriced and second-rate meals."

"I have to meet this LaPointe," Blake murmured as he stood. "You'll get what you want, Summer." As a satisfied smile formed on her lips, he narrowed his eyes. "And you damn well better deliver what you promised."

The fire leapt back, accenting the gold in her irises. And as he saw it, he wanted.

"I've given you my word. Your middle-class restaurant with its mediocre prime rib and soggy pastries will be serving the finest in haute cuisine within six months."

"Or?"

So he wanted collateral, Summer thought, and heaved a breath. "Or my services for the term of the contract are gratis. Does that satisfy you?"

"Completely." Blake held out a hand. "As I said, you'll have precisely what you've asked for, down to the last egg beater."

"A pleasure doing business with you." Summer tried to draw her hand away and found it caught firm. "Perhaps you don't," she began, "but I have work to do. You'll excuse me?"

"I want to see you."

She let her hand remain passively in his rather than risk a struggle she might lose. "You have seen me."

"Tonight."

"Sorry." She smiled again, though her teeth were beginning to clench. "I have a date."

She felt the quick increase in pressure of his fingers over hers and was perversely pleased. "All right, when?"

"I'll be in the kitchen every day, and some evenings, to oversee the remodeling. You need only ride the elevator down."

He drew her closer, and though the desk remained between them, Summer felt that the ground beneath was a bit less firm. "I want to see you alone," he said quietly. Lifting her hand to his lips, he kissed her fingers slowly, one by one. "Away from here, outside of business hours."

If Blake Cocharan II had been anything like Blake Cocharan III in his youth, Summer could understand how her mother had become so quickly, so heatedly involved. The yearning was there, and the temptation—but she wasn't Monique. In this case, she was determined history would not repeat itself. "I've explained to you why that's not possible. I don't enjoy covering the same ground twice."

"Your pulse is racing," Blake pointed out as he ran a finger across her wrist.

"It generally does when I become annoyed."

"Or aroused."

Tilting her head, she sent him a killing look. "Would you amuse yourself with LaPointe in this way?"

Temper stirred and he suppressed it, knowing she wanted him to be angry. "At the moment, I don't care whether you're a chef or a plumber or a brain surgeon. At the moment," he repeated, "I only care that you're a woman, and one who I desire very much."

She wanted to swallow because her throat had gone dry but fought off the need. "At the moment I *am* a chef with a specific job to do. I'll ask you again to excuse me so I can begin to do it."

This time, Blake thought as he released her hand. But, by God, this time was the last time. "Sooner or later, Summer."

"Perhaps," she agreed as she picked up her leather folder. "Perhaps not." In one quick gesture, she zipped it closed. "Enjoy your day, Blake." As if her legs weren't weak and watery, she strolled to the door and out.

Summer continued to walk calmly through the outer office, over the plush carpet, past the busy secretaries and through the reception area. Once in the elevator, she leaned back against the wall and let out the long, tense breath she'd been holding. Nerves jumping, she began the ride down.

That was over, she told herself. She'd faced him in his office and won every point.

Sooner or later, Summer.

She let out another breath. Almost every point, she corrected. The important thing now was to concentrate on her kitchen, and to keep busy. It wasn't going to help matters if she allowed herself to think of him as she had over the weekend.

As her nerves began to calm, Summer straightened away from the wall. She'd handled herself well, she'd made herself clear and *she'd* walked out on him. All in all, a successful morning. She pressed a hand against her stomach, where a few muscles were still jumping. Damn it, things would be simpler if she didn't want him so badly.

When the doors slid open she stepped out, then wound her way around to the kitchen. In the prelunch bustle, she went unnoticed. She approved of the noise. A quiet kitchen to Summer meant there was no communication. Without that, there was no cooperation. For a moment, she stood just inside the doorway to watch.

She approved of the smells. It was a mixture of lunchtime aromas over the still-lingering odors of breakfast. Bacon, sausage and coffee. She caught the scent of baking chicken, of grilled meat, of cakes fresh from the oven. Narrowing her eyes, she envisioned the room as it would be in a short time. Made to her order. Better, Summer decided with a nod.

"Ms. Lyndon."

Distracted, she frowned up at a big man in white apron and cap. "Yes?"

"I'm Max." His chest expanded, his voice stiffened. "Head chef."

Ego in danger, she thought as she extended a hand. "How do you do, Max. I missed you when I was in last week."

"Mr. Cocharan has instructed me to give you full cooperation during this—transition period."

Marvelous, she thought with an inward moan. Resentment in a kitchen was as difficult to deal with as a deflated soufflé. Left to herself, she might have been able to keep injured feelings to a minimum, but the damage had already been done. She made a mental note to give Blake her opinion of his tact and diplomacy.

"Well, Max, I'd like to go over the proposed structural changes with you, since you know the routine here better than anyone else."

"Structural changes?" he repeated. His full, round face flushed. The moustache over his mouth quivered. She caught the gleam of a single gold tooth. "In *my* kitchen?"

My kitchen, Summer mentally corrected, but smiled. "I'm sure you'll be pleased with the improvements— and the new equipment. You must have found it frustrating trying to create something special with outdated appliances."

"This oven," he said and gestured dramatically toward it, "this range—both have been here since I began at Cocharan. We are none of us outdated."

So much for cooperation, Summer thought wryly. If it was too late for a friendly transition of authority, she'd have to go with the *coup*. "We'll be receiving three new ovens," she began briskly. "Two gas, one electric. The electric will be used exclusively for desserts and pastries. This counter," she continued, walking toward it without looking back to see if Max was following, "will be removed and the ranges I specified built into a new counter—butcher block. The grill remains. There'll be an island here to provide more working area and to make use of what is now essentially wasted space."

"There is no wasted space in my kitchen."

Summer turned and aimed her haughtiest stare. "That isn't a matter for debate. Creativity will be the first priority of this kitchen, efficiency the second. We'll be expected to produce quality meals during the remodeling—difficult but not impossible if everyone makes the necessary adjustments. In the meantime, you and I will go over the current menu with an eye toward adding excitement and flair to what is now pedestrian."

She heard him suck in his breath but continued before he could rage. "Mr. Cocharan contracted me to turn this restaurant into the finest establishment in the city. I fully intend to do just that. Now, I'd like to observe the staff in lunch preparations." Unzipping her leather folder, Summer pulled out a note pad and pen. Without another word she began walking through the busy kitchen.

The staff, she decided after a few moments, was well trained and more orderly than many. Credit Max. Cleanliness was obviously a first priority. Another point for Max. She watched a cook expertly bone a chicken. Not bad, Summer decided. The grill was sizzling, pots steaming. Lifting a lid, she ladeled out a small portion of the soup du jour. She sampled it, holding the taste on her tongue a moment.

"Basil," she said simply, then walked away. Another cook drew apple pies from an oven. The scent was strong and wholesome. Good, she mused, but any experienced grandmother could do the same. What was needed was some pizzazz. People would come to this restaurant for what they wouldn't get at home. Charlottes, Clafouti, flambécs.

The structural changes came from her practical side, but the menu—the menu stemmed from her creativity, which was always paramount.

As she surveyed the kitchen, the staff, drew in the smells, absorbed the sounds, Summer felt the first real stirrings of excitement. She would do it, and she would do it for her own satisfaction just as much as in answer to Blake's challenge. When she was finished, this kitchen would bear her mark. It would be different entirely from jetting from one place to the next to create a single memorable dish. This would have continuity, stability. A year from now, five years from now, this kitchen would still retain her touch, her influence.

The thought pleased her more than she'd expected. She'd never looked for continuity, only the flash of an individual triumph. And wouldn't she be behind the scenes here? She might be in the kitchen in Milan or Athens, but the guests in the dining room knew who was preparing the Charlotte Royal. Clients wouldn't come into the restaurant anticipating a Summer Lyndon dessert, but a Cocharan Hotel meal.

Even as she mulled the thought over in her mind, she found it didn't matter. Why, she was still unsure. For now, she only knew the pleasurable excitement of planning. *Think about it later,* she advised herself as she made a final note. There were months to worry about consequences, reasons, pitfalls. She wanted to begin, get elbow deep in a project she now, for whatever reason, considered peculiarly her own.

Slipping her folder under her arm, she walked out. She couldn't wait to start working on menus.

Chapter 6

Russian Beluga Malasol Caviar—that should be available from lunch to late-night dining. All night through
room service.

Summer made another scrawled note. During the
past two weeks, she'd changed the projected menu a
dozen times. After one abortive session with Max, she'd
opted to go solo on the task. She knew the ambience
she wanted to create, and how to do so through food.

To save herself time, she'd set up a small office in a
storage room off the kitchen. There, she could oversee
the staff and the beginnings of the remodeling while
having enough privacy to work on what was now her
pet project.

Avoiding Blake had been easy because she'd kept
herself so thoroughly busy. And it appeared he was just
as involved in some complicated corporate deal. Buying out another hotel chain, if rumor were fact. Summer

had little interest in that, for her concentration focused on items like medallions of veal in champagne sauce.

As long as the remodeling was going on, the staff remained in a constant state of panic or near panic. She'd come to accept that. Most of the kitchens she'd worked in were full of the tension and terror only a cook would understand. Perhaps it was that creative tension, and the terror of failure, that helped form the best meals.

For the most part, she left the staff supervision to Max. She interfered with the routine he'd established as little as possible, incorporating the changes she'd initiated unobtrusively. She'd learned the qualities of diplomacy and power from her father. If it placated Max at all, it wasn't apparent in his attitude toward Summer. That remained icily polite. Summer shrugged this off and concentrated on perfecting the entrées her kitchen would offer.

Calf's Liver Berlinoise. An excellent entrée, not as popular certainly as a broiled filet or prime rib, but excellent. As long as she didn't have to eat it, Summer thought with a smirk as she noted it down.

Once she'd organized the meat and poultry, she'd put her mind to the seafood. And naturally there had to be a cold buffet available twenty-four hours a day through room service. That was something else to work out. Soups, appetizers, salads—all of those had to be considered, decided on and confirmed before she began on the desserts. And at the moment, she'd have traded any of the elegant offerings jotted down in front of her for a cheeseburger on a sesame seed bun and a bag of chips.

"So this is where you've been hiding." Blake leaned against the doorway. He'd just completed a grueling four-hour meeting and had fully intended to go up to his suite for a long shower and a quiet, solitary meal. Instead, he'd found himself heading for the kitchen, and Summer.

She looked as she had the first time he'd seen her— her hair down, her feet bare. On the table in front of her were reams of scrawled-on paper and a half-empty glass of diluted soda. Behind her, boxes were stacked, sacks piled. The room smelled faintly of pine cleaner and cardboard. In her own way, she looked competent and completely in charge.

"Not hiding," she corrected. "Working." Tired, she thought. He looked tired. It showed around the eyes. "Been busy? We haven't seen you down here for the past couple of weeks."

"Busy enough." Stepping inside, he began to poke through her notes.

"Wheeling and dealing from what I hear." She leaned back, realizing all at once that her back ached. "Taking over the Hamilton chain."

He glanced up, then shrugged and looked back at her notes again. "It's a possibility."

"Discreet." She smiled, wishing she weren't quite so glad to see him again. "Well, while you've been playing Monopoly, I've been dealing with more intimate matters." When he glanced at her again, with his brow raised exactly as she'd expected it to be, she laughed. "Food, Blake, is the most basic and personal of desires, no matter what anyone might say to the contrary. For many, eating is a ritual experienced three times a day. It's a chef's job to make each experience memorable."

"For you, eating's a jaunt through adolescence."

"As I said," Summer continued mildly, "food is very personal."

"Agreed." After another glance around the room, he looked back at her. "Summer, it's not necessary for you to work in a storage room. It's a simple matter to set you up in a suite."

She pushed through the papers, looking for her list on poultry. "This is convenient to the kitchen."

"There's not even a window. The place is packed with boxes."

"No distractions." She shrugged. "If I'd wanted a suite, I'd have asked for one. For the moment, this suits me." And it's several hundred feet away from you, she added silently. "Since you're here, you might want to see what I've been doing."

He lifted a sheet of paper that listed appetizers. "*Coquilles St. Jacques, Escargots Bourguignonne, Pâté de Campagne.* Is it too personal a question to ask if you ever eat what you recommend?"

"From time to time, if I trust the chef. You'll see, if you go more thoroughly through my notes, that I want to offer a more sophisticated menu, because the American palate is becoming more sophisticated."

Blake smiled at the term *American,* and the way she said it, before he sat across from her. "Is it?"

"It's been a slow process," she said dryly. "Today, you can find a good food processor in almost every kitchen. With one, and a competent cookbook, even you could make an acceptable mousse."

"Amazing."

"Therefore," she continued, ignoring him, "to lure people into a restaurant where they'll pay, and pay well to be fed, you have to offer them the superb. A few blocks down the street, they can get a wholesome, filling meal for a fraction of what they'll pay in the

Cocharan House." Summer folded her hands and rested her chin on them. "So you have to give them a very special ambience, incomparable service and exquisite food." She picked up her soda and sipped. "Personally, I'd rather pick up a take-out pizza and eat it at home, but…" She shrugged.

Blake scanned the next sheet. "Because you like pizza, or you like being alone?"

"Both. Now—"

"Do you stay out of restaurants because you spend so much time in a kitchen behind them or because you simply don't like being in a group?"

She opened her mouth to answer and found she didn't know. Uncomfortable, she toyed with her soda. "You're getting more personal, and off the point."

"I don't think so. You're telling me we have to appeal to people who're becoming sophisticated enough to make dishes that were once almost exclusively professionally prepared, as well as draw in clientele who might prefer a quick, less expensive meal around the corner. You, due to your profession and your taste, fall into both categories. What would a restaurant have to offer not only to bring you in, but to make you want to come back?"

A logical question. Summer frowned at it. She hated logical questions because they left you no choice but to answer. "Privacy," she answered at length. "It isn't an easy thing to accomplish in a restaurant, and of course, not everyone looks for it. Many go out to eat to see and be seen. Some, like myself, prefer at least the illusion of solitude. To accomplish both, you have to have a certain number of tables situated in such a way that they seem removed from the rest."

"Easily enough done with the right lighting, a clever arrangement of foliage."

"The key words are right and clever."

"And privacy is your prerequisite in choosing a restaurant."

"I don't generally eat in them," Summer said with a restless movement of her shoulders. "But if I do, privacy ranks equally with atmosphere, food and service."

"Why?"

She began to push the papers together on her desk and stack them. "That's definitely a personal question."

"Yes." He covered her hands with one of his to still them. "Why?"

She stared at him a moment, certain she wouldn't answer. Then she found herself drawn by the quiet look and the gentle touch. "I suppose it stems back to eating in so many restaurants as a child. And I suppose one of the reasons I first became interested in cooking was as a defense against the interminable ritual of eating out. My mother was—is—of the type who goes out to see and be seen. My father often considered eating out a business. So much of my parents' lives, and therefore mine, was public. I simply prefer my own way."

Now that he was touching her, he wanted more. Now that he was learning of her, he wanted all. He should have known better than to believe it would be otherwise. He'd nearly convinced himself that he had his feelings for her under control. But now, sitting in the cramped storage room with kitchen sounds just outside the door, he wanted her as much—more—than ever.

"I wouldn't consider you an introvert, or a recluse."

"No." She didn't even notice that she'd laced her fingers with his. There was something so comfortable, so right about the gesture. "I simply like to keep my private life just that. Mine and private."

"Yet, in your field, you're quite a celebrity." He shifted and under the table his leg brushed against hers. He felt the warmth glow through him and the need double.

Without thinking, she moved her leg so that it brushed his again. The muscles in her thighs loosened. "Perhaps. Or you might say my desserts are celebrities."

Blake lifted their joined hands and studied them. Hers was shades lighter than his, inches smaller and more narrow. She wore a sapphire, oval, deeply blue in an ornate antique setting that made her fingers look that much more elegant. "Is that what you want?"

She moistened her lips, because when his eyes came back to hers they were intense and as darkly blue as the stone on her hand. "I want to be successful. I want to be considered the very best at what I do."

"Nothing more?"

"No, nothing." Why was she breathless? she asked herself frantically. Young girls got breathless—or romantics. She was neither.

"When you have that?" Blake rose, drawing her to her feet without effort. "What else?"

Because they were standing, she had to angle her head to keep her eyes level with his. "It's enough." As she said it, Summer had her first doubts of the truth of that statement. "What about you?" she countered. "Aren't you looking for success—more success? The finest hotels, the finest restaurants."

"I'm a businessman." Slowly, he walked around the table until nothing separated them. Their hands were still joined. "I have a standard to maintain or improve.

I'm also a man." He reached for her hair, then let it flow through his fingers. "And there're things other than account books I think about."

They were close now. Her body brushed his and caused her skin to hum. She forgot all the rules she'd set out for both of them and reached up to touch his cheek. "What else do you think about?"

"You." His hand was at her waist, then sliding gently up her back as he drew her closer. "I think very much about you, and this."

Lips touched—softly. Eyes remained open and aware. Pulses throbbed. Desire tugged.

Lips parted—slowly. A look said everything there was to say. Pulses hammered. Desire tore free.

She was in his arms, clinging, greedy, burning. Every hour of the past two weeks, all the work, the planning, the rules, melted away under a blaze of passion. If she sensed impatience in him, it only matched her own. The kiss was hard, long, desperate. Body strained against body in exquisite torment.

Tighter. Whether she said the word aloud or merely thought it, he seemed to understand. His arms curved around her, crushing her to him as she wanted to be. She felt the lines and planes of his body mold to hers even as his mouth molded to hers, and somehow she seemed softer than she'd ever imagined herself to be.

Feminine, sultry, delicate, passionate. Was it possible to be all at once? The need grew and expanded—for him—for a taste and touch she'd found nowhere else. The sound she made against his lips came as much from confusion as from pleasure.

Good God, how could a woman take him so far with only a kiss? He was already more than half-mad for her.

Control was losing its meaning in a need that was much more imperative. Her skin would slide like silk under his hands—he knew it. He had to feel it.

He slipped a hand under her sweater and found her. Beneath his palm, her heartbeat pounded. Not enough. The thought raced through his mind that it would never be enough. But questions, reason, were for later. Burying his face against her throat he tasted her skin. The scent he remembered lingered there, enticing him further, drawing him closer to the edge where there could be no turning back. The fatigue he'd felt when he'd entered the room vanished. The tension he felt whenever she was near evaporated. At that moment, he considered her completely his without realizing he'd wanted exclusive possession.

Her hair brushed over his face, cloud soft, fragrant. It made him think of Paris, right before the heat of summer took over from spring. But her skin was hot and vibrating, making him envision long humid nights when lovemaking would be slow, endlessly slow. He wanted her there, in the cramped little room where the floor was littered with boxes.

She couldn't think. Summer could feel her bones dissolve and her mind empty. Sensation after sensation poured over her. She could have drowned in them. Yet she wanted more—she could feel her body craving more, wanting all. Storm, thunder, heat. Just once…the longing seeped into her with whispering promises and dark pleasure. She could let herself be his, take him as hers. Just once. And then…

With a moan, she tore her mouth from his and buried her face against his shoulder. Once with Blake would haunt her for the rest of her life.

"Come upstairs," Blake murmured. Tilting her head back, he ran kisses over her face. "Come up with me where I can make love with you properly. I want you in my bed, Summer. Soft, naked, mine."

"Blake..." She turned her face away and tried to steady her breathing. What had happened to her—when—how? "This is a mistake—for both of us."

"No." Taking her by the shoulders, he kept her facing him. "This is right—for both of us."

"I can't get involved—"

"You already are."

She let out a deep breath. "No further than this. It's already more than I intended."

When she started to back away, he held her firmly in front of him. "I need a reason, Summer, a damn good one."

"You confuse me." Summer blurted it out before she realized it, then swore at the admission. "Damn it, I don't like to be confused."

"And I ache for you." His voice was as impatient as hers, his body as tense. "I don't like to ache."

"We've got a problem," she managed, dragging a hand through her hair.

"I want you." Something in the way he said it made her hand pause in midair and her gaze lift to his. There was nothing casual in those three words. "I want you more than I've ever wanted anyone. I'm not comfortable with that."

"A big problem," she whispered and sat unsteadily on the edge of the table.

"There's one way to solve it."

She managed a smile. "Two ways," she corrected. "And I think mine's the safest."

"Safest." Reaching down, he ran a fingertip over the curve of her cheek. "You want safety, Summer?"

"Yes." It was easily said because she'd discovered it was true. Safety was something she'd never thought about until Blake, because she'd never felt endangered until then. "I've made myself a lot of promises, Blake, set a lot of goals. Instinct tells me you could interfere. I always go with my instincts."

"I've no intention of interfering with your goals."

"Nevertheless, I have a few very strict rules. One of them is never to become intimate with a business associate or a client. In one point of view, you fall into both categories."

"How do you intend to prevent it from happening? Intimacies come in a lot of degrees, Summer. You and I have already reached some of them."

How could she deny it? She wanted to run from it. "We managed to keep out of each other's way for two weeks," she pointed out. "It's simply a matter of continuing to do so. Both of us are very busy at the moment, so it shouldn't be too difficult."

"Eventually one of us is going to break the rules."

And it could be me just as easily as it could be him, she thought. "I can't think about eventually, only about now. I'll stay downstairs and do my job. You stay upstairs and do yours."

"Like hell," Blake muttered and took a step forward. Summer was halfway to her feet when a knock sounded on her door.

"Mr. Cocharan, there's a phone call for you. Your secretary says it's urgent."

Blake controlled his fury. "I'll be there." He gave Summer a long, hard look. "We're not finished."

She waited until he'd reached the door. "I can turn this place into a palace or a greasy spoon," she said quietly. "It's your choice."

Turning around, he measured her. "Blackmail?"

"Insurance," she corrected and smiled. "Play it my way, Blake and everybody's happy."

"Your point, Summer," he acknowledged with a nod. "This time."

When the door closed behind him, she sat again. She may have outmaneuvered him this time, she mused, but the game was far from over.

Summer gave herself another hour before she left her temporary office to go back to the kitchen. Busboys wheeled in and out with trays of dirty dishes. The dishwasher hummed busily. Pots simmered. Someone sang as she basted a chicken. Two hours to the dinner rush. In another hour, the panic and confusion would set in.

It was then, when the scent of food hit her, that Summer realized she hadn't eaten. Deciding to kill two birds with one stone, she began to root through the cupboards. She'd find something for a late lunch, and see just how provisions were organized.

She couldn't complain about the latter. The cupboards were not only well stocked, they were systematically stocked. Max had a number of excellent qualities, she thought. A pity an open mind wasn't among them. She continued to scan shelf after shelf, but the item she was looking for was nowhere to be found.

"Ms. Lyndon?"

Hearing Max's voice behind her, Summer slowly closed the cabinet door. She didn't have to turn around to see the cold politeness in his eyes or the tight disapproval of his mouth. She was going to have to do something about this situation before long, she decided. But at the moment she was a bit tired, quite a bit hungry and not in the mood to deal with it.

"Yes, Max." She opened the next door and surveyed the stock.

"Perhaps I can help you find what you're looking for."

"Perhaps. Actually, I'm checking to see how well stocked we are while searching out a jar of peanut butter. Apparently——" she closed that door and went on to the next "——we're very well stocked indeed, and very well organized."

"My kitchen is completely organized," Max began stiffly. "Even in the midst of all this—this carpentry."

"The carpentry's almost finished," she said easily. "I think the new ovens are working out well."

"To some, new is always better."

"To some," she countered, "progress is always a death knell. Where do I find the peanut butter, Max? I really want a sandwich."

This time she did turn, in time to see his eyebrows rise and his mouth purse. "Below," he said with a hint of a smirk as he pointed. "We keep such things on hand for the children's menu."

"Good." Unoffended, Summer crouched down and found it. "Would you like to join me?"

"Thank you, no. I have work to do."

"Fine." Summer took two slices of bread and began to spread the peanut butter. "Tomorrow, nine o'clock, you and I will go over the proposed menus in my office."

"I'm very busy at nine."

"No," she corrected mildly. "We're very busy from seven to nine, then things tend to ease off, particularly midweek, until the lunch rush. Nine o'clock," she repeated over his huff of breath. "Excuse me, I have to get some jelly for this."

Leaving Max gritting his teeth, Summer went to one of the large refrigerators. Pompous, narrow-minded ass, she thought as she found a restaurant-sized jar of grape jelly. As long as he continued to be uncooperative and stiff, things were going to be difficult. More than once, she'd expected Max to turn in his resignation—and there were times, though she hated to be so hard line, that she wished he would.

The changes in the kitchen were already making a difference, she thought as she closed the second slice of bread over the jelly and peanut butter. Any fool could see that the extra range, the more efficient equipment, tightened the flow of preparation and improved the quality of food. Annoyed, she bit into her sandwich just as excited chatter broke out behind her.

"Max'll be furious. *Fur-i-ous.*"

"Nothing he can do about it now."

"Except yell and throw things."

Perhaps it was the underlying glee in the last statement that made Summer turn. She saw two cooks huddled over the stove. "What'll Max be furious about?" she asked over another mouthful of sandwich.

The two faces turned to her. Both were flushed either from the heat of the stove or excitement. "Maybe you ought to tell him, Ms. Lyndon," one of the cooks said after a moment of indecision. The glee was still there, she noticed, barely suppressed.

"Tell him what?"

"Julio and Georgia eloped—we just got word from Julio's brother. They took off for Hawaii."

Julio and Georgia? After a quick flip through her mental file, Summer placed them as two cooks who worked the four-to-eleven shift. A glance at her watch told her they were already fifteen minutes late.

"I take it they won't be coming in today."

"They quit." One of the cooks snapped his fingers. "Just like that." He glanced across the room where Max was babying a rack of lamb. "Max'll hit the roof."

"He won't solve anything up there," she murmured. "So we're two short for the dinner shift."

"Three," the second cook corrected. "Charlie called in sick an hour ago."

"Wonderful." Summer finished off her sandwich, then rolled up her sleeves. "Then the rest of us better get to work."

With an apron covering her jeans and sweater, Summer took over one section of the new counter. Perhaps it wasn't her usual style, she mused as she began mixing the first oversized bowl of cake batter, but circumstances called for immediate action. And, she thought as she licked some batter from her knuckle, they damn well better get the stereo speakers in before the end of the week. Summer might bake without Chopin in an emergency once, but she wouldn't do it twice.

She was arranging several layers of Black Forest cake in the oven when Max spoke over her shoulder.

"You're making yourself some dessert now?" he began.

"No." Summer set the timer, then moved back to the counter to start preparations on chocolate mousse. "It seems there's been a wedding and an illness—though

I don't think the first has anything to do with the second. We're shorthanded tonight. I'm taking over the desserts, Max, and I don't exchange small talk when I'm working."

"Wedding? What wedding?"

"Julio and Georgia eloped to Hawaii, and Charlie's sick. I have this mousse to deal with at the moment."

"Eloped!" he exploded. "Eloped without my permission?"

She took the time to look over her shoulder. "I suppose Charlie should have checked with you before he got sick as well. Save the hysterics, Max, and have someone peel me some apples. I want to do a *Charlotte de Pommes* after this."

"Now you're changing my menu!" he exploded.

She whirled, fire in her eyes. "I have a dozen different desserts to make in a very short time. I'd advise you to stay out of my way while I do it. I'm not known for graciousness when I'm cooking."

He sucked in his stomach and pulled back his shoulders. "We'll see what Mr. Cocharan has to say about this."

"Terrific. Keep him out of my way, too, for the next three hours or someone's going to end up with a face full of my best whipped cream." Spinning back around, she went to work.

There wasn't time, she couldn't take the time, to study and approve each dessert as it was completed. Later, Summer would think of the hours as assembly line work. At the moment, she was too pressed to think. Julio and Georgia had been the dessert chefs. It was now up to her to do the work of two people in the same amount of time.

She ignored the menu and went with what she knew she could make from memory. The diners that evening were in for a surprise, but as she finished topping the second Black Forest cake, Summer decided it would be a pleasant one. She arranged the cherries quickly, cursing the need to rush. Impossible to create when one was on such a ridiculous timetable, she thought, and muttered bad temperedly under her breath.

By six, the bulk of the baking was done and she concentrated on the finishing touches of a line of desserts designed to satisfy an army. Chocolate icing there, a dab of cream here, a garnish, a spoon of jam or jelly. She was hot, her arms aching. Her once-white apron was streaked and splashed. No one spoke to her, because she wouldn't answer. No one approached her, because she tended to snarl.

Occasionally she would indicate with a wave of her arm a section of dishes that were to be taken away. This was done instantly, and without a sound. If there was talk, it was done in undertones and out of her hearing. None of them had ever seen anything quite like Summer Lyndon on a roll.

"Problems?"

Summer heard Blake speak quietly over her shoulder but didn't turn. "Cars are made this way," she mumbled, "not desserts."

"Early reports from the dining room are more than favorable."

She grunted and rolled out pastry dough for tarts. "The next time I'm in Hawaii, I'm going to look up Julio and Georgia and knock their heads together."

"A bit testy, aren't you?" he murmured and earned

a lethal glare. "And hot." He touched her cheek with a fingertip. "How long have you been at it?"

"Since a bit after four." After shrugging his hand away she began to rapidly cut out pastry shells. Blake watched, surprised. He'd never seen her work quickly before. "Move."

He stepped back but continued to watch her. By his calculations, she'd worked on the menus in the windowless storage room for more than six hours, and had now been on her feet for nearly three. Too small, he thought as a protective urge moved through him. Too delicate.

"Summer, can't someone else take over now? You should rest."

"No one touches my desserts." This was said in such a strong, authoritative voice that the image of a delicate flower vanished. He grinned despite himself.

"Anything I can do?"

"I'll want some champagne in an hour. Dom Perignon, '73."

He nodded as an idea began to form in his mind. She smelled like the desserts lined on the counter in front of her. Tempting, delicious. Since he'd met her, Blake had discovered he possessed a very demanding sweet tooth. "Have you eaten?"

"A sandwich a few hours ago," she said testily. "Do you think I could eat at a time like this?"

He glanced at the sumptuous array of cakes and pastries. He could smell delicately roasted meats, spicy sauces. Blake shook his head. "No, of course not. I'll be back."

Summer muttered something, then fluted the edges of her pastry shells.

Chapter 7

By eight o'clock, Summer was finished, and not in the best of humors. For nearly four hours, she'd whipped, rolled, fluted and baked. Often, she'd spent twice that time, and twice that effort, perfecting one single dish. That was art. This, on the other hand, had been labor, plain and simple.

She felt no flash of triumph, no glow of self-satisfaction, but simply fatigue. An army cook, she thought disdainfully; it was hardly different from producing the quickest and easiest for the masses. At the moment, if she never saw the inside of another egg again, it would be too soon.

"There should be enough made up to get us through the dinner hour, and room service tonight," she told Max briskly as she pulled off her soiled apron. Critically she frowned at a line of fruit tarts. More than one of them were less than perfect in shape. If there'd been time, she'd have discarded them and made others. "I want someone in touch with personnel first thing in the morning to see about hiring two more dessert chefs."

"Mr. Cocharan has already contacted personnel." Max stood stiffly, not wanting to give an inch, though he'd been impressed with how quickly and efficiently she'd avoided what could easily have been a catastrophe. He clung tightly to his resentment, even though he had to admit—to himself—that she baked the best apricot tart he'd ever tasted.

"Fine." Summer ran a hand over the back of her neck. The skin there was damp, the muscles drawn taut. "Nine o'clock tomorrow, Max, in my office. Let's see if we can get organized. I'm going home to soak in a hot tub until morning."

Blake had been leaning against the wall, watching her work. It had been fascinating to see just how quickly the temperamental artist had put her nose to the grindstone and produced.

She'd shown him two things he hadn't expected—a speed and lack of histrionics when she'd been forced to deal with a less than ideal situation, and a calm acceptance of what was obviously a touchy area with Max. However much she played the role of prima donna, when her back was against the wall, she handled herself very well.

When she removed her apron, he stepped forward. "Give you a lift?"

Summer glanced over at him as she pulled the pins from her hair. It fell to her shoulders, tousled, and a bit damp at the ends from the heat. "I have my car."

"And I have mine." The arrogance, with that trace of aloofness, was still there, even when he smiled.

"And a bottle of Dom Perignon, '73. My driver can pick you up in the morning."

She told herself she was only interested in the wine. The cool smile had nothing to do with her decision. "Properly chilled?" she asked, arching her brow. "The champagne, that is."

"Of course."

"You're on, Mr. Cocharan. I never turn down champagne."

"The car's out in the back." He took her hand rather than her arm as she'd expected. Before she could make any counter move, he was leading her from the kitchen. "Would it embarrass you if I said I was very impressed with what you did this evening?"

She was used to accolades, even expected them. Somehow, she couldn't remember ever getting so much pleasure from one before. She moved her shoulders, hoping to lighten her own response. "I make it my business to be impressive. It doesn't embarrass me."

Perhaps if she hadn't been tired, he wouldn't have seen through the glib answer so easily. When they reached his car, Blake turned and took her by the shoulders. "You worked very hard in there."

"Just part of the service."

"No," he corrected, soothing the muscles. "That's not what you were hired for."

"When I signed the contract, that became my kitchen. What goes out of it has to satisfy my standards, my pride."

"Not an easy job."

"You wanted the best."

"Apparently I got it."

She smiled, though she wanted badly just to sit down. "You definitely got it. Now, you did say something about champagne?"

"Yes, I did." He opened the door for her. "You smell of vanilla."

"I earned it." When she sat, she let out a long, pleasurable sigh. Champagne, she thought, a hot bath with mountains of bubbles, and smooth, cool sheets. In that order. "Chances are," she murmured, "even as we speak, someone in there is taking the first bite of my Black Forest cake."

Blake shut the driver's door, then glanced at her as he started the ignition. "Does it feel odd?" he asked. "Having strangers eat something you spent so much time and care creating?"

"Odd?" Summer stretched back, enjoying the plush luxury of the seat and the view of the dusky sky through the sun roof. "A painter creates on canvas for whoever will look, a composer creates a symphony for whoever will listen."

"True enough." Blake maneuvered his way onto the street and into the traffic. The sun was red and low. The night promised to be clear. "But wouldn't it be more gratifying to be there when your desserts are served?"

She closed her eyes, completely relaxed for the first time in hours. "When one cooks in one's own kitchen for friends, relatives, it can be a pleasure or a duty. Then there might be the satisfaction of watching something you've cooked being appreciated. But again, it's a pleasure or a duty, not a profession."

"You rarely eat what you cook."

"I rarely cook for myself," she countered. "Except the simpler things."

"Why?"

"When you cook for yourself, there's no one there to clean up the mess."

He laughed and turned into a parking lot. "In your own odd way you're a very practical woman."

"In every way I'm a practical woman." Lazily, she opened her eyes. "Why did we stop?"

"Hungry?"

"I'm always hungry after I work." Turning her head, she saw the blue neon sign of a pizza parlor.

"Knowing your tastes by now, I thought you'd find this the perfect accompaniment to the champagne."

She grinned as the fatigue was replaced with the first real stirrings of hunger. "Absolutely perfect."

"Wait here," he told her as he opened the door. "I had someone call ahead and order it when I saw you were nearly finished."

Grateful, and touched, Summer leaned back and closed her eyes again. When was the last time she'd allowed anyone to take care of her? she wondered. If memory served her, the last time she'd been pampered she'd been eight, and cranky with a case of chicken pox. Independence had always been expected of her, by her parents, and by herself. But tonight, this one time, it was a rather sweet feeling to let someone else make the arrangements with her comfort in mind.

And she had to admit, she hadn't expected simple consideration from Blake. Style, yes, credit where credit was due, yes—but not consideration. He'd put in a hard day himself, she thought, remembering how tired he'd looked that afternoon. Still, he'd waited long past the time when he could have had his own dinner in comfort, relaxed in his own way. He'd waited until she was finished.

Surprises, she mused. Blake Cocharan III definitely had some surprises up his sleeve. She'd always been a sucker for them.

When Blake opened the car door, the scent of pizza rolled pleasurably inside. Summer took the box from him, then leaned over and kissed his cheek. "Thanks."

"I should've tried pizza before," he murmured.

She settled back again, letting her eyes close and her lips curve. "Don't forget the champagne. Those are two of my biggest weaknesses."

"I've made a note of it." Blake pulled out of the parking lot and joined the traffic again. Her simple gratitude shouldn't have surprised him. It certainly shouldn't have moved him. He had the feeling she would have had the same low-key, pleased reaction if he'd presented her with a full-length sable or a bracelet of blue-white diamonds. With Summer, it wouldn't be the gift, but the nature of the giving. He found he liked that idea very much. She wasn't a woman who was easily impressed, he mused, yet she was a woman who could be easily pleased.

Summer did something she rarely did unless she was completely alone. She relaxed, fully. Though her eyes were closed, she was no longer sleepy, but aware. She could feel the smooth motion of the car beneath her, hear the rumble of traffic outside the windows. She had only to draw in a breath to smell the tangy scent of sauce and spice. The car was spacious, but she could sense the warmth of Blake's body across the seat.

Pleasant. That was the word that drifted through her

mind. So pleasant, there seemed to be no need for caution, for defenses. It was a pity, she reflected, that they weren't driving aimlessly....

Strange, she'd never chosen to do anything aimlessly. And yet, tonight, to drive...along a long, deserted beach—with the moon full, shining off the water, and the sand white. You'd be able to hear the surf ebb and flow, and see the hundreds of stars you so rarely noticed in the city. You'd smell the salt and feel the spray. The moist, warm air would flow over your skin.

She felt the car swing off the road, then purr to a stop. For an extra moment, Summer held on to the fantasy.

"What're you thinking?"

"About the beach," she answered. "Stars." She caught herself, surprised that she'd indulged in what could only be termed romanticism. "I'll take the pizza," she said, straightening. "You can bring the champagne."

He put a hand on her arm, lightly but it stopped her. Slowly he ran a finger down it. "You like the beach?"

"I never really thought about it." At the moment, she found she'd like nothing better than to rest her head against his shoulder and watch waves surge against the shore. Star counting. Why should she want to indulge in something so foolish now when she never had before? "For some reason, it just seemed like the night for it." And she wondered if she were answering his question or her own.

"Since there's no beach, we'll just have to come up with something else. How's your imagination?"

"Good enough." Quite good enough, Summer thought, to see where she'd end up if she didn't change the mood—hers as well as his. "And at the moment, I imagine the pizza's getting cold, and the champagne warm." Opening the door, she climbed out with the box in hand. Once inside the building, Summer started up the stairs.

"Does the elevator ever work?" Blake shifted the bag in his arm and joined her.

"Off and on—mostly it's off. Personally, I don't trust it."

"In that case, why'd you pick the fourth floor?"

She smiled as they rounded the second landing. "I like the view—and the fact that salesmen are usually discouraged when they're faced with more than two flights of steps."

"You could've chosen a more modern building, with a view, a security system and a working elevator."

"I look at modern tools as essential, a new car, well tuned, as imperative." Drawing out her keys, Summer jiggled them lightly as they approached her door. "As to living arrangements, I'm a bit more open-minded. My flat in Paris has temperamental plumbing and the most exquisite cornices I've ever seen."

When she opened the door, the scent of roses was overwhelming. There were a dozen white in a straw basket, a dozen red in a Sevres vase, a dozen yellow in a pottery jug and a dozen pink in Venetian glass.

"Run into a special at the florist's?"

Summer raised her brows as she set the pizza on the dinette. "I never buy flowers for myself. These are from Enrico."

Blake set the bag next to the box and drew out the champagne. "All?"

"He's a bit flamboyant—Enrico Gravanti—you might've heard of him. Italian shoes and bags."

Two hundred million dollars worth of shoes and bags, as Blake recalled. He flicked a finger down a rose petal. "I hadn't heard Gravanti was in town. He normally stays at the Cocharan House."

"No, he's in Rome." As she spoke, Summer went into the kitchen for plates and glasses. "He wired these when I agreed to make the cake for his birthday next month."

"Four dozen roses for a cake?"

"Five," Summer corrected as she came back in. "There's another dozen in the bedroom. They're rather lovely, a kind of peach color." In anticipation, she held out both glasses. "And, after all, it is one of my cakes."

With a nod of acknowledgment, Blake loosened the cork. Air fizzed out while the champagne bubbled toward the lip of the bottle. "So, I take it you'll be going to Italy to bake it."

"I don't intend to ship it air freight." She watched the pale gold liquid rise in the glass as Blake poured. "I should only be in Rome two days, three at most." Raising the glass to her lips, she sipped, eyes closed, senses keen. "Excellent." She sipped again before she opened her eyes and smiled. "I'm starving." After lifting the lid on the box, she breathed deep. "Pepperoni."

"Somehow I thought it suited you."

With a laugh, an easy one, she sat down. "Very perceptive. Shall I serve?"

"Please." And as she began to, Blake flicked on his lighter and set the three staggered-length tapers she had on the table burning. "Champagne and pizza," he said as he turned off the lights. "That demands candlelight, don't you think?"

"If you like." When he sat, Summer lifted her first

piece. The cheese was hot enough to make her catch her breath, the sauce tangy. "Mmmm. Wonderful."

"Has it occurred to you that we spend a great deal of our time together eating?"

"Hmm—well, it's something I thoroughly enjoy. I always try to look at eating as a pleasure rather than a physical necessity. It adds something."

"Pounds, usually."

She shrugged and reached for the champagne. "Of course, if one isn't wise enough to take one's pleasure in small doses. Greed is what adds pounds, ruins the complexion and makes one miserable."

"You don't succumb to greed?"

She remembered abruptly that it had been just that, exactly that, that she'd felt for him. But she'd controlled it, Summer reminded herself. She hadn't succumbed. "No." She ate slowly, savoring. "I don't. In my profession, it would be disastrous."

"How do you keep your pleasure in small doses?"

She wasn't sure she trusted the way the question came out. Taking her time, she set a second piece on each plate. "I'd rather have one spoonful of a superb chocolate soufflé than an entire plateful of food that doesn't have flair."

Blake took another bite of pizza. "And this has flair?"

She smiled because it was so obviously not the sort of meal he was used to. "An excellent balance of spices— perhaps just a tad heavy on the oregano—a good marriage of sauce and crust, the proper handling of cheese and the bite of pepperoni. With the proper use of the senses, almost any meal can be memorable."

"With the proper use of the senses," Blake countered, "other things can be memorable."

She reached for her glass again, her eyes laughing over the rim. "We're speaking of food. Taste, of course, is paramount, but appearance…" He linked his hand with hers and she found herself watching him. "Your eyes tell you first of the desire to taste." His face was lean, the eyes a deep blue she found continuously compelling.…

"Then a scent teases you, entices you." His was dark, woodsy, tempting.…

"You hear the way champagne bubbles into a glass and you want to experience it." Or the way he said her name, quietly.

"After all this," she continued in a voice that was beginning to take on a faint huskiness, a faint trace of feeling, "you have the taste, the texture to explore." And his mouth held a flavor she couldn't forget.

"So—" he lifted her hand and pressed his mouth to the palm "—your advice is to savor every aspect of the experience in order to absorb all the pleasure. Then…" Turning her hand over, he brushed his lips, then the tip of his tongue, over her knuckles. "The most basic of desires becomes unique."

In an arrow-straight line, the heat shot up her arm. "No experience is acceptable otherwise."

"And atmosphere?" Lightly, with just a fingertip, he traced the shape of her ear. "Wouldn't you agree that the proper setting can enhance the same experience? Candlelight, for instance."

Their faces were closer now. She could see the soft shifting light casting shadows, mysteries. "Outside devices can often add more intensity to a mood."

"You could call it romance." He took his fingertip down the length of her jawline.

"You could." Champagne never went to her head, yet her head was light. Slowly, luxuriously, her body was softening. She made an effort to remember why she should allow neither to happen, but no answer came.

"And romance, for some, is another very elemental need."

"For some," he murmured when his lips followed the trail of his fingertip.

"But not for you." He nipped at her lips and found them soft, and warm.

"No, not for me." But her sigh was as soft and warm as her lips

"A practical woman." He was raising her to her feet so that their bodies could touch.

"Yes." She tilted her head back, inviting the exploration of his lips.

"Candlelight doesn't move you?"

"It's only an attractive device." She curved her arms up his back to bring him closer. "As chefs, we're taught that such things can lend the right mood to our meals."

"And it wouldn't matter if I told you that you were beautiful? In the full sun where your skin's flawless— in candlelight, which turns it to porcelain. It wouldn't matter," he continued as he ran a line of moist heat down her throat, "if I told you you excite me as no other woman ever has? Just looking at you makes me want, touching you drives me mad."

"Words," she managed, though her head was spinning. "I don't need—"

Then his mouth covered hers. The one long, deep kiss made lies of all her practical claims. Tonight, though she'd never wanted such things before, she wanted the romance of soft words, soft lights. She wanted the slow, savoring loving that emptied the mind and made a furnace of the body. Tonight she wanted, and there was only one man. If tomorrow there were consequences, tomorrow was hours away. He was here.

She didn't resist as he lifted her. Tonight, if only for a short while, she'd be fragile, soft. She heard him blow out the candles and the light scent of melted wax followed them toward the bedroom.

Moonlight. The silvery sorcery of moonlight slipped through the windows. Roses. The fragile fragrance of roses floated on the air. Music. The muted magic of Beethoven drifted in from the apartment below.

There was a breeze. Summer felt it whisper over her face as he placed her on the bed. Atmosphere, she thought hazily. If she had planned on a night of lovemaking, she could have set the stage no better. Perhaps... She drew him down to join her.... Perhaps it was fate.

She could see his eyes. Deep blue, direct, involving. He watched her while doing no more than tracing the shape of her face, of her lips, with his finger. Had anyone ever shown her that kind of tenderness? Had she ever wanted it?

No. And if the answer was no, the answer had abruptly changed. She wanted this new experience, the sweetness she'd always disregarded, and she wanted the man who would bring her both.

Taking his face in her hands, she studied him. This was the man she would share this one completely private moment with, the one who would soon know her body as well as her vulnerabilities. She might have wavered over the trust, reminded herself of the pitfalls—

if she'd been able to resist the need, and the strength, she saw in his eyes.

"Kiss me again," she murmured. "No one's ever made me feel the way you do when you kiss me."

He felt a surge of pleasure, intense, stunning. Lowering his head, he touched his lips to hers, toying with them, watching her as she watched him while their emotions heightened and their need sharpened. Should he have known she'd be even more beautiful in the moonlight, with her hair spread over a pillow? Could he have known that desire for her would be an ache unlike any desire he'd known? Was it still as simple as desire, or had he crossed some line he'd been unaware of? There were no answers now. Answers were for the daylight.

With a moan, he deepened the kiss and felt her body yield beneath his even as her mouth grew avid. Little tongues of passion flickered, still subdued beneath a gentleness they both seemed to need. Odd, because neither of them had needed it before, or often thought to show it.

Her hands were light on his face, over his neck, then slowly combing through his hair. Though his body was hard on hers, there was no demand yet.

Savor me. The thought ran silkily through her mind even as Blake's lips journeyed over her face. Slowly. She'd never known a man with such patience or an arousal so heady. Mouth against mouth, then mouth against skin—each drew her deeper and still deeper into a languor that encompassed both body and mind.

Touch me. And he seemed to understand this fresh need. His hands moved, but still without hurry, over her shoulders, down her sides, then up again to whisper over her breasts—until it was no longer enough for either of them. Then wordlessly they began to undress each other.

Fingers of moonlight fell across exposed flesh—a shoulder, the length of an arm, a lean torso. Luxuriously, Summer ran her hands over Blake's chest and learned the muscle and form. Lazily, he explored the length of her and learned the subtle curves and silk. Even when the last barrier of clothing was drawn away, they didn't rush. So much to touch, taste—and time had no meaning.

The breeze flitted in, but they grew warmer. Wherever her fingers wandered, his flesh would burn, then cool only to burn again. As he took his lips over her, finding pleasure, learning secrets, she began to heat. And demand crept into both of them.

More urgently now, with quick moans, trembling breaths, they took each other further. He hadn't known he could be led, and she'd always refused to be, yet now, one guided the other to the same destination.

Summer felt reality slipping away from her, but had no will to stop it. The music penetrated only faintly into her consciousness, but his murmurs were easily heard. It was his scent, no longer the roses, that titillated. She would feel whatever she was meant to feel, go wherever she was meant to go, as long as he was with her. Along with the strongest physical desire she'd ever known was an emotional need that exploded inside her. She couldn't question it, couldn't refuse it. Her body, mind, heart, ached for him.

With his name trembling on her lips, she took him into her. Then, for both of them, the pleasure was so acute that sanity was forgotten. Sensation—waves, floods, storms—whipped through her. The calm had become a hurricane to revel in. Together, they were swept away.

Had hours passed or minutes? Summer lay in the filtered moonlight and tried to orient herself. She'd never felt quite like this. Sated, exhilarated, exhausted. Once she'd have said it was impossible to be all at once.

She could feel the brush of Blake's hair against her shoulder, the whisper of his breath against her cheek. His scent and hers were mixed now, so that the roses were only an accent. The music had stopped, but she thought she could still hear the echo. His body was pressed into hers, but his weight was a pleasure. She knew, without effort, she could wrap her arms around him and stay just so for the rest of her life. So through the hazy pleasure came the first stirrings of fear.

Oh, God, how far had she gone in such a short time? She'd always been so certain her emotions were perfectly safe. It wasn't the first time she'd been with a man, but she was too aware that it was the first time she'd made love in the true sense of the word.

Mistake. She forced the word into her head even as her heart tried to block it. She had to think, had to be practical. Hadn't she seen what uncontrolled emotions and dreams had done to two intelligent people? Both her parents had spent years moving from relationship to relationship looking for...what?

This, her heart told her, but again she blocked it out. She knew better than to look for something she didn't believe existed. Permanency, commitment—they were illusions. And illusions had no place in her life.

Closing her eyes a moment, she waited for herself to

settle. She was a grown woman, sophisticated enough to understand and accept mutual desire that held no strings. *Treat it lightly,* she warned herself. *Don't pretend it's more than it is.*

But she couldn't resist smoothing his hair as she spoke. "Odd how pizza and champagne affect me."

Raising his head, Blake grinned at her. At the moment, he felt he could've taken on the world. "I think it should be your staple diet." He kissed the curve of her shoulder. "It's going to be mine. Want some more?"

"Pizza and champagne?"

Laughing, he nuzzled her neck. "That, too." He shifted, drawing her against his side. It was one more gesture of intimacy that had something inside her trembling.

Set out the rules, Summer told herself. *Do it now, before...before it would be much too easy to forget.*

"I like being with you," she said quietly.

"And I you." He could see the shadows play on the ceiling, hear the muted sound of traffic outside, but he was still saturated with her.

"Now that we've been together like this, it's going to affect our relationship one of two ways."

Puzzled, he turned his head to look at her. "One of two ways?"

"It's either going to increase the tension while we're working, or alleviate it. I'm hoping it alleviates it."

In the darkness he frowned at her. "What happened just now had absolutely nothing to do with business."

"Whatever you and I do together is bound to affect our working relationship." Moistening her lips, she tried to continue in the same light way. "Making love with you was...personal, but tomorrow morning we're back to being associates. This can't change that—I think it'd be a mistake to let it change the tone of our business dealings." Was she rambling? Was she making sense? She wished desperately that he would say something, anything at all. "I think we both knew this was bound to happen. Now that it has, it's cleared the air."

"Cleared the air?" Infuriated, and to his surprise, hurt, he rose on his elbow. "It did a damn sight more than that, Summer. We both know that, too."

"Let's keep it in perspective." How had she begun this so badly? And how could she keep rambling on when she only wanted to curl up next to him and hold on? "We're both unattached adults who're attracted to each other. On that level, we shouldn't expect any more from each other than's reasonable. On a business level, we both have to expect total involvement."

He wanted to push the business level down her throat. Violently. The emotion didn't please him, nor did the sudden realization that he wanted total involvement on a very personal level. With an effort, he controlled the fury. He needed to ask, and answer, some questions for himself—soon. In the meantime, he needed to keep a cool head.

"Summer, I intend to make love with you often, and when I do, business can go to hell." He ran a hand down her side and felt her body respond. If she wanted rules, he thought furiously, he'd give her rules. His. "When we're here, there isn't any hotel or any restaurant. There's just you and me. Back at Cocharan House, we'll be as professional as you want."

She wasn't certain if she wanted to calmly agree with him or scream in protest. She remained silent.

"And now," he continued, drawing her still closer, "I

want to make love with you again, then I want to sleep with you. At nine o'clock tomorrow, we'll get back to business."

She might have spoken then, but his mouth touched hers. Tomorrow was hours away.

Chapter 8

Damn, it was frustrating. Blake had heard men complain about women, calling them incomprehensible, contradictory, baffling. Because he'd always found it possible to deal with women on a sensible level, he'd never put much credence in any of it, until Summer. Now, he found himself searching for more adjectives. Rising from his desk, Blake paced to the window and frowned out at his view of the city.

When they'd made love the first time, he realized that he'd never known that a woman could be that soft, that giving. Strong—still strong, yes, but with a fragility that had a man lying in velvet. Had it been his imagination, or had she been totally his in every way one person could belong to another? He'd have sworn that for that space of time she'd thought of nothing but him, wanted nothing but him. And yet, before their bodies had cooled, she'd been so practical, so…unemotional.

Damn, wasn't a man supposed to be grateful for that—a man who wanted the pleasure and companionship of a woman without all the complications? He could remember other relationships where a neat set of rules had proven invaluable, but now...

Below, a couple walked along the sidewalk, their arms slung around each other's shoulders. As he watched he imagined them laughing at something no one else would understand. And as he watched, Blake thought of his own statement of the degrees of intimacy. Instinct told him that he and Summer had shared an intimacy as deep as any two people could experience. Not just a merging of bodies, but a touching, a twining, of thoughts and needs and wants that was absolute. But if his instincts had told him one thing, she had told him another. Which was he to believe?

Frustrating, he thought again and turned away from the window. He couldn't deny that he'd gone to her apartment the night before with the idea of seducing her, and putting an end to the tension between them. But he couldn't deny that he'd been seduced after five minutes alone with her. He couldn't see her and not want to touch her. He couldn't hear her laugh without wanting to taste the curve of her lips. Now that he'd made love with her, he wasn't certain a night would pass without his wanting her again.

There must be a term for what he was experiencing. Blake was always more comfortable when he could label something and therefore file it properly. The most efficient heading, the most logical category. What was it called when you thought of a woman when you should be thinking about something else? What name did you give to this constant edgy feeling?

Love... The word crept up on him, not entirely pleasantly. Good God. Uneasy, Blake sat again and stared at the far wall. He was in love with her. It was just as simple—and just as terrifying—as that. He wanted to be with her, to make her laugh, to make her tremble with desire. He wanted to see her eyes glow with temper, and with passion. He wanted to spend quiet evenings, and wild nights, with her. And he was deadly sure he'd want the same thing twenty years down the road.

Since the first time he'd walked down those four flights of stairs from her apartment, he hadn't thought of another woman. Love, if it could ever be considered logical, was the logical conclusion. And he was stuck with it. Taking out a cigarette, Blake ran his fingers down the length of it. He didn't light it, but continued to stare at the wall.

Now what? he asked himself. He was in love with a woman who'd made herself crystal clear on her feelings about commitments and relationships. She wanted no part of either. He, on the other hand, believed in the permanency, and even the romance, of marriage—though he'd never considered it specifically applying to himself.

Things were different now. He was a man too well ordered, both outwardly and mentally, not to see marriage as the direct result of love. With love, you wanted stability, vows, endurance. He wanted Summer. Blake leaned back in his chair. And he firmly believed there was always a way to get what you wanted.

If he even mentioned the word love, she'd be gone in a flash. Even he wasn't completely comfortable with it as yet. Strategy, he told himself. It was all a matter of strategy—or so he hoped. He simply had to convince her that he was essential to her life, that theirs was the relationship designed to break her set of rules.

Apparently the game was still on—and he still intended to win. Frowning at the wall, he began to work his way through the problem.

Summer was having problems of her own. Four cups of strong black coffee hadn't quite brought her up to maximum working level. Ten hours' sleep suited her well, eight could be tolerated. With less than that, and she'd had a good deal less than that the night before, she edged perilously close to nastiness. Add to that a state of emotional turmoil, and Max's frigid resentment, and it didn't promise to be the most pleasant or productive morning.

"By using one of the traditional French garnitures for the roast of lamb, we'll add something European and attractive to the entrée." Summer folded her hands on some of the scattered papers on her desk. She'd brought a few of Enrico's flowers in and set them in a water glass. They helped cover some of the dusty smell.

"My roast of lamb is perfect as it is."

"For some tastes," Summer said evenly. "For mine it's only adequate. I don't accept adequate." Their eyes warred, violently. As neither gave way, she continued. "I prefer to go with *clamart,* artichoke hearts filled with buttered peas, and potatoes sautéed in butter."

"We've always used watercress and mushrooms."

Meticulously, she changed the angle of a rosebud. The small distraction helped her keep her temper. "Now, we use *clamart.*" Summer noted it down, underlined it, then went on. "As to the prime rib—"

"You will not touch my prime rib."

She started to snap back but managed to grit her teeth instead. It was common knowledge in the kitchen that the prime rib was Max's specialty, one might say his baby. The wisest course was to give in graciously on this point, and hold a hard line on others. Her British heritage of fair play came through.

"The prime rib remains precisely as it is," she told him. "My function here is to improve what needs improving while incorporating the Cocharan House standard." Well said, Summer congratulated herself while Max huffed and subsided. "In addition, we'll keep the New York strip and the filet." Sensing he was mollified, Summer hit him with the poultry entrée. "We'll continue to serve the very simple roast chicken, with the choice of potatoes or rice and the vegetables of the day, but we add pressed duck."

"Pressed duck?" Max blustered. "We have no one on staff who's capable of preparing that dish properly, nor do we have a duck press."

"No, which is why I've ordered one, and why I'm hiring someone who can use it."

"You're bringing someone into my kitchen just for this!"

"I'm bringing someone into *my* kitchen," she corrected, "to prepare the pressed duck and the lamb dish among other things. He's leaving his current job in Chicago to come here because he trusts my judgment. You might begin to do the same." With this, she began to tidy papers. "That's all for today, Max. I'd like you to take along these notes." While the headache began to drum inside her head, she handed him a stack of papers. "If you have any suggestions on what I've listed, please jot them down." She bent back over her work as he rose and strode silently out of the room.

Perhaps she shouldn't have been so abrupt. Summer understood injured feelings and fragile egos. She might have handled it better. Yes, she might have—with a weary sigh, she rubbed her temple—if she wasn't feeling a bit injured and fragile herself. Your own fault, she reminded herself; then propping her elbows on the table, she dropped her head into the cupped hands.

Now that it was tomorrow, she had to face the consequences. She'd broken one of her own primary rules. Never become intimate with a business associate. She should have been able to shrug and say rules were made to be broken, but… It worried her more that it wasn't that particular rule that was causing the turmoil, but another she'd broken. Never let anyone who could really matter get too close. Blake, if she didn't draw in the lines now and hold them, could really matter.

Drinking more coffee and wishing for an aspirin, she began to go over everything again. She was certain she'd been casual enough, and clear enough, the night before over the lack of ties and obligations. But when they'd made love again, nothing she'd said had made sense. She shook her head, trying to block that out. That morning they'd been perfectly at ease with each other—two adults preparing for a workday without any morning-after awkwardness. That's what she wanted.

Too many times, she'd seen her mother glowing and bubbling at the beginning of an affair. This man was *the* man—this man was the most exciting, the most considerate, the most poetic. Until the bloom faded. Summer's belief was that if you didn't glow, you didn't fade, and life was a lot simpler.

Yet she still wanted him.

After a brief knock, one of the kitchen staff stuck his head around her door. "Ms. Lyndon, Mr. Cocharan would like to see you in his office."

Summer finished off her rapidly cooling coffee. "Yes? When?"

"Immediately."

She lifted a brow. No one summoned her immediately. People requested her, at her leisure. "I see." Her smile was icy enough to make the messenger shrink back. "Thank you."

When the door closed again she sat perfectly still. These were working hours, she reflected, and she was under contract. It was reasonable and right that he should ask her to come to his office. That was acceptable. But she was still Summer Lyndon—she went to no one immediately.

She spent the next fifteen minutes deliberately dawdling over her papers before she rose. After strolling through the kitchen, and taking the time to check on the contents of a pot or skillet on the way, she went to an elevator. On the ride up, she glanced at her watch, pleased to note that she'd arrive nearly twenty-five minutes after the call. As the doors opened she flicked a speck of lint from the sleeve of her blouse, then sauntered out.

"Mr. Cocharan would like to speak to me?" She gave the words the intonation of a question as she smiled down at the receptionist.

"Yes, Ms. Lyndon, you're to go right through. He's been waiting."

Unsure if the last statement had been censure or warning, Summer continued down the hall to Blake's door. She gave a peremptory knock before going in. "Good morning, Blake."

When she entered, he set aside the file in front of him and leaned back in his chair. "Have trouble finding an elevator?"

"No." Crossing the room, she chose a chair and settled down. He looked, she thought, as he had the first time she'd come into his office—aloof, aristocratic. This then was the perfect level for them to deal on. "This is one of the few hotels that has elevators one doesn't grow old waiting for."

"You're aware what the term immediately means."

"I'm aware of it. I was busy."

"Perhaps I should make it clear that I don't tolerate being kept waiting by an employee."

"And I'll make two things clear," she tossed back. "I'm not merely an employee, but an artist. Secondly, I don't come at the snap of anyone's fingers."

"It's eleven-twenty," Blake began with a mildness Summer instantly suspected. "On a workday. My signature is at the base of your checks. Therefore, you do answer to me."

The faint, telltale flush crept along her cheekbones. "You'd turn my work into something to be measured in dollars and cents and minute by minute—"

"Business is business," he countered, spreading his hands. "I think you were quite clear on that subject."

She'd maneuvered herself successfully toward that particular corner, and he'd given her a helpful shove into it. As a result, her attitude only became more haughty. "You'll notice I *am* here at present. You're wasting time."

As an ice queen, she was magnificent, Blake thought.

He wondered if she realized how a change of expression, a tone of voice, could alter her image. She could be half a dozen women in the course of a day. Whether she knew it or not, Summer had her mother's talent. "I received another dissatisfied call from Max," he told her flatly.

She arched a brow and looked like royalty about to dispense a beheading. "Yes?"

"He objects—strongly—to some of the proposed changes in the menu. Ah—" Blake glanced down at the pad on his desk "—pressed duck seems to be the current problem, though several others were tossed in around it."

Summer sat straighter in her chair, tilting up her chin. "I believe you contracted me to improve the quality of Cocharan House dining."

"I did."

"That is precisely what I'm doing."

The French was beginning to seep into the intonation of her voice, her eyes were beginning to glow. Despite the fact it annoyed him, she was undeniably at her most attractive this way. "I also contracted you to manage the kitchen—which means you should be able to control your staff."

"Control?" She was up, and the ice queeen was now the enraged artist. Her gestures were broad, her movements dramatic. "I would need a whip and chain to control such a narrow-minded, ill-tempered old woman who worries only about his own egocentricities. *His* way is the only way. *His* menu is carved in stone, sacrosanct. Pah!" It was a peculiarly French expletive that would have been ridiculous coming from anyone else. From Summer, it was perfect.

Blake tapped his pen against the edge of his desk while he watched the performance. He was nearly tempted to applaud. "Is this what's known as artistic temperament?"

She drew in a breath. Mockery? Would he dare? "You've yet to see true temperament, *mon ami.*"

He only nodded. It was tempting to push her into full gear—but business was business. "Max has worked for Cocharan for over twenty-five years." Blake set down the pen and folded his hands—calm, in direct contrast to Summer's temper. "He's loyal and efficient, and obviously sensitive."

"Sensitive." She nearly spat the word. "I give him his prime rib and his precious chicken, but still, he's not satisfied. I will have my pressed duck and my *clamart. My* menu won't read like something from the corner diner."

He wondered if he recorded the conversation and played it back to her, she'd see the absurdity of it. At the moment, though he had to clear his throat to disguise a chuckle, he doubted it. "Exactly," Blake said and kept his face expressionless. "I've no desire to interfere with the menu. The point is, I've no desire to interfere at all."

Far from mollified, Summer tossed her hair behind her shoulders and glared at him. "Then why do you bother me with these trivialities?"

"These trivialities," he countered, "are your problem, not mine. As manager, part of your function is to do simply that. Manage. If your supervisory chef is consistently dissatisfied, you're not doing your job. You're free to make whatever compromises you think necessary."

"Compromises?" Her whole body stiffened. Again, he thought she looked magnificent. "I don't make compromises."

"Being hardheaded won't bring peace to your kitchen."

She let out her breath in a hiss. "Hardheaded!"

"Exactly. Now, the problem of Max is back in your court. I don't want any more phone calls."

In a low, dangerous voice, she let out a stream of French, and though he was certain it was colloquial, he caught the drift. With a toss of her head, she started toward the door.

"Summer."

She turned, and the stance reminded him of one of the mythical female archers whose aim was killingly true. She wouldn't even wince as her arrow went straight through the heart. Ice queen or warrior, he wanted her. "I want to see you tonight."

Her eyes went to slits. "You dare."

"Now that we've tabled the first issue, it's time to go onto the second. We might have dinner."

"You tabled the first issue," she retorted. "I don't table things so easily. Dinner? Have dinner with your account book. That's what you understand."

He rose and approached her without hurry. "We agreed that when we're away from here, we're not business associates."

"We're not away from here." Her chin was still angled. "I'm standing in your office, where I was summoned."

"You won't be standing in my office tonight."

"I stand wherever I choose tonight."

"So tonight," he continued easily, "we won't be business associates. Weren't those your rules?"

Personal and professional, and that tangible line of demarcation. Yes, that's the way she'd wanted it, but it wasn't as easy for her to make the separation as she'd thought it would be. "Tonight," she said with a shrug, "I may be busy."

Blake glanced at his watch. "It's nearly noon. We might consider this lunch hour." He looked back at her, half smiling. Lifting a hand, he tangled it in her hair. "During lunch hour, there's no business between us, Summer. And tonight, I want to be with you." He touched his lips to one corner of her mouth, then the other. "I want to spend long—" his lips slanted over hers softly "—private hours with you."

She wanted it too, why pretend otherwise? She'd never believed in pretenses, only in defenses. In any event, she'd already decided to handle Max and the kitchen in her own way. Linking her hands around his neck, she smiled back at him. "Then tonight, we'll be together. You'll bring the champagne?"

She was softening, but not yielding. Blake found it infinitely more exciting than submission. "For a price."

Her laugh was wicked and warm. "A price?"

"I want you to do something for me you haven't done before."

She tilted her head, then touched the tip of her tongue to her lip. "Such as?"

"Cook for me."

Surprise lit her eyes before the laughter sprang out again. "Cook for you? Well, that's a much different request from what I expected."

"After dinner I might come up with a few others."

"So you want Summer Lyndon to prepare your dinner." She considered it as she drew away. "Perhaps I will, though such a thing usually costs much more than a bottle of champagne. Once in Houston I prepared a meal for an oil man and his new bride. I was paid in stock certificates. Blue chip."

Blake took her hand and brought it to his lips. "I bought you a pizza. Pepperoni."

"That's true. Eight o'clock then. And I'd advise you to eat a very light lunch today." She reached for the door handle, then glanced over her shoulder with a grin. "You do like *Cervelles Braisées?*"

"I might, if I knew what it was."

Still smiling, she opened the door. "Braised calf's brains. *Au revoir.*"

Blake stared at the door. She'd certainly had the last word that time.

The kitchen smelled of cooking and sounded like a drawing room. Strains of Chopin were muted as Summer rolled the boneless breasts of chicken in flour. On the range, the clarified butter was just beginning to deepen in color. Perfect. Stuffed tomatoes were already prepared and waiting in the refrigerator. Buttered peas were just beginning to simmer. She would sauté the potato balls while she sautéed the *suprêmes*.

Timing, of course, was critical. *Suprêmes de Volaille à Brun* had to be done to the instant, even a minute of overcooking and she would, like any temperamental cook, throw them out in disgust. Hot butter sizzled as she slipped the floured chicken into it.

She heard the knock but remained where she was. "It's open," she called out. Meticulously, she adjusted the heat under the skillet. "I'll take the champagne in here."

"*Chérie,* if I'd only thought to bring some."

Stunned, Summer turned and saw Monique, glorious in midnight black and silver, framed by her kitchen doorway. "Mother!" With the kitchen fork still in her hand, Summer closed the distance and enveloped her mother.

With that part bubbling, part sultry laugh she was famous for, Monique kissed both of Summer's cheeks, then drew her daughter back. "You are surprised, *oui?* I adore surprises."

"I'm astonished," Summer countered. "What're you doing in town?"

Monique glanced toward the range. "At the moment, apparently interrupting the preparations for an intimate *tête à tête.*"

"Oh!" Whipping around, Summer dashed back to the skillet and turned the chicken breasts, not a second too soon. "What I meant was, what are you doing in Philadelphia?" She checked the flame again, and was satisfied. "Didn't you once say you'd never set foot in the town of the hardware king again?"

"Time mellows one," Monique claimed with a characteristic flick of the wrist. "And I wanted to see my daughter. You are not so often in Paris these days."

"No, it doesn't seem so, does it?" Summer split her attention between her mother and her range, something she would have done for no one else. "You look wonderful."

Monique's smooth cheeks dimpled. "I feel wonderful, *mignonne.* In six weeks, I start a new picture."

"A new picture." Carefully Summer pressed a finger to the top of the chicken. When they sprang back, she removed them to a hot platter. "Where?"

"In Hollywood. They have pestered me, and at last I give in." Monique's infectious laugh bubbled out again.

"The script is superb. The director himself came to Paris to woo me. Keil Morrison."

Tall, somewhat gangly, intelligent face, fiftyish. Summer had a clear enough picture from the glossies, and from a party for a reigning box office queen where she'd prepared *île Flottante.* From her mother's tone of voice, Summer knew the answer before she asked the question. "And the director?"

"He, too, is superb. How would you feel about a new step poppa, *chérie?*"

"Resigned," Summer said, then smiled. That was too hard a word. "Pleased, of course, if you're happy, Mother." She began to prepare the brown butter sauce while Monique expounded.

"Oh, but he is brilliant and so sensitive! I've never met a man who so understands a woman. At last, I've found my perfect match. The man who finally brings everything I need and want into my life. The man who makes me feel like a woman."

Nodding, Summer removed the skillet from the heat and stirred in the parsley and lemon juice. "When's the wedding?"

"Last week." Monique smiled brilliantly as Summer glanced up. "We were married quietly in a little churchyard outside Paris. There were doves—a good sign. I tore myself away from Keil because I wanted to tell you in person." Stepping forward, she flashed a thin diamond-crusted band. "Elegant, *oui?* Keil doesn't believe in the—how do you say?—ostentatious."

So, for the moment, neither would Monique DuBois Lyndon Smith Clarion Morrison. She supposed, when the news broke, the glossies and trades would have a field day. Monique would eat up every line of publicity. Summer kissed her mother's cheek. "Be happy, *ma mère.*"

"I'm ecstatic. You must come to California and meet my Keil, and then—" She broke off as the knock interrupted her. "Ah, this must be your dinner guest. Shall I answer for you?"

"Please." With the tongue caught between her teeth, Summer poured the sauce over the *suprêmes.* She'd serve them within five minutes or dump them down the sink.

When the door opened, Blake was treated to a slightly more voluptuous, slightly more glossy, version of Summer. The candlelight disguised the years and enhanced the classic features. Her lips curved slowly, in the way her daughter's did, as she offered her hand.

"Hello, Summer is busy in the kitchen. I'm her mother, Monique." She paused a moment as their hands met. "But you are familiar to me, yes. But yes!" she continued before Blake could speak. "The Cocharan House. You are the son—B.C.'s son. We've met before."

"A pleasure to see you again, Mademoiselle Dubois."

"This is odd, *oui?* And amusing. I stay in your hotel while in Philadelphia. Already my bags are checked in and my bed turned down."

"You'll let me know personally if there's anything I can do for you while you stay with us."

"Of course." She studied him in the brief but thorough way a woman of experience has. Like mother, like daughter, she mused. Each had excellent taste. "Please, come in. Summer is putting the finishing touches on your meal. I've always admired her skill in the kitchen. Myself, I'm helpless."

"Diabolically helpless," Summer put in as she entered with the hot platter. "She always made sure she burned things beyond recognition, and therefore, no one asked her to cook."

"An intelligent move, to my thinking," Monique said easily. "And now, I'll leave you to your dinner."

"You're welcome to join us, Mother."

"Sweet." Monique framed Summer's face in her hands and kissed both cheeks again. "But I need my beauty rest after the long flight. Tomorrow, we catch up, *non?* Monsieur Cocharan, we will all have dinner at your wonderful hotel before I go?" In her sweeping way, she was at the door. *"Bon appétit."*

"A spectacular woman," Blake commented.

"Yes." Summer went back to the kitchen for the rest of the meal. "She continually amazes me." After placing the vegetables on the table, she picked up her glass. "She's just taken her fourth husband. Shall we drink to them?"

He began to remove the foil from the bottle, but her tone had him pausing. "A bit cynical?"

"Realistic. In any case, I do wish her happiness." When he removed the cork, she took it and absently waved it under her nose. "And I envy her perennial optimism." After both glasses were filled, Summer touched hers to his. "To the new Mrs. Morrison."

"To optimism," Blake countered before he drank.

"If you like," Summer said with a shrug as she sat. She transferred one of the *suprêmes* from the platter to his plate. "Unfortunately the calf's brains looked poor today, so we have to settle for chicken."

"A pity." The first bite was tender and perfect. "Would you like some time off to spend with your mother while she's in town?"

"No, it's not necessary. Mother'll divide her time between shopping and the health spa during the day. She tells me she's about to begin a new film."

"Really." It only took him a minute to put things together. "Morrison—the director?"

"You're very quick," Summer acknowledged, toasting him.

"Summer." He laid a hand over hers. "Do you object?"

She opened her mouth to answer quickly, then thought it over. "No. No, object isn't the word. Her life's her own. I simply can't understand how or why she continually plunges into relationships, tying herself up into marriages which on the average have lasted 5.2 years apiece. Is the word optimism, I wonder, or gullibility?"

"Monique doesn't strike me as a gullible woman."

"Perhaps it's a synonym for romantic."

"No, but romantic might be synonymous with hope. Her way isn't yours."

Yet we both chose lovers from the same bloodline, Summer reminded herself. Just what would Blake's reaction be to that little gem? Keep the past in the past, Summer advised herself. And concentrate on the moment. She smiled at him. "No, it's not. And how do you find my cooking?"

Perhaps it was best to let the subject die, for a time. He needed to ease her over that block gently. "As I find everything about you," Blake told her. "Magnificent."

She laughed as she began to eat again. "It wouldn't be advisable for you to become too used to it. I rarely prepare meals for only compliments."

"That had occured to me. So I brought what I thought was the proper token."

Summer tasted the wine again. "Yes, the champagne is excellent."

"But an inadequate token for a Summer Lyndon meal."

When she shot him a puzzled look, he reached in his inside pocket and drew out a small thin box.

"Ah, presents." Amused, she accepted the box.

"You mentioned a fondness for them." Blake saw the amusement fade as she opened the box.

Inside were diamonds—elegant, even delicate in the form of a slender bracelet. They lay white and regal against the dark velvet of the box.

She wasn't often overwhelmed. Now, she found herself struggling through waves of astonishment. "The meal's too simple for a token like this," she managed. "If I'd known, I'd've prepared something spectacular."

"I wouldn't have thought art ever simple."

"Perhaps not, but..." She looked up, telling herself she wasn't supposed to be moved by such things. They were only pretty stones after all. But her heart was full. "Blake, it's lovely, exquisite. I think you've taken me too seriously when I talk of payments and gifts. I didn't do this tonight for any reason more than I wanted to do it."

"This made me think of you," he said as if she hadn't spoken. "See how cool and haughty the stones are? But..." He slipped the bracelet out of the box. "If you look closely, if you hold it to light, there's warmth, even fire." As he spoke, he let the bracelet dangle from his fingers so that it caught and glittered with the flames from the candles. At that moment, it might have been alive.

"So many dimensions, from every angle you can see something different. A strong stone, and more elegant than any other." Laying the bracelet over her wrist, he clasped it. His gaze lifted and locked on hers. "I didn't do this tonight for any reason other than I wanted to do it."

She was breathless, vulnerable. Would it be like this every time he looked at her? "You begin to worry me," Summer whispered.

The one quiet statement had the need whipping through him almost out of control. He rose, then, drawing her to her feet, crushed her against him before she could agree or protest. "Good."

His mouth wasn't patient this time. There seemed to be a desperate need to hurry, take all, take everything. Hunger that had nothing to do with the meal still unfinished on the table sped through him. She was every desire, and every answer. Biting off an oath, he pulled her to the floor.

This was the whirlwind. She'd never been here before, trapped, exhilarated. Elated by the speed, trembling from the power, Summer moved with him. There was no patience with clothes this time. They were tugged and pulled and tossed aside until flesh could meet flesh. Hot and eager, her body arched against his. She wanted the wind and the fury that only he could bring her.

As his hands sped over her, she delighted in their firmness, in the strength of each individual finger. Her own demands raged equally. Her mouth raced down his throat, teeth nipping, tongue darting. Each unsteady breath told her that she drove him just as he drove her. There was pleasure in that, she discovered. To give passion, and to have it returned to you. Even though her mind clouded, she knew the instant his control snapped. He was rough, but she delighted in it. She had taken him beyond the civilized only by being. His mouth was everywhere, tasting, on a crazed journey from her lips to her breasts—lingering—then lower, still lower, until she caught her breath in astonished excitement.

The world peeled away, the floor, the walls, ceiling, then the sky and the ground itself. She was beyond all that, in some spiraling tunnel where only the senses ruled. Her body had no bounds, and she had no control. She moaned, struggling for a moment to pull it back, but the first peak swept her up, tossing her blindly. Even the illusion of reason shattered.

He wanted her like this. Some dark, primitive part of him needed to know he could bring her to this throbbing, mindless world of sensations. She shuddered beneath him, gasping, yet he continued to drive her up again and again with hands and mouth only. He could see her face in the candlelight—those flickers of passion, of pleasure, of need. She was moist and heated. And he was greedy.

Her skin pulsed under him everywhere he touched. When he touched his mouth to the sensitive curve where thigh meets hip, she arched and moaned his name. The sound of it tore through him, pounding in his blood long after there was silence.

"Tell me you want me," he demanded as he raced up her shuddering body again. "And only me."

"I want you." She could think of nothing. She would have given him anything. "Only you."

They joined in a violence that went on and on, then shattered into a crystal contentment.

She lay beneath him knowing she'd never gather the strength to move. There was barely the strength to breathe. It didn't seem to matter. For the first time, she noticed the floor was hard beneath her, but it didn't inspire her to shift to a more comfortable position. Sighing, she closed her eyes. Without too much effort, she could sleep exactly where she was.

Blake moved, only to draw himself up and take his weight on his own arms. She seemed so fragile suddenly, so completely without defense. He hadn't been gentle with her, yet during the loving, she'd seemed so strong, so full of fire.

He gave himself the enjoyment of looking at her while she half dozed, wearing nothing more than diamonds at her wrist. As he watched, her eyes fluttered open and she watched him, catlike from half-lowered lids. Her lips curved. He grinned at her, then kissed them.

"What's for dessert?"

Chapter 9

Unfortunately, Summer was going to need a phone in her office. She preferred to work undisturbed, and phones had a habit of disturbing, but the final menu was almost completed. She was approaching the practical stage of selective marketing. With so many new things—and difficult-to-come-by items—on the bill of fare, she would have to begin the process of finding the best suppliers. It was a job she would have loved to have delegated, but she trusted her own negotiating skills, and her own intuition, more than anyone else's. When choosing a supplier of the best oysters or okra, you needed both.

After tidying her morning's work, Summer gave the stack of papers a satisifed nod. Her instincts about taking this very different sort of job had been valid. She was doing it, and doing it well. The kitchen remodeling was exactly what she'd envisioned, the staff was well trained—and with her carefully screened and selected additions would be only more so. The two new pastry chefs were better than she'd expected them to be. Julio and Georgia had sent a postcard from Hawaii, and it had been taped, with some honor, to the front of a refrigerator. Summer had only had a moment's temptation to throw darts at it.

She'd interfered very little with the setup in the dining room. The lighting there was excellent, the linen impeccable. The food—her food—alone would be all the refreshing the restaurant required.

Soon, she thought, she'd be able to have the new menus printed. She had only to pin down a few prices first and haggle over terms and delivery hours. The next step was the installation of a phone. Choosing to deal with it immediately, she headed for the door. She entered the kitchen from one end as Monique entered from the other. All work ceased.

It amused Summer, and rather pleased her, that her mother had that stunning effect on people. She could see Max standing, staring, with a kitchen spoon in one hand that dripped sauce unheeded onto the floor. And, of course, Monique knew how to make an entrance. It might be said she was a woman made for entrances.

She smiled slowly—it almost appeared hesitantly—as she stepped in, bringing the scent of Paris and spring with her. Her eyes were more gray than her daughter's and, despite the difference in years and experience, held more innocence. Summer had yet to decide if it was calculated or innate.

"Perhaps someone could help me?"

Six men stepped forward. Max came perilously close

to allowing the stock from the spoon to drip on Monique's shoulder. Summer decided it was time to restore order. "Mother." She brushed her way through the circle of bodies surrounding Monique.

"Ah, Summer, just who I was looking for." Even as she took her daughter's hands, she gave the group of male faces a sweeping smile. "How fascinating. I don't believe I've ever been in a hotel kitchen before. It's so—ah—large, *oui?*"

"Please, Ms. Dubois—madame." Unable to contain himself, Max took Monique's hand. "I'd be honored to show you whatever you'd like to see. Perhaps you'd care to sample some of the soup?"

"How kind." Her smile would have melted chocolate at fifty yards. "Of course, I must see everything where my daughter works."

"Daughter?"

Obviously, Summer mused, Max had heard nothing but violins since Monique walked into the room. "My mother," Summer said clearly, "Monique Dubois. This is Max, who's in charge of the kitchen staff."

Mother? Max thought dumbly. But of course the resemblance was so strong he felt like a fool for not seeing it before. There wasn't a Dubois film he hadn't seen at least three times. "A pleasure." Rather gallantly, he kissed the offered hand. "An honor."

"How comforting to know my daughter works with such a gentleman." Though Summer's lip curled, she said nothing. "And I would love to see everything, just everything—perhaps later today?" she added before Max could begin again. "Now, I must steal Summer away for just a short time. Tell me, would it be possible to have some champagne and caviar delivered to my suite?"

"Caviar isn't on the menu," Summer put in with an arch look at Max. "As yet."

"Oh." Prettily, Monique pouted. "I suppose some pâté, or some cheese would do."

"I'll see to it personally. Right away, madame."

"So kind." With a flutter of lashes, Monique slipped her arm through Summer's and swept from the room.

"Laying it on a bit thick," Summer muttered.

Monique threw back her head and gave a bubbling laugh. "Don't be so British, *chérie.* I just did you an enormous service. I learned from the delightful young Cocharan this morning that not only is my daughter an employee at this very hotel—which you didn't bother to tell me—but that you had a few internal problems in the kitchen."

"I didn't tell you because it's only a temporary arrangement, and because it's been keeping me quite busy. As to the internal problems…"

"In the form of one very large Max." Monique glided into the elevator.

"I can handle them just fine by myself," Summer finished.

"But it doesn't hurt to have him impressed by your parentage." After pressing the button for her floor, Monique turned to study her daughter. "So, I look at you in the light and see that you've grown more lovely. That pleases me. If one must have a grown daughter, one should have a beautiful grown daughter."

Laughing, Summer shook her head. "You're as vain as ever."

"I'll always be vain," Monique said simply. "God

willing I'll always have a reason to be. Now—" she motioned Summer out of the elevator "—I've had my morning coffee and croissants, and my massage. I'm ready to hear about this new job of yours and your new lover. From the look of you, both agree with you."

"I believe it's customary for mothers and daughters to discuss new jobs, but not new lovers."

"Pooh." Monique tossed open the door to her suite. "We were never just mother and daughter, but friends, *n'est-ce pas?* And *chère amies* always discuss new lovers."

"The job," Summer said distinctly as she dropped into a butter-soft daybed and brought up her legs, "is working out quite well. I took it originally because it intrigued me and—well because Blake threw LaPointe up in my face."

"LaPointe? The beady-eyed little man you detest so much? The one who told the Paris papers you were his…"

"Mistress," Summer said violently.

"Ah, yes, such a foolish word, mistress, so antiquated, don't you agree? Unless one considers that mistress is the feminine term for master." Monique smiled serenely as she draped herself on the sofa. "And were you?"

"Certainly not. I wouldn't have let him put his pudgy little hands on me if he'd been half the chef he claims to be."

"You might have sued."

"Then more people would've snickered and said where there's smoke there's fire. The little French swine would've loved that." She was gritting her teeth, so she deliberately relaxed her jaw. "Don't get me started on

LaPointe. It was enough that Blake maneuvered me into this job with him as an edge."

"A very clever man—your Blake, that is."

"He's not my Blake," Summer said pointedly. "He's his own man, just as I'm my own woman. You know I don't believe in that sort of thing." The discreet knock had Monique waving negligently and Summer rising to answer. She thought, as the tray of cheeses and fresh fruit and the bucket of iced champagne was wheeled in, that Max must have dashed around like a madman to have it served so promptly. Summer signed the check with a flourish and dismissed the waiter.

Idly Monique inspected the tray before choosing a single cube of cheese. "But you're in love with him."

Busy with the champagne cork, Summer glanced over. "What?"

"You're in love with the young Cocharan."

The cork exploded out, champagne fizzed and geysered from the bottle. Monique merely lifted her glass to be filled. "I'm not in love with him," Summer said with an underlying desperation her mother recognized.

"One is always in love with one's lover."

"No, one is not." With a bit more control, Summer poured the wine. "Affairs don't have to be romantic and flowery. I'm fond of Blake, I respect him. I consider him an attractive, intelligent man and enjoy his company."

"It's possible to say the same of a brother, or an uncle. Even perhaps an ex-husband," Monique commented. "This is not what I think you feel for Blake."

"I feel passion for him," Summer said impatiently. "Passion is not to be equated with love."

"Ah, Summer." Amused, Monique chose a grape. "You can think with your British mind, but you feel with your French heart. This young Cocharan isn't a man any woman would lightly dismiss."

"Like father like son?" The moment it was said, Summer regretted it.

But Monique only smiled, softly, reminiscently. "It occurred to me. I haven't forgotten B.C."

"Nor he you."

Interested, Monique flipped back from the past. "You've met Blake's father?"

"Briefly. When your name was mentioned he looked as though he'd been struck by lightning."

The soft smile became brilliant. "How flattering. A woman likes to believe she remains in a man's memory long after they part."

"You may be flattered. I can tell you I was damned uncomfortable."

"But why?"

"Mother." Restless, Summer rose again and began to pace. "I was attracted to Blake—very much attracted—and he to me. How do you think I felt when I was talking to his father, and both B.C. and I were thinking about the fact that you'd been lovers? I don't think Blake has any idea. If he did, do you realize how awkward the situation would be?"

"Why?"

On a long breath, Summer turned to her mother again. "B.C. was and is married to Blake's mother. I get the impression Blake's rather fond of his mother, and of his father."

"What does that have to do with it?" Monique's gesture was typically French—a slight shrug, a slight lifting of the hand, palm out. "I was fond of his father too. Listen to me," she continued before Summer could retort. "B.C. was always in love with his wife. I knew that then. We consoled each other, made each other laugh in what was a miserable time for both of us. I'm grateful for it, not ashamed of it. Neither should you be."

"I'm not ashamed." Frustrated, Summer dragged a hand through her hair. "I don't ask you to be, but—damn it, Mother, it's awkward."

"Life often is. You'll remind me there are rules, and so there are." She threw back her head and took on the regal haughtiness her daughter had inherited. "I don't play by the rules, and I don't apologize."

"Mother." Cursing herself, Summer went and knelt beside the couch. "I wasn't criticizing you. It's only that what's right for you, what's good for you, isn't right and good for me."

"You think I don't know that? You think I'd have you live my life?" Monique laid a hand on her daughter's head. "Perhaps I've seen more deep happiness than you've seen. But I've also seen more deep despair. I can't wish you the first without knowing you'd face the second. I want for you only what you wish for yourself."

"Some things you're afraid to wish for."

"No, but some things are more carefully wished for. I will give you some advice." She patted Summer's head, then drew her up to sit on the sofa. "When you were a little girl, I gave you none because small children have always been a mystery to me. When you grew up, you wouldn't have listened to any. Perhaps now we've come to the point between mother and daughter when each understands the other is intelligent."

With a laugh, Summer picked a strawberry from the tray. "All right, I'll listen."

"It does not make you less of a woman to need a

man." When Summer frowned, she continued. "To need one to exist, yes, this is nonsense. To need one to give one scope and importance, this is dishonest. But to need a man, one man, to bring joy and passion? This is life."

"There can be joy and passion in a woman's life without a man."

"Some joy, some passion," Monique agreed. "Why settle for some? What is it that you prove by cutting off what is a natural need? Perhaps it's a foolish woman who takes a different man as a husband, four times. Again, I don't apologize, but only remind you that Summer Lyndon is not Monique Dubois. We look for different things in different ways. But we are both women. I don't regret my choices."

With a sigh, Summer laid her head on her mother's shoulder. "I want to be able to say that for myself. I've always thought I could."

"You're an intelligent woman. What choice you make will be right for you."

"My greatest fear has always been to make a mistake."

"Perhaps your greatest fear is your greatest mistake." She touched Summer's cheek again. "Come, pour me some more champagne. I'll tell you of my Keil."

When Summer returned to the kitchen, her mind was still playing back her conversation with Monique. It was rare that Monique pressed her for details about her personal life, and rarer still for her to offer advice. It was true that most of the hour they'd spent together had been devoted to a listing of Keil Morrison's virtues, but in those first few moments, Monique had said things designed to make Summer think—designed to make her begin to doubt her own list of priorities.

But when she approached the swinging doors leading into the kitchen, and the sounds of the argument met her, she knew her thinking would have to wait.

"My casserole's perfect."

"Too much milk, too little cheese."

"You've never been able to admit that my casseroles are better than yours."

Perhaps the scene was laughable—huge Max and little Charlie, the undersized Korean cook who came no higher than his superior's breastbone. They stood, glaring at each other, while both of them held a solid grip on a spinach casserole. It might have been laughable, Summer thought wearily, if the rest of the kitchen staff hadn't already been choosing up sides while the luncheon orders were ignored.

"Inferior work," Max retorted. He'd yet to forgive Charlie for being out sick three days running.

"Your casseroles are always inferior work. Mine are perfect."

"Too much milk," Max said solidly. "Not enough cheese."

"Problem?" Summer stepped up, lining herself between them.

"This scrawny little man who masquerades as a cook is trying to pass this mass of soggy leaves off as a spinach casserole." Max tried to tug the glass dish away and found that the scrawny little man was surprisingly strong.

"This big lump of dough who calls himself a chef is jealous because I know more about vegetables than he does."

Summer bit down hard on her bottom lip. Damn it, it was funny, but the timing was all wrong. "Perhaps the rest of you might get back to work," she began coolly, "before what clientele we have left in the dining room evacuates to the nearest golden arches for decent service. Now…" She turned back to the two opponents. Any moment, she decided, there'd be bared teeth and snarls. "This, I take it, is the casserole in question."

"The dish is a casserole," Max tossed back. "What's in it is garbage." He tugged again.

"Garbage!" The little cook squealed in outrage, then curled his lip. "Garbage is what you pass off as prime rib. The only thing edible on the plate is the tiny spring of parsley you part with." He tugged back.

"Gentlemen, might I ask a question?" Without waiting for an answer, she touched a finger to the dish. It was still warm, but cooling fast. "Has anyone tasted the casserole?"

"I don't taste poison." Max gave the dish another yank. "I pour poison down the sink."

"I wouldn't have this—this ox taste one spoonful of my spinach." Charlie yanked right back. "He'd contaminate it."

"All right, children," Summer said in sweet tones that had both men's annoyance turning on her. "Why don't I do the testing?"

Both men eyed each other warily. "Tell him to let go of my spinach," Charlie insisted.

"Max—"

"He lets go first. I'm his superior."

"Charlie—"

"The only thing superior is his weight." And the tug-of-war began again.

Out of patience, Summer tossed up her hands. "All right, *enough!*"

It might have been the shock of having her raise her voice, something she'd never done in the kitchen—or it might have been that the dish itself was becoming slippery from so much handling. Either way, at her word, the dish fell out of both men's hands with force. It struck the edge of the counter, shattering, so that glass flew even before the casserole and its contents hit the floor. In unison, Max and Charlie erupted with abuse and accusations.

Summer, distracted by the pain in her right arm, glanced down and saw the blood begin to seep from a four-inch gash. Amazed, she stared at it for a full three seconds while her mind completely rejected the idea that blood, her blood, could pour out so quickly.

"Excuse me," she managed at length. "Do you think the two of you could finish this round after I stop bleeding to death?"

Charlie looked over, a torrent of abuse trembling on his tongue. Instead, he stared wide-eyed at the wound, then broke into an excited ramble of Korean.

"If you'd stop interfering," Max began, even as he caught sight of the blood running down Summer's arm. He blanched, then to everyone's surprise, moved like lightning. Grabbing a clean cloth, he pressed it against the gash in Summer's arm. "Sit," he ordered and nudged her onto a kitchen stool. "You," he bellowed at no one in particular, "clean up this mess." Already he was fashioning a tourniquet. "Relax," he said to Summer with unaccustomed gentleness. "I want to see how deep it is."

Giddy, she nodded and kept her eyes trained on the steam from a pot across the room. It didn't really hurt so very much, she thought as her vision blurred then refocused. She'd probably imagined all that blood.

"What the hell's going on in here?" She heard Blake's voice vaguely behind her. "You can hear the commotion in here clear out to the dining room." He strode over, intending to give both Summer and Max the choice of unemployment or peaceful coexistence. The red-stained cloth stopped him cold. "Summer?"

"An accident," Max said hurriedly while Summer shook her head to clear it. "The cut's deep—she'll need stitches."

Blake was already grabbing the cloth from Max and pushing him aside. "Summer. How the hell did this happen?"

She focused on his face and registered concern and perhaps temper in his eyes before everything started to swim again. Then she made the mistake of looking down at her arm. "Spinach casserole," she said foolishly before she slid from the stool in a dead faint.

The next thing she heard was an argument. *Isn't this where I came in?* she thought vaguely. It only took her a moment to recognize Blake's voice, but the other, female and dry, was a stranger.

"I'm staying."

"Mr. Cocharan, you aren't a relative. It's against hospital policy for you to remain while we treat Ms. Lyndon. Believe me, it's only a matter of a few stitches."

A few stitches? Summer's stomach rolled. She didn't like to admit it, but when it came to needles—the kind the medical profession liked to poke into flesh—she was a complete coward. And if her sense of smell wasn't playing tricks on her, she knew where she was. The odor of antiseptics was much too recognizable. Perhaps if she just sat up and quietly walked away, no one would notice.

When she did sit up, she found herself in a small, curtained examining room. Her gaze lit on a tray that held all the shiny, terrifying tools of the trade.

Blake caught the movement out of the corner of his eye, and was beside her. "Summer, just relax."

Moistening her lips, she studied the room again. "Hospital?"

"Emergency Room. They're going to fix your arm."

She managed a smile, but kept her gaze locked on the tray. "I'd just as soon not." When she started to swing her legs over the side of the examining table, the doctor was there to stop her.

"Lie still, Ms. Lyndon."

Summer stared back at the tough, lined female face. She had frizzy hair the color of a peach, and wire-rim glasses. Summer gauged her own strength against the doctor's and decided she could win. "I'm going home now," she said simply.

"You're going to lie right there and get that arm sewed up. Now be quiet."

Well, perhaps if she recruited an ally. "Blake?"

"You need stitches, love."

"I don't want them."

"Need," the doctor corrected, briskly. "Nurse!" While she scrubbed her hands in a tiny sink, she looked back over her shoulder. "Mr. Cocharan, you'll have to wait outside."

"No." Summer managed to struggle back into a sitting position. "I don't know you," she told the white-coated woman at the sink. "And I don't know her," she added when the nurse pushed passed the curtains. "If

I'm going to have to sit here while you sew up my arm with cat gut or whatever it is you use, I'm going to have someone here that I know." She tightened her grip on Blake's hand. "I know him." She lay back down but kept the death hold on Blake's hand.

"Very well." Recognizing both a strong will and basic fear, the doctor gave in. "Just turn your head away," she advised. "This won't take long. I've already used yards of cat gut today."

"Blake." Summer took a deep breath and looked straight into his eyes. She wouldn't think about what the two women on the other side of the table were doing to her arm. "I have a confession to make. I don't deal very well with this sort of thing." She swallowed again when she felt the pressure on her skin. "I have to be tranquilized to get through a dental appointment."

Out of the corner of his eye, he saw the doctor take the first stitch. "We almost had to do the same thing for Max." He ran his thumb soothingly over his knuckles. "After this, you could tell him you're going to put in a wood-burning stove and a hearth and he wouldn't give you any trouble."

"A hell of a way to get cooperation." She winced, felt her stomach roll and swallowed desperately. "Talk to me—about anything."

"We should take a weekend, soon, and go to the beach. Some place quiet, right on the ocean."

It was a good image, she struggled to focus on it. "Which ocean?"

"Any one you want. We'll do nothing for three days but lie in the sun, make love."

The young nurse glanced over, and a sigh escaped before the doctor caught her eye.

"As soon as I'm back from Rome. All you have to do is find some little island in the Pacific while I'm gone. I'd like a few palm trees and friendly natives."

"I'll look into it."

"In the meantime," the doctor put in as she snipped off a length of bandage, "keep this dressing dry, have it changed every third day and come back in two weeks to have the stitches removed. A nasty slice," she added, giving the bandage a last professional adjustment. "But you'll live."

Cautiously Summer turned her head. The wound was now covered in the sterile white gauze. It looked neat, trim and somehow competent. The nausea faded instantly. "I thought they made the stitches so they dissolved."

"It's a nice arm." The doctor rinsed off her hands in the sink. "We wouldn't want a scar on it. I'll give you a prescription for some pain pills."

Summer set her jaw. "I won't take them."

With a shrug, the doctor dried her hands. "Suit yourself. Oh, and you might try the Solomon Islands off New Guinea." Whipping back the curtain, she strode out.

"Quite a lady," Summer muttered as Blake helped her off the table. "Terrific bedside manner. I can't think why I don't hire her as my personal physician."

The spunk was back, Blake thought with a grin, but kept a supportive arm around her waist. "She was exactly what you needed. You didn't need any more sympathy, or worry, than you were getting from me."

She frowned up at him as he led her into the parking lot. "When I bleed," she corrected, "I need a great deal of sympathy and worry."

"What you need—" he kissed her forehead before

opening the car door "—is a bed, a dark room and a few hours' rest."

"I'm going back to work," she corrected. "The kitchen's probably chaos, and I have a long list of phone calls to make—as soon as you arrange to have a phone hooked up for me."

"You're going home, to bed."

"I've stopped bleeding," Summer reminded him. "And though I admit I'm a complete baby when it comes to blood and needles and doctors in white coats, that's done now. I'm fine."

"You're pale." He stopped at a light and turned to her. It wasn't entirely clear to him how he'd gotten through the last hour himself. "You arm's certainly throbbing now, or soon will be. I make it a policy—whenever one of my staff faints on the job, they have the rest of the day off."

"Very liberal and humanitarian of you. I wouldn't have fainted if I hadn't looked."

"Home, Summer."

She sat up, folded her hands and took a deep breath. Her arm *was* throbbing, but she wouldn't have admitted it now for anything. With the new ache, and annoyance, it was easy to forget that she'd clung to his hand a short time before. "Blake, I realize I've mentioned this before, but sometimes it doesn't hurt to reiterate. I don't take orders."

Silence reigned in the car for almost a full minute. Blake turned west, away from Cocharan House and toward Summer's apartment building.

"I'll just take a cab," she said lightly.

"What you'll take is a couple of aspirin, right before I draw the shades and tuck you into bed."

God, that sounded like heaven. Ignoring the image, she set her chin. "Just because I depended on you—a little—while that woman was plying her needle, doesn't mean I need a keeper."

There was a way to convince her to do as he wanted. Blake considered it. Perhaps the direct way was the best way. "I don't suppose you noticed how many stitches she put in your arm."

"No." Summer looked out the window.

"I did. I counted them as she sewed. Fifteen. You didn't notice the size of the needle, either?"

"No." Pressing a hand to her stomach she glared at him. "Dirty pool, Blake."

"If it works…" Then he slipped a hand over hers. "A nap, Summer. I'll stay with you if you like."

How was she supposed to deal with him when he went from being kind, to filthy, to gentle? How was she supposed to deal with herself when all she really wanted was to curl up beside him where she knew it would be safe and warm? "I'll rest." All at once, she felt she needed to, badly, but it no longer had anything to do with her arm. If he continually stirred her emotions like this, the next few months were going to be impossible. "Alone," she finished firmly. "You have enough to do back at the hotel."

When he pulled up in front of her building, she put out a hand to stop him from turning off the engine. "No, you needn't bother to come up. I'll go to bed, I promise." Because she could feel him tense with an objection, she smiled and squeezed his hand. I have to go up alone, she realized. If he came with her now, everything could change. "I'm going to take those aspirin, turn on the stereo and lie down. I'd feel better if you'd go by the kitchen and make certain everything's all right there."

He studied her face. Her skin was pale, her eyes weary. He wanted to stay with her, have her hold onto him for support again. Even as he sat beside her, he could feel the distance she was putting between them. No, he wouldn't allow that—but for now, she needed rest more than she needed him.

"If that's what you want. I'll call you tonight."

Leaning over, she kissed his cheek, then climbed from the car quickly. "Thanks for holding my hand."

Chapter 10

It was beginning to grate on her nerves. It wasn't as though Summer didn't enjoy attention. More than enjoying it, she'd come to expect it as a matter of course in her career. It wasn't as if she didn't enjoy being catered to. That was something she'd developed a taste for early on, growing up in households with servants. But as any good cook knows, sugar has to be dispensed with a careful hand.

Monique had extended her stay a full week, claiming that she couldn't possibly leave Philadelphia while Summer was still recovering from an injury. The more Summer tried to play down the entire incident of her arm and the stitches, the more Monique looked at her with admiration and concern. The more admiration and concern she received, the more Summer worried about that next visit to the doctor.

Though it wasn't in character, Monique had gotten into the habit of coming by Summer's office every day with healing cups of tea and bowls of healthy soup—then standing over her daughter until everything was consumed.

For the first few days, Summer had found it rather sweet—though tea and soup weren't regulars on her diet. As far as she could remember, Monique had always been loving and certainly kind, but never maternal. For this reason alone, Summer drank the tea, ate the soup and swallowed complaints along with them. But as it continued, and as Monique consistently interrupted the final stages of her planning, Summer began to lose patience. She might have been able to tolerate Monique's overreaction and mothering, if it hadn't been for the same treatment by the kitchen staff, headed by Max.

She was permitted to do nothing for herself. If she started to brew a pot of coffee, someone was there, taking over, insisting that she sit and rest. Every day at precisely noon, Max himself brought her in a tray with the luncheon speciality of the day. Poached salmon, lobster soufflé, stuffed eggplant. Summer ate—because like her mother, he hovered over her—while she had visions of a bacon double cheeseburger with a generous side order of onion rings.

Doors were opened for her, concerned looks thrown her way, conciliatory phrases heaped on her until she wanted to scream. Once when she'd been unnerved enough to snap that she had some stitches in her arm, not a terminal illness, she'd been brought yet another soothing cup of tea—with a saucer of plain vanilla cookies.

They were killing her with kindness.

Every time she thought she'd reached her limit, Blake managed to level things for her again. He wasn't callous of her injury or even unkind, but he certainly wasn't treating her as though she were the star attraction at a deathbed.

He had an uncanny instinct for choosing the right time to phone or drop in on the kitchen. He was there, calm when she needed calm, ordered when she yearned for order. He demanded things of her when everyone else insisted she couldn't lift a finger for herself. When he annoyed her, it was in an entirely different way, a way that tested and stretched her abilities rather than smothered them.

And with Blake, Summer didn't have that hampering guilt about letting loose with her temper. She could shout at him knowing she wouldn't see the bottomless patience in his eyes that she saw in Max's. She could be unreasonable and not be worried that his feelings would be hurt like her mother's.

Without realizing it, she began to see him as a pillar of solidity and sense in a world of nonsense. And, for perhaps the first time in her life, she felt an intrinsic need for that pillar.

Along with Blake, Summer had her work to keep her temper and her nerve ends under some kind of control. She poured herself into it. There were long sessions with the printer to design the perfect menu—an elegant slate gray with the words COCHARAN HOUSE embossed on the front—thick creamy parchment paper inside listing her final choices in delicate script. Then there were the room service menus that would go into each unit—not quite so luxurious, perhaps, but Summer saw to it that they were distinguished in their own right.

She talked for hours with suppliers, haggling, demanding and enjoying herself more than she would ever have guessed, until she got precisely the terms she wanted.

It gave her a glow of success—perhaps not the flash she felt on completing some spectacular dish—but a definite glow. She found that in a different way, it was equally satisfying.

And it was unpardonably annoying to be told, after the completion of a particularly long and successful negotiation, that she should take a little nap.

"Chérie." Monique glided into the storage room, just as Summer hung up the phone with the butcher, bearing the inevitable cup of herbal tea. "It's time you had a break. You mustn't push yourself so."

"I'm fine, Mother." Glancing at the tea, Summer sincerely hoped she wouldn't gag. She wanted something carbonated and cold, preferably loaded with caffeine. "I'm just going over the contracts with the suppliers. It's a bit complicated and I've still got one or two calls to make."

If she'd hoped that would be a gentle hint that she needed privacy to work, she was disappointed. "Too complicated when you've already worked so many hours today," Monique insisted and took a seat on the other side of the desk. "You forget, you've had a shock."

"I cut my arm," Summer said with strained patience.

"Fifteen stitches," Monique reminded her, then frowned with disapproval as Summer reached for a cigarette. "Those are so bad for your health, Summer."

"So's nervous tension," she muttered, then doggedly cleared her throat. "Mother, I'm sure Keil's missing you desperately just as you must be missing him. You shouldn't be away from your new husband for so long."

"Ah, yes." Monique sighed and looked dreamily at the ceiling. "For a new bride, a day away from her husband is like a week, a week can be a year." Abruptly, she pressed her hands together, shaking her head. "But my Keil, he is the most understanding of men. He knows I must stay when my daughter needs me."

Summer opened her mouth, then shut it again. Diplomacy, she reminded herself. Tact. "You've been wonderful," she began, a bit guiltily, because it was true. "I can't tell you how much I appreciate all the time, all the trouble, you've taken over this past week or so. But my arm's nearly healed now. I'm really fine. I feel terribly guilty holding you here when you should be enjoying your honeymoon."

With her light, sexy laugh, Monique waved a hand. "My sweet, you'll learn that a honeymoon isn't a time or a trip, but a state of mind. Don't concern yourself with that. Besides, do you think I could leave before they take those nasty stitches out of your arm?"

"Mother—" Summer felt the hitch in her stomach and reached for the tea in defense.

"No, no. I wasn't there for you when the doctor treated you, but—" here, her eyes filled and her lips trembled "—I will be by your side when she removes them—one at a time."

Summer had an all-too-vivid picture of herself lying once again on the examining table, the tough-faced doctor over her. Monique, frail in black, would be standing by, dabbing at her eyes with a lacy handkerchief. She wasn't sure if she wanted to scream, or just drop her head between her knees.

"Mother, you'll have to excuse me. I've just remembered, I have an appointment with Blake in his office."

Without waiting for an answer, Summer dashed from the storage room.

Almost immediately Monique's eyes were dry and her lips curved. Leaning back in her chair, she laughed in delight. Perhaps she hadn't always known just what to do with a daughter when Summer had been a child, but now… Woman to woman, she knew precisely how to nudge her daughter along. And she was nudging her along to Blake, where Monique had no doubt her strong-willed, practical and much-loved daughter belonged.

"À l'amour," she said and lifted the tea in a toast.

It didn't matter to Summer that she didn't have an appointment, only that she see Blake, talk to him and restore her sanity. "I have to see Mr. Cocharan," she said desperately as she pushed right past the receptionist.

"But, Ms. Lyndon—"

Heedless, Summer dashed through the outer office and tossed open his door without knocking. "Blake!"

He lifted a brow, motioned her inside, then continued with his telephone conversation. She looked, he thought, as if she were on the last stages of a manhunt, and on the wrong side of the bloodhounds. His first instinct might have been to comfort, to soothe, but common sense prevailed. It was all too obvious that she was getting enough of that, and detesting it.

Frustrated, she whirled around the room. Nervous energy flowed from her. She stalked to the window, then, restless, turned away from the view. Ultimately she walked to the bar and poured herself a defiant portion of vermouth. The moment she heard the phone click back on the cradle, she turned to him.

"Something has to be done!"

"If you're going to wave that around," he said mildly,

indicating her glass, "you'd better drink some first. It'll be all over you."

Scowling, Summer look a long sip. "Blake, my mother has to go back to California."

"Oh?" He finished scrawling a memo. "Well, we'll be sorry to see her go."

"*No!* No, she has to go back, but she won't. She insists on staying here and nursing me into catatonia. And Max," she continued before he could comment. "Something has to be done about Max. Today—today it was shrimp salad and avocado. I can't take much more." She sucked in a breath, then continued in a dazed rambling of complaints. "Charlie looks at me as if I were Joan of Arc, and the rest of the kitchen staff is just as bad—if not worse. They're driving me crazy."

"I can see that."

The tone of voice had her pacing coming to a quick halt and her eyes narrowing. "Don't aim that coolly amused smile at me."

"Was I smiling?"

"Or that innocent look, either," she snapped back. "You were smiling inside, and nervous breakdowns are definitely not funny."

"You're absolutely right." He folded his hands on the desk. "Why don't you sit down and start from the beginning."

"Listen—" She dropped into a chair, sipped the vermouth, then was up and pacing again. "It's not that I don't appreciate kindness, but there's a saying about too much of a good thing."

"I think I've heard that."

Ignoring him, she plunged on. "You can ruin a

dessert with too much pampering, too much attention, you know."

He nodded. "The same's sometimes said of a child."

"Just stop trying to be cute, damn it."

"It doesn't seem to take any effort." He smiled. She scowled.

"Are you listening to me?" she demanded.

"Every word."

"I wasn't cut out to be pampered, that's all. My mother—every day it's cup after cup of herbal tea until I have visions of sloshing when I walk. 'You should rest, Summer. You're not strong yet, Summer.' Damn it, I'm strong as an ox!"

He took out a cigarette, enjoying the show. "I'd've said so myself."

"And Max! The man's positively smothering me with good will. Lunch every day, twelve on the dot." With a groan, she pressed a hand against her stomach. "I haven't had a real meal in a week. I keep getting these insane cravings for tacos, but I'm so full of tea and lobster bisque I can't do anything about it. If one more person tells me to put up my feet and rest, I swear, I'm going to punch them right in the mouth."

Blake scrutinized the end of his cigarette. "I'll make sure I don't mention it."

"That's just it, you don't." She spun around the desk, then sat on it directly in front of him. "You're the only one around here who's treated me like a normal person since this ridiculous thing happened. You even shouted at me yesterday. I appreciate that."

"Think nothing of it."

With a half laugh, she took his hand. "I'm serious. I feel foolish enough for being so careless as to let an accident like that happen in my kitchen. You don't constantly remind me of it with pats on the head and concerned looks."

"I understand you." Blake linked his fingers with hers. "I've been making a study of you almost from the first instant we met."

The way he said it had her pulse fluctuating. "I'm not an easy person to understand."

"No?"

"I don't always understand."

"Let me tell you about Summer Lyndon, then." He measured her hand against his before he linked their fingers. "She's a beautiful woman, a bit spoiled from her upbringing and her own success." He smiled when her brows drew together. "She's strong and opinionated and intensely feminine without being calculating. She's ambitious and dedicated with a skill for concentration that reminded me once of a surgeon. And she's romantic, though she'll claim otherwise."

"That's not true," Summer began.

"She listens to Chopin when she works. Even while she chooses to have an office in a storage room, she keeps roses on her desk."

"There're reasons why—"

"Stop interrupting," he told her simply, and with a huff, she subsided. "What fears she has are kept way below the surface because she doesn't like to admit to having any. She's tough enough to hold her own against anyone, and compassionate enough to tolerate an uncomfortable situation rather than hurt someone's feelings. She's controlled, and she's passionate. She has a taste for the best champagne and junk food. There's no one I've known who's annoyed me quite so much, or who I'd trust quite so implicitly."

She let out a long breath. It wasn't the first time he'd put her in a position where words were hard to come by. "Not an entirely admirable woman."

"Not entirely," Blake agreed. "But a fascinating one."

She smiled, then sat on his lap. "I've always wanted to do this," she murmured, snuggling. "Sit on some big corporate executive's lap in an elegant office. I'm suddenly quite sure I'd rather be fascinating than admirable."

"I prefer you that way." He kissed her, but lightly.

"You've chased off my nervous breakdown again."

He brushed at her hair, thinking he was close—very close—to winning her completely. "We aim to please."

"Now if I just didn't have to go back down and face all that sugar." She sighed. "And all those earnestly concerned faces."

"What would you rather do?"

Linking her hands around his neck, she laughed and drew back. "If I could do anything I wanted?"

"Anything."

Thoughtfully she ran her tongue over her teeth then grinned. "I'd like to go to the movies, a perfectly dreadful movie, and eat pounds of buttered popcorn with too much salt."

"Okay." He gave her a friendly slap on the bottom. "Let's go find a dreadful movie."

"You mean now?"

"Right now."

"But it's only four o'clock."

He kissed her, then hauled her to her feet. "It's known as playing hookey. I'll fill you in on the way."

* * *

She made him feel young, foolishly young and ir-responsible, sitting in a darkened corner of the theater with a huge barrel of popcorn on his lap and her hand in his. When he looked back over his life, Blake could remember no time when he hadn't felt secure—but ir-responsible? Never that. Having a multimillion dollar business behind him had ingrained in him a very de-manding sense of obligation. However much he'd ben-efited growing up, having enough and always the best, there'd always been the unspoken pressure to maintain that standard—for himself, and for the family business.

Because he'd always taken that position seriously, he was a cautious man. Impulsiveness had never been part of his style. But perhaps that was changing a bit—with Summer. He'd had the impulse to give her what-ever she'd wanted that afternoon. If it had been a trip to Paris to eat supper at Maxim's, he'd have arranged it then and there. Then again, he should have known that a box of popcorn and a movie were more her style.

It was that style—the contrast of elegance and sim-plicity—that had drawn him in from the first. He knew, without question, that there would never be another woman who would move him in the same way.

Summer knew it had been days since she had fully relaxed. In fact, she hadn't been able to relax at all since the accident with anyone but Blake. He'd given her sup-port, but more important, he'd given her space. They hadn't been together often over the past week, and she knew Blake was closing the deal with the Hamilton chain. They'd both been busy, preoccupied, pressured, yet when they were alone and away from Cocharan House, they didn't talk business. She knew how hard he'd worked on this purchase—the negotiations, the paperwork, the endless meetings. Yet he'd put all that aside—for her.

Summer leaned toward him. "Sweet."

"Hmm?"

"You," she whispered under the dialogue on the screen. "You're sweet."

"Because I found a dreadful movie?"

With a chuckle, she reached for more popcorn. "It is dreadful, isn't it?"

"Terrible, which is why the theater's nearly empty. I like it this way."

"Antisocial?"

"No, it just makes it easier—" leaning closer, he caught the lobe of her ear between his teeth "—to indulge in this sort of thing."

"Oh." Summer felt the thrill of pleasure start at her toes and climb upward.

"And this sort of thing." He nipped at the cord of her neck, enjoying her quick little intake of breath. "You taste better than the popcorn."

"And it's excellent popcorn." Summer turned her head so that her mouth could find his.

So warm, so right. Summer felt it was almost possible to say that her lips were made to fit his. If she'd believed in such things… If she'd believed in such things, she might have said that they'd been meant to find each other at this stage of their lives. To meet, to clash, to attract, to merge. One man to one woman, enduringly. When they were close, when his lips were heated on hers, she could almost believe it. She wanted to believe it.

He ran a hand down her hair. Soft, fresh. Just the

touch of that and no more could make him want her unreasonably. He never felt stronger than when he was with her. And he never felt more vulnerable. He didn't hear the explosion of sound and music from the speakers. She didn't see the sudden kaleidoscope of color and movement on the screen. Hampered by the small seats, they shifted in an effort to get that much closer.

"Excuse me." The young usher, who had the job until September when school started up again, shifted his feet in the aisle. Then he cleared his throat. "Excuse me."

Glancing up, Blake noticed that the house lights were on and the screen was blank. After a surprised moment, Summer pressed her mouth against his shoulder to muffle a laugh.

"Movie's over," the boy said uncomfortably. "We have to—ah—clear the theater after every show." Glancing at Summer, he decided any man might lose interest in a movie with someone like her around. Then Blake stood, tall, broad shouldered, with that one aloofly raised eyebrow. The boy swallowed. And a lot of guys didn't like to be interrupted.

"Ah—that's the rule, you know. The manager—"

"And reasonable enough," Blake interrupted when he noticed the boy's Adam's apple working.

"We'll just take the popcorn along," Summer said as she rose. She tucked the barrel under one arm and slid her other through Blake's. "Have a nice evening," she told the usher over her shoulder as they walked out.

When they were outside, she burst out laughing. "Poor child, he thought you were going to manhandle him."

"The thought crossed my mind, but only very briefly."

"Long enough for him to get nervous about it." After

climbing into the car, she placed the popcorn in her lap. "You know what he thought, don't you?"

"What?"

"That we were having an illicit affair." Leaning over, she nipped at Blake's ear. "The kind where your wife thinks you're at the office, and my husband thinks I'm shopping."

"Why didn't we go to a motel?"

"That's where we're going now." Nibbling on popcorn again, she sent him a wicked glance. "Though I think in our case we might substitute my apartment."

"I'm willing to be flexible. Summer..." He drew her against his side as they breezed through a light. "Just what was that movie about?"

Laughing, she let her head lay against his shoulder. "I haven't the vaguest idea."

Later, they lay naked in her bed, the curtains open to let in the light, the windows up to let in the breeze. From the apartment below came the repetitive sound of scales being played, a bit unsteadily, on the piano. Perhaps she'd dozed for a short time, because the sunlight seemed softer now, almost rosy. But she wasn't in any hurry for night to fall.

The sheets were warm and wrinkled from their bodies. The air was ripe with supper smells—grilling pork from the piano teacher's apartment, spaghetti sauce from the newlyweds next door. The breeze carried the mix of both, appealingly.

"It's nice," Summer murmured, with her head nestled in the curve of her lover's shoulder. "Just being here like this, knowing that anything there is to do can be done just as well tomorrow. You probably haven't played hookey enough." She was quite sure she hadn't.

"If I did, the business would suffer and the board would begin to grumble. Complaining's one of their favorite things."

Absently, she rubbed the bottom of her foot over the top of one of his. "I haven't asked you about the Hamilton chain because I thought you probably got enough of that at the office, and from the press, but I'd like to know if you got what you wanted."

He thought about reaching for a cigarette then decided it wasn't worth the effort. "I wanted those hotels. As it turned out, the deal satisfied all parties in the end. You can't ask for more than that."

"No." Thoughtfully, she rolled over so that she could look at him directly. Her hair brushed over his chest. "Why did you want them? Is it the acquisition itself, the property or just a matter of enjoying the wheeling and dealing? The strategy of negotiations?"

"It's all of that. Part of the enjoyment in business is setting up deals, working out the flaws, following through until you've gotten what you were aiming for. In some ways it's not that different from art."

"Business isn't art," Summer corrected archly.

"There are parallels. You set up an idea, work out the flaws, then follow through until you've created what you wanted."

"You're being logical again. In art you use the emotion in equal parts with the mind. You can't do that in business." Her shrug was typically French. Somehow she became more French whenever her craft was under discussion. "This is all facts and figures."

"You left out instinct. Facts and figures aren't enough without that."

She frowned, considering. "Perhaps, but you wouldn't follow instinct over a solid set of facts."

"Even a solid set of facts varies according to the circumstances and the players." He was thinking of her now, and himself. Reaching up, he tucked her hair behind her ear. "Instincts are very often more reliable."

And she was thinking of him now, and herself. "Often more," Summer murmured, "but not always more. That leaves room for failure."

"No amount of planning, no amount of facts, precludes failure."

"No." She laid her head on his shoulder again, trying to ward off the little trickle of panic that was trying to creep in.

He ran a hand down her back. She was still so cautious, he thought. A little more time, a little more room—a change of subject. "I have twenty new hotels to oversee, to reorganize," he began. "That means twenty more kitchens that have to be studied and graded. I'll need an expert."

She smiled a little as she lifted her head again. "Twenty is a very demanding and time-consuming number."

"Not for the best."

Tilting her head, she looked down her straight, elegant nose. "Naturally not, but the best is very difficult to come by."

"The best is currently very soft and very naked in my arms."

Her lips curved slowly, the way he most enjoyed them. "Very true. But this, I think, is not a negotiating table."

"You've a better idea how to spend the evening?"

She ran a fingertip along his jawline. "Much better."

He caught her hand in his and, drawing her finger into his mouth, nipped lightly. "Show me."

The idea appealed, and excited. It seemed that whenever they made love she was quickly dominated by her own emotions and his skill. This time, she would set the pace, and in her own time, in her own way, she would destroy the innate control that brought her both admiration and frustration. Just the thought of it sent a thrill racing up her spine.

She brought her mouth close to his, but used her tongue to taste. Slowly, very slowly, she traced his lips. Already she could feel the heat rising. With a lazy sigh, she shifted so that her body moved over his as she trailed kisses down his jaw.

A strong face, she thought, aristocratic but not soft, intelligent, but not cold. It was a face some women would find haughty—until they looked into the eyes. She did so now and saw the intensity, the heat, even the ruthlessness.

"I want you more than I should," she heard herself say. "I have you less than I want."

Before he could speak, she crushed her mouth to his and started the journey for both of them.

He was still throbbing from her words alone. He'd wanted to hear that kind of admission from her; he'd waited to hear it. Just as he'd waited to feel this strong, pure emotion from her. It was that emotion that stripped away all his defenses even as her seeking hands and mouth exploited the weaknesses.

She touched. His skin heated.

She tasted. His blood sang.

She encompassed. His mind swam.

Vulnerable. Blake discovered the new sensation in himself. She made him so. In the soft, lowering light—near dusk—he was trapped in that midnight world of quietly raging powers. Her fingers were cool and very sure as they stroked, enticed. He could feel them slide leisurely over him, pausing to linger while she sighed. And while she sighed, she exploited. His body was weighed down with layer after layer of pleasures—to be seduced so carefully, to be desired so fully.

With long, lengthy, openmouthed kisses, she explored all of him, reveling in the firm masculinity of his body—knowing she would soon rip apart that impenetrable control. She was obsessed with it, and with him. Could it be that now, after she'd made love with him, after she'd begun to understand the powers and weaknesses in his body, she would find even more delight in learning of them again?

There seemed to be no end to the variations of her feelings, to the changes of sensations she could experience when she was with him like this. Each time, every time, was as vital and unique as the first had been. If this was a contradiction to everything she'd ever believed was true about a man and woman, she didn't question it now. She exalted in it.

He was hers. Body and mind—she felt it. Almost tangibly she could sense the polish, the civilized sheen, that was so much a part of him melt away. It was what she wanted.

There was little sanity left. As she roamed over him the need became more primitive, more primal. He wanted more, endlessly more, but the blood was drumming in his head. She was so agile, so relentless. He experienced a wave of pure helplessness for the first time in his life. Her hands were clever—so clever he couldn't hear the quick unsteadiness of her breathing. He could feel her tormenting him exquisitely, but he couldn't see the flickers of passion or depth of desire in her eyes. He was blind and deaf to everything.

Then her mouth was devouring his and everything savage that civilized men restrain tore from him. He was mad for her. In his mind were dark swirling colors, in his ears was a wild rushing like a sea crazed by a storm. Her name ripped from him like an oath as he gripped her, rolling her to her back, enclosing her, possessing her.

And there was nothing but her, to take, to drown in, to ravage and to worship until passion spun from its peak and emptied him.

Chapter 11

"I'm starving."

It was full dark, with no moon to shed any trickle of light into the room. The darkness itself was comfortable and easy. They were still naked and tangled on Summer's bed, but the piano had been silent for an hour. There were no more supper smells in the air. Blake drew her a bit closer and kept his eyes shut, though it wasn't sleep he sought. Somehow in the silence, in the darkness, he felt closer to her.

"I'm starving," Summer repeated, a bit sulkily this time.

"You're the chef."

"Oh, no, not this time." Rising on her elbow, Summer glared at him. She could see the silhouette of his profile, the long line of chin, the straight nose, the sweep of brow. She wanted to kiss all of them again, but knew it was time to make a stand. "It's definitely your turn to cook."

"My turn?" He opened one eye, cautiously. "I could send out for pizza."

"Takes too long." She rolled on top of him to give him a smacking kiss—and a quick jab in the ribs. "I said I was starving. That's an immediate problem."

He folded his arms behind his head. He, too, could see only a silhouette—the drape of her hair, slope of her shoulder, the curve of her breasts. It was enough. "I don't cook."

"Everyone cooks something," she insisted.

"Scrambled eggs," he said, hoping it would discourage her. "That's about it."

"That'll do." Before he could think of anything to change her mind, she was off the bed and switching on the bedside lamp.

"Summer!" He tossed his arm over his eyes to shield them and tried a halfhearted moan. She grinned at that before she turned to the closet to find a robe.

"I have eggs, and a skillet."

"I make very bad eggs."

"That's okay." She found his slacks, shook them out briefly, then tossed them on top of him. "Real hunger makes allowances."

Resigned, Blake put his feet on the floor. "Then I don't expect a critique afterward."

While she waited, he slipped into a pair of brief jockey shorts. They were dark blue, cut low at the waist, high at the thigh. Very sexy, she mused, and very discreet. Strange how such an incidental thing could reflect a personality.

"Cooks like to be cooked for," she told him as he drew on his slacks.

He shrugged into his shirt, leaving it unbuttoned. "Then don't interfere."

"Wouldn't dream of it." Hooking her arm through his, Summer led him to the kitchen. Again, she switched on lights and made him wince. "Make yourself at home," she invited.

"Aren't you going to assist?"

"No, indeed." Summer took the top off the cookie jar and plucked out the familiar sandwich cookie. "I don't work overtime and I never assist."

"Union rules?"

"My rules."

"You're going to eat cookies?" he asked as he rummaged for a bowl. "And eggs?"

"This is just the appetizer," she said with her mouth full. "Want one?"

"I'll pass." Sticking his head in the refrigerator, he found a carton of eggs and a quart of milk.

"You might want to grate a bit of cheese," Summer began, then shrugged when he sent her an arch look. "Sorry. Carry on." Blake broke four eggs into the bowl then added a dollop of milk. "One should measure, you know."

"One shouldn't talk with one's mouth full," he said mildly and began to beat the eggs.

Overbeating them, she thought but managed to restrain herself. But when it came to cooking, willpower wasn't her strong suit. "You haven't heated up the pan, either." Undaunted by being totally ignored, she took another cookie. "I can see you're going to need lessons."

"If you want something to do, make some toast."

Obligingly she took a loaf of bread from the bin and popped two pieces in the toaster. "It's characteristic of cooks to get a bit testy when they're watched, but a good chef has to overcome that—and distractions." She waited until he'd poured the egg mixture into a skillet before going to him. Wrapping her arms around his waist, she pressed her lips to the back of his neck. "All manner of distraction. And you've got the flame up too high."

"Do you like your eggs singed or burned clear through?"

With a laugh, she ran her hands up his bare chest. "Singed is fine. I have a nice little white Bordeaux you might've put in the eggs, but since you didn't, I'll just pour some into glasses." She left him to cook and, by the time Blake had finished the eggs, she had buttered toast on a plate and chilled wine in glasses. "Impressive," Summer decided as she sat at the dinette. "And aromatic."

But it's the eyes that tell you first, he remembered. "Attractive?" He watched as she spooned eggs on her plate.

"Very, and—" she took a first testing bite "—yes, and quite good, all in all. I might consider putting you on the breakfast shift, on a trial basis."

"I might consider the job, if cold cereal were the basic menu."

"You'll have to expand your horizons." She continued to eat, enjoying the hot, simple food on an empty stomach. "I believe you could be quite good at this with a few rudimentary lessons."

"From you?"

She lifted her wine, and her eyes laughed over the

rim. "If you like. You certainly couldn't have a better teacher."

Her hair was still rumpled around her face—his hands had done that. Her cheeks were flushed, her eyes bright and flecked with gold. The robe threatened to slip off one shoulder, and left a teasing hint of skin exposed. As passion had stripped away his control, now emotions stripped away all logic.

"I love you, Summer."

She stared at him while the smile faded slowly. What went through her she didn't recognize. It didn't seem to be any one sensation, but a cornucopia of fears, excitement, disbelief and longings. Oddly, no one of them seemed dominant at first, but were so mixed and muddled she tried to grip any one of them and hold on to it. Not knowing what else to do, she set the glass down precisely, then stared at the wine shimmering inside.

"That wasn't a threat." He took her hand, holding it until she looked up at him again. "I don't see how it could come as that much of a surprise to you."

But it had. She expected affection. That was something she could deal with. She understood respect. But love—that was such a fragile word. Such an easily broken word. And something inside her begged for it to be taken from him, cherished, protected. Summer struggled against it.

"Blake, I don't need to hear that sort of thing the way other women do. Please—"

"Maybe you don't." He hadn't started the way he'd intended to, but now that he had, he'd finish. "But I need to say it. I've needed to for a long time now."

She drew her hand from his and nervously picked up

her glass again. "I've always thought that words are the first thing that can damage a relationship."

"When they're not said," Blake countered. "It's a lack of words, a lack of meaning, that damages a relationship. This one isn't a word I use casually."

"No." She could believe that. It might have been the belief that had the fear growing stronger. Love, when it was given demanded some kind of return. She wasn't ready—she was sure she wasn't ready. "I think it's best, if we want things to go on as they are, that we—"

"I don't want things to go on as they are," he interrupted. He'd rather have felt annoyance than this panic that was sneaking in. He took a moment, trying to alleviate both. "I want you to marry me."

"No." Summer's own panic became full-blown. She stood quickly, as if that would erase the words, put back the distance. "No, that's impossible."

"It's very possible." He rose too, unwilling to have her draw away from him. "I want you to share my life, my name. I want to share children with you and all the years it takes to watch them grow."

"Stop." She threw up her hand, desperate to halt the words. They were moving her, and she knew it would be too easy to say yes and make that ultimate mistake.

"Why?" Before she could prevent it, he'd taken her face in his hands. The touch was gentle, though there was steel beneath. "Because you're afraid to admit it's something you want, too?"

"No, it's not something I want—it's not something I believe in. Marriage—it's a license that costs a few dollars. A piece of paper. For a few thousand dollars more, you can get a divorce decree. Another piece of paper."

He could feel her trembling and cursed himself for

not knowing how to get through. "You know better than that. Marriage is two people who make promises to each other, and who make the effort to keep them. A divorce is giving up."

"I'm not interested in promises." Desperate, she pushed his hands from her face and stepped back. "I don't want any made to me, and I don't want to make any. I'm happy with my life just as it is. I have my career to think of."

"That's not enough for you, and we both know it. You can't tell me you don't feel for me. I can see it. Every time I'm with you it shows in your eyes, more each time." He was handling it badly, but saw no other course open but straight ahead. The closer he came, the further away she drew. "Damn it, Summer, I've waited long enough. If my timing's not as perfect as I wanted it to be, it can't be helped."

"Timing?" She dragged a hand through her hair. "What are you talking about? You've waited?" Dropping her hands, she began to pace the room. "Has this been one of your long-term plans, all neatly thought out, all meticulously outlined? Oh, I can see it." She let out a trembling breath and whirled back to him. It no longer made any difference to her if she were unreasonable. "Did you sit in your office and go over your strategy point by point? Was this the setting up, the looking for flaws, the following through?"

"Don't be ridiculous—"

"Ridiculous?" she tossed back. "No, I think not. You'd play the game well—disarming, confusing, charming, supportive. Patience, you'd have a lot of that. Did you wait until you thought I was at my most vulnerable?" Her breath was heaving now, and the words were tumbling out on each one. "Let me tell you something, Blake, I'm not a hotel chain you can acquire by waiting until the market's ripe."

In a slanted way she'd been killingly accurate. And the accuracy put him on the defensive. "Damn it, Summer, I want to marry you, not acquire you."

"The words are often one and the same, to my way of thinking. Your plan's a little off the mark this time, Blake. No deal. Now, I want you to leave me alone."

"We have a hell of a lot of talking to do."

"No, we have no talking to do, not about this. I work for you, for the term of the contract. That's all."

"Damn the contract." He took her by the shoulders, shaking her once in frustration. "And damn you for being so stubborn. I love you. That's not something you can brush aside as if it doesn't exist."

To their mutual surprise, her eyes filled abruptly, poignantly. "Leave me alone," she managed as the first tears spilled out. "Leave me completely alone."

The tears undermined him as her temper never would have done. "I can't do that." But he released her when he wanted to hold her. "I'll give you some time, maybe we both need time, but we'll have to come back to this."

"Just go away." She never allowed tears in front of anyone. Though she tried to dash them away, others fell quickly. "Go away." On the repetition she turned from him, holding herself stiff until she heard the click of the door.

She looked around, and though he was gone, he was everywhere. Dropping to the couch, she let herself weep and wished she were anywhere else.

She hadn't come to Rome for the cathedrals or the fountains or the art. Nor had she come for culture or history. As Summer took a wicked cab ride from the airport into the city, she was more grateful for the crowded streets and noise than the antiquity. Perhaps she'd stayed in America too long this time. Europe was fast cars, crumbling ruins and palaces. She needed Europe again, Summer told herself. As she zipped past the Trevi Fountain she thought of Philadelphia.

A few days away, she thought. Just a few days away, doing what she was best at, and everything would fall back into perspective again. She'd made a mistake with Blake—she'd known from the beginning it had been a mistake to get involved. Now it was up to her to break it off, quickly, completely. Before long he'd be grateful to her for preventing him from making an even larger mistake. Marriage—to her. Yes, she imagined he'd be vastly relieved, within even a few weeks.

Summer sat in the back of the cab watching Rome skim by and was more miserable than she'd ever been in her life.

When the cab squealed to a halt at the curb she climbed out. She stood for a moment, a slender woman in white fedora and jacket with a snakeskin bag slung carelessly over one shoulder. She was dressed like a woman of confidence and experience. In her eyes was a child who was lost.

Mechanically she paid off the driver, accepted her bag and his bow, then turned away. It was only just past 10:00 a.m. in Rome, and already hot under a spectacular sky. She remembered she'd left Philadelphia in a thunderstorm. Walking up the steps to an old, distinguished building, she knocked sharply five times. After a reasonable wait, she knocked again, harder.

When the door opened, she looked at the man in the

short silk robe. It was embroidered, she noticed, with peacocks. On anyone else it would've looked absurd. His hair was tousled, his eyes half-closed. A night's growth of beard shadowed his chin.

"Hello, Carlo. Wake you up?"

"Summer!" He swallowed the string of Italian abuse that had been on his tongue and grabbed her. "A surprise, *sì?*" He kissed her soundly, twice, then drew her away. "But why do you bring me a surprise at dawn?"

"It's after ten."

"Ten is dawn when you don't begin to sleep until five. But come in, come in. I don't forget you come for Gravanti's birthday."

Outside, Carlo's home was distinguished. Inside it was opulent. Dominated by marble and gold, the entrance hall only demonstrated the beginning of his penchant for the luxurious. They walked through and under arches into a living area crowded with treasures, small and large. Most of them had been given to him by pleased clients—or women. Carlo had a talent for picking lovers who remained amiable even when they were no longer lovers.

There was a brocade at the windows, Oriental carpets on the floor and a Tintoretto on the wall. Two sofas were piled with cushions deep enough to swim in. An alabaster lion, nearly two feet in height, sat beside one. A three-tiered chandelier shot out splinters of refracted light from its crystals.

She ran her finger down a porcelain ewer in delicate Chinese blue and white. "New?"

"Sì."

"Medici?"

"But of course. A gift from a…friend."

"Your friends are always remarkably generous."

He grinned. "But then, so am I."

"Carlo?"

The husky, impatient voice came from up the curving marble stairs. Carlo glanced up, then looked back at Summer and grinned again.

Summer removed her white fedora. "A friend, I take it."

"You'll give me a moment, *cara*." He was heading for the steps as he spoke. "Perhaps you could go into the kitchen, make coffee."

"And stay out of the way," Summer finished as Carlo disappeared upstairs. She started toward the kitchen, then went back to take her suitcase with her. There wasn't any use leaving Carlo with something like luggage to explain to his friend.

The kitchen was as spectacular as the rest of the house and as large as the average hotel room. Summer knew it as well as she knew her own. It was all in ebonies and ivories with what appeared to be acres of counter space. It boasted two ovens, a restaurant-sized refrigerator, two sinks and a dishwasher that could handle the aftermath of an embassy dinner. Carlo Franconi had never been one to do anything in a small way.

Summer opened a cabinet for the coffee beans and grinder. On impulse, she decided to make crêpes. Carlo, she mused, might be just a little while.

When he did come, she was just finishing up at the stove. "Ah, *bella,* you cook for me. I'm honored."

"I had a twinge of guilt about disrupting your morning. Besides—" She slipped crêpes, pregnant with warm apples and cinnamon, onto plates. "I'm hungry." Summer set them on a scrubbed worktable while Carlo pulled up chairs. "I should apologize for coming like this without warning. Was your friend annoyed?"

He flashed a grin as he sat. "You don't give me enough credit."

"Scusi." She passed the small pitcher of cream. "So, we'll be working together for Enrico's birthday."

"My veal, with spaghetti. Enrico has a weakness for my spaghetti. Every Friday, he is in my restaurant eating." Carlo started immediately on the crêpe. "And you make the dessert."

"A birthday cake." Summer drank coffee while her crêpe cooled untouched. Suddenly, she had no appetite for it. "Enrico requested something special, created just for him. Knowing his vanity, and his fondness for chocolate and whipped cream, it was easy to come up with it."

"But the dinner isn't for two more days. You come early?"

She shrugged and toyed with her coffee. "I wanted to spend some time in Europe."

"I see." And he thought he did. She was looking a bit hollow around the eyes. A sign of romantic trouble. "Everything goes well in Philadelphia?"

"The remodeling's done, the new menus printed. I think the kitchen staff is going to do very well. I hired Maurice from Chicago. You remember?"

"Oh, yes, pressed duck."

"It's an exciting menu," she went on. "Just the sort I'd have if I ever decided to have a place of my own. I suppose I developed a bit of respect for you, Carlo, when I started to deal with the paperwork."

"Paperwork." He finished off his crêpes and eyed hers. "Ugly but necessary. You aren't eating, Summer."

"Hmm? No, I guess it's a touch of jet lag." She waved at her plate. "Go ahead."

Taking her at her word, he switched plates. "You solved the problem of Max?"

Absently she touched her arm. The stitches, thank God, were a thing of the past. "We're managing. Mother came to visit for a while. She always makes an impression."

"Monique! So, how is she?"

"Married again," Summer said simply and lifted her coffee. "A director this time, another American."

"She's happy?"

"Naturally." The coffee was strong—stronger than she'd grown used to in America. She thought in frustration that nothing was as it once was for her. "They're starting a film together in another few weeks."

"Perhaps her wisest choice. Someone who would understand her artistic temperament, her needs." He lingered over the perfect melding of spices and fruit. "And how is your American?"

Summer set down her coffee and stared at Carlo. "He wants to marry me."

Carlo choked on a bite of crêpe and grabbed for his cup. "So—congratulations."

"Don't be silly." Unable to sit, she rose, sticking her hands in the pockets of her long, loose jacket. "I'm not going to."

"No?" Going to the stove, Carlo poured them both more coffee. "Why not? You find him unattractive, maybe? Bad tempered, stupid?"

"Of course not." Impatient, she curled and uncurled her fingers inside the jacket pockets. "That has nothing to do with it."

"What has?"

"I've no intention of getting married to anyone. That's one merry-go-round I can do without."

"You don't choose to grab for the brass ring, maybe because you're afraid you'd miss."

She lifted her chin. "Be careful, Carlo."

He shrugged at the icy tone. "You know I say what I think. If you'd wanted to hear something else, you wouldn't have come here."

"I came here because I wanted a few days with a friend, not to discuss marriage."

"You're losing sleep over it."

She'd picked up her cup and now slammed it down again. Coffee spilled over the sides. "It was a long flight and I've been working hard. And, yes, maybe I'm upset over the whole thing," she continued before Carlo could speak. "I hadn't expected this from him, hadn't wanted it. He's an honest man, and I know when he says he loves me and wants to marry me, he means it. For the moment. That doesn't make it any easier to say no."

Her fury didn't unnerve him. Carlo was well used to passionate emotions from women—he preferred them. "And you—how do you feel about him?"

She hesitated, then walked to the window. She could look out on Carlo's garden from there—a quiet, isolated spot that served as a border between the house and the busy streets of Rome. "I have feelings for him," Summer murmured. "Stronger feelings than are wise. If anything, they only make it more important that I break things off now. I don't want to hurt him, Carlo, any more than I want to be hurt myself."

"You're so sure love and marriage would hurt?" He put his hands on her shoulders and kneaded them lightly. "When you look so hard at the what-ifs in life, *cara mia,* you miss much living. You have someone who loves you, and though you won't say the words, I think you love him back. Why do you deny yourself?"

"Marriage, Carlo." She turned, her eyes earnest. "It's not for people like us, is it?"

"People like us?"

"We're so wrapped up in what it is we do. We're used to coming and going as we please, when we please. We have no one to answer to, no one to consider but ourselves. Isn't that why you've never married?"

"I could say I'm a generous man, and feel it would be too selfish to limit my gifts to only one woman." She smiled, fully, the way he'd wanted to see her smile. Gently, he brushed the hair away from her face. "But to you, the truth is I've never found anyone who could make my heart tremble. I've looked. If I found her, I'd run for a license and a priest quickly."

With a sigh, she turned back to the window. The flowers were a tapestry of color in the strong sun. "Marriage is a fairy tale, Carlo, full of princes and peasants and toads. I've seen too many of those fairy tales fade."

"We write our own stories, Summer. A woman like you knows that because you've always done so."

"Maybe. But this time I just don't know if I have the courage to turn the next page."

"Take your time. There's no better place to think about life and love than *Roma.* No better man to think about them with than Franconi. Tonight, I cook for you. Linguini—" he kissed the tips of his fingers "—to die for. You can make me one of your babas—just like when we were students, *sì?*"

Turning back to him, Summer wrapped her arms

around his neck. "You know, Carlo, if I were the marrying kind, I'd take you, for your pasta alone."

He grinned. "*Carissima,* even my pasta is nothing compared to my—"

"I'm sure," she interrupted dryly. "Why don't you get dressed and take me shopping? I need to buy something fantastic while I'm in Rome. I haven't given my mother a wedding present yet."

How could he have been so stupid? Blake flicked on his lighter and watched the flame cut through the darkness. It wouldn't be dawn for an hour yet, but he'd given up on sleep. He'd given up on trying to imagine what Summer was doing in Rome while he sat wakeful in an empty suite of rooms and thought of her. If he went to Rome…

No, he'd promised himself he'd give her some room, especially since he'd handled everything so badly. He'd given them both some room.

More strategy, he thought derisively and drew hard on the cigarette. Was that what the whole thing was about? He'd always enjoyed challenges, problems. Summer was certainly both. Was that the reason he wanted her? If she'd agreed to marry him, he could have congratulated himself on a plan well thought out and perfectly executed. Another Cocharan acquisition. Damn it.

He rose. He paced. Smoke curled from the cigarette between his fingers, then disappeared into the half-light. He knew better than that, even if she didn't. If it were true that he'd treated the whole affair like a problem to be carefully solved, it was only because that was his make-up. But he loved her, and if he were sure of anything, it was that she loved him too. How was he going to get over that wall she'd erected?

Go back to the way things were? Impossible. He looked out at the city as the darkness began to soften. In the east, the sky was just beginning to lighten with the first hints of pink. Suddenly he realized he'd watched too many sunrises alone. Too much had changed between them now, Blake mused. Too much had been said. You couldn't take love back and lock it away for convenience's sake.

He'd stayed away from her for a full week before she'd gone to Rome. It had been much harder than he'd imagined it would be, but her tears that night had pushed him to it. Now he wondered if that had been yet another mistake. Perhaps if he'd gone to her the next day...

Shaking his head, he moved away from the window again. All along, his mistake had been trying to treat the situation with logic. There wasn't any logic in loving someone, only feelings. Without logic, he lost all advantage.

Madly in love. Yes, he thought the term very apt. It was all madness, an incurable madness. If she'd been with him, he could have shown her. Somehow, when she came back, he thought violently, he'd take that damn wall down piece by piece until she was forced to face the madness, too.

When the phone rang he stared at it. Summer? "Hello."

"Blake?" The voice was a little too sulky, a little too French.

"Yes. Monique?"

"I'm sorry to disturb you, but I always forget how

much time is different between west and east. I was just going to bed. You were up?"

"Yes." The sun was slowly rising, the room was pale with light. Most of the city wasn't yet awake, but he was. "Did you have a good trip back to California?"

"I slept almost the whole way. Thank God, because there have been so many parties. So little changes in Hollywood—some of the names, some of the faces. Now, to be chic, one must wear sunglasses on a string. My mother did this, but only to keep from losing them."

He smiled because Monique demanded smiles. "You don't need trends to be chic."

"How flattering." Her voice was very young and very pleased.

"What can I do for you, Monique?"

"Oh, so sweet. First I must tell you how lovely it was to stay in your hotel again. Always the service is impeccable. And Summer's arm, it's better, no?"

"Apparently. She's in Rome."

"Oh, yes, my memory. Well, she was never one to sit too long in one space, my Summer. I saw her only briefly before I left. She seemed...preoccupied."

He felt his stomach muscles knotting, his jaw tightening. Deliberately he relaxed both. "She's been working very hard on the kitchen."

Monique's lips curved. He gives away nothing, this one, she thought with approval. "Yes, well I may see her again for a short time. I must ask you a favor, Blake. You were so kind during my visit."

"Whatever I can do."

"The suite where I stayed, I found it so restful, so *agréable*. I wonder if you could reserve it for me again, in two days' time."

"Two days?" His brow creased, but he automatically reached for a pen to jot it down. "You're coming back east?"

"I'm so foolish, so—what is it?—absent-minded, *oui?* I have business to take care of there, and with Summer's accident, it all went out of my head. I must come back and tie up the ends that are loose. And the suite?"

"Of course, I'll see to it."

"*Merci.* And perhaps, I could ask one more thing of you. I will have a small party on Saturday evening— just a few old friends and some wine. I'd be very grateful if you could stop by for a few minutes. Around eight?"

There was nothing he wanted less at the moment than a party. But manners, upbringing and business left him only one answer. Again, he automatically noted down the date and time. "I'd be happy to."

"Marvelous. Till Saturday then, *au revoir.*"

After hanging up the phone, Monique gave a tinkle of laughter. True, she was an actress, not a screenwriter, but she thought her little scenario was brilliant. Yes, absolutely brilliant.

Picking up the phone, she prepared to send a cablegram. To Rome.

Chapter 12

Chérie. Must return to Philadelphia for some unfinished business before filming begins. Will be at Cocharan House in my suite over the weekend. Having a little soirée Saturday evening. Do come. 8:30. A bientôt. Mother.

And just what was she up to? Summer glanced over the cable again as she cruised above the Atlantic. Unfinished business? Summer could think of no business Monique would have in Philadelphia, unless it involved husband number two. But that was ancient history, and Monique always had someone else handle her business dealings. She'd always claimed a good actress was a child at heart and had no head for business. It was another one of her diabolically helpless ways that made it possible for her to do only exactly as she wanted. What

Summer couldn't figure out was why Monique would want to come back east.

With a shrug, Summer slipped the cable back into her bag.

She didn't feel like hassling with people and cocktail talk in just over five hours. The day before, she'd outdone herself with the creation of a birthday cake shaped like Enrico's palatial home outside Rome, and filled with a wickedly wonderful combination of chocolate and cream. It had taken her twelve hours. And for once, at the host's insistence, she'd remained and joined the party for champagne and dessert.

She'd thought it would be good for her. The people, the elegance, the celebratory atmosphere. It had done no more than show her that she didn't want to be in Rome exchanging small talk and drinking wine. She wanted to be home. Home, though it surprised her, was Philadelphia.

She didn't long for Paris and her odd little flat on the Left Bank. She wanted her fourth-floor apartment in Philadelphia, where there were memories of Blake in every corner. However foolish it made her, however unwise or impractical it was, she wanted Blake.

Now, flying home, she found that hadn't changed. It was Blake she wanted to go to when she was on the ground again. It was to Blake she wanted to tell all the foolish stories she'd heard in Enrico's dining room. It was Blake she wanted to hear laugh. It was Blake she wanted to curl up next to now that the nervous energy of the past few days was draining.

Sighing, she tilted her seat back and closed her eyes. But she would do her duty and go to her mother's suite. Perhaps Monique's little party was the perfect diversion. It would give Summer just a bit more time before she faced Blake again. Blake, and the decision she had thought was already made.

B.C. ran a finger around the inside of the snug collar of his shirt and hoped he didn't look as nervous as he felt. Seeing Monique again after all these years—having to introduce Lillian to her. *Monique, my wife, Lillian. Lillian, Monique Dubois, a former lover. Small world, isn't it?*

Though he was a man who appreciated a good joke, this one eluded him.

It seemed there was no statute of limitations on marital transgressions. It was true that he'd only strayed once, and then during an unofficial separation from his wife that had left him angry, bitter and frightened. A crime committed once, was still a crime committed.

He loved Lillian, had always loved her, but he'd never be able to deny that the brief affair with Monique had happened. And he couldn't deny that it had been exciting, passionate and memorable.

They'd never contacted each other again, though once or twice he'd seen her when he was still actively working in the business. Even that had been so long ago.

So, why had she called him now, twenty years later, insisting that he come—with his wife—to her suite at the Philadelphia Cocharan House? He ran his finger around his collar once again. Something was choking him. Monique's only explanation had been that it concerned the happiness of his son and her daughter.

That had left him with the problem of fabricating a reason for coming into town and insisting that Lillian accompany him. That hadn't been a piece of cake, because he'd married a sharp-minded, independent woman, but it was nothing compared with the next ordeal.

"Are you going to fuss with that tie all day?" B.C. jumped as his wife came up behind him. "Easy." With a laugh, she brushed the back of his jacket, smoothing it over his shoulders in a habit that took him back to their honeymoon. "You'd think you'd never spent an evening with a celebrity before. Or is it just French actresses that make you nervous?"

This one French actress, B.C. thought and turned to his wife. She'd always been lovely, not the breath-catching beauty Monique had been, but lovely with the kind of quiet looks that remain lovely through the years. Her pure, rich brunette hair was liberally streaked with gray, but styled in such a way that the contrasting colors enhanced her looks.

Lillian had always had style. She'd been his partner, always, had stood up to him, stood by him. A strong woman. He'd needed a strong woman. She was the best damn first mate a man could ask for. He put his hands on her shoulders and kissed her, quite tenderly.

"I love you, Lily." When she touched his cheek and smiled, he took her hand, feeling like the condemned man walking his last mile. "We'd better go. We'll be late."

Blake hung up the phone in disgust. He was certain Summer would be back that evening. But though he'd called her apartment off and on for over an hour, there'd been no answer. He was out of patience, and in no mood to go down and be sociable in Monique's suite. Much like his father had done, he tugged on his tie.

When all this was over, when she was back, he was going to find a way to convince her to go away with him. He'd find that damn island in the Pacific if that's what it took. He'd *buy* the damn island and set up house-keeping. Build a chain of pizza parlors or fast-food restaurants. Maybe that would satisfy the woman.

Feeling unreasonable, and just a little mean, he strode out of the apartment.

Monique surveyed the suite and nodded. The flowers were a nice touch—not too many, just a few buds here and there to give the rooms a whiff of a garden. A touch—only a touch of romance. The wine was chilling, the glasses sparkling in the subdued lighting. And Max had outdone himself with the hors d'oeuvres, she decided. A little caviar, a little pâté, some miniature quiches—very elegant. She must remember to pay a visit to the kitchen.

As for herself—Monique touched a hand to the chignon at the base of her neck. Not her usual style, but she wanted to add the air of dignity. She felt the evening might call for it. But the black silk pants and off-the-shoulder blouse were sexy and chic. She simply couldn't resist the urge to dress with a bit of flair for the part.

The scene was set, she decided. Now it was only a matter for the players....

The knock came. With a slow smile, Monique went toward the door. Act one was about to begin.

"B.C.!" Her smile was brilliant, her hands thrown out to him. "How wonderful to see you again after all this time."

Her beauty was as stunning as ever. There was no resisting that smile. Though he'd been determined to be very aloof and very polite, his voice warmed. "Monique, you don't look a minute older."

"Always the charmer." She laughed, then kissed his cheek before she turned to the woman beside him. "And you are Lillian. How lovely that we meet at last. B.C. has told me so much of you, I feel we're old friends."

Lillian measured the woman across the threshold and lifted a brow. "Oh?"

No fool, this one, Monique decided instantly, and liked her. "Of course, that was all so long ago, so we must get to know each other all over again. Now please come in. B.C., you'd be kind enough to open a bottle of champagne."

A bundle of nerves, B.C. crossed the room to comply. A drink would be an excellent idea. He'd have preferred bourbon, straight up.

"Of course, I've seen you many times," Lillian began. "I'm sure you haven't made a movie I've missed, Ms. Dubois."

"Monique, please." In a simple, gracious gesture, she plucked a rosebud from a vase and handed it to Lillian. "And I'm flattered. From time to time I would retire, this last occasion has been the longest. But always, going back to the film is like going back to an old lover."

The cork blew out of the bottle like a missile and bounced off the ceiling. Calmly Monique slipped an arm through Lillian's. Inside she was giggling like a girl. "Such an exciting sound, is it not? It always makes me happy to hear champagne being opened. We must have a toast, *n'est-ce pas?*"

She lifted a glass with a flourish, and looked, to Lillian's thinking, just like the character she'd played in *Yesterday's Dream.*

"To fate, I think," Monique decided. "And the strange way it twists us all together." She clinked her glass against B.C.'s, then his wife's, before drinking. "So tell me, you are still enchanted with sailing, B.C.?"

He cleared his throat, no longer certain if he should watch his wife or Monique. Both of them were definitely watching him. "Ah, yes. As a matter of fact, Lillian and I just got back from Tahiti."

"How charming. A perfect place for lovers, *oui?*"

Lillian sipped her wine. "Perfect."

"Et voilà," Monique said when the knock sounded. "The next guest. Please help yourself." It was now Act Two. Having the time of her life, Monique went to answer. "Blake, so kind of you to come, and how charming you look."

"Monique." He took the hand she extended and brought it to his lips even as he calculated just how long it would be before he could make his escape. "Welcome back."

"I must be certain not to wear out the welcome. You'll be surprised by my other guests, I think." With this she gestured inside.

The last two people he'd expected to see in Monique's suite were his parents. He crossed the room and bent to kiss his mother. "Very surprised. I didn't know you were in town."

"We only got in a little while ago." Lillian handed her son a glass of champagne. "We did call your suite, but the phone was busy." Just what stage is this woman setting? Lillian wondered as Monique joined them.

"Families," she said grandly, helping herself to some caviar. "I have a great fondness for them. I must tell you both how I admire your son. The young Cochran carries on the tradition, is it not so?"

For an instant, only an instant, Lillian's eyes narrowed. She wanted to know just what tradition the French actress referred to.

"We're both very proud of Blake," B.C. said with some relief. "He's not only maintained the Cochran standard, but expanded it. The Hamilton chain was an excellent move." He toasted his son. "Excellent. How's the turnover in the kitchen going?"

"Very smoothly." And it was the last thing he wanted to discuss. "We start serving from the new menu tomorrow."

"Then we timed our visit well," Lillian put in. "We'll have a chance to test it firsthand."

"Do you know the coincidence?" Monique asked Lillian as she offered the tray of quiches.

"Coincidence?"

"But it is amusing. It is my daughter who now manages your son's kitchen."

"Your daughter." Lillian glanced at her husband. "No, it wasn't mentioned to me."

"She is a superb chef. You would agree, Blake? She often cooks for him," she added with a deliberate smile before he could make any comment.

Lillian held the rosebud under her nose. Interesting. "Really?"

"A charming girl," B.C. put in. "She has your looks, Monique, though I could hardly credit that you had a grown daughter."

"And I was just as surprised when I first met your son." She smiled at him. "Isn't it strange where the years go?"

B.C. cleared his throat and poured more wine.

Weeks before, Blake had wondered what messages had passed between Summer and his father. Now he had no trouble recognizing what wasn't being said between B.C. and Monique. He looked at his mother first and saw her calmly drinking champagne.

His father and Summer's mother? When? he wondered as he tried to digest it. For as long as he could remember, his parents had been devoted, almost inseparable. No—abruptly he remembered a short, turbulent time during his early teens. The house had been full of tension, arguments in undertones. Then B.C. had been gone for two weeks—three? A business trip, his mother had told him, but even then he'd known better. But it had been over so quickly, he'd rarely thought of it since. Now...now he had a definite idea where his father had spent at least some of that time away from home. And with whom.

He caught his father's eye—the uncomfortable, half-defiant look. The man, Blake mused, was certainly paying for a slip in fidelity that was two decades old. He saw Monique smile, slowly. Just what the hell was she trying to stir up?

Almost before the anger could fully form, she laid a hand on his arm. It was a gesture that asked him to wait, to be patient. Then came another knock. "Ah, excuse me. You would pour another glass?" Monique asked B.C. "We have one more guest tonight."

When she opened the door, Monique couldn't have been more pleased with her daughter. The simple jade silk dress was soft, narrow and subtly sexy. It made her slight pallor very romantic. "*Chérie,* so good of you not to disappoint me."

"I can't stay long, Mother, I have to get some sleep." She held out a pink-ribboned box. "But I wanted to bring you a wedding gift."

"So sweet." Monique brushed her lips over Summer's cheek. "And I have something for you. Something I hope you'll always treasure." Stepping aside, she drew Summer in.

Not like this, Summer thought desperately when the first shock of seeing Blake again rippled through her. She'd wanted to be prepared, rested, confident. She didn't want to see him here, now. And his parents— one look at the woman beside Blake and she knew she had to be B.C.'s wife. Nothing else made sense—Monique's kind of sense.

"Your game isn't amusing, Mother," she murmured in French.

"On the contrary, it might be the most important thing I've ever done. B.C.," she said in gay tones, "you've met my daughter, *oui?*"

"Yes, indeed." With a smile, he handed Summer a glass of champagne. "Nice to see you again."

"And Blake's mother," Monique continued. "Lillian, may I present my only child, Summer."

"I'm very pleased to meet you." Lillian took her hand warmly. She wasn't blind and had seen the stunned look that had passed between her son and the actress's daughter. There'd been surprise, longing and uncertainty. If Monique had set the stage for this, Lilian would do her best to help. "I've just been hearing that you're a chef and responsible for the new menu we'll be boasting of tomorrow."

"Yes." She searched for something to say. "Did you enjoy your sailing? Tahiti, wasn't it?"

"We had a marvelous time, even though B.C. tends to become Captain Bligh if you don't watch him."

"Nonsense." He slipped his arm around his wife's shoulders. "This is the only woman I'd ever trust at the wheel of one of my ships."

They adore each other. Summer realized it and found it surprised her. Their marriage was nearing its fortieth year, and obviously hadn't been without storms... yet they adored each other.

"It's rather beautiful, is it not, when a husband and wife can share an interest and yet be—separate people?" Monique beamed at them, then looked at Blake. "You would agree that such things keep a man and woman together, even when they have to struggle through hard times and misunderstandings?"

"I would." He looked directly at Summer. "It's a matter of love, and of respect and perhaps of...optimism."

"Optimism!" Monique clearly found the word perfect. "Yes, this I like. I, of course, am always so— perhaps too much. I've had four husbands, clearly too optimistic." She laughed at herself. "But then, I think I looked always first, and perhaps only, for romance. Would you say, Lillian, that it's a mistake not to look beyond that?"

"We all look for romance, love, passion." She touched her husband's arm lightly, in a gesture so natural neither of them noticed it. "Then of course respect. I suppose I'd have to add two things to that." She looked up at her husband. "Tolerance and tenacity. Marriage needs them all."

She knew. As B.C. saw the look in his wife's eyes he realized she'd always known. For twenty years, she'd known.

"Excellent." Rather pleased with herself, Monique set her gift on the table. "This is the perfect time then to open a gift celebrating my marriage. This time I intend to put all those things into it."

She wanted to leave. Summer told herself it was only a matter of turning around and walking to the door. She stood rooted, with her eyes locked on Blake's.

"Oh, but it's beautiful." Reverently, Monique lifted the tiny hand-crafted merry-go-round from the bed of tissue. The horses were ivory, trimmed in gilt—each one perfect, each one unique. At the turn of the base, it played a romantic Chopin Prelude. "But, darling, how perfect. A carousel to celebrate a marriage. The horses should be named romance, love, tenacity and so forth. I shall treasure it."

"I—" Summer looked at her mother, and suddenly none of the practicalities, none of the mistakes mattered. "Be happy, *ma mére*."

Monique touched her cheek with a fingertip, then brushed it with her lips. "And you, *mignonne*."

B.C. leaned down to whisper in his wife's ear. "You know, don't you?"

Amused, she lifted her glass. "Of course," she answered in an undertone. "You've never been able to keep secrets from me."

"But—"

"I knew then and hated you for almost a day. Do you remember whose fault it was? I don't anymore."

"God, Lily, if you'd known how guilty I was. Tonight, I was nearly suffocating with—"

"Good," she said simply. "Now, you old fool, let's get out of here so these children can iron things out. Monique—" She held out her hand, and as hands met, eyes met, things passed between them that would never have to be said. "Thank you for a lovely evening, and my best wishes to you and your husband."

"And mine to you." With a smile reminiscent of the past, she held out her arms to B.C. *"Au revoir, mon ami."*

He accepted the embrace, feeling like a man who'd just been granted amnesty. He wanted nothing more than to go up to his own suite and show his wife how much he loved her. "Perhaps we'll have lunch tomorrow," he said absently to the room at large. "Good night."

Monique began to giggle as the door shut behind him. "Love, it will always make me laugh. So—" Briskly, she began to rewrap her gift and box it. "My bags are being held for me downstairs and my plane leaves in one hour."

"An hour?" Summer began. "But—"

"My business is done." Tucking the box under her arm, she rose on her toes to kiss Blake. "You have the good fortune of possessing excellent parents." Then she kissed Summer. "And so, my sweet, do you, though they weren't suited to remain husband and wife. The suite is paid for through the night, the champagne's still cold." She glided for the door leaving a trail of Paris in her wake. Pausing in the doorway, she looked back. *"Bon appétit, mes enfants."* Monique considered it one of her very finest exits.

When the door closed, Summer stood where she was, unsure if she wanted to applaud or throw something.

"Quite a performance," Blake commented. "More wine?"

She could be as urbane and casual as he. "All right."

"And how was Rome?"

"Hot."

"And your cake?"

"Magnificent." Lifting her freshly filled glass, she took two steps away. It was always better to talk of the unimportant when so many urgent needs were pressing. "Things running smoothly here?"

"Amazingly so. Though I think everyone'll be relieved that you're here for the first run tomorrow. Tell me—" he sipped his own wine, approving it "—when did you first know that my father and your mother had had an affair?"

That was blunt enough, she thought. Well, she would be equally blunt. "When it was happening. I was only a child, but children are astute. You could say I suspected it then. I was sure of it when I first mentioned my mother's name to your father."

He nodded, remembering the meeting in his office. "Just how much have you let that bother you?"

"It was awkward." Restlessly she moved her shoulders.

"And you were determined not to let history repeat itself."

His perception was too often killingly accurate. "Perhaps."

"But then, in a matter of speaking, it did."

With another attempt at casualness, she spread some caviar on a cracker. "But then, neither of us was married."

As if it were only general cocktail talk, Blake chose a quiche. "You know why your mother did this tonight."

Summer shook her head when he offered the tray. "Monique could never resist a scene of any kind. She set the stage, brought in the players, to show me, I think, that while marriage might not be perfect, it can be durable."

"Was she successful?" When she didn't speak, Blake set down his glass. It was time they stopped hedging, time they stopped speaking in generalities. "There hasn't been an hour since the last time I saw you that I haven't thought of you."

Her eyes met his. Helplessly she shook her head. "Blake, I don't think you should—"

"Damn it, you're going to hear me out. We're good for each other. You can't tell me you don't believe that. Maybe you were right before about the way I planned out my...courtship," he decided for a lack of a better word. "Maybe I was too smug about it, too sure that if I waited for just the right moment, I'd have exactly what I wanted with the least amount of trouble. I had to be sure or I'd've gone insane trying to give you enough time to see just what we could have together."

"I was too hard that night." She wrapped her arms around herself then dropped them to her sides. "I said things because you frightened me. I didn't mean them, not all of them."

"Summer." He touched her cheek. "I meant everything I said that night. I want you now as much as I wanted you the first time."

"I'm here." She stepped closer. "We're alone."

The need twisted inside him. "I want to make love with you, but not until I know what it is you want from me. Do you want only a few nights, a few memories, like our parents had together?"

She turned away then. "I don't know how to explain."

"Tell me how you feel."

She took a moment to steady herself. "All right. When I cook, I take this ingredient and that. I have my own hands, my own skill, and putting these together, I make something perfect. If I don't find it perfect, I toss it out. There's little patience in me." She paused a moment, wondering if he could possibly understand this kind of analogy. "I've thought that if I ever decided to become involved in a relationship, there would be this ingredient and that, and again I'd put them together. But I knew it would never be perfect. So…" She let out a long breath. "I wondered if that too would be something to toss out."

"A relationship isn't something that has to be created in a day, or perfected in a day. Part of the game is to keep working on it. Fifty years still isn't long enough."

"A long time to work on something that'll always be just a little flawed."

"Too much of a challenge?"

She whirled, then stopped. "You know me too well," she murmured. "Too well for my own good. Maybe too well for your own."

"You're wrong," he said quietly. "You are my own good."

Her mouth trembled open, then closed. "Please," she managed, "I want to finish this. When I was in Rome, I tried to tell myself that this was what I wanted—to go back to flying here, there, without anyone to worry about but myself and the next dish I would create. When I was in Rome," she added with a sigh, "I was more miserable than I've ever been in my life."

He couldn't prevent the grin. "Sorry to hear it."

"No, I think you're not." Turning away, she ran her fingertip around and around the rim of a champagne glass. Since she would only explain once, she wanted to be certain she explained well. "On the plane, I told myself that when I came back, we would talk, reasonably, logically. We'd work the situation out in the best manner. In my head, I thought that would be a continuation of our relationship as it was. Intimacy without strings, which is perhaps not intimacy at all." She lifted the glass and sipped some of the cold, frothy wine. "When I walked in here tonight and saw you, I knew that would be impossible. We can't see each other as we have been. In the end, that would damage us both."

"You're not walking out of my life."

Turning back, she stood toe-to-toe with him. "I would, if I could. And damn it, you're not the one who's stopping me. It's me! None of your planning, none of your logic could've changed what was inside me. Only I could change it, only what I feel could change it."

She took his hands. She took a deep breath. "I want to ride that merry-go-round with you, and I want my shot at the brass ring."

His hands slid up her arms, into her hair. "Why? Just tell me why."

"Because sometime between the moment you walked in my front door and now, I fell in love with you. No matter how foolish it is, I want to take a chance on that."

"We're going to win." His mouth sought hers, and when she trembled he knew it was as much from nerves as passion. Soon they'd face the passion, now he would soothe the nerves. "If you like, we'll take a trial period." He began to roam her face with kisses. "We can even put it in contract form—more practical."

"Trial?" She started to draw away from him, but he held her close.

"Yes, and if during the trial period either of us wants a divorce, they simply have to wait until the end of the contract term."

Her brows came together. Could he speak of business now? Would he dare? Her chin tilted challengingly. "How long is the contract term?"

"Fifty years."

Laughing, she threw her arms around his neck. "Deal. I want it drawn up tomorrow, in triplicate. But tonight—" she began to nibble on his lips as she ran her hands beneath his jacket "—tonight we're only lovers. Truly lovers now. And the suite is ours till morning."

The kiss was long—it was slow—it was lingering.

"Remind me to send Monique a case of champagne," Blake said as he lifted Summer into his arms.

"Speaking of it…" Leaning over—a bit precariously—she lifted the two half-full glasses from the table. "We shouldn't let it get flat. And later," she continued as he carried her toward the bedroom, "much later, perhaps we can send out for pizza."

* * * * *

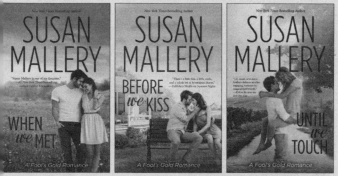

The women of Bliss County are ready to meet the men of their dreams! See how it all begins in this enchanting new series by #1 *New York Times* bestselling author

LINDA LAEL MILLER

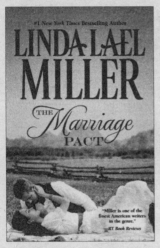

Ten years ago, Hadleigh Stevens was eighteen and *this* close to saying "I do," when Tripp Galloway interrupted her walk down the aisle. Now that she's recovered from her youthful mistake *and* Tripp's interference, Hadleigh and her single friends form a marriage pact. She doesn't expect Tripp to meddle with her new plan to find Mr. Right—or to discover that she's more attracted to him than ever!

Divorced and eager to reconnect with his cowboy roots, Tripp returns to Bliss County to save his ailing father's ranch. He's not looking for another wife—certainly not his best friend's little sister. But he's never been able to forget Hadleigh. And this time, if she ends up in his arms, he won't be walking away!

Available now wherever books are sold!

Be sure to connect with us at:

Harlequin.com/Newsletters
Facebook.com/HarlequinBooks
Twitter.com/HarlequinBooks

www.Harlequin.com

TERI WILSON

Ever since she was a little girl learning to make decadent truffles in her family's chocolate shop, Juliet Arabella has been aware of the bitter feud between the Arabellas and the Mezzanottes. With their rival chocolate boutiques on the same street in Napa Valley, these families *never* mix. Until one night, when Juliet anonymously attends the annual masquerade ball. In a moonlit vineyard, she finds herself falling for a gorgeous stranger, a man who reminds her what passion is like outside the kitchen. But her bliss is short-lived when she discovers her masked prince is actually Leo Mezzanotte, newly returned from Paris and the heir to her archenemy's confection dynasty.

With her mind in a whirl, Juliet leaves for Italy to represent the Arabellas in a prestigious chocolate competition. The prize money will help her family's struggling business, and Juliet figures it's a perfect opportunity to forget Leo…only to find him already there and gunning for victory. As they compete head-to-head, Leo and Juliet's fervent attraction boils over. But Juliet's not sure whether to trust her adversary, or give up on the sweetest love she's ever tasted….

Available now wherever books are sold!

Be sure to connect with us at:

Harlequin.com/Newsletters
Facebook.com/HarlequinBooks
Twitter.com/HarlequinBooks

www.Harlequin.com

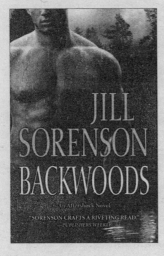

REQUEST YOUR FREE BOOKS!

2 FREE NOVELS
FROM THE ROMANCE COLLECTION
PLUS 2 FREE GIFTS!

YES! Please send me 2 FREE novels from the Romance Collection and my 2 FREE gifts (gifts are worth about $10). After receiving them, if I don't wish to receive any more books, I can return the shipping statement marked "cancel." If I don't cancel, I will receive 4 brand-new novels every month and be billed just $6.24 per book in the U.S. or $6.74 per book in Canada. That's a savings of at least 22% off the cover price. It's quite a bargain! Shipping and handling is just 50¢ per book in the U.S. and 75¢ per book in Canada.* I understand that accepting the 2 free books and gifts places me under no obligation to buy anything. I can always return a shipment and cancel at any time. Even if I never buy another book, the two free books and gifts are mine to keep forever.

194/394 MDN F4XY

Name _____ (PLEASE PRINT) _____

Address _____ Apt. # _____

City _____ State/Prov. _____ Zip/Postal Code _____

Signature (if under 18, a parent or guardian must sign)

Mail to the Harlequin® Reader Service:
IN U.S.A.: P.O. Box 1867, Buffalo, NY 14240-1867
IN CANADA: P.O. Box 609, Fort Erie, Ontario L2A 5X3

Want to try two free books from another line?
Call 1-800-873-8635 or visit www.ReaderService.com.

* Terms and prices subject to change without notice. Prices do not include applicable taxes. Sales tax applicable in N.Y. Canadian residents will be charged applicable taxes. Offer not valid in Quebec. This offer is limited to one order per household. Not valid for current subscribers to the Romance Collection or the Romance/Suspense Collection. All orders subject to credit approval. Credit or debit balances in a customer's account(s) may be offset by any other outstanding balance owed by or to the customer. Please allow 4 to 6 weeks for delivery. Offer available while quantities last.

Your Privacy—The Harlequin® Reader Service is committed to protecting your privacy. Our Privacy Policy is available online at www.ReaderService.com or upon request from the Harlequin Reader Service.

We make a portion of our mailing list available to reputable third parties that offer products we believe may interest you. If you prefer that we not exchange your name with third parties, or if you wish to clarify or modify your communication preferences, please visit us at www.ReaderService.com/consumerschoice or write to us at Harlequin Reader Service Preference Service, P.O. Box 9062, Buffalo, NY 14269. Include your complete name and address.

ROM13R

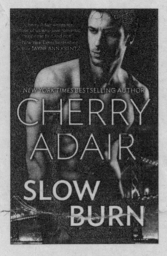

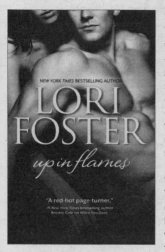

NORA ROBERTS

28594	O'HURLEY'S RETURN	___	$7.99 U.S.	___	$9.99 CAN.
28592	O'HURLEY BORN	___	$7.99 U.S.	___	$9.99 CAN.
28590	SWEET RAINS	___	$7.99 U.S.	___	$9.99 CAN.
28588	NIGHT TALES: NIGHT SHIELD & NIGHT MOVES	___	$7.99 U.S.	___	$9.99 CAN.
28587	NIGHT TALES: NIGHTSHADE & NIGHT SMOKE	___	$7.99 U.S.	___	$9.99 CAN.
28586	NIGHT TALES: NIGHT SHIFT & NIGHT SHADOW	___	$7.99 U.S.	___	$9.99 CAN.
28578	THE LAW OF LOVE	___	$7.99 U.S.	___	$8.99 CAN.
28172	WHISPERED PROMISES	___	$7.99 U.S.	___	$8.99 CAN.
28171	FOREVER	___	$7.99 U.S.	___	$9.99 CAN.
28170	REFLECTIONS & DREAMS	___	$7.99 U.S.	___	$8.99 CAN.
28169	HAPPY ENDINGS	___	$7.99 U.S.	___	$9.99 CAN.
28168	CHANGE OF HEART	___	$7.99 U.S.	___	$9.99 CAN.
28167	CHARMED & ENCHANTED	___	$7.99 U.S.	___	$9.99 CAN.
28166	PLAYING FOR KEEPS	___	$7.99 U.S.	___	$8.99 CAN.
28165	CAPTIVATED & ENTRANCED	___	$7.99 U.S.	___	$9.99 CAN.
28164	FIRST IMPRESSIONS	___	$7.99 U.S.	___	$9.99 CAN.
28162	A DAY AWAY	___	$7.99 U.S.	___	$9.99 CAN.
28161	MYSTERIOUS	___	$7.99 U.S.	___	$9.99 CAN.
28160	THE MacGREGOR GROOMS	___	$7.99 U.S.	___	$9.99 CAN.
28158	ROBERT & CYBIL	___	$7.99 U.S.	___	$9.99 CAN.
28156	DANIEL & IAN	___	$7.99 U.S.	___	$9.99 CAN.
28154	GABRIELLA & ALEXANDER	___	$7.99 U.S.	___	$9.99 CAN.
28150	IRISH HEARTS	___	$7.99 U.S.	___	$9.99 CAN.
28137	PERFECT HARMONY	___	$7.99 U.S.	___	$8.99 CAN.
28133	THE MacGREGORS: SERENA & CAINE	___	$7.99 U.S.	___	$9.99 CAN.

(limited quantities available)

TOTAL AMOUNT	$	_____
POSTAGE & HANDLING	$	_____
($1.00 FOR 1 BOOK, 50¢ for each additional)		
APPLICABLE TAXES*	$	_____
TOTAL PAYABLE	$	_____

(check or money order—please do not send cash)

To order, complete this form and send it, along with a check or money order for the total above, payable to Harlequin Books, to: **In the U.S.:** 3010 Walden Avenue, P.O. Box 9077, Buffalo, NY 14269-9077; **In Canada:** P.O. Box 636, Fort Erie, Ontario, L2A 5X3.

Name: _____

Address: _____ City: _____

State/Prov.: _____ Zip/Postal Code: _____

Account Number (if applicable): _____

075 CSAS

*New York residents remit applicable sales taxes.
*Canadian residents remit applicable GST and provincial taxes.

Silhouette®
Where love comes alive™

Visit Silhouette Books at www.Harlequin.com

PSNR0514B